The Orphan *of* Florence

ALSO BY JEANNE KALOGRIDIS

The Borgia Bride

I, Mona Lisa

The Devil's Queen

The Scarlet Contessa

The Inquisitor's Wife

The
Orphan
of Florence

Jeanne Kalogridis

St. Martin's Griffin ﹡ New York

THE ORPHAN OF FLORENCE. Copyright © 2017 by Jeanne Kalogridis. All rights reserved. Printed in the United States of America. For information, address St. Martin's Press, 175 Fifth Avenue, New York, N.Y. 10010.

www.stmartins.com

Library of Congress Cataloging-in-Publication Data

Names: Kalogridis, Jeanne, author.
Title: The orphan of florence / Jeanne Kalogridis.
Description: First edition. | New York: St. Martin's Griffin, [2017]
Identifiers: LCCN 2017018868| ISBN 9780312675479 (trade pbk.) | ISBN 9781466850231 (ebook)
Subjects: | GSAFD: Suspense fiction. | Mystery fiction.
Classification: LCC PS3561.A41675 O77 2017 | DDC 813/.54—dc23
LC record available at https://lccn.loc.gov/2017018868

Our books may be purchased in bulk for promotional, educational, or business use. Please contact your local bookseller or the Macmillan Corporate and Premium Sales Department at 1-800-221-7945, extension 5442, or by email at MacmillanSpecialMarkets@macmillan.com.

First Edition: October 2017

10 9 8 7 6 5 4 3 2 1

For my father,
William Andrew Dillard,
Who loved in secret from afar

Acknowledgments

The following people have my undying gratitude, and deserve special mention here; without them, you would not be holding this book in your hands:

Irwin Rumler
Russell Galen
Charles Spicer
April Osborn
David Blixt

I'd like to thank each of the following individuals for supporting me in finishing this novel:

George A. Kalogridis
Jan Davis and Mitchell Kalogridis
Keith Macksey
Melissa Clepper-Faith
Jerry Miller
Kathy, Matt, Daemon, and Lily Prorok
C. W. Gortner
Jackie Sewell
Tim Waggoner
Dimitri LaBarge
Teresa Bigbee

Trent Zelazny
Dawn Rice
Laura Lewis
Matt Phillips
M. J. Rose
Vidura Barrios
Warren Lapine
Andy Michael
Nat P.
Sarah Waterhouse
Karen Essex

Kent Burden

Frank Carbone

David Tocher

Samina Patel Sharp

Bob Dev

J. Martin

Kristina Butke

Mike Cobley

H. W. Shannon

sidhekist

kayaking.gram

jcpete

hardboiledbaby

dolleygurl

Leslie Carrol

Jonah Kit

Laura Watkins

Bob Moats

Winston

Gio Pompele

Vincent Docherty

Richard Dansky

edidep

dlteana.graham9

lesliegski

usmantm

cesc.rosello

hfvrtualbooktours

My special thanks, also, to those who contributed anonymously; you know who you are.

Magic is only as black as the heart that practices it.

Abramo Fiorentino

Real magic is the transformation of self.

J.M. Dillard

The Orphan *of* Florence

Florence, Italy

Late November 1478

One

The night I was caught with my hand in a gentleman's pocket—the night my life completely changed—it was burning cold, so bitter I'd never felt anything like it before or since. I would have stayed inside if we hadn't been out of food and coin, or if the moon, whose light I could never bear to waste, hadn't been full. So out we went, Tommaso and I, onto mostly quiet cobblestone streets in the pale blue light, the moon huge and glorious in a clear star-riddled sky, the air perfectly still and burning where it touched my exposed face. Because of the cold, I walked so fast I may as well have been running; Tommaso gasped and whined because his little legs couldn't keep up. I ignored him, of course, and increased my pace until he was too breathless to complain. I didn't make our usual stop at the Fico Tavern, where the marks were plentiful if not wealthy, but headed straight for the Buco Tavern instead. Our chances of cutting a single fat purse were better there; I wanted to be home and warm fast as a blink.

We were barreling down a side street with tall narrow houses crammed side by side, uninterrupted walls of stone and stucco on either side of us, when Tommaso yelled something that finally made me slow.

"Paolo!" he called out, in that piping baby voice of his. "Wake up! You can't sleep out here tonight!"

Impatient, I stopped and turned around to see Tommaso

addressing someone's front door. He looked like a cherub then, Tommaso did, though he was emphatically not on the side of the angels. Six years old at most, blond as a German weaver, and thin, a sprinkling of freckles across his nose and cheeks, his head too large for his body, his pale faintly blue eyes too large for his face. He was wrapped in a hole-pocked horse blanket, because the Game made it necessary for him to look as pathetic as possible. Pathetic and adorable, able to melt any heart—save mine, of course. He had a talent for deceit and adored the Game; he'd have gone barefoot if I'd let him, just for the effect. I'd had to insist that he keep his woolen cap on that night, especially since I kept his hair cut close to his scalp, just like my own, the better to keep down the lice and fleas. Keeping mine short had an additional advantage, that of convincing dangerous souls that they were dealing with a streetwise lad, not a fragile young lady.

I came two strides closer and saw the seated figure, its spine pressed to the doorjamb in hopes of catching a waft of heat escaping from the hearth inside. I'd passed by it but paid it no mind; just another poor homeless wretch dying of starvation and cold on the streets of Florence. If I stopped for every one of them, I'd be the one starving. And on this night, especially, I'd die of cold.

But we knew this poor homeless wretch.

Everybody in Florence knew young Paolo and his cat Old Sot, a red tabby now curled in his owner's lap, both apparently sleeping—the latter's head dropped, chin on chest. Paolo and Old Sot were fixtures on the steps of the city cathedral. The former did good business there, as his missing lower leg, cheer, and drunken cat coaxed alms out of the stoniest hearts. Paolo could hobble on well enough on a wooden leg, but when begging he sat with his legs sprawled in front of him, the stump pointedly visible. Regular contributors always remembered to bring a bit of ale for Old Sot, and pour it in the little bowl his owner kept for him. One bowl for the coins, one for the cat. Old Sot would yowl for his treat, lap the ale up promptly, then shake his head to flick the foam from his whiskers.

My throat tightened. I had a fond spot in my heart for Old Sot and Paolo, but fond spots were a dangerous luxury for poor folk scrabbling to survive.

"Come away, Tommaso," I said in a low voice, hoping to spare him grief. "Paolo knows what he's doing." I knew where this was unhappily headed; no point in getting Tommaso upset. He had to keep his wits about him for the Game. *I* had to keep my wits about me for the Game.

Tommaso pretended not to hear. He stepped up and jostled the lad's shoulder. "Wake up," he said. "You'll freeze to death. So will Old Sot."

Paolo and his cat didn't stir.

Tommaso shook his shoulder harder.

I raised my voice. "Come away *now,* Tommaso!"

Too late. Tommaso gave a push, causing Paolo to fall on his side; the cat went with him, still curled, and hit the cobblestone beside his master, the two frozen stiff.

A moment of silence passed after Paolo's body fell; Tommaso was stunned, but I'd known the instant I'd seen them that Paolo and his cat were dead. I waited a respectful second, then patted the corpse down looking for coins and found none. Paolo's fall had revealed the bottom half of the wooden door, where someone had painted the words, *Death to the pope,* and a second wag had come along and painted beneath it, *Lorenzo beds his mother.*

Actually, I didn't quote the second phrase word for word, but you get the gist. Lorenzo de' Medici, the wealthiest, most powerful, and theoretically most revered citizen, was at war with the pope and Rome, which meant that Florence was at war with them, too. The enemy armies were fighting only a few days' ride from our city walls, which meant food and goods were becoming scarce and more people like Paolo were starving and freezing to death on the streets. Fewer people gave money or food to beggars, and the middle class had less money to be stolen. Impolite graffiti became a common sight in the city and lately was increasingly directed at Lorenzo for not putting a stop to the war, even though it was all Pope Sixtus's fault. There had been bread riots, and calls for Lorenzo to surrender himself, and rumors that he was thinking of abandoning the city to save his own neck. Don't get me wrong, I'd always been loyal to Lorenzo, but I was angry with both men for the war, which was hard on the wealthy and middle class and deadly to us poor. When food was scarce, guess who got it?

Work or starve. Why else would Paolo have risked being out in such weather?

Why else would we?

That was when I realized Paolo's wooden leg was gone; he couldn't have walked to safety if he'd tried. Some bastard had to have taken his money and the leg as well, so Paolo couldn't follow. I felt a surge of sadness and rage, but turned my face from the emotion; it wouldn't do Paolo, and especially not Tommaso, any good.

Tommaso began to wail.

I snatched his hand and pulled him along with me as I resumed my former pace.

"Stop sniveling," I hissed, as Tommaso gasped and sobbed beside me. "It won't make him any less dead. You don't see me crying, do you?"

I had to say it; he had to be taught. Otherwise, his heart would break so many times he'd give in to despair, a sure way to wind up like poor Paolo.

Two days before we'd found a skeletal mother and her infant

frozen in an alleyway, and Tommaso had cried all night long. I'd had to hold him and soothe him to shut him up. But, as I tried to tell him, you can't let yourself be affected by these things, because they're going to happen all the time on the streets. I'd liked Paolo, who was cheerful and charming despite his circumstances, but I couldn't let myself care about what happened to him. All of us unwanted folks on the street were going to meet an early death. As I'd explained to Tommaso, any day might find me hauled off to prison or killed by a mark, competitor, or rapist, or stricken dead by plague. Caring for anyone, including me, was just stupid—because once he let himself do it, he'd cry until he went mad, and that would just make him easier prey.

I don't care, he'd sobbed, clinging to me. *I love you anyway. Don't you love me back?*

I didn't answer, which made him cry all the harder, but I held him until he finally gave up and went to sleep. I didn't want him thinking of me as his mother. I'd seen too many times what happens to mothers and their children on the streets.

When it comes to naming taverns, we Florentines take a practical approach. Take the two most notorious taverns in town, the Buco and the Fico, both of which generate far more capital from human flesh than from ale. They're named for the specific type of flesh they peddle.

The word *buco* can mean many things in the Florentine dialect, *hole* being chief among them and, in less polite company—particularly among the men frequenting this particular tavern—it refers to a highly puckered part of the anatomy. *Fico,* on the other hand, means *fig,* which is also the rudest way in our Tuscan tongue of referring to the sweetest part of a woman. Want a lad? Visit the Buco. Looking for women? Go to the Fico.

I never much liked working near the Buco, even though it caters to a wealthier clientele. Not because I had anything against gentlemen who prefer lads; local wisdom says all boys go through the submissive phase, which they supposedly grow out of by the time they're married. And no one thinks twice about older men, especially bachelors or widowers, visiting the Buco looking for a tender young morsel. Two grown men together, now *that's* taboo in this wicked town. Those are the sort that earn the attention of the Eight of the Night and get arrested for sodomy. But if one of the partners is a boy just past puberty, like Paolo, it's considered perfectly natural; the Church frowns on it, of course, but the police look the other way.

Me, I'm a thief and damned myself, so I don't judge other people's business. I never liked going to the Buco simply because the tight alleyway leading to it didn't offer a lot of options for escape; I preferred playing the Game where the odds of getting away were better. But it was cold and I wanted my one fat purse.

Tommaso had quit sniveling by the time we reached the alleyway outside the Buco, because I'd told him silly stories about Paolo and Old Sot in heaven—how Paolo had both his legs and was chasing after young wenches and catching them because he was so speedy, and how Old Sot had his very own keg and was lying on his back with his tongue to the tap, lapping up all the ale he could hold and becoming very inebriated in the process. I'd had Tommaso grinning, but he'd stopped and said sadly, "But you don't believe in heaven."

What I really believed was that heaven wasn't for people like Tommaso and me, because God all too obviously didn't care about us. It was just easier to say I didn't believe than to explain that I felt God especially had it in for me in particular. Why else had my life turned out so rotten? God and heaven were for good people, kind people, people who could afford to care. My problem was I had cared too much, and I'd have slit my own throat early on if it hadn't been for Tommaso; I had to learn to guard my heart, and the least I could do was teach Tommaso to guard his, so that it would never break.

I shrugged. "Maybe I'm wrong," I said, and that was enough to make him thoughtful instead of weepy.

Oddly enough, by the time we took our places on opposite sides of the alleyway near the tavern door, I'd grown nervous, as if I'd known something was about to go wrong. I was clutching the unsheathed razor hidden in my cloak pocket so hard that my gloved hand ached. I focused on creating my best come-hither male prostitute expression while ignoring Tommaso. It was a Saturday and, despite the weather, the Buco was fairly busy; every minute or so, yellow light spilled out into the alley when the door opened or closed as sober men went walking in and pairs of drunken men came stumbling out.

As I stood on the side of the alleyway opposite Tommaso, trying not to watch the torchlight glint off the trickle of clear snot running from his little nose, someone walked up to share the alleyway with us. A man in his early twenties, shoddily dressed and shivering. And handsome, though I usually never allowed myself to notice such things. I would have called him pretty, given his bow-shaped upper lip and strikingly pale eyes set in a nest of effeminately long dark lashes. I don't like pretty men— sometimes I have to pull myself short and remind myself that I can't afford to like men, period—but I judged this one undeniably attractive, despite his unfashionably long, straight copper hair and bangs covering his eyebrows.

He may have been good-looking enough to get a lot of business, but he was ten years too old to still be peddling his wares outside the Buco. Young male prostitutes always grow into men and have to find more honest employment, which is why they're on the lookout for wealthy patrons to pay for their education. This handsome prowler was obviously one of the unlucky ones, but he should've had the good sense to realize he'd outgrown the passive sexual role and needed to get into some other line of work.

He barely gave Tommaso a glance, but then he caught sight of me standing near the door and gave me a fleeting look of interest, which he instantly corrected with a frown. No point in flirting with one of his younger peers. I scowled back. I'd never let a man catch me looking at him starry-eyed. I held my ground, forcing him to stand farther from the tavern door than he probably wanted; I didn't like that he was close enough to interfere with the Game if things went badly.

The heavy tavern door swung open again, letting out the warmth, the light, and the roars of men wagering on dice or on the doomed birds in the cockpit. They tie spurs and sometimes razors to the cocks' feet, and last week, one of the birds here turned on its owner and slashed his throat for putting it in the ring too many times. The man fell dead on the spot. They dragged the body away and went to get the cock, to kill it. But some sly competitor had already stolen the bird.

A couple emerged from the tavern. Typical patrons, one a well-dressed man in his thirties, his red felt toque marking a successful merchant, and the other a lad of perhaps seventeen— my age, in a thin gray cloak shiny with wear. Both were drunk and singing a carnival song loaded with double-entendres; the older, shorter man's head was lolling on the shoulder of the lad's, their arms wrapped around each other's waists. They didn't notice me or the handsome competitor, or Tommaso, who by then had managed to work up some more tears—dishonest ones now, for the patrons—that were trickling down his dirty cheeks.

Our handsome prostitute watched the couple pass with a sigh. I barely noticed; I was too busy eyeing the solitary figure headed through the alleyway toward us, in the direction of the tavern.

Leaning heavily on his cane, the man shuffled slowly into the arc of light cast by the torches. A very old man, judging from the stooped shoulders beneath his black cloak and the straggly white hair hanging over his ears. He wore a traditionally Florentine red felt toque, the kind that fits tightly over the ears and temples, but flares out a bit at the crown, like bread dough rising in a round pan. His face was lean and narrow with a sharp chin and a long, thin crooked nose, big enough but nothing like those gigantic twisted monsters sported by the cream of Florentine society, the Tornabuoni and Medici. But what set him apart most was the narrow swath of fine black silk tied around his head, covering one eye. I'm good at guessing professions and I took him for a banker.

The drunken couple emerging from the tavern staggered past the old man, jostling him so that he wobbled and had to struggle to regain his balance. He scowled in disapproval at the handsome prostitute's solicitous smile.

As the old man drew nearer to me, the handle of his cane glinted in the torchlight. Pure gold: I spot it the way a soaring falcon spots a hare in the forest below. His cloak was of the finest quality heavy wool, simply but exquisitely tailored. And he was alone, no doubt with a purse full of coins intended for the pleasures of the Buco.

A juicy mark—rich, feeble, and half blind, hallelujah—had just dropped into our laps like manna from the sky. My one fat purse. It was too sweet, too easy.

So I worried. The cane was a potential weapon, and the handsome prostitute was still nearby. Granted, the old man needed the cane for balance, and I was sure the younger man would run at the sight of my razor. If we were lucky, this would be our first and only Game of the evening.

I let go a discreet cough, one just loud enough for Tommaso to hear. When he glanced at me, I inclined my head slightly toward the old man and drew my left forefinger beneath my nose, as if wiping it. It was the signal.

The Game had begun.

Tommaso went into action, wailing as he ran up to the old man. "Signore!" he called in that high little-girl voice of his. "Signore, please!" He was shivering, clutching the horse blanket tighter about him with his bare hands, his little legs thin as sticks. "My mother has died, and I'm *starving*! Only one denari, signore, only one for the love of Jesus and the Virgin . . . !"

The old man stopped, his expression one of senile confusion, and stared down at the boy. "Eh," he said. "Eh . . ." and patted his purse, hidden in a side interior pocket of his cloak. The right side—by a gift of heaven, his *blind* side, and the very place a pickpocket would go looking for it.

As luck—or in my case, skill and experience—would have it, I was standing on the old man's right side. And gloating to myself that this was a gift. A harmless old man, one patting his purse to reveal exactly where it was; usually, I had to do a bump and fan to find it. Better yet, the handsome prostitute had disappeared completely, perhaps sensing that we were about to make a lift and wanting nothing to do with it.

I tried not to smile as I closed in on my target.

Tommaso was prone to improvisation and that night was no exception. Rather than cry harder and drop to his knees in order to further distract the mark, which was the plan, he went on all fours and reached for something invisible on the filthy cobblestones.

"But look!" he crowed. "Look here, signore! It's a miracle!"

"Eh?" the old man said, stooping down as far as his unsteady legs would permit. "Eh?"

"A coin, a whole *soldi*! A miracle from the Virgin! She heard my prayer! Look!"

I brushed past the old man, our cloaks grazing each other; he was more solid than he looked. Then I pretended to lose my balance a bit, as if I'd been drunk, and performed a bump. I jostled him just hard enough so that he didn't feel me slitting his cloak with the razor. With two fingers, I slipped the deliciously heavy velvet purse up and out of the pocket as I muttered, "Excuse me." In a blink, it was safe inside my own cloak pocket.

The instant I palmed the purse, Tommaso's angelic voice said, with heartrending disappointment, "Oh! I imagined it! Oh no! Wait! Is that it?"

He continued scrabbling in the dirt while I pivoted on one foot, turning my back to the old man and preparing to move quickly and quietly back down the alleyway, away from the mark, away from the Buco, toward home.

Except that while I was pivoting, a hand clamped down on my wrist, the guilty one attached to the very fingers that had just lifted the purse.

I tried to pull away, but the grip was too strong. It belonged to the old man, who had dropped his cane and was standing perfectly upright, shoulders square. He was actually tall and burly, the filthy trickster.

"Thief!" he bellowed, in a powerful bass. "Thief! Someone help me!"

I pulled out my razor and brandished it at him—it's not big or impressive looking, but it's dangerous enough to make most marks unhand me. This man paid not a whit of attention to it; he was looking into my eyes with a gaze commanding and fearless, as if he'd been an emperor and I a worm that had crawled into his path. He had me in his power, and he wanted me to know it.

I struggled to pull free. I didn't want to use the razor unless I absolutely had to—once things get bloody, there's no turning back—so I made swiping motions with it in the air that gradually came closer and closer to his hand.

I swept my gaze briefly over the area and saw that Tommaso had already run off. I'd told him that if one of us got caught, the other one should run like hell and never look back; every man for himself. Even if I'd been prone to worry about what could happen to a lone six-year-old on the street, I wouldn't have, because Tommaso had an invisible advantage. Under his rags, he was wearing my most precious possession: a truly magical talisman of silver, one that I'd wished devoutly in that instant I'd been wearing.

Ten years ago in the orphanage, when I wasn't much older than Tommaso, Sister Anna Maria took me aside in the garden, behind a tall juniper where no one else could see, and showed me the amulet.

What is it? I'd demanded, full of curiosity, staring at her palm, which held what looked to be a large silver coin on a leather thong. If I'd spoken that way—with juvenile bluntness—to the abbess who ran the orphanage, I'd have gotten my teeth knocked down my throat. Directness was not tolerated in little girls. But Sister Anna Maria was patient and usually kind.

It's a talisman, she'd explained. *A charm, probably meant to keep you safe, although good Christians oughtn't put faith in such things. But it's right that you should have it.*

I looked up at her in surprise. She wore a white habit because it was summer, and she'd crouched on her haunches so that we could speak face-to-face. Her face was very narrow and lean, with a nose that was too big and lips that were too thin, but her eyes were large and beautiful.

Why, Sister? I'd asked.

Because you were wearing it the day I found you outside in the little basin, she said.

Here in Florence, abandoned infants are left in the basin—a cranny, really, carved into the handsome marble work of the fountain in the square that faces the orphanage. Before sunrise, the mother or relative would leave the baby there, where the nuns would be sure to find it in the morning. No other city in Italy, or probably all Europe, was as progressive as ours. No mother had to feel shame or despair, because the Hospital for the Innocents, the Ospedale degli Innocenti, was not only new and clean, it was also an architectural masterpiece. Its benefactors were exceedingly wealthy, and the children were therefore well fed and dressed.

My mother had apparently felt some ambivalence about whether I should have survived; I was left naked in the stone cold basin in winter. Naked, except for the talisman. Had I not been discovered and whisked inside quickly, I would have died.

I looked at the shiny metal in the sister's palm.

Why didn't you tell me before? I asked.

It's very, very rare and dear. You weren't old enough to care for it properly, she replied.

You mean, to hide it from the abbess. I was referring to that sour Servant of Mary Sister Maria Ignatia, the abbess of the convent attached to the orphanage. She would have snatched it off my neck and beaten me for having such an accursed thing.

Sister Anna Maria nodded wistfully. *You have to make sure she never sees it. You can't show it to any of the children either, or she'll find out about it and take it away.*

It's from my parents, I said slowly. My cheeks and neck began to burn; my voice wavered. The talisman was rare; it was dear. Which meant my parents had been—or still were—wealthy. I'd always assumed they'd been poor, which meant they'd either died early from the plagues that always swept through the bleaker quarters of the city or had been starving and hadn't had so much as a rag to wrap their infant daughter in.

In other words, I'd believed that they had abandoned me either because they were dead and couldn't help it or because they loved me and wished me well.

But no, my parents had been rich folk. Which meant that they could have given me a much better life. Even if both my parents had died, or I was a bastard child, there was still an obligated wealthy family in Florence who found me inconvenient.

Sister Anna Maria gestured, smiling, for me to take the silver disc from her hand. I took it all right, and hurled it furiously to the earth. I was grinding it in with my heel when she caught my arms and pulled me away.

They loved you, she said with stern certainty, *or you wouldn't have been wearing it. It's very dear. You must keep it; your mother's hand touched it.*

I spat on it clumsily, with most of the saliva winding up on my chin. *If they had loved me,* I retorted bitterly, *I wouldn't be here. If she touched it, I don't want it.*

I ran away.

I wouldn't look at Sister Anna Maria for a week, but not long after, I found myself starting to think about the charm. It was mine, and the sister had said that it was worth a lot of money. I could tuck it away for the day I left the orphanage and sell it.

So I began to drop hints with the good sister that I had reconsidered and wanted it back. She ignored me for a few days, but when I persisted, she finally delivered it to me. In secret, of course.

Take good care of this, she said, as she handed it over. *This is no ordinary charm. Look: It bears the stamp of the Magician of Florence. That little sun and moon conjoined—do you see the tiny crescent moon there?* She pointed with a fingernail. *It embraces the sun, that circle with a dot in its center. See how they both rest on the inner point of the M, next to the F?*

It was a beautiful, heavy coin with legends standing out in bas-relief. Curious lines and symbols marked the front, and on the back, a square with several rows of apparently random numbers.

I let out a childish gasp of fear when she mentioned the Magician and wondered how a nun would know such things.

Isn't it wicked? I asked. I wasn't really afraid it was wicked, but I *was* afraid that I'd spit on it and some demon might appear and punish me for doing it.

Sister Anna Maria smiled in gentle amusement. *It was made to protect you, Giulia, so how could it be wicked? And it did. Of course, you shouldn't speak to the abbess about it . . .*

I'd figured out a long time ago that the abbess was a complete idiot, so there was no chance of me telling her anything. I took the talisman in my hand and stared at it.

There were other magicians in the city—the bulk of them charlatans, but there was only one legendary Magician of Florence. Even us orphans, sheltered as we were from the world beyond the convent walls, knew: He was ancient, immortal, and the most dangerous man in the city because his power knew no bounds. He could force people to kill against their will, to fall in love, to do his bidding. His clientele were those who lusted for power, those who wished their enemies dead, those who desired unholy control over another. Rumor said the Medici family had become the wealthiest and most prominent in town only because they paid dearly for the Magician's talismans; all of his customers paid dearly for his talismans because they always worked. No one, including his rich clients, had ever seen the Magician in person because he had the talent of making himself invisible, which led to a lot of speculation about whether he was walking among us without anyone having a clue.

You couldn't impress anyone more than by announcing that you were wearing a charm enchanted by the Magician of Florence.

Even if you were wearing it because your parents wanted to be rid of you.

Back in front of the Buco Tavern, I was desperately wishing the very dear amulet was hanging from my neck.

"Thief!" the old man bellowed at me once again, and instantly the handsome prostitute materialized out of the dark, long red hair glinting in the torchlight.

Before I could react, the not-really-so-very-old man squeezed my wrist so hard that I dropped my razor onto the cobblestones. The handsome young prostitute bounded forward wielding a double-bladed knife half the length of his thigh, the sort of knife men carry when they mean business. I glanced down at my little razor in the street, then back up at his big knife.

"Eight of Public Safety," Handsome said, identifying himself as a policeman to the old man, who finally let go of my other hand. "Search the boy, my lord; I'm sure your purse is in his cloak."

The bastard. Both of them: two rotten stinking bastards, tricking a poor lad this way, neither of them what they had seemed. The Eight of Public Safety—a division of Florence's city government, so named for the fact that eight guildsmen sat on the council—dealt with thievery and assault and like crimes; it would have made much more sense to encounter someone from the council of the Eight of the Night, which handled sodomy. Why go to elaborate lengths to catch a petty thief like me?

The old man patted me down and finally found his velvet purse in my extra-long inside front pocket. He also found a small folded square of paper.

"It's a Bible verse," I lied. "For luck."

The old man unfolded it and read it silently.

"Anything I should see?" the policeman asked.

My intended victim smiled as he pocketed it. "As he says: *Suffer the little children to come unto me, and forbid them not, for of such is the kingdom of God.* Probably stolen from a nun or priest. The boy certainly can't read."

I looked at him dumbfounded; he was a criminally smooth liar. An honest citizen would have shown it to the officer.

"And your money?" the redheaded policeman asked.

The old man loosened the drawstring of his purse and peered into it. "All there," he said, and tucked it away inside his cloak.

"Well, then." The officer took my upper arm and gave me a shake. "You'll be sleeping in jail tonight. That is, if the other inmates let you. A small boy with a pretty face like yours should know better."

"Why are you arresting *me*?" I snapped. "Don't you have better things to do than pick on a poor lad? Why isn't someone from the Eight of the Watch here instead of you?"

"Hah!" the policeman sneered. "You've got a lot of—"

"One moment, please, Officer," the old man interrupted, with upper-upper-class diction and accent. "No harm was done. I have my purse. Must you arrest him?"

"I can't let a pickpocket go free!" Officer Handsome growled. "Besides, we've had too many complaints about this one with the accursed eyes."

Accursed eyes was right. Even I cursed my own eyes frequently, just as I did at that very moment, because they identified me resoundingly and without question to anyone who got close enough to see that my left eye was an unremarkable brown, while the right was a pale and most remarkable green. God had marked me, which made most people—including my parents, no doubt—look on me with suspicious superstition. The trait smelled of witchcraft and possession.

"But what if you were to place him in my custody?" the old man asked. "If I promise to care for and rehabilitate him?"

I was immediately suspicious of such generosity, especially from a man headed for the Buco. Because, as the officer had pointed out, I appeared to be a small boy with a pretty face.

Handsome lifted his chin and rolled his eyes in a "you don't really expect me to believe that" gesture. "And how can I be sure you intend only that, Signore?"

"I live on the Via de' Gori, just west of the Church of San Lorenzo," the old man answered, his tone disdainful at the officer's implication. The Via de' Gori was smack in the richest part of town. "Ask for me, Ser Giovanni the banker, tomorrow morning. The boy will be at my palazzo, and he'll tell you that no mischief was involved—that he was, in fact, well fed and offered decent employment, enough to keep him from continuing in his current line of . . . work."

I stared at the old man in disbelief, and at the cop with a pleading expression. I stared at the sea monster and the whirlpool, neither of them good choices. I certainly didn't want to go to jail, where my fate was certain, but by tomorrow morning, the not-feeble old man could have had his way with me a dozen times over nowhere near the Via de' Gori. That is, if he hadn't killed me for being disappointingly female.

Officer Handsome was likewise not buying the old man's story. "Look, even if I trusted you, and I'm not sure I do, signore, there's the matter of the boy. What makes you think he won't slit your throat in your sleep and rob you of everything?"

He had a point. Because I had decided to go with the old man and had been dreaming of that very scenario—save for the throat-slitting part. It probably wouldn't happen because the man was an impressive liar, which boded ill, but at least he wasn't an officer with a long knife bent on hauling me to prison. Once Handsome was out of the picture, I'd give my former mark the slip. I knew all the little tunnels and alleyways that only the children of Florence's streets know, and like Tommaso, I had a knack for disappearing.

The old man laughed. "He won't be a problem, Officer. I have a bodyguard at my house to protect me."

At that point, I piped up. "I'll go with him," I told the officer. "I'm not in my line of work because I want to be. I was forced into it because I'm an orphan."

"Really?" Handsome asked, in a tone that said he trusted me not at all. "Because I *will* check on you in the morning. And if any harm's been done to this gentleman, or anything in his home is missing, I'll see you're tossed in *Le Stinche* for the rest of your short life."

The words *Le Stinche* made my bowels contract. The most notorious prison in Florence, built for debtors and small-time criminals like me, was famed not only for its innovative torture devices, but for fleas the size of rats and rats the size of dogs.

I dropped my gaze and forced a tear. "Please, Officer," I begged. "I swear, if I only could have one chance . . . I'll do exactly as the gentleman says. I'm not a bad person, just hungry. It's been so . . . hard lately, trying to get food."

Out of the corner of my welling eye, I saw Handsome's lips twist because he knew it *was* hard for my kind to find food. "Well," he said, and I realized, with well-concealed joy, that I would eventually be sleeping at home that night. "All right," he said to the old man, who smiled. "But I will call on you in the morning, and the boy had better be safe and well fed."

"You're a man of compassion, Officer," the old man said. "You shan't regret it."

"Thank you, Officer," I said. "It's true, you won't regret it. I swear by the Virgin's blue."

"Hmmph," Officer Handsome said, his tone one of irritated dismissal. "Ser Giovanni, I'll call on you in the morning."

Pleased, Ser Giovanni gave a slight bow and caught my elbow with a politely firm grip. I let him lead me out of the alleyway to the street, in the direction of the Via de' Calzaiuoli, on which stood Florence's famous cathedral, the Duomo. So long as the policeman was within earshot, I remained compliant and silently focused on how to snatch the gold-handled cane without getting beaten with it.

We were finally out of Officer Handsome's earshot, almost off the side road and onto the broad Via de' Calzaiuoli, which bisected the city from north to south. I was just getting ready to stick my foot out to trip the old man so I could snatch the cane and run. But in the breath between my decision and its execution, Ser Giovanni came to a sudden stop.

Before I could blink, he dropped my arm and pulled on the gold handle of his cane. A wicked-looking stiletto came hissing out as the wooden part of the cane clattered to the cobblestones. The dagger was double-edged, narrower than a finger but as long as my arm from elbow to fingertips. Long enough to pass right through me with room to spare.

I tried to run, but he caught hold of me again, grasping my cloak and tunic at the neck. And then he lifted me off my feet *with one hand* and shoved me against the front wall of an armorer's shop. The exquisitely fine tip of the stiletto—sharper than my razor—rested against my bare cheek.

We were nose to nose. Struggling for breath as my collar tightened around my neck, I saw the deep lines etched on either side of his thin lips, and the finer, feathery ones about his one exposed eye, which had pronounced bags beneath it. But his eyebrow and the stubble on his chin and hollow cheeks were mostly black. He was past middle age, old enough to be my grandfather, but definitely not weakened by age. Nor was he, I realized, a banker.

Officer Handsome and I had been thoroughly duped. I whispered my favorite curse word, the one about what should be done to someone else's mother.

"I could cut you so fast, you'd be shaking hands with the devil before you knew you were dead," he hissed in my ear, his breath warm and therefore welcome, his words not. "So before you think of running off or causing any trouble, think on this." And he whipped the stiletto through the air just outside my ear. I squeezed my eyes shut and flinched as it whistled.

Abruptly, he let go of my cloak. I landed clumsily on my feet, too terrified to think, and opened my eyes to discover him giving me a look, one that said he was an emperor—no, more imperious than even that. One that said he was God, and held the power of life and death. I tried to look away from that gaze and found I couldn't.

"Pick up the cane," he ordered, aiming the point of the stiletto at my throat.

I slowly picked up the cane. He held out his free hand, and I gave it to him, my eyes wide, my lips smaller than they've ever been. They weren't the only things puckered.

"I won't run," I said weakly, as he slid the empty cane into a sheath hidden beneath his cloak.

"Now," he commanded, "walk closely beside me. If you decide to run . . . Well, as you've seen, I can move faster than you can."

He took my upper arm firmly, but not so hard that anyone would notice anything amiss. They'd think we were a couple coming from the Buco Tavern. Which, after all, we were.

I oriented my body toward the northeast, where the Via de' Gori and his supposed banker's palazzo lay. But he steered me the opposite way around—to the southeast, and the Old Bridge, the Ponte Vecchio, over the Arno River.

Toward a whole new world of trouble.

Two

I'm not a superstitious sort, but shortly after leaving the orphanage, I discovered the Magician's talisman really worked. The first summer Tommaso and I were together, the worst sort of plague was making its fatal rounds in the poorer neighborhoods. Our neighborhood, in fact, and Tommaso caught it. He was only four, an innocent clinging little thing, and I felt helpless watching him suffer, coughing up his own blood, flailing in delirium as he fought for each breath.

It wasn't that I really cared about the boy, mind you. (At least, that's what I told myself to stay sane.) It's just that I would never have been able to find another accomplice who trusted me, whom I could trust, and who did everything I told him to.

I'd learned early on that God never answered prayers—at least not mine. I figured my prayers might even kill the boy. So when Tommaso just kept getting sicker, I slipped the silver talisman around his neck.

His fever broke within the hour.

When he came to, he discovered the talisman and asked, *Why am I wearing your lucky charm, Giuliano?*

He always called me *Giuliano* because I told him that was my name. No point in telling him it was actually the feminine *Giuliana*, because I didn't want him slipping up and using it on the street. That would cause real trouble, and the police would haul me off even if I hadn't been doing anything nefarious at the time.

A young woman unescorted on the street was either a servant or a whore, and I was too rough-looking to be mistaken for someone's servant.

I gave it to you because I got tired of it, I answered Tommaso.

He wouldn't drop the subject. *But, it's supposed to keep you safe. It's magic.*

There's no such thing as magic, I'd said wearily. Even though by that point, I had no doubt it had saved Tommaso's life. I just hated admitting I was superstitious.

He silently digested this, long enough for me—who'd been sitting up with him for two nights—to doze off as I sat cross-legged on the floor beside our straw mattress.

You love me, he said, startling me awake. I blinked at him, too disoriented to speak. He looked at me with his huge pale eyes, then back at the coin in his small hand. I felt a sudden welling of tears and became angry with myself for growing soft until I remembered that exhaustion made people weepy for no good reason.

You gave this to me to get me well, he said thoughtfully. *And it worked. But you could've gotten sick yourself. You love me, Guiliano, even if you won't say it.*

I made a disgusted face and said, *You're delirious. Go back to sleep.* And promptly fell asleep myself.

I made Tommaso keep wearing the talisman. Once he was better and we were getting ready to go play the Game one evening, he tried to give it back.

I don't want it, I said. *You keep it.*

He looked up at me with his cherub face. *You do love me, Giuliano. Even if you won't say it. You used to wear the charm to keep you safe during the Game. But now you've given it to me.*

I curled my lip. *I gave it to you, you little shite, because you're likelier to screw up and get caught. I can take care of myself. You can't.*

I love you, he said, and grabbed me so tightly I could barely breathe. He was hopeless, really; all my passionate warnings to guard his heart had no effect on him. And that was sad, because in this life, loss and abandonment are guaranteed.

Several times during the two years that had passed since, food and money grew scarce and I had plenty of opportunities to sell the talisman. I'd planned to do it right after Tommaso and I got together. The proceeds would have made us very comfortable for a few months, I reasoned, but its loss might cost me a partner. Loyal, honest partners—and there were none so pathetically loyal and honest as Tommaso—were nearly impossible to come by. In the long run, it made more sense to keep him safe and well.

It had nothing to do with adoring him. Nothing at all.

So there I was with my abductor gripping my arm as I cursed myself for letting Tommaso wear the talisman. The further south we headed through the city, the faster his pace grew. He was in a hurry to get where we were going and clearly didn't want to be seen.

I'm fast on my feet, but I had to work to keep up with him as we made our way into an alleyway, dodging stray dogs and cats, stones and garbage, and the occasional drunk staggering toward home. My man knew his way and didn't slow once, as if it'd been full daylight and he'd memorized every rat and pebble.

Soon we were crossing onto the narrow Old Bridge, so crowded with run-down shops that you couldn't see the Arno River beneath it. Even in the cold, I had to cover my nose with my free hand at the smell coming from the tanners' establishments, where they use piss and dung to treat the rotting skins. It can make your eyes water. And then there are the butchers' shops, with the blood and offal from carcasses; I don't need to tell you how bad *that* smells. They're all on the river because it's easier to dump all the nasty stuff in there. Ser Giovanni ducked his head against the stench and increased his speed.

We arrived panting on the other side of the river, in the southern quarter known as the Oltrarno, a less populated place than the city proper. The houses were fewer and not so crowded together, and the streets broader, marked by the occasional walled estate of a wealthy merchant, a few smaller churches, and shops. My abductor had a nose for alleyways, and we soon found ourselves in an empty one between two houses so close to each other that I could easily have pressed a palm to both buildings at the same time. The narrow space was muddy and even the bitter weather failed to lessen the stink of recently emptied chamber pots.

Ser Giovanni set a huge paw on my chest and thrust me against an icy wall, then seized my collar so tightly I struggled to catch my breath. He stared down into my face; flickering yellow light from an upstairs window lit him ghoulishly from above, so that his face was in shadow. The silk patch covering his right eye added to the sinister effect.

"The paper," he said. He took it from his pocket with his free hand and waved it in front of my nose. "Who gave it to you? And who were you delivering it to?"

"No one gave it to me," I said, bristling faintly, a bit irritated, despite my terror, that he would assume I was too ignorant to have written it myself. It was a perfectly reasonable assumption, but it annoyed me anyway. "I wrote something down so I wouldn't forget it. It's just an address."

He let go a laugh that was more a bark. "Please. For a pickpocket, you're a very stupid liar. It's written in code. You're work-ing for spies."

"If you're so honest, why did you lie about it to the police?"

He glared at me, unmoved; the heat of his one-eyed gaze was so intense that I yielded.

"No one gave it to me," I said emphatically. "It's a note to myself."

See, I'd created a secret alphabet when I lived at the orphan-age, to keep the nuns from deciphering my message to a certain lad in the building adjacent to the girls' dormitory. It was simple, really; I'd taken some symbols—squares, squiggles, punctuation marks, the few Greek letters that I knew—and changed their de-sign a bit to create something new. And then I substituted a sym-bol for a particular letter of the alphabet. *A*, for example, was represented by a star, *b* by a backward 5, and so on.

"In *code*?" he hissed. I could hear him slip his hand into his pocket. He was reaching for the stiletto. "Where did you get this? Tell me *now*."

He truly seemed ready to murder me; I caved. "It's my fence's address," I said. "It's my little alphabet, so people can't read what I don't want them to."

"Prove it," he said. "Write it down and decipher it for me."

"I have no pen," I said.

He pointed down at the mud beneath our feet.

I had no choice. I knelt on the cold stinking ground, slipped off a glove, and after a panicked moment when I had trouble re-membering the fence's new address, I scribed my secret symbols in the wet earth.

I glanced up expecting to find him impressed by my penman-ship, but his expression was unreadable. I wiped my filthy finger on my cloak and began to rise.

"Not yet," he said. "Now write the decryption beneath it."

"The de— what?"

"Write down what it really says."

I hesitated; if I gave him my fence's location, then he could easily turn both of us over to the police. And my fence would see to it that I didn't survive a day in jail with him.

But looking up at Ser Giovanni—if that was indeed his name— I got the impression that he was planning an even worse fate for me if I didn't comply.

I wrote the address down, putting each letter beneath the symbol that represented it, and, still on my knees, looked up at his face again.

It was motionless and totally devoid of emotion save for a slight widening of the eyes, which were no longer staring at me, but something oddly distant.

He returned to himself and gestured for me to rise; I ran the sole of my boot over the mud first, smearing it until my secret disappeared. Without a word, he gripped my elbow and pulled me along at a breakneck pace, leading me away from the populated area and out toward the countryside. We took a little dirt path through a sparsely wooded field, with winter-browned grass and shrubs and the clawing fingers of oaks that snagged on my cap. The ground was uneven, thanks to stones and the work of moles in warmer days, before they burrowed deeper beneath the surface. I turned my ankle stepping into a hole, but my captor didn't let me slow; fortunately, the pain lessened the farther we walked. Soon we came to a clearing. On the near horizon stood the outskirts of a heavy forest.

I feared we were headed there, where he would ravish and murder me, but instead he veered to the right until we came to a rusticated stone wall, a good head taller than he and covered in tangles of winter-naked woody vines. The wall seemed to stretch on forever, and we walked along its forbidding periphery until Ser Giovanni finally came to a stop.

I felt the ugly thrill of an animal before the slaughter and girded myself to break away. Just as I began to turn away, Giovanni dropped my arm, drew the stiletto, and placed its tip at my throat, just firmly enough to make an impression on my skin. If I ran in any direction except directly backward—not the fastest way to escape—I'd cut myself on it.

"Don't move," he growled, and I, a pickpocket born to disappear in a wink, found myself frozen, breathless.

With his gaze hard on me, he used his free hand to dig beneath the neck of his tunic and slip out a very long leather thong that hung from his neck. The thong held several skeleton keys, which jingled as he felt beneath the tangle of vines. Without looking away from me, he picked one of the keys from the thong and slipped it into a hole hidden deep within the rock. I could hear the muffled click as the lock turned. He gave a mighty one-armed shove against the stone, and it groaned slowly open like a door. In fact, it *was* a door, a heavy wooden one, cleverly covered in a thin layer of stone and vines to match the wall. I expected to see light coming from a house, but what lay inside the wall was as dark as what lay outside.

At the very moment Ser Giovanni pushed the door open wide enough for us to pass, his attention was compromised when he leaned inward a bit, and the tip of the stiletto leaned with him half a hand's span away from my throat.

I took a long awkward step backward, pivoted, and began to run. I had no intention of waiting to see what the bastard had planned for me, here in the middle of nowhere, in the dark.

He barked a curse behind me, but I didn't look back. I ran full tilt, the cold air stinging my lungs, my gait like a reeling drunk's thanks to the moles. My gaze was fastened on the weed- and vine-covered ground just in front of me, eerily lit by the moon's blue light as it floated above the Arno.

I got several paces ahead of him and might have gotten away, but the toe of my boot found the edge of a large rock and I was taken down, arms spread-eagle. My knees took the brunt of the fall, a sharp stone slicing into one. I didn't pause to take inventory but scrambled back to my feet and ran, gritting my teeth every time I put weight on the injured knee. I managed several painful, hitching strides over the uneven terrain, knowing that my pace was too slow. I stared up at the moon, thinking that I looked on it for the last time. As scared as I was, I was also angry. It wasn't fair, my living such a short, miserable, loveless life, and now I was on my way to spend eternity in hell.

I propelled myself forward on my good leg just as a leather-gloved hand caught my elbow with crushing force and yanked me off balance. I flailed, struggling to stay on my feet, but in the end, even my captor couldn't hold me up. I fell backward, landing hard on my arse, shrieking at the realization that my dignity and my life were about to be taken here, in this desolate stretch of thatch and rocks and mole holes.

"For God's sake," Ser Giovanni said, with matter-of-fact disgust. "Keep your mouth shut. No one will hear you if you don't, but it's damned irritating. You're shrill as a little girl."

He dragged me limping back over the uneven ground, through the open secret door and onto an estate, with a square three-story palazzo as big as a Medici's sitting in the middle of a sprawling compound. The building was relatively new and in good repair, but not a single light shone through any of the windows. The fountain—several tiered marble bowls that grew gradually larger from top to bottom, each decorated with a *fleur de lis,* the stylized lily that represented Florence—had been dry for some time. The entire landscape was as wild and tangled as the weedy, hole-pocked field outside the walls.

My captor pushed the door shut, the stiletto in his hand, his one eye on me, and slid a bolt, locking it to those outside. He then took another of the keys on the thong and turned it in a crevice somewhere in the rock. Locking *me* in.

"Come on," he said quietly, lowering the stiletto to his side, and took my arm again. Now that I was safely his, his grip was polite but steadying, his pace slow.

I hobbled with him past the great palazzo, past empty stables, an abandoned kitchen garden, and a family chapel topped by a statue of the serene Virgin, her open arms draped fetchingly in stone. This property had once belonged to an extremely wealthy family; I couldn't imagine why it had been abandoned, unless everyone inside had died from plague. Even then, some relative, however distant, should have appeared to claim it.

We crossed a property as large as a public square, my bruised, aching knee grateful for the slower pace; the legging over it felt damp. It still didn't have my full attention, as I was busy trying to figure out how to get to the keys around my captor's neck. Preferably *after* I'd gotten my hands on the stiletto.

We soon came to another wall much like the one we'd just passed. I figured we'd come to the end of the property, so I was puzzled when Ser Giovanni let go of my arm, and *without* holding the stiletto on me, lifted the vines and applied yet another key to a lock hidden in the rusticated stone. This time he pulled the door open—it swung outward—and gestured for me to limp ahead of him. I stepped into another unkempt walled landscape, this one smaller, with a withered kitchen garden covered in frost, a small pond, and a typical Florentine three-storied house—a stone and stucco rectangle with a flat roof—that had probably once served as the head gardener's dwelling (a very well-paid head gardener on a very prestigious estate). Like the grand palazzo, the house was fairly new and in good shape, more than comfortable enough for the family of a successful merchant.

But its windows, too, were distressingly black.

Once again, Ser Giovanni pulled the gate shut, bolted it, and then locked it with one of the keys. I was doubly locked in now, with no hope of escape, which was no doubt why he slid his stiletto back into the gold-handled cane.

He caught my shoulder again, this time lightly. "Watch your step," he said, his tone more relaxed. "The moles have been at work here, too."

We made our way at a pace that allowed me to catch my breath and realize that the legging over my aching knee was damp with blood. A cut, however small, could kill a healthy person in a week if it wasn't properly looked after. But I'd worry about that only if I survived the night.

Despite myself, I had to lean heavily on him. Fortunately, the ground leveled out onto a path packed into the dirt beneath the dead and dying weeds. He headed straight toward the two-story house, but instead of approaching the front door, he took me around to the back, where tall evergreen shrubs half hid the servants' entrance.

This time, he turned his back to me as he unlocked the door. It was a solid arched door, its wooden center bound with a band of bronze, and as it swung outward I could see how very thick and sturdy it was.

"Inside," he said, gesturing for me to enter.

I stepped inside and froze, disoriented; the place was as dark as death, so black I couldn't see what lay in front of me. There was no moon in here to light the way.

Behind me, Ser Giovanni's boots sounded briefly against the stone floor; the door groaned faintly as he closed it.

"Don't move," he said softly. "Stand right there."

I sensed that we were in a room, and not a very big one given that his words were muted by what were surely walls. For an instant, I thought to run because he could see no better than I, but I realized fast enough that he knew his way about and I didn't. There might have been furniture to stumble over, or a torture rack, or wild dogs in the room, for all I knew.

And so I stood there like a fool and listened for the third time to the sound of a bolt sliding to keep others out, and the key turning in the lock to keep me in. I listened, and in my mind saw sour old Sister Maria Ignatia at the orphanage, shaking her head and telling me I'd come to no good. Apparently she'd been right.

She'd often said it, and she'd repeated it the week before my fifteenth birthday—or more accurately, the fifteenth anniversary of my discovery—when I was going to be turned out. Boys were supposed to leave the orphanage at age eighteen and girls at fifteen, though really, the Abbess Sister Maria Ignatia bent the rules to suit herself, including the primary one of taking in all orphans.

Take Tommaso for instance: He'd been abandoned at the tender age of four when his mother died, right at the time the nuns were getting ready to kick me out. It had been a particularly bad summer for plague that year in Florence, and the nuns were terrified of an outbreak at the orphanage. So when Tommaso showed up crying near the front portico, next to the little basin where I and other abandoned babies had been left, Sister Maria Ignatia said he was too old and refused to let the other nuns bring him in. Technically, the Hospital for the Innocents had originally been intended for infants, but over the years, the nuns had begun to take in children of all ages without exception. I knew the abbess refused because she was afraid that Tommaso had come to us courtesy of the plague. It didn't help that he was wearing rags and clearly from the poorest part of town, where the corpses were piling up the fastest.

That was the week of my fifteenth birthday, according to the abbess. When boys were booted out, they could become an apprentice or find work at a shop or, if they were deemed of good character, could borrow money to open their own shop. A few of the smartest were sometimes taken in by wealthy benefactors to be educated. Girls had two choices: marriage or the cloister.

Those were what Sister Maria Ignatia offered when she made her little speech to me, the way she did to all the girls who were about to be cast to the wolves. Of course, the nuns all knew that no convent would ever survive me—their nickname for me was the Terror. And I had no intention of marrying. So I nicked some summer clothes from one of the boys, a pair of scissors, and a blanket. I guess I was a natural-born thief even then.

The very next day, after I'd wrapped up the stolen goods in the blanket and was waiting for lunch so that I could run away on a full belly, Sister Maria Ignatia came and told me she had a man who wanted to marry me.

First off, he was a tanner. You could smell the stink on him before he took his first step into the room. He held his cap in hands that were stained dark brown; his equally stained tunic was patched in several places, and his leggings bore holes. He was poor and bald as a baby, with big floppy ears that were hairier than a cat's. And he was old, twice a widower. No surprise there: He'd made his wives work "hard," he said, "at least as hard as I did. It's a difficult life, which is why I need someone young and strong. Someone to bear me more children"—he had five still at home, and five dead of plague—"while helping me run the business."

And he smiled at me with big brown rabbit teeth. What was left of them, anyway.

Now I have nothing against tanners. I just don't want that life for myself. I don't ever want to get used to that smell.

And I was spoiled, I admit. The orphanage was large and airy and fairly new, its façade an architectural masterpiece, and we were all well fed and clothed and taught the basics of running a household. Going to the tannery would be a far more miserable life than the one I knew.

I stared daggers at Sister Maria Ignatia. She'd always hated me, and I her; at first I thought it was because of what the other girls whispered, that I was a witch because of my different colored eyes—one brown, one green. But it hadn't taken me long to realize that I was also the brightest girl in the orphanage and a hundred times smarter than she was. It wasn't my fault that the fact became apparent in front of the other children, because I don't keep my mouth shut when someone does something stupid or unkind. Like beating children who didn't deserve it, which Sister Maria Ignatia did often. She had another reason to hate me: No matter how often she punished me, I always managed to stay one up on her, to make a cheeky comment to or about her that made the other girls giggle.

The day I turned fifteen, Sister Maria Ignatia was smiling. A pursed little smile on her wrinkled face, and gloating in her eyes.

There were richer men who came to the orphanage offering far better marriage proposals to us girls. In fact, most were merchants and shopkeepers, because the Ospedale generally produced well-mannered young women. But Sister Maria Ignatia had saved the tanner for me.

I was the only one in the room who was scowling.

The tanner noticed, and asked tentatively, "But you're a good

Christian, I hope, of virtuous character. Will you work hard for me, bear my children, and obey me faithfully?"

I looked straight into Sister Maria Ignatia's eyes as I answered. "The hell I will!"

I didn't wait for her response or permission to leave. I stalked out of the office, went into the room I shared with twenty other girls, and for the first time ever hung my precious silver amulet around my neck for all the world to see. I took my blanket with its stolen booty tied inside and slung it over my shoulder.

No one stopped me from leaving, although by the time I was stomping toward the front door, Sister Maria Ignatia was leaning against the wall, smiling, her hands hidden beneath her white summer apron.

"You'll come to no good," the abbess whispered triumphantly as I passed. I knew what she meant—a lot of the orphans, boys and girls, who took to the street wound up as prostitutes—and for once, I was too mad to think of a proper retort.

As I stormed away from the orphanage where I'd spent my entire life—away from the graceful arched colonnades that made it look more like a Roman monument than a foundling hospital—Tommaso was still sitting in the hot sun near the basin by the portico, begging pitifully for coins from passersby. He was such a timid creature then, too stunned and frightened to stray far from his place in front of the orphanage and easy prey for those with bad intentions. I marched up to him and when he looked up, grateful that someone had come to make a contribution, I grabbed his hand and yanked him to his feet.

"You're coming with me now," I said.

So Sister Maria Ignatia had been right: Here I was, headed for no good end, stark blind beside a one-eyed man who'd kidnapped me at knifepoint. I thought of how Tommaso would wind up dying sooner rather than later on the streets and wondered whether he had enough sense to go stay with my friend Cecilia. I couldn't help wondering whether my fate would have been different if I'd been the one wearing the talisman.

My captor took my arm again and slowly led me through the darkened room. I inched forward haltingly, my free hand out in front of me searching for objects. The room was cool, but not as cold as outside, and as we took a few more steps, I felt the temperature rise. Ser Giovanni squeezed my arm and I paused, listening to the sound of heavy cloth being drawn back—dark drapes, I realized, as sudden slivers of light revealed the outline of a doorway.

He pushed open the door. I squinted at the sudden appearance of yellow lamplight; my body shuddered at the rush of warm air. We stepped into a kitchen where coals glowed beneath the andirons in the cooking hearth, still uncovered for the night as if awaiting our arrival. There was a lit sconce by the door and one over the long working table across from the hearth. A cauldron perfumed with rabbit and rosemary hung on a hook in the hearth, high enough so that the contents would stay hot but not scorch on the bottom. An upper shelf on the hearth held two fragrant rounds of bread on a wooden peel.

Whatever I'd expected to find, it hadn't been this drool-inducing kitchen. We passed through it into a large windowless sitting room, where another hearth held glowing coals. My attendant ignored me and heaped fresh kindling onto them and gave it all a stir with the iron poker. The fire leapt with a whoosh, and he stared into the flames for a few seconds, his face glowing coral.

I gauged my chances of snatching the poker and beaning him with it—but I knew they were nil, and I cursed myself for

not carrying a second razor. In lieu of one, I took in my surroundings, well lit by more sconces, and looked for a way out.
There was a door to the left of a wall pocked with niches, but it
was bolted; I wouldn't be able to slide the bolt fast enough before
I was caught. I glanced around and spied two large tapestries on
the walls, one of a group of women picking oranges, glistening
with real thread of gold, and one of a unicorn and stag drinking
from a fountain while men spied on them from behind a wall.
There were oil paintings, too, from the very best artists in town,
of battles and nymphs and Abraham about to slaughter his son
Isaac. A candelabrum sat on the high dark mantel—a very odd
candelabrum, with eight holders that formed four concentric *U*s,
and a straight one that bisected the center of all the *U*s; on either
side of it stood goblets carved from precious stones: purple, blue,
an emerald one swirled with darker green and a glittering red
one that had to be ruby. Niches built into the opposite wall held
marble busts of Roman emperors and Athenian philosophers, all
crumbling with age, and a modern bronze bust of Mars. Beneath
my filthy boots lay an exotic carpet covered in vaguely floral vines
in scarlet, evergreen, and gold.

All works of the finest artisans, tucked into this deserted
house. All just sitting there for the taking, a pickpocket's dream.
But given the circumstance, one with a nightmarish cast. I promised myself that if I made it out alive, as much of that treasure as
I could carry was going with me.

My host set the poker down and turned from the fire. "Sit,"
he said, gesturing at a cluster of four daybeds covered in green
silk and gold brocade. I sat on the very edge of one nearest the
hearth and the kitchen, unwilling to lie back against the velvet
pillows, even though my knee was aching.

The stirred fire cast off marvelous heat, but I couldn't relax and enjoy it. There was a reason this man had a home tucked in a secret a place, one no one could find on his own, and a reason he had pretended to be old and feeble, tricking me. Most of all, there was a reason he handled his stiletto like a professional assassin.

Ser Giovanni held out his hand. "Your cloak, please."

His tone was polite and faintly businesslike, as though he were speaking to a colleague come for a financial transaction, not someone he'd kidnaped by force. I decided he was being nice now simply because he didn't want a struggle. Less work to have a willing victim—but he'd soon discover that I wasn't going to let him have an easy time of it.

I slipped off my short cloak and handed it to him, oddly ashamed of the grease stains on my patched rumpled tunic and of the smell of my own body. It'd been so cold lately that Tommaso and I had skipped three of our monthly baths so far; I'm usually a stickler for cleanliness, to keep down the fleas and lice, but they're not bad in winter. Still, there are always some, because I keep the room warm enough and Tommaso is always bringing home stray kittens.

I thought my man was going to make me strip naked on the spot—not that I would—but instead he draped the cloak over his arm and said, "That cut on your knee needs cleaning."

I followed his gaze. My legging had split right over the center of my knee and the torn wool edges were stuck to the skin beneath by drying blood.

"Hmm," he said noncommittally. "I'll be back shortly."

My daybed was the closest one to the fire, and I held my now gloveless hands out toward the hearth, feeling my nose and thighs and fingers tingle as they warmed. Meanwhile, he went off into another room. I was astounded that he left the poker propped against the brick wall by the hearth—had he left it there intentionally? Was it some sort of trick? Or was he really that careless?

It didn't matter; I had to take the chance. I took two silent steps over to the hearth, picked up the poker, and suddenly realized that where there was a kitchen, there were bound to be knives. I tiptoed into the other room, poker in hand, to take quick inventory. No weapons on the long wooden table or on the wall, just a second poker by the oven. There were several cupboards against the wall opposite the hearth and a closet.

Just as I chose the cabinet nearest the oven, a door in one of the rooms opened and closed, followed by approaching tread. The poker would have to serve. I hurried back into the sitting room to retake my seat, clutching my weapon low next to the chaise longue, on the side my captor couldn't see as he entered.

His steps, muted by carpet, came nearer, accompanied by another's lighter tread. "Steady, Leo," he murmured. "I know; I can smell him, too."

So. I had more than one captor to deal with. I gripped the poker harder and tried to keep breathing as I readied myself to spring.

Ser Giovanni appeared in the archway. His cap, cloak, gloves, cane, and stiletto were gone. So was the fringe of white hair. His head had been shaved a week or two ago, and salt and pepper stubble had started to grow back, revealing a hairline that receded at each temple. The deep creases on either side of his thin lips were real, as was the silk eyepatch and the bags under his uncovered eye: He was still old enough to be my grandfather, if a hale and hearty one. A gleaming gray tunic hung to his mid-thigh, covering fine black woolen leggings. The satiny silk draped closely over the skin, hinting at thick muscles as powerful as a blacksmith's on his chest and arms. A round talisman of bright gold on a black thong hung shamelessly over his heart.

He held an empty basin in his hands and a folded towel over one forearm.

Next to him, at the level of his hip, stood a gray velvet giant of a dog, with a broad muscular chest like its owner, a handsome square muzzle, and close-docked ears. Its eyes were clear amber, expressionless and intensely focused on me. And I was intensely focused on the fact that the animal was unleashed.

Living on the street as I do along with all the other strays, I've learned to read dogs and befriend even the ones who first act as if they'd like to sink their teeth into my leg. But the one breed I've always feared is the Neapolitan mastiff, which is not just smart, suspicious, and protective by nature, but larger and much heavier than I am. People keep them when they're looking for a guard animal that will defend them and their property—to the death.

And I don't mean the mastiff's death. On the street, they still talk about a young thief who made the mistake of trying to cut the purse of a rich man with a Neapolitan mastiff in the cathedral plaza. The dog tore the boy open and ate his intestines as if they were sausages.

This dog looked capable of doing the same. It lunged at me with a bowel-loosening snarl.

I cringed and raised the poker as my captor said, in a voice ludicrously calm for the situation, "Stop, Leo."

Leo stopped in mid-lunge, sat, and looked curiously back at his master, who had glimpsed the poker in my hand. The latter gave a short laugh and said, in a tone as soft and unworried as he'd used with the mastiff, "Oh, good God. What're you going to do with that?"

His accent had shifted. It was that of the streets, and he spoke it easily, naturally. Just like I spoke it then, even though the nuns—most of them from wealthy families—had raised us to sound like members of the merchant class.

"I'm afraid of the dog," I said in a small voice.

He sighed, his tone long-suffering. "Put down the poker. And hold out your hand, knuckles first."

I stared at the dog. If Ser Giovanni wanted to, he could tell it to attack. Mastiffs are known for being impervious to pain, and it wouldn't even have felt a few blows with an iron poker before it tore out my throat.

Something about the way the dog looked adoringly up at his master convinced me to set the poker down on the lovely carpet. I held out my unsteady hand, knuckles first.

Ser Giovanni looked at the patiently waiting animal. A glistening ribbon of thick saliva welled from its pendulous muzzle, dangled for an instant a finger's length from its chin, and gradually thinned all the way down to the floor, like a spider dropping from the ceiling. I knew it was drooling with the desire to eat my innards.

"Now, Leo," he said, as if speaking to a person. "This is . . ." He frowned and glanced up at me suddenly. "What's your name, lad?"

"Giuliano," I said. Close enough.

"Leo, this is Giuliano, a friend. Go sniff."

The obedient animal lumbered over to me. It stank, but probably smelled a lot better than I did that night. I tried to keep my fist from trembling as the dog snuffled it with its glistening black nose. Ser Giovanni could give it the order to attack at any instant.

"Good boy, Leo," his master soothed. The mastiff's stub of a tail wagged. "Stand up easily and pet him now, Giuliano. Let him smell you as much as he wants."

I stood up and slowly opened my hand. Leo—whose shoulder came to my waist—sat panting, mouth half open in a friendly grin, huge tongue lolling to one side with endearing gracelessness.

For an instant, I was confused. Why was I making friends with the dog? And then I realized: Leo was learning my scent in case I tried to run.

"He'll protect you, too, now," Ser Giovanni said, "so long as you don't try to hurt me. Even without Leo, you wouldn't have much luck." He pointed to the gold charm at his heart. "Protection. Made by the Magician of Florence."

I stared at the charm as it flashed with firelight. It was fine jewelry made with exquisite skill and, save for the fact that it was gold, it looked very like the one Tommaso now wore. For the umpteenth time that night, I fervently wished I'd been wearing it instead.

"You know my name," I said to my captor at last. "But I'm not so sure of yours."

"Eh," he said. "That will come later, if at all. It depends."

"Depends on what?"

He drew a breath and released it as he sank into a squat in front of the fire and warmed his hands. "How you respond to my . . . business proposition, and whether we come to trust each other."

I stared at him. The stiletto, his strength, his dragging me out here . . . He was certainly an uncommon criminal. A master of crime, given his wealth.

"Trust each other?" I retorted. "I'm a lad with no means of protection, and you're a brute with many. A man like you doesn't bring pickpockets in from the street out of charity."

He scowled. "You're too cynical for your age."

"With good reason. Say your piece, then I'll be on my way."

Leo raised a paw as big as my hand and rested it heavily on

my forearm, directing me to scratch the front of his chest. I didn't dare disobey. I scratched the dog until he thumped his rear leg in ecstasy.

"I'm in a business that requires an assistant with fast feet and hands, and the ability to keep his mouth shut," my captor said. "I'm sorry I had to scare you to get you here. But you'd never have believed me and considered my proposition otherwise."

I still didn't believe him. No one lurking around the Buco in disguise had honest business in mind. But the mastiff was right next to me, drooling on my boot, so I pretended to take Ser Giovanni seriously.

"What sort of work?" I asked.

Ignoring the question, he stood up. "We need to take care of that knee before it starts rotting. Come with me into the kitchen and we'll clean it up. Besides, it's past time for my supper, and I'm starving. Let's eat now and talk later."

I would have insisted on an answer, but I'd been starving before I picked his pocket at the Buco. If I was going to die, at least I'd have a full belly.

I rose. Sitting down had made my joint stiffer. I half limped behind my captor into the kitchen, the dog following.

Ser Giovanni ambled into the kitchen and pulled a stool up to the middle of the long working table, right under a sconce.

"Off with the leggings," he said.

There it was. He was a rotten lying bastard, and I had no razor, no space to run. He was after a lad; he'd be enraged to discover I was a girl.

"I can't," I said, hiding my rage, making my voice sound tearful.

He sighed and rolled his eyes. "Don't flatter yourself; I'm not interested in you that way. How else can we clean the knee? Unless you want to die in a week when it festers."

I'm very good at lies, but at that moment, I couldn't think of a single good one. "I *can't*," I repeated.

Curious, he squinted at me. "I never knew an urchin could be such a prude."

"Please don't make me," I begged.

He gestured at the stool, his tone firm. "Leave the damned leggings on, then. But sit down."

Relieved, I did.

He went to the cupboard nearest the oven and pulled out a paring knife, put the blade between his teeth and rummaged in a cupboard before pulling out a corked jug.

He set it down on the table and gestured for me to lift my knee off the stool. I did, and he slipped a clean rag under it. Then he uncorked the jug before lifting it again.

"Ready?" he asked. "This will sting."

I nodded, catching a whiff of yeast just before he poured the wine on my knee. It stung all right; I gritted my teeth while he poured until the dried blood was mostly dissolved. He would have yanked the wool away from the wound, but I pushed his hand away and did it myself. Then I dabbed at the gash with the dry edge of the rag.

It was a game he was playing, trying to get me to trust him. Maybe he preferred a willing victim.

He set the jug of wine down, took up the paring knife, and cut the dirty bit of legging away to expose the gash.

"That'll keep it from putrefying for the moment," he said. "And now . . ." He went to one of the cupboards, clattered about inside, and returned with two spoons and two bowls. One of the spoons he handed to me.

I stared as he went over to the cauldron hung over the kitchen fire and ladled stew into each bowl, then broke some chunks of bread from the loaves on the hearth and set them atop the soup.

"Where are the servants?" I asked, trying not to sound as suspicious as I felt. No wealthy man served himself supper, and no wealthy man with good intentions served it to a pauper.

He didn't answer; I had no choice but to limp after him.

He led me to a small dining room off the kitchen, already lit by tapers burning on the table, as if we'd been expected. The room was shadowy, but not quite enough to hide the oil paintings on the wall.

Or the gold candelabrum that held the burning tapers. My fear warred with the sheer agony of being near such valuable things without the means of hauling them off; it was as cruel as making a starving man watch others eat a banquet.

Leo flopped down beside the chair Ser Giovanni took.

He lifted a thick black brow. "Pray if you like. My God isn't particular about such things." And he tucked into his stew.

It was thick with rabbit meat, vegetables, and raviolini, and the smell of it made me drool like the mastiff. It could have been drugged or poisoned, but if I was doomed, I might as well appreciate such a succulent last meal.

As I ate, my captor looked up from his dish. "If you work for me," he said, munching his bread, "I'll pay you well. Ridiculously well. But the condition is that you sleep here. You'll need the protection this place provides."

I studied his brown eye and saw tiny candle flames reflected there, but nothing else; I might as well have been trying to read stone. He could have been a madman, a murderer, the world's most dangerous criminal. With the black silk patch over the other eye, he certainly looked the part.

"And what exactly is the ridiculous pay?"

"A florin if you agree to stay and train for an . . . errand, to be accomplished in a few weeks. More, after that, if the arrangement becomes permanent," he answered.

I choked on my bread and barely managed to cough it up. He was a madman, then, to think I would believe such an outrageous lie. A gold florin was more than most well-fed merchants made in a year.

"Bullshit," I said before I could stop myself.

My host grinned, slipped a hand into an invisible pocket and drew out a coin. I knew counterfeits when I saw them, and this florin was pure gold, just like the candelabrum. He held it up to the candlelight so that it glittered.

"Here." He handed it across the table to me. "Your first payment in advance."

I snatched it and bit into it; the soft gold yielded slightly to my teeth. It was a real florin, right there in my hand. I wasn't so stupid as to think he'd let me walk out alive with it, but instinct took over; I folded my fingers over it tightly and slipped it into the waist of my leggings.

I played along. "A whole florin for a few weeks' work?"

He nodded, letting his spoonful of soup rest midway between his lips and the bowl. "If you perform the errand well, there'll be a second florin as a reward—and, if we get along, more permanent employment of a florin per year. Perhaps more."

I held back a sneer of contempt. He was an idiot to think I'd believe such a stupid lie.

He saw my disbelief and continued, "As I said, it's dangerous work—but then, no more dangerous than your line of work. As a skilled pickpocket, you're well suited. I've been watching you. And as you proved in the alley, you're very, very smart in a way no other pickpocket on the streets is. That's a unique set of talents I can use."

The skin on my upper arms pricked. If he really had been watching me, then he knew about Tommaso. I shook off the ridiculous fear, reminding myself that he couldn't win me over by threatening the boy. Nothing could break my heart.

"What is it exactly that you're asking me to do, Ser Giovanni?"

His expression remained unreadable. "We'll talk about that after you agree to take the job."

"That's not fair," I said. "What if you're lying and it's more dangerous than my current line of work? I'd have to refuse."

He grinned as if I'd just told a very funny joke. His teeth were small but only a little yellowed, in good shape for someone his age. "You won't refuse me," he said jovially.

I lifted my chin, defiant. "How can you know that I won't say no?" It was all bluster, of course, and he knew it. He had his physical strength, the weapons, the dog.

His confident smile broadened. "I know. Because I, dear lad, am the Magician of Florence."

Three

When I could catch my breath, I said, "I don't believe you. You're going to have to prove it."

He was a madman, surely. I sensed he wasn't lying, that he believed what he said.

But it couldn't be true. Although . . . there was the convincing disguise, the way he had seemed so old and feeble, and the omnipotent way he had *looked* at me when he'd held the stiletto to my throat, as if he were God. And there was the priceless gold talisman over his heart, the talisman that looked so much like mine.

"If you're the Magician," I ventured, "you wouldn't need all the elaborate security."

All the locks might have made sense if he'd lived in Rome, where the Church's influence was strong and anyone found practicing sorcery would be burned as a heretic. But the Florentine government usually looked the other way, especially when the wealthy were involved.

He didn't take offense, didn't argue, didn't respond; his tone was purely practical. "I'll give you proof if you agree to take the job now," he said. "It requires a little playacting and acrobatics for now, and later, perhaps, some assistance to me in my work. But you must swear first on whatever you hold dear never to reveal what I show you. Otherwise, you can go home and tell everyone you were abducted by the Magician of Florence and not a soul will believe you."

He leaned over his bowl and attacked his stew again, then stuffed a wad of bread into his mouth.

I couldn't believe him, but there was that damned talisman staring me in the face. To know whether he was a lunatic, a criminal, or the Magician, I'd have to take the next step.

"All right," I said finally. "I'll take the job. I swear on my own life not to reveal anything you show me, anything you say."

He set down his spoon. "Good. Now first, explain it to me. Your literacy. The secret alphabet."

When I was around six or so, Sister Maria Ignatia announced that we girls were finally old enough to be schooled. I was terribly excited. And terribly disappointed when the schooling turned out to be sewing, embroidery, etiquette, cooking, and household finances—but *no* reading or writing. Those, according to the abbess, were the province of men.

I found this unacceptable. I'd been born with a love of words and an ease in learning them. I'd been dreaming of the day I'd hold a quill in my hand and form my first letters.

And, I suppose, I'd been born with the sort of stubbornness and disregard for authority that makes a good thief. So when the boys and girls met for dance lessons after chapel—the only time the sexes were allow to intermingle, under the nonexistent watch of tipsy dozing priests from the boys' orphanage—I managed to befriend a lad who recognized my intelligence and was sympathetic. Lauro was several years older than I. At the dances he would trace the letters on my palm with his finger and pronounce them for me; later, we became daring and he led me off to the library. He'd been given a key because he was the brightest boy in the orphanage, bored with the regular lessons, and was no doubt destined for university. On those Sunday afternoons, he tutored me briefly and abetted me during my first theft, watching the entrance to the library while I stole a reading and writing primer. Lauro smuggled quill, ink, and paper to me at intervals, leaving them in various hiding places for me to find; that was when I developed my secret alphabet, using stars, circles, squares, and made-up symbols, each representing a different letter of the Roman alphabet, so that we could communicate in safety. Upon seeing it, Lauro proclaimed me a genius of his stature. I was never so proud.

I thrived under these circumstances for a few years, even though the only days I could study the purloined books came when I pretended to be sick and the nuns were busy with the other children while I read my stolen treasures under the sheets. Eventually Lauro taught me a smattering of Latin; I took to it enthusiastically and would have become proficient except that one day, a benefactor rescued Lauro from the orphanage. Once again, I was abandoned.

I found a note from him in one of our hiding places saying that he had already gone; the letter was folded inside a small parchment leaflet excerpting some of Plato's work in Latin, a parting gift. I worked hard to translate every word and succeeded, but having been spared an education in philosophy, its content—about a cave and fire and shadows—left me mystified.

In the end, the little pamphlet was discovered and Sister Maria Ignatia made a public spectacle of my whipping, even though it never occurred to her that I was actually able to read it.

I didn't tell my captor the real story, of course; I told him that the "abbot" so hated me that "he'd" ignored my quickness and learning and instead of finding me a benefactor, had apprenticed me to a tanner.

Ser Giovanni listened to the story with reserve and commanded me to follow him. With Leo padding alongside, he led me out of the kitchen through the sitting room and into a cooler office that smelled of paper, parchment, and dust. A chair sat beside a desk and a cupboard; on one wall, tall wooden shelves held ledgers, quills, and vials of ink. The opposite wall was entirely covered with large maps of Tuscany, the Marches, the Papal States, and the Romagna, as well as detailed street maps of Florence, Naples, and Rome—the three cities at war. A glass-covered lamp on the desk cast flickering light onto the maps; Ser Giovanni picked it up by its brass handle and cranked up the wick; the room brightened.

And then he bent down and retrieved the gold-handled cane—the one that held the long, deadly stiletto—that was propped against the desk. With the lamp in one hand, he gestured casually with the cane in his other for me to walk ahead of him.

A thrill of dread passed through me. It had all been a ruse, this foolish talk of the Magician and florins, and I, who'd thought I was the most street-smart person in the world, was actually the most gullible. By demanding proof, I'd just pushed things toward the very end I'd feared.

The lamplight lit his lean face from beneath, gleaming on every ridge and shading every hollow, making him look ghoulish. "Go on, then," he said, his tone still amiably matter-of-fact, as if the cane had not just changed everything.

I staggered into the next room, a bare-walled storage area, the floor littered with trunks and crates; ropes, tools, and buckets sat in haphazard piles. There were no doors leading further, only a wall; no other way out save the entrance Ser Giovanni and his dog now blocked. My dead end.

Ser Giovanni handed me the lamp and lifted up a corner of the plain gray carpet. He rolled it far back on itself so that it would stay put. Beneath it sat a wooden hatch, the sort that leads down to a wine cellar. He gave the thick rope handle a tug; the hatch lifted to reveal a sturdy ladder leading down into darkness.

I stared down into a black abyss, a dungeon that might have held a private torture chamber and the skeletons of other unfortunates like myself. What if Ser Giovanni simply abandoned me there, my shrieks unheard, to languish and starve?

"I'm not going down there," I said, aware that my voice was trembling and I could not stop it.

"Yes, you are," Ser Giovanni said, faintly amused. "For a tough little thief, you frighten easily."

He handed me the cane, the one that hid the wicked stiletto, and I stared at it, thunderstruck—until I realized that he had to have switched canes.

I pulled on the cane's gilded handle enough to expose the deadly sharp blade; I couldn't have been more mystified and gaped up at Ser Giovanni.

"I've given you no reason to trust me yet," he said. "Call it a sign of good faith."

Good faith, indeed; if I'd threatened him with the stiletto, the dog would have eaten me alive.

He gestured at the mastiff. "Leo, stay."

Leo settled like a sphinx beside the open hatch and stared mournfully down into the blackness, his brow puckering.

"Now," his master said to me, "follow."

Clutching the lamp in one hand, Ser Giovanni began to climb down the ladder. Watching, Leo rested his great chin sadly between his front paws; his jowls spread out onto the exposed stone floor and began to generate a slowly spreading slick of spittle.

"Damn it," I muttered. I tucked the cane under one arm and stepped carefully onto the first rung of the ladder. As I moved onto the second and caught hold of the first with my hands, I glanced down between my legs at the receding lamp.

As I moved down, the air grew colder. The ladder wasn't long, and when I stepped off the final rung, Ser Giovanni caught my elbow to help me balance; the lamp in his hand revealed only stony ground beneath our feet and more blackness.

He gestured for me to take his arm, the one that held the lamp.

I rested my hand in the crook of his bent elbow and took half a dozen measured steps with him before he stopped. Fabric rustled as he parted black drapes, just like the ones that had blocked the light of the kitchen from the outer entry room. They hid an arched door; Ser Giovanni felt beneath his collar and pulled out the long necklace that held the skeleton keys. He unlocked the door, gave it a firm one-handed push, and motioned me inside.

I stepped in and winced a bit at the chill; Ser Giovanni followed and lifted the lamp so that the arc of light it cast expanded to reveal a cellar with earthen walls and floors. Instead of wine, it held a cabinet, worktable, shelves, and various implements of a craftsman. At its far end stood a Moorish-looking tent with a canopy, made of the same heavy black fabric as the drapes. Its curtained entrance was pulled shut, but a sliver of light escaped at the seam. I put my hand on his arm again, and we began moving toward it.

Near the cellar's entrance, a tall narrow cabinet stood beside bundles of drying herbs suspended from a hook. The cabinet was divided into a few dozen tiny drawers, all identified by small squares of yellowed paper glued to the outside, each square labeled in neat, measured script. An apothecary; every Italian family that could afford one had one, and Ser Giovanni's was well stocked, as one would expect of a wealthy man.

Next to it a trio of high bookshelves held several dozen leather tomes with gilded titles on their spines and stacks of scrolls, some of them with tarnished silver finials; beside the shelves sat a chair, a small table, and an unlit lamp.

I tried to catch some of the titles as we passed and would have stumbled right into a hole in the ground had Ser Giovanni not quickly steered me away. The lamplight revealed a small, shallow pit the breadth of both my hands, edged on all sides with steel strips. I'd been in many a shop to sell stolen trinkets and recognized it as a jeweler's furnace. Beside it lay a poker, bellows, and a large bin of coal; against the nearest wall rested a shelf holding jars of white powder, slabs of ocher beeswax, and stacks of bars: gold, silver, iron, copper, and lead. In front of the shelf, a worn, scratched worktable was littered with metal files, delicate engraving tools, a small beeswax mold, and a tiny heap of metal shavings.

A bright new silver talisman on a leather thong sat beside the shavings.

My mouth opened at the gold bars, a king's fortune; my gaze moved involuntarily from the silver talisman on the table to the gold talisman on Ser Giovanni's broad chest, then up at his face. He seemed suddenly to have increased in stature, in solidity. His exposed eye was lit not only by the lamp's glow, but also by an internal fire, an infinite confidence born of ancient wisdom.

He saw my expression of awe and the corners of his lips stretched faintly, grimly upward, not in a smile as much as an acknowledgment that he was worthy of it.

He moved to the worktable, took up the silver talisman in his free hand, and gestured for me to accompany him.

I nursed no thoughts of escape now; I had to see what awaited us. He stopped a few steps from the black velvet tent, where a few hooded black capes hung from wooden pegs.

A sheathed Turkish scimitar was propped beneath them.

For some reason, I remembered Tommaso's favorite Bible story, the story of Abraham and Isaac, and in my mind's eye saw Isaac strapped to the stone altar, struggling vainly as his father raised the knife above him, ready to strike.

I was being led to slaughter. How could I have forgotten that the blackest magic required blood?

I pulled the cane from under my arm and unsheathed the stiletto just as Ser Giovanni was setting the lamp down on the ground. He rose slowly and raised his hands, palms facing me to show he meant no harm.

"Relax, lad," he said softly, without any fear. "You can hold on to the weapon, if it gives you comfort. You can even keep it unsheathed. The whole purpose of bringing you down here is to protect you, not cause you harm."

I wanted to whip the stiletto through the air in front of him, to make it sing as shrilly as it had when he'd brandished it at me. I wanted to be gone, with as many gold bars as I could carry. I lifted it and pointed it at his chest.

Utterly unimpressed, he took a cloak from a peg and tossed it at me; it landed silently in a heap at my feet.

"Take your cap and boots off and put this on," he directed. "And raise the hood." Then he took another cloak and, turning his back to the dagger's tip, began to pull it on.

"You're a fool to trust me," I said, angry that my voice was quivering. "I'll run you through and take those bars with me."

"No you won't," he said blithely, pulling off his boot.

"What's to stop me?"

Once the boot was off, he turned back toward me, his one foot bare, his other shod, and his gaze fastened on mine as if the blade between us didn't exist.

"Me," he answered, his tone even and calm. "And the dog. And the gates. But most of all . . ." He lifted the gold talisman hung around his neck and held it up for me to see. "This."

I thought of Tommaso and the plague and sheathed the dagger, then set the cane against the wall and picked up the cloak. It was so long the fabric pooled around my feet; the sleeves fell half an arm's length beyond my hands.

Ser Giovanni proceeded to pull off his other boot, then pulled the hood over his face and studied me in the wavering light as I removed my boots. Shadows hid his eye and the upper bridge of his nose; I could see only its long tip, the black, skeletal hollows of his cheeks, and the deep crevices on either side of his mouth. Give him a scythe, and he was Death personified.

"When we're inside, don't speak," he said, his tone still hushed. "Or move unless I tell you to. Do *not* touch anything. Keep your hands at your side."

I nodded and scuffled behind him, trying not to trip over folds of my robe's fabric, as he parted the black drape and went inside the tent.

I entered a different world.

The walls and carpet were black, and the high black ceiling had been speckled with gold paint to resemble the night sky, giving the illusion that we stood beneath the stars in a place that had no boundaries. A ceiling lamp shone down on objects that seemed to float in the air: a white candle, a brass thurible, a gilded goblet, a steel dagger. Miraculously, Ser Giovanni set the silver talisman beside the goblet, where it hung, motionless, suspended.

Above the objects, a painting floated, a diagram comprised of ten carefully spaced circles divided into three columns: four circles in the center row, flanked by three circles on either side, all connected by thick lines painted in different colors, all containing different mysterious symbols.

Ser Giovanni took his place in front of the altar and used a striking steel to light the incense in the thurible. He began to chant what sounded like a very ancient prayer in a very foreign tongue. The air came alive, as if a lightning bolt had just struck the ground we were standing on. I felt tingling in my feet and spine and grew lightheaded, as though I'd drunk a large cup of unwatered wine. Of course he couldn't be *the* Magician; such a thing could never happen to me, and he seemed quite the mortal sitting at the dinner table. But there was no doubt he was *a* magician. And a powerful one at that.

He struck the steel again, and a spark caught the wick of the white candle and flared. Only when he struck the steel a third time and set it to an invisible wick did I realize that there was a black candle opposite the white one and that the objects that seemed to be floating in space were actually resting on two square black boxes, one stacked atop the other.

By the time he picked up the steel dagger and began to walk around the perimeter of the tent with it, pointing it straight ahead sometimes and other times swiping at the empty air with it, I was swaying on my feet like a bridegroom about to faint. Although my body felt drunk, my mind seemed curiously clear. I marked each action he took and listened to his strange gibberish.

I'm normally not superstitious, but I was entranced. Even though he spoke softly, Ser Giovanni's deep voice vibrated with such power that it filled the tent and thundered in my ears. After he made a full circle, he returned to the altar, made some motions with the knife over the silver talisman, then set down the knife, took up the small vial, and coaxed a drop from it onto the talisman's center. He was casting a spell upon it, imbuing it with magical power right before my eyes. Preparing it as only a real magician could.

He picked up the talisman and vial and turned back to me. In the flickering light, I caught sight of his gaze.

It was fierce, magnificent, compelling, filled with otherworldly power. I lowered my eyes to the ground, feeling uneasy, unworthy. Whatever was happening here was either very wicked or very holy. I could feel the tingling energy of it in my freezing toes, up my legs, into my spine.

But he wasn't *the* Magician. He couldn't be. The Magician would never reveal himself to a lowly urchin; besides, amazing things never happened to me.

He put one palm over the talisman and vial in his other hand and uttered a short prayer. Then he spoke to me, his tone distant, otherworldly.

"Lower your hood, please."

My heart began to race. He'd made the amulet well before going to the Buco Tavern this evening to find me and bring me here. *I've been watching you for a while.* He had prepared his tent for this ritual. All of his efforts this night had been to bring me here to this moment, this instant.

My long robes would trip me up before I ever made it out of the tent, and so I wormed my hands out of the long sleeves and complied. At least he didn't have a knife in his hand—yet. He slipped the leather thong over my head, and the silver amulet fell over my heart, exactly where the other one had hung.

Ser Giovanni put his forefinger to the open vial and upended it briefly. He stretched out his hand, his fingertip cold as the ground, and traced a symbol on my forehead. I smelled cinnamon and clove; my forehead tingled and began to burn, but I dared not wipe the oil away.

He returned to the altar, put down the vial, and took up the dagger, and did some swiping with it. When he had circled the entire tent, he put out the candles with the flat of his blade.

We were done, and I wasn't dead.

The minute we stepped outside the tent, I rubbed my irritated brow on my sleeve.

Ser Giovanni laughed as he pulled back his hood. He was mortal again, with a human voice; he no longer seemed so tall.

"It burns, I know," he said. "It's for protection, like the talisman. The least I could do, putting you in this line of work."

I didn't believe a word. People don't take young thieves home in order to protect them—not without a darker motive.

On the way out of the dungeon, Ser Giovanni paused at the worktable to pick up a blunt knife, then headed for the cabinet beneath the drying herbs and opened one of the tiny compartments. He drew out a small glass jar containing a dark brown gummy substance with an unpleasant chemical smell and took out a dab of it—smaller than a quarter of a pea—with the edge of the knife. He rolled it between his thumb and forefinger to produce a tiny ball and popped it into his pocket. I stared quizzically at him, but he said only:

"For that knee of yours."

He went first as we climbed back up the ladder, toward the welcome warmth. Leo was waiting for us in the storeroom, his ghost-gray stump of a tail wagging, a viscous pool of spittle lying on the stone floor where he'd rested his chin.

"Mind that, it's slippery," Ser Giovanni said, taking my arm as I stepped up from the ladder, wincing at the stab of pain beneath my throbbing knee. With Leo in tow, we walked back out the way we came, the air growing warmer with each step. But instead of leading me back to the lavish sitting room, he guided me to a staircase leading to the upper floors.

"You'll be sleeping in a real bed in your own room tonight," he said. "You'll bathe first, though."

"No," I said stoutly.

He sighed. "Lad, I already told you I've no interest in you that way. Those filthy rags you're wearing are going into the fire and you'll bathe before you lie down in a clean bed. It's not just that you stink. I won't have your lice and fleas in my house."

He stepped onto the landing, turned to the left, and opened a door.

I followed him into a bedchamber ten times the size of the attic Tommaso and I shared, where a thigh-high wooden tub sat beside a sputtering hearth; steam hung over the bathwater.

It had to be magic. How else could the water still be hot?

A neatly folded towel and a lump of soap rested on the floor next to the tub, as did a stack of boy's clothing—unnerving proof that my captor had been watching me, and planning, for some time. Ser Giovanni took kindling from the pile and tossed it onto the glowing coals, then stirred it with the poker. The fire came fully to life, casting its orange glow onto us, onto the walls.

A large bed with sumptuous covers and drawn-back curtains stood against one wall, but I was too nervous to notice much else. My gaze was on the magician, who propped the poker against the hearth as though he had no fear I'd try to brain him with it. He held out his hand, and when I recoiled from it, he sighed and turned his face away to give me my privacy. Leo pressed against his legs like a magnet.

"Off with it, now," he ordered, not looking at me. "Everything."

"Stand on the other side of the door," I told him. "You don't have to close it all the way."

When he didn't budge, I worked up false tears until one spilled down my cheek. "Please," I said.

He pressed fingers to his temple and rubbed it as if his head hurt. "Good God. All right. But give me your boots."

I complied quickly. He took the boots and wrinkled his nose.

"Awfully small feet to have created such a stench," he said. He held the boots at arm's length by the back cuffs and went back through the doorway, the dog following. He pulled the door two-thirds shut behind him.

Shielded from his sight, I set the florin on the night table, then shed my clothes and hurled them at the door.

My undergarments were a problem. I always wore a ragged piece of cotton around my waist and folded one edge into a proper-looking codpiece, the better to fool people into thinking I was male. I also wore a length of linen fabric wound four times, tight as a shroud, around my chest. I unfastened the false codpiece, then unwound the linen around my breasts and squelched an appreciative sigh at the lack of pressure. I kicked both under the bed.

Ser Giovanni called at the door. "Where are your undergarments?"

"Haven't got any," I replied. I tiptoed over to the poker and took it, just in case, and sloshed the water with it so he'd think I was getting in. Then I raised it over my shoulder, ready to bring it down on his head the instant he set foot inside the room to take advantage of my freshly bathed nakedness.

Instead, the door slammed closed, and Ser Giovanni and Leo's footfalls receded down the stairs until I heard nothing at all.

I couldn't bring myself to get into the tub, although the water looked beckoning. Even though my feet were still aching from walking unshod on the freezing dungeon floor, warming them thoroughly—for the first time all winter—seemed a delicious notion. In the orphanage, I'd never seen clean, hot water in a tub, only the dirty, tepid dregs left by several predecessors before my turn came.

I propped the poker against the tub and turned toward the fire to study the new silver talisman around my neck. Other than the fact that the metal was dazzling and untarnished, it looked extremely similar to the one I'd given Tommaso to wear, although the rows of numbers on the back were different, as were a few of the symbols on the front.

But one was not: a small *M*, with an *F* growing out of its left leg.

See there? Sister Anna Maria had urged, on that long-ago day in the orphanage. *That little sun and moon conjoined—so you see the tiny crescent moon there? It embraces the sun, that circle with a dot in it.*

It was the stamp of the Magician of Florence.

Just as it had in the starry-skied black tent, the hair on the back of my neck lifted. This time, the hair on my forearms rose as well, because I *knew*.

I dropped the talisman and it fell between my breasts. I was so stunned I forgot the poker and my treacherous situation and stood frozen, staring into the fire, trying not to believe and utterly failing.

I was naked; I couldn't flee out into the fatal cold. Mindless, numb, I propped the poker beside the fireplace, where it belonged, and set the towel and soap beside the tub, within easy reach.

I sat down in the water and gasped at its warmth, then picked up the honey-colored bar lying beside the towel. Soap was dear, and Tommaso and I always went without. It was scented with lavender and rosewater, and I lathered myself up with it mechanically, hardly realizing what I was doing, because I was so afraid.

It had nothing to do with the Magician's possibly nefarious plans for me or his drooling monster of a dog. I could accept that my host was *a* magician, but I didn't want to know that he was *the* Magician.

Because if he really was *the* Magician . . .

My talisman had been my one link to my parents—a silent, metal one. Now here was one of flesh and blood. He might have seen my mother and father face-to-face. Spoken to them. His hand might have brushed against theirs.

Which meant that my parents had been real people, not faceless monsters. People who had gone to the Magician for help because they'd wanted to protect their child. And *that* was too horrible, too painful to contemplate for an instant.

Better hatred than grief. Hatred at least keeps you moving.

At that moment of crystalline certainty, my plans changed drastically. I was no longer interested only in escaping with as much booty as I could carry. As terrified as I was of learning it, I would stay with Ser Giovanni until I learned the truth about my parents. I would take the job and earn my florin, if necessary.

And *then* I would escape with as much treasure as I could carry.

I dunked my head into the filmy water and felt the fleas begin scrambling across my scalp. I held my breath under the water until I was sure they'd all drowned, then came up for air and began scrubbing my close-cropped mane.

Taking the job made more and more sense to me. Tommaso and Cecilia would be worried that night, but in the morning I could explain everything to them. Money could change our lives. Cecilia could dress the part of a respectable widow and pass Tommaso off as her child. They'd never be cold or hungry. I could buy Tommaso the best education Florence could provide; he could grow up to become a wealthy merchant or shopkeeper. He could provide comfortably for a wife and children and live a happy life.

Not that I cared, mind you. The best thing about the money was what it could do for me.

As I dunked my head back in the filmy water and massaged it to rinse away the soap, I still wondered whether I was being played for a fool—whether, now that I was clean and less physically offensive, Ser Giovanni would suddenly bound in and ravish me. But the door didn't open, not a crack, as I stepped out of the tub and grabbed my damp towel to cover myself. No pickpocket had ever smelled so sweet.

I put on the clothes—all of fine, dark blue wool, and comically large on my small frame; the felt cap dropped past my eyebrows instead of resting snugly just below my hairline.

My boots were still gone, so I padded across the floor in my leggings and went downstairs looking for Ser Giovanni. Leo was sitting in the doorway leading to the kitchen and wagged his stump of a tail as I passed. I found his owner standing at the working table rubbing lard into my boots.

"Stop it!" I exclaimed, scandalized to see such a wealthy man at such a menial task. "I'll do that!"

"Too late," he said. "Already done." He handed the gleaming boots to me. "So, are you going to work for me?"

"Yes," I said firmly. "I want to work for the Magician of Florence. I don't want to go back to the streets, and I certainly don't want to end up a tanner. But . . ." I hesitated. I didn't want to look weak, and I also worried he wouldn't believe me.

"But?" he prompted.

"I have a couple of friends," I said, trying to sound as truthful as I actually was. "They rely on me. I need to tell them I'm all right. And I need to give them this florin."

I watched distrust flicker across his face. He knew I could just take the money and be gone forever. I held his keen one-eyed gaze for a while and tried to emanate sincerity from every pore in my skin.

"All right," he said at last. "Visit your friends in the morning and tell them you've obtained legitimate employment. But one thing I insist on: that you never return to your old life. You'll be living here so long as you work for me, and you'll never need to steal again."

I gave a small smile of triumph. Of course, working for a magician meant my eternal damnation, but then, I was already well and damned as a pickpocket. I offered my hand like a man, to seal the deal.

He stared at it for a moment. "First, your name. Your real one, please."

"It really is Giuliano," I answered, somewhat truthfully.

"Giuliano it is, then," he echoed. "I'm Abramo." He offered his hand.

Of *course* Giovanni wasn't his real name.

"Ser Abramo," I said, and shook it. Of course, if I'd known the real truth, about the magic and the Medici and what I was really volunteering for, I'd never have taken his hand. "Can I ask you a question?"

"So long as you quit calling me *Ser*."

"Are you really three hundred years old?"

He laughed so hard I never did get an answer.

Lamp in one hand, cup in the other, and a man's woolen nightshirt draped over one arm, Ser Abramo led me back up the stairs to the bedroom with the tub beside the hearth. Leo padded beside us, half grinning in apparent approval.

"You'll sleep here tonight," the Magician said, as he set the cup and lamp on the night table and the folded nightshirt on the bed while I watched, squatting beside the fire. "There's a chamber pot beneath the bed and a basin and pitcher of water over in the corner. I'll give you the choice of drinking the wine or not." Ser Abramo gestured with his chin at the cup on the night table. "It'll taste bitter because I mixed that bit of opium with it. But drink it down quick and it won't be too bad."

"Opium?"

"Poppy. Don't try to tell me that knee of yours doesn't hurt; I've seen you limping a bit. If you have trouble sleeping because of the pain, this will ease it."

I stiffened with mistrust.

He saw it and shrugged. "Your choice. If the ache begins to argue with you tonight, the cup is there. It'll make you drowsy, but too much of it can put you to sleep forever, so mind you don't get any ideas of sneaking downstairs for more."

"Yes, sir." I looked at the four-poster bed in front of me, with its expensive brocade canopy and velvet bed curtains. It was large enough to hold half a dozen orphans. I'd never slept in a bed without someone else in it, and the thought was daunting.

"The hearth should keep you warm enough," Abramo said. "I'll show you the privy in the morning. Good night then," he said, and turned toward the door, but a thought stopped him. He reached for one of the thongs around his neck, lifted it up over his head, and held it out to me.

Skeleton keys; the way onto the property, and the way out. They jangled as he dropped them into my palm.

"Here," he said. "I have other copies. I think it's important to trust each other, don't you?"

I was still staring down at the keys when he left, closing the door softly behind him.

I stripped, threw the keys on the night table, pulled on the ridiculously big nightshirt, and bolted the door—I didn't want to
have to spend the night wondering just how much I trusted Ser
Abramo.

And then I crawled into the magnificent bed. A real feather
bed. I sank into it the way a raisin sinks into rising dough. The
brocade cover was stiff, but the thick wool blanket was heavy and
soft and clean, not at all scratchy and questionable-smelling like
the one Tommaso and I shared. The sheets were silk, and the sensation of them against my clean perfumed skin, along with the
warmth of the blanket and the hearth, was so delicious that I
almost forgot my aching knee.

I fell asleep quickly. But a few hours later, I must have shifted
my weight back onto the knee because the pain woke me. I suffered with it an hour or so until I finally decided it was probably
safe to drink from the cup on the night table.

The wine itself was finer than I'd ever tasted—not the sour,
watered-down stuff I'd tasted on occasion—but smooth and
delicious, except for the slightly bitter aftertaste. I snuggled back
under the blanket and waited for the throbbing in my knee to
ease. I remember wondering if it ever would, when I suddenly
awoke from a dream of Ser Abramo talking earnestly to another man.

The poppy-tinged wine left me so giddy that I laughed, re-
membering all that had happened that night—the stiletto at my
throat, the magical ceremony, the displays of priceless art, the
Magician of Florence. It had to all be a dream or a vision brought
on by fever. I sat up in the bed, pushing against all-too-real feathers and down. The blanket was real, and the cup on the night
table, and the washtub, and the dying embers in the hearth.

Maybe the voices had been real, too. I held my breath and
strained to listen.

A moment of silence passed, but then—very faint but undeniable—came a sound. Muffled, unintelligible, but definitely a human voice. Ser Abramo's, perhaps.

And then that of another man. Had I not been listening so intently, however, I would never have heard them.

If I hadn't been so torn about whether to trust Ser Abramo, or just so damned curious about what was going on, I might have yielded to the sweet drowsiness and gone back to sleep.

Instead, I folded back the covers and slipped from the bed. The floor was cold beneath my bare feet. I crept to the door—movement made me slightly queasy, but that mild discomfort paled compared to the velvet sensation of air against my skin and the slow, delicious throb of my heart. I unbolted the door, opened it, and slipped onto the small landing at the top of the stairs. Ser Abramo's chamber was nearby to my left, and the door to the darkened room was cracked. I put my ear next to it and listened.

The voices were definitely emanating from the room, along with the louder sound of Leo snoring. And yet . . .

The closer I leaned toward the opening and the harder I strained to hear, the more convinced I became that only Leo was actually inside. The voices were coming from inside the room, yet muffled as though they were farther away.

I pressed gently against the heavy wooden door until it opened enough for me to see inside the room.

The heap of glowing ash in the fireplace eased the darkness just enough for me to make out the shapes of cabinets and night tables, black against the grayish light. I could hear Leo snuffling in his sleep on the other side of the large bed.

The *empty* large bed, which hadn't been slept in. Ser Abramo was nowhere to be seen.

But faintly, ever so faintly, I could hear men's muted voices coming from the wall next to the fireplace.

From *within* the wall.

Lorenzo is fleeing to France, someone said.

And another voice replied, mysteriously, *Lorenzo is the fool.*

I tried, but could make out no other words.

Mind you, there were no other rooms—at least, no other rooms visible to my eyes—on the second level except for my bedchamber and Ser Abramo's. It was impossible for there to be voices droning on in the wall, but there they were.

I pushed away the thought that Ser Abramo had become disembodied and was having an invisible conversation with a magical being. There was a logical explanation. There had to be.

Such as a hidden room.

I stood, listening to the unintelligible conversation until I began to feel lightheaded; I backed out onto the landing and silently pulled the door back to its original position, then stole quietly back to my room.

As I stirred the fire back to life—staring fixedly at the beautiful glints of blue and green hidden within the sputtering orange flames—thoughts swirled in my head.

Ser Abramo already had a huge jeweler's shop and magical circle down in the cellar. The voice inside the wall was not his, but another man's—or was it a demon, conjured to tell the future?

I wasn't sure I wanted to find out.

I remembered the keys on the night table.

I think it's important to trust each other, don't you?

I pondered Ser Abramo's words and felt a sudden, sobering thrill of fear.

He'd done everything to make sure I trusted him. Fed me, tended to my wound, gave a stirring magical performance, and made me feel special, chosen, wanted . . . all the things an orphan craved most to be. He'd even given me what supposedly were the keys to the estate.

Having so thoroughly courted my trust, he had also given me the wine mixed with the fruit of the poppy.

My choice, he'd said. Knowing that I was in pain and would almost certainly reach for the cup.

It was a Game, just like the one Tommaso and I played. It had to be. Ser Abramo—if that was really his name—was just performing another role, like the one of the old man Ser Giovanni, hunched over his cane. He wasn't the Magician of Florence. He *couldn't* be; the Magician would never let a cur like me come near him. He certainly wouldn't *choose* me, of all pickpockets, to work with him.

Abramo was playing a game with me either to indulge his twisted personal pleasure or to entrap me into becoming something worse than a pickpocket. If life had taught me anything, it was that no one was trustworthy—especially the rich, who hated us poor.

A whole florin. What had I been thinking? It was too good to be true.

Panicked, I pulled on my clothes and took the florin and the keys. I was out the door and down the stairs as quickly as my sluggish limbs could move. I was in sedated terror the whole way down, sure that Leo would wake up and hear me.

I made my way to the bolted door leading to the sitting room, which Ser Abramo had locked earlier. I lifted the bolt and slipped one of the skeleton keys into the lock. I expected to make several tries with different keys and discover none worked, but to my surprise, the door was already unlocked.

I pushed it open and entered the sitting room. The ebbing light from the hearth allowed me to steer around the daybeds and chairs, past the busts of ancient philosophers, the tapestries, and the paintings.

Terrified or not, the thief in me couldn't resist slipping two of the gemstone goblets into the waistband of my leggings.

I moved through the kitchen, the soup cauldron still hanging above the glowing coals. The door where Ser Abramo and I had entered the house was still bolted from the inside; I lifted the bolt and pushed . . .

It was open, as was the door leading outdoors.

I stepped out into the night and drew in a lungful of cold, bracing air. There weren't many hours of darkness left; the glowing white moon was easing itself down into the western sky. I limped up to the heavy stone wall surrounding the property and put my shoulder to it. It slowly slid open.

Beyond lay the pockmarked field and, across the river, the moon hovered just above the black skyline of the city.

Adjusting the heavy precious goblets to keep them from sliding down into my leggings, I moved in the direction of the river, the limbs of barren trees casting ghoulish shadows onto the pockmarked earth. I was halfway to the River Arno when I planted my foot into another mole hole. I went down screeching.

I sat on the freezing ground staring up at the moon, once again certain that it would be the last thing I saw, certain that any second, I would hear the thrum of four-legged footfall, the gasping of canine breath.

But there was only silence and the sound of my own panting. I was free to go back to Tommaso, to return to my unsafe, unhappy life on the streets. To let my past remain a mystery, and my future stunted and miserable.

I stood up and turned to look back, for one last time, at the distant walls covered with their thicket of dead vines. Did they enclose a trap or the secret of my past and a chance for a better life?

I turned my face back to the Arno, tasting freedom. Then turned it back toward the stone wall, considering that a different sort of freedom might have been lying there.

Either direction held the risk of an early demise. But only one held the promise of something good happening to me, a concept so foreign it frightened me.

I drew a deep breath and started moving back the way I'd come, toward the vine-covered wall.

I carefully bolted each gate and then each door in the house behind me. I replaced the precious goblets on the hearth mantel. When I came to the stairs—my tread clumsy because of the poppy—Leo's silhouette was waiting at the top, on the landing.

It was the final test of the Magician's unmerited trust in me. The mastiff stood perfectly motionless, a pale gray ghost; his stillness could have been calm or the prelude to a vicious lunge. I spoke softly to him as I came up toward him, trying not to quake.

Queasy with fear, I stopped two steps from the landing, almost close enough to pet him, certainly close enough for him to tear out my throat with a single move. Suddenly, he grinned, tongue lolling over monstrous teeth, and his stubby tail and backside began to wiggle.

Ser Abramo really had taught Leo my scent so that the dog would know and trust me, not so that he could hunt me down.

"Good boy," I whispered as I climbed up to stand beside him, stunned by the possibility that a stranger I'd met on the streets of Florence meant me well. The Magician of Florence, no less.

Still, there had to be a catch. It scared me to believe that something so good could happen. I didn't want to trust Ser Abramo. And I certainly didn't want to care, because then God and the Devil would conspire to take him away from me.

But there was magic in Abramo's house, a magic deeper than any talisman or incantation. I didn't understand it then, but it was beginning to stir inside of me.

"Hello, Leo," I murmured, and reached out to touch his soft velvet head.

Four

I woke from a dead sleep to sharp rapping, and opened my eyes to see Ser Abramo in my doorway with a lamp in hand, Leo at his side. When I'd returned to bed the previous night, I'd unintentionally left my bedchamber door open, thanks to exhaustion and the poppy's effects.

I sat up in the glorious feather bed, pulling the sheets and blanket up to my collarbone, and noted that, other than my knee, my body was unharmed, my virginity intact. The very real new talisman between my breasts was warm from my body heat. I ran a hand through my close-cropped hair, still amazed by how soft and clean it felt and by the aromas of rose and lavender wafting from it.

My dreams had been so vivid that had I not been in the feather bed staring at Ser Abramo, I wouldn't have believed he or his house existed. Leo and the open doors had been real, I decided, but the voices in the wall had definitely been the product of my opium-fueled imagination. Still, I felt a stirring of anger at the very thought that Lorenzo would abandon Florence for France.

"Good morning," Ser Abramo said. His voice held a warm lilt. He glanced at the open doorway then at me, and smiled in a way that hinted my supposed trust had touched him. He had no clue that I'd meant to bolt it again.

"You slept through the bells," he said. "I expect they must be deafening where you live. Get dressed and come down to the kitchen. You'll hear footsteps; it's just the chambermaid, using the back stairs to get to our rooms. She knows to stay out of our way, so don't go looking for her. She'll be off before we finish breakfast. Cook's already been and gone."

He paused. "I'm glad you decided to come back last night," he said knowingly.

I made my expression as blank and innocent as possible.

"The goblets over the fireplace. You switched them when you put them back."

I felt heat on my face. He was, after all, the dangerously power-ful Magician, and if angered, God knows what punishment he could inflict.

"I *am* sorry about the goblets," I mumbled. "I'll never steal from you again."

"See that you don't," he said, suddenly all business and brush-ing the topic away with faint impatience. "I'll lead you back toward the city today until you learn your way. You have an hour and a half to see your friends and tell them you'll be sleeping else-where. Then we'll meet at the foot of the Old Bridge, on the east side of the Oltrarno shore. Don't worry, I'll find you."

My best friend, Cecilia, lived in a room above the potter's shop next door to the Porco Tavern on the Via de' Calzaiuoli, in the center of town, right across the street from the infamous Fico. I'd tried to get her apprenticed to the potter when she moved in; he produced excellent *maiolica*—the tin-glazed pottery decorated in bright shades of cobalt, antimony yellow, and rust—and made a good living. Unfortunately, his wife was too jealous to permit it, though not jealous enough to refuse the rent money I paid her, even though she rightly suspected Cecilia of having plied the prostitute's trade. She needn't have worried, though; Cecilia would never have dreamed of seducing another woman's husband. She was a shy girl, never one to run after boys.

Cecilia looked like a painting of Venus or an angel—skin like pearl, huge blue eyes, pale golden hair that fell in loose curls past her waist, although when she became a mother, she wore it pinned up. She would have been impossibly beautiful if it hadn't been for her small round button of a nose. She grew up, but that little nose never did keep pace. Even so, men still turned their heads to gape at her like fools.

Girls like me, with plain long noses and heavy eyebrows and thin lips, we were the ones that people called "handsome" when they were feeling kind. We could get away with masquerading as young men. But then there were curvy goddesses like Cecilia, with her sweet feminine face, impressive bosom, and impossibly delicate hands. If she'd dressed like a lad, people would have laughed.

Her landlord thought I was her boyfriend and kept asking her when I was going to propose.

Because a decent woman couldn't be seen traipsing the streets by herself, Tommaso and I accompanied her to Mass at the big domed cathedral, the Duomo, every Sunday, and she took to teaching him the sung responses in the liturgy, and how to cross himself.

"Just because the nuns were awful to us," she always said, "doesn't mean there isn't a loving God."

After Mass, when most of the people had cleared out, we would stay behind so Tommaso could stare up at the enormous cupola until his neck ached. You can't believe it if you haven't seen it; it's the largest one in the whole world, too big to describe, and it rises to an impossible height. The architect must have used pure magic to keep it from caving in. I would stare up at it, too, and the shaft of light that filtered down from the opening at the very top. If ever I came close to believing in heaven, it was then.

"And who designed the dome?" Cecilia always asked Tommaso.

"Brunelleschi!" he'd crow.

"And what else did Brunelleschi design?"

"The orphanage!"

Then we'd troop across the street to the Baptistery, because Tommaso loved to look at the different brass bas-relief panels on the three famous doors, each panel telling a different biblical story.

"And who designed this door?" Cecilia would ask.

"Ghiberti!" Tommaso would shout, depending on the door. Or: "Pisano!"

Cecilia would point to the different panels and make Tommaso name them: John the Baptist baptizing Jesus. Salome dancing. Flagellation. Tommaso's favorite panel was the one of the angel staying Abraham's hand before he killed his son Isaac. It made him happy, he said, that Isaac didn't die and went back to live with his father. My favorite panel was the one of Salome holding John the Baptist's head on a dish. Cecilia said my choice showed a lot of anger toward men. Her favorite was the one of Jesus walking on the water, rescuing Saint Peter from drowning. I said her choice showed a lot of wishful thinking.

The frames around the panels were decorated with vining designs and flowers, and the brass heads of men that projected right off the door. Tommaso always had to go to the north door and look down near the bottom for the fat balding head of Ghiberti, the man who designed the best doors. All the other heads wore solemn expressions and stared off into the distance, but old Ghiberti looked right at you with a sly little smirk. Most of the brass was still somewhat bright on the doors, but the top of Ghiberti's round head was completely dull. Like everyone else in the city, Tommaso liked to rub it for luck.

That's the thing about Florence. Even the poorest of us are proud of our architecture and our art. Ask any street urchin, and he'll take you on a grand tour, rattling off the names of the creators and explaining the symbolism as if he had built or painted it himself. Tommaso got excited and proud about learning all these things, and Cecilia was a good teacher.

She was two years older than me; we grew up sharing a bed with four other girls. We joked we were sisters, although we couldn't have been more different. I remember the first time (out of hundreds) that I went without supper for some cheeky remark. I must have been about five, and the abbess had said in front of all the other girls that I was wicked and bound for hell. I was banished to the big orphan's chamber and standing defiantly on the bed while all of the other children were eating in the refectory. Cecilia left supper early, saying she felt sick, but she really left so that she could smuggle me some bread.

I remember sitting on the bed across from her and eating it with gusto when she said, in her quiet way, "You're not wicked, and you're not going to hell. Don't ever listen to what Sister Maria Ignatia says. She doesn't like you because she's not very bright, and you are."

That was all it took for me to be loyal to Cecilia forever. Up to that point, I'd never realized I was smart. I'd just thought most grown-ups were dumb.

But I was never smart enough to keep my mouth shut, especially when Sister Maria Ignatia's nasty comments caused some of the girls to burst into tears. *Stupid cow* was one of her favorite expressions, and more than once I made the sobbing girl laugh by telling Sister Maria Ignatia to her face, *Actually, we're calves, which makes you sisters the cows. And you're abbess, so you're the biggest—*

I never got to finish the sentence without being slapped so hard I bit my tongue. Or punished in some other physical way that would have scandalized the educated Florentines who funded the orphanage. They considered beatings cruel and low class. So did I. I'd rather die than raise my hand against Tommaso, and he knows it, the little shite.

Sister Maria Ignatia wasn't swift enough to come up with a different phrase, and it got to the point where every time she uttered *stupid cow*, the girls would start to giggle, because they knew I wouldn't let it rest. Over the years, Cecilia became the only thing standing between me and hunger. I stopped minding getting slapped, because I looked forward to Cecilia bringing me a bit of food, and most of all, to talking alone with her.

One day, when we were alone and I was ranting bitterly against God for allowing children to go without parents, Cecilia said, "I think God makes orphans so we can choose our own families. When we finally leave this place, can I tell people you're my little sister?"

The day I left the orphanage, I dragged Tommaso with me to the first vacant alleyway, where I donned the boy's clothing that I'd nicked and chopped off my hair with stolen scissors. Then straightaway, I went looking for Cecilia. I knew she had married an old baker when she left the orphanage, and I went from shop to shop asking where I could find her. Turned out the bastard had beaten her so badly that she ran away and wouldn't go back. I finally found her on the Via de' Calzaiuoli halfway between the Duomo and the Old Bridge, wearing her legally required little bells like a necklace and bracelets, tottering around in those dangerous high-heeled slippers. Her golden hair was scandalously uncovered and hung down her shoulders to show off those beautiful loose curls. I spotted her leaning back against the side wall of the Berteluccie tavern, fluttering her blond lashes at a wealthy, overfed man. The look on his face made me want to retch.

We figured out that she was already pregnant the day I found her.

I couldn't bear the thought of her having to be a prostitute for another second, but at the time, I was broke with no place to stay. Tommaso and I bunked in tiny rat-infested little room for a few nights until I ran into Rafael on the street. I guess he was around seventeen or eighteen then. He tried to pick my pockets, but when he saw I didn't have a single coin on me, he took pity and became my teacher. And . . .

Back in the orphanage, I swore that I would never give my heart to another human being, because even my own parents didn't love me enough to keep me. No one could be trusted. Then came Rafael, and I broke my own rule for him. I let myself care— and of course, he met a terrible, tragic end.

Lesson taken: Love exists only to break your heart. Therefore, I do my best not to care.

Loyalty, now, that's another matter, one of personal honor. A heartless thief I may be, a heretic and a sinner, but I am loyal. Prove yourself to me, and I will never desert you. I'm stupid that way.

So that morning, I walked into the crockery maker's shop; he and his wife were working a well-off customer for a large sale and didn't give me a glance. I walked up the stairs behind the counter and through the series of rooms that led back to Cecilia's. I gave a rap on the door and Cecilia unbolted and flung open the door so fast, I knew she'd been hoping it was me.

She'd wound a long scarf tightly around her head and pulled one end through the top opening, so that the rest of the scarf hung down her back. It wasn't a flattering look, but it was popular among working-class wives, which is what Cecilia wanted to look like. She was still beautiful anyway, even in her overlarge gray kirtle, a used one I found for her at the clothier's, and an underdress of old yellowed wool.

"Don't wake the baby," she whispered out of habit, and then immediately cried out, "Oh thank God, Giuli, we were so worried!" She planted a kiss on both of my cheeks and hugged me so tightly I couldn't breathe.

Just when I thought I was going to faint for lack of air, she loosened her grip on me enough to call out, "Tommaso! Tommaso, look! It's Giuli!"

The baby started crying of course, and Tommaso flew at me like a stone loosed from a slingshot.

"Giuliano!" he cried, happy and indignant at the same time. "Giuliano, you scared me!"

We collided with such force that I staggered backward, nearly knocked off my feet. I couldn't help but laugh. He wound his thin, surprisingly strong little arms around my waist and burrowed his face there, crying for a few seconds, and then he punched me square in the gut the way boys do when they're mad. It was symbolic, not serious, and didn't hurt that much. I held him at arm's length by his shoulders while I squatted down to his level.

"I got caught last night," I said, growing serious. "You know I'd never stay away on purpose. I like to keep my word."

He hugged me again. I clicked my tongue in annoyance, but hugged him back anyway in order to keep my balance. He smelled like a little boy—that slightly sour smell of sweat that isn't objectionable because it comes from a child. Thank God the room was warm enough, allowing Cecilia to coax him out of that flea-ridden old horse blanket he'd been wearing the night before.

"I missed you," Tommaso said, his voice taut as he struggled not to cry anymore.

"I came as soon as I could," I said. "The old man in front of the Buco caught me, and there was a cop, too, and they kept me. I couldn't get away until this very minute."

"Did they hurt you?" he asked, his huge pale eyes brimming. I turned my face toward Cecilia, to prove to him that his tears would have no effect on me.

"They didn't put you in jail, did they?" Cecilia asked.

I gave a nonchalant shrug. "No, they didn't throw me in jail. I just sat in an office and they asked me a lot of questions. It was boring, actually."

"He was crying so hard last night," Cecilia said softly, "and this morning, too." I looked up at her to share the knowing gaze that grown-ups give each other when talking about their children. She'd picked up her baby, Ginevra, who wasn't quite old enough to walk, and was jiggling her on one hip; Ginevra had hushed and stared at me solemnly with her pale eyes, her sparse golden brown hair brushed up into a single large ringlet that fell onto her forehead. Her hair was black when she was born, but it keeps getting lighter and lighter. If it keeps up, she'll be as blond as her mother soon.

"Hi, Ginevra," I said softly and wiggled my fingers at her; she was still at that shy stage and hid her face in her mother's hip. But she smiled first.

"I told him you'd be back, but he didn't believe me," Cecilia went on. "I got some supper into him last night."

She pulled the door all the way open and I stood. "No, they didn't hurt me," I growled, in a pretend-bear voice. "They can't hurt me! I'm too strong and too fast!"

Tommaso finally grinned. He was too big for me to pick up, really, but I spun him about so that his back was pressed against my front, and I slipped my arms under his. With a bit of effort, I managed to lift his feet off the ground as we crossed the threshold; the action reminded me of my injured knee.

Cecilia's room was nothing to brag about, but she had a big blanket covering the straw mattress and a nice porcelain basin and pitcher I bought for her from the shop downstairs. She kept the place tidy and there were hardly any rats at all. She had a slightly wobbly night table to set the basin on, a mirror, and two stools, which made the place seem a palace compared to the tiny hovel Tommaso and I shared. She'd used some of the money I gave her for food to buy a wooden crucifix that hung over the night table.

Once we were inside and Cecilia shut the door, Tommaso sniffed my clothes.

"You smell funny," he said, his spirits lifted. "All sweet, like a whore."

"Tommaso!" Cecilia and I both snapped in unison, as I dropped him.

"Don't let me hear you use that word again," I scolded. "It's an ugly one, not one polite people use." I took his shoulders so he would turn around and listen, and finally noticed that he'd lost one of his front teeth, one he'd been worrying with his tongue over the past few days. I felt an odd pang that I'd missed the event.

"Are we polite people?" he asked innocently. "We're thieves, after all."

"Well," I said, recognizing an opening. "I've found an honest job. One that will make us rich, so that you and Cecilia will never have to work again. I'm going to buy us a house in a safe neighborhood, with a yard for a kitchen garden and chickens, and I'm going to get you a tutor."

Tommaso wrinkled his nose at the word *tutor*, while Cecilia clapped a hand to her mouth in astonishment.

"Are you *serious*, Giuli?" she asked, drawing it away. "Where on earth would you find work that paid that well?"

"Well . . ." I said, thinking fast. I wasn't in the mood to argue, so I couldn't tell them all the details. "The old man who caught me last night. Tommaso must have told you about him. Turns out that he's rich as a Medici and as generous as one to the poor. He offered me a job that pays a florin a year." I had meant to say *a lot* instead of *florin*, but I was too busy trying to concoct a suitable lie. I knew the instant I said it, it would lead to trouble.

"A florin?" Tommaso's piping voice took on a scornful tone. "Giuliano, you're teasing!"

"You *are* teasing," Cecilia said, but it was as much a question as a statement. She stopped jiggling Ginevra, who popped a thumb into her drooling mouth. "What sort of job could possibly pay a florin, unless you own a bank?"

A very good question, one I still didn't have an explanation for. But I did my best to look confident, for Cecilia's sake.

"Like I said, he's rich as a Medici. Take a whiff, Cecilia. I took a warm bath with perfumed soap last night." I extended my neck in her direction. She leaned forward to sniff it.

"You *do* smell wonderful," she admitted. Her voice grew soft, and her expression suspicious—not in a disapproving way, but a protective one. "So you weren't in a police office last night, were you? What exactly would you have to do for this man, Giuli?"

We both knew what she was referring to, although Tommaso hadn't a clue. We never talked about Cecilia's former profession in front of him.

"Nothing like *that*," I said. "He's a very nice man. And he needs a . . . courier. It's very busy work and requires good knowledge of the city." I drew in a breath, and released it with another half truth. "He knows about you three, and he's very generous to the poor. He wants to help us start a new life. He's a saint, really."

Cecilia set the baby down on the bed and sat down heavily beside her. "It's too good to be true."

I grinned. "Yes, it's too good to be true, but it really is."

For emphasis, I took the gold florin Ser Abramo had given me and pressed it into her palm. She sucked in air with a short, high-pitched shriek, as if the pope himself had just walked into the room. Tommaso ran to her side, crowding her as he tried to get a good look.

She stared at it, her eyes very wide. And because she still couldn't quite believe it, she sank her teeth into it and started when she saw that they had made a slight impression in the soft gold. When she could finally speak, she asked, still gazing down at the coin, "How soon can we start looking for a house?"

"Tomorrow, I think," I said. "Around this same time. But I'll need to check with my employer first."

She looked up at me, her gaze bright with affection. "All of us together in a house. Like a real family. Giuli, you're so amazing!"

"Really?" Tommaso looked up at me with a not-so-toothy grin. "A real house?"

I cleared my throat and gave a little shrug, trying to sound casual. "Yes, all of us together. It'll be wonderful. I'll just be spending the night at Ser Giovanni's place for a little while, but I'll come by every day."

"You mean you'll be staying there?" Cecilia asked.

"You're not going to stay with me?" Tommaso echoed immediately. His voice sounded very, very small.

"Not in the beginning," I answered briskly. "I'll be busy earning a lot of money so we'll all be rich. I can't help it, Tommaso. You know I'd stay if I could. But I'll see you as often as I can. Things will be just the same, except that we won't have to play the Game anymore. Cecilia and Ginevra will keep you company at night."

Tommaso was smart, like me, and wasn't fooled for an instant.

His eyes filled and his pale, freckled face contorted, the lips drawing up in a grimace to reveal the red-pink gap where his front tooth had been.

"You're leaving me," he said. His voice shook. "You're moving in with a rich man, and you're leaving me with Cecilia."

He threw himself facedown on the bed and began to wail, heartbroken, his butterfly-wing shoulder blades shuddering. Baby Ginevra joined in.

"No, no, no," I said sternly. "Don't say that, Tommaso. I promised I wouldn't leave you and I keep my promises."

I went over to the bed and tried to get him to roll over; he did, but buried his head in his arms to try to hide the fact that his face was red and dripping with tears. He can produce an amazing amount of them in a very short time.

"I'm only doing it long enough so we can afford a nice house," I said. "I won't be gone forever. I'll try to take you and Cecilia to look for one tomorrow."

"That'll be fun, won't it, Tommaso?" Cecilia ventured brightly. "A house where we can live together forever!" To me, she whispered, "He really took it very hard last night when you didn't show."

Tommaso was beside himself sobbing. "You promised you wouldn't leave me," he gasped. "You *promised*, Giuliano."

"Tommaso, no," I said, and put my hand on his shoulder. He flailed out blindly, one arm covering his eyes, the hand of the other slapping the air around me—a symbolic gesture, nothing more. He didn't mean to hit me, but I leaned in too close, and the edge of his sharp little fingernails broke the skin at my cheekbone.

"My mother said she'd never leave me, too," he wept.

"Tommaso!" Cecilia cautioned. "Don't you dare strike Giuli ever again, or I'll give you a whipping! You're just going to have to spend the nights with Ginevra and me for a little while longer. You're a big boy, so quit acting like a baby."

Cecilia'd been out working the streets the first week I stayed with Tommaso. She didn't know that his mother had died of plague in the night, that he had stumbled, terrified, over her body. She hadn't been with me when Tommaso woke screaming from nightmares, and later trembled in my arms. She didn't know just how horribly afraid he'd been of the dark, until the only way to get him to sleep was to swear that I'd never leave him.

But letting myself get choked up about it wasn't going to help any of us.

"He'll come around," Cecilia said softly to me.

"Tommaso," I said urgently.

He stopped weeping in order to listen.

"I'll come back as soon as I can," I said. "I promise."

"I don't want you to," he said coldly, his words muffled by the mattress. "I can't believe you anymore."

Cecilia lowered her voice. "Tomorrow will be a different story, Giuli. I'll make him apologize to you." She unfolded her fist to look at the gold in her palm again. "I can't really believe it," she said, looking up at me and smiling. "Giuli, a house! You're so amazing! How can I ever repay you?"

"You already paid," I said listlessly, and headed for the door.

Cecilia opened it for me. "We should be celebrating," she said. "I just pray that whatever you're doing, it's nothing terribly dangerous. That you don't get hurt. Then we would all have reason to cry."

"I won't get hurt," I said. "I'll try to come back tomorrow."

Before I could turn to leave, she whispered, "You have to tell me, Giuli. What sort of job requires you to spend the night with your employer?"

"I told you," I said. "I'm to be his courier."

"Of what?"

I opened my mouth and closed it again. At last I said, "You wouldn't believe me if I told you."

I left her standing in the doorway as I went back down the stairs and headed into the streets, telling myself firmly that I did *not* feel like crying for Tommaso. No one, I thought, could ever make me cry.

I would soon be proven wrong.

Five

I made my way south through the city, past the Duomo and the more distant toothy tower of the Signoria, and over the Old Bridge, so preoccupied with Tommaso's reaction that I saw little of it and barely heard the indignant comments of the passersby I nearly collided with. I had to figure out a way to reassure him, or he'd be hell to live with from here on out.

I moved off the bridge and passed under the arched stone portal onto the cobblestone street—the broadest street in all Florence, the Via Maggio—separated from the river by built up banks and a low stone wall meant to hold back the floods to which the Arno was prone. The Duomo's midday bells began to chime as if cued and were joined by a hundred different bells from a hundred lesser churches all over Florence, including the near-deafening ones of the nearby cathedral of Santo Spirito.

I squinted in the bright winter sun, standing still as a tide of purposeful pedestrians swept by on the busy street, including a group of Franciscan monks near running as they hurried to Santo Spirito for noon Mass. I was surprised that Ser Abramo wasn't already waiting for me just beyond the gate. I'd expected him to be prompt.

Just as I was debating whether I'd misunderstood his message, a hand gripped my shoulder from behind. I let go a yelp of surprise and wheeled about.

An elderly Franciscan stood before me, a finger raised to his lips. His brown hood covered a fringe of black-and-silver hair, chopped so that it just covered the tips of his ears. His shaved crown was covered by a little brown skullcap, and his face was lean and stubbly, with a markedly prominent nose, its tip reddened by the cold.

"Giuliano," Ser Abramo said softly. "I didn't mean to startle you."

Still disguised, Ser Abramo lead me on a circuitous path beyond the cobblestone streets of the Oltrarno, into the thick of the woods and back out again, pointing out landmarks that weren't at all obvious to the uninitiated eye. He, too, was preoccupied and spoke the fewest words possible. We covered a good bit of ground before he came out of his reverie.

"That oak trunk there," he finally said, pointing. "Orient yourself to the southeast, on a diagonal and keep walking until you come upon the remnants of an abandoned well. Then proceed due east from there until you come upon the mole-pocked field; in spring and summer, it'll be a meadow, but you'll know from the holes."

He indicated other landmarks, too, a poplar tree in the middle of a copse of oaks, a barn visible in the far distance, and a pond. I did my best to concentrate, even though my thoughts kept returning to Tommaso. We eventually arrived at the high brick walls of the abandoned estate.

Each worn stone in the high wall looked the same as the other, and the woody vines covered the top half of the wall as far as I could see. Yet Ser Abramo didn't hesitate as he drew his necklace of keys out from beneath the brown cassock with one hand; with the other, he pointed at the spot where the lock was hidden beneath the thicket.

"Right there," he said. And to prove his point, he lifted the vines and thrust the key right into the lock. I heard it click.

"But how do you know where?" I asked.

"Look." He pointed down at the spot where the wall met the earth, directly beneath the lock. The very bottom stone was cracked vertically in two, right down the middle. If I'd drawn a straight line up from the crack, it would have intersected the lock perfectly.

He handed me the keys and let me run my hand over the cold stone to find the lock, then stood back as he waited for me to get the door open. The lock was old and rusting, and I had difficulty fitting the key into it. Trying to turn the key was even harder; I jiggled it several different ways without success before trying to use so much force that I finally feared I would break it in two.

I half turned to Ser Abramo, who was watching me carefully, his expression suddenly sad. I opened my mouth to say, *I can't do it*. But I never got the chance.

The world went black and I couldn't breathe. The keys crashed to the earth. I clawed at the fabric pulled down over my head, at the large hands that instantly cinched and tied it around my neck.

"Abramo!" I screamed, muffled. "Abramo, help me!"

"Gently!" he shouted at someone else. "Gently!"

I flailed out blindly, lost my balance, and stumbled against a large male body that caught my wrists and held me fast. "You *bastard*!" I screamed, muffled. "You lying filthy *bastard*!"

But the body that pinned me wasn't Abramo's, which always smelled of rosemary; this man was stout and stunk of sweat and rancid lard. He pushed me against a likewise foul-smelling cohort, who held me fast as the first bound my wrists together. I was knocked to my feet and managed to connect the heels of my boots against an invisible face. I wasn't about to let them take me down easily.

"Abramo! Help me!" I yelled, but there was only silence save for the sound of my struggling and the collision of strange flesh against mine.

I roared, drowning in rage—at the Magician, at God, at the fact that I would never get to see Tommaso's front tooth grow back in.

At the fact that he would always believe I had abandoned him on purpose. That I was disloyal.

Most of all, I raged at myself: How, how could I ever have been so stupid as to let myself trust anyone?

I kicked; I howled; I cursed all three men hideously and called for help, but none of it availed. I was pushed and pulled into the woods, into a cart, and set facedown on mounds of soft fabric. More was laid over me, until I was covered and gasping. I turned my head to one side, the better to get air. A man cried *hee-yah,* a donkey brayed, and the cart lurched forward, creaking and rumbling over uneven earth.

The earth gave way to cobblestone, the rural quiet to the muffled singsong of vendors and babble of pedestrians, the clops of a hundred other hooves, the creaks of a hundred other wagons. We were in the heart of the city proper, but in my disoriented shock, I could not have said where.

The noise abruptly faded; the cart stopped.

The tarp was thrown back, the folded piles of fabrics removed, and my ankles unbound. Still blinded, I could walk. My captors flanked me, each clutching one of my arms, and pulled me along with them. From the echo of our steps, I judged we were inside a large open building—and not a fancy one at that. Wooden planks creaked beneath our feet, and a draft of cold air wafted over me; it smelled faintly of sulfur, like the arms of freshly dyed fabric that had covered me in the wagon bed. A warehouse, then.

We walked a fair ways before we moved into a slightly warmer area. I was pushed down onto a stool. One man pressed his hand firmly down on my shoulder, to keep me seated, while the other pulled a door shut behind us.

Fingers fussed at my neck; the film of black cloth disappeared as a captor pulled the hood from my head.

I sat in front of a large wooden desk, once grand but now worn and pitted. On the other side sat one of my abductors, a man so stout his great belly kept him from resting his elbows on the desk. He smiled grimly at me, his clean-shaven cheeks red and puffed from drink; far leaner by comparison, his accomplice stood beside me, motionless, his face still hidden by his cowl, a dagger prominently displayed in the hand that wasn't holding me down.

"Don't be afraid, we're one of you," Stout said, as I tried to make sense of his grammar; his accent was that of a Florentine laborer. "Giuseppe sent us." He paused. "You can trust me, y'know. Giuseppe tol' me you was all right, that you'd be loyal to our cause. 'Cause you have a head on your shoulders."

"Giuseppe?" I asked, confused. I'd never heard of the man.

"The same," Stout confirmed. "C'mon, you don't have to pretend with us. Surely you've had some . . . interaction?"

I shook my head.

"Here then," he said, and made a strange symbol, a sort of *t* made by raising one hand, palm forward, as if to swear an oath, and laying his opposite hand, palm down, atop it.

My expression was apparently so perplexed that he took my response as genuine.

"It don't matter, then," he said, folding his hands over his belly. "Even if he din' speak to you yet, we still have an offer." He cleared his throat. "So here's the part about the money, laddie. You knew this were coming, din' you?"

"What about the money?" I scowled at him to show I had no fear, but my shaking voice betrayed me.

Stout grinned at me, revealing a missing front tooth; I thought of Tommaso teasing the pink little gap with his tongue and felt a pang. "You think he were lying about the florins, din' you?"

He was speaking of *Ser Abramo*. The Magician hadn't defended me; he had set me up. These goons were his.

"The son of a bitch!" I exclaimed involuntarily.

"You're angry at 'im, I get that. So maybe you din' expect this. But did you think he were lyin' about the florins?"

"Probably," I allowed.

Stout nodded, pleased at my reply.

"He's not," he said. "You strike me as quick for a lad. Now Florence may be a rich city, but people ain't so keen to toss a florin at the feet of a little thief like you, eh?" His smile vanished along with his jovial tone. "Florence is dyin'. Starvin' to death for Lorenzo's sin. You bit of skin and bone, you look like your belly's never been full. And now the merchants is coming to know hunger, too. Even the wealthy is feelin' the pinch."

He leaned forward toward me—as far as his corpulence allowed—his gaze intense. "There's no way our handful of soldiers can win against the likes of Rome and Naples. No way at all, and everyone knows it. Even Lorenzo's fine fat friends. And what happens when *they* start hurtin'?"

I stared back at him, mute.

"I'll tell you what," Stout said confidently. "Revolution. If the pope's army don't come in and slaughter you all to a man first."

"What do you mean *you all*?" I asked gruffly. "You're Florentine, too."

"But I ain't stupid, now, is I?" he countered.

I didn't dare reply.

"And you ain't stupid neither," he continued. "We see the writin' on the wall, you and me. Besides, them as has suffered like you—the poor, the outcast—this life is cruel. But in death you got eternal riches in heaven. It's all poor folk has to look forward to, innit?

"But every soul in Florence are excommunicated now, all because of one man's sin. So you don't even got that to look forward to. And Lorenzo, he's got all the money he can spend and then some, so why should he worry with the likes of you?"

Lorenzo didn't sin, I wanted to tell him. *We were excommunicated because the pope is mad at Lorenzo. Lorenzo wouldn't sell him the property he wanted, and so Pope Sixtus sent people to murder Lorenzo and his brother. And now Sixtus is punishing all of us Florentines until Lorenzo gives himself up—to be killed.*

Sixtus was no real pope. He was a politician of the greediest kind. He wanted not just the one property; he wanted all of Italy to rule. Lorenzo knew the sale would dangerously shift the balance of power toward Rome. Thank God he had escaped—barely—with his life. His younger brother, Giuliano—with the same name as me—hadn't been so lucky.

Stout continued his monologue. "No one in Florence would ever toss you a denarius now, because things are so bad. But," he paused for emphasis. "There *is* the wealthiest man in Italy. *He* cares enough to share his blessings with a pauper like you."

I had to ask, even though I was pretty sure of the answer. "And who is this wealthiest man?"

Stout smiled beatifically. "The Holy Father. Who's invitin' you to work on the side of God, for riches now and eternal, you might say. We seen what smarts you have, with letters and codes and such. Astonishin', that the Almighty would give such wits to a street cur like you, but mysterious is His ways."

He searched my face for a reaction; finding none, he continued. "And then there's the fact you has quick fingers. You can lift things off people easy without anyone noticin'. And you can just as easily slip 'em into someone's pocket."

Steal things. Deliver them on the sly. That was what the Magician had hired me to do, but I had never imagined he would use his powers against Florence. If he did, then our city was surely doomed.

"You want me to spy for Rome. To be a courier." I tried to say it matter-of-factly, without utter disgust.

"Maybe, even someday, to read code. Or make it. They say you have a way with letters and such."

Who knows what the Magician had originally intended for me? But then he had seen my secret alphabet. I'd stupidly written it in the cold mud for him. He had pegged me for a spy, and now his cohorts were trying to recruit me to the enemy side.

All those kindnesses he showed me, all those lies, all that so-called "trust," were intended to sway me to treason.

"Don't think of it as spyin' for Rome," Stout wheedled. "It's for God. For the Holy Father. For Florence, really—it's the best thing for her. You'd be savin' not only every citizen's life, but every citizen's soul."

Except Lorenzo's, I thought. Like every other pauper, I was irritated with him; hunger will do that to a person. But like I said, I'm loyal. Loyal to Lorenzo and loyal to Florence, which to my mind were the same.

"I don't know what you're talking about, I truly don't," I said innocently. "I'll just leave now and forget this conversation. Who'd believe me, anyway? I'm a thief."

I took a deep breath and moved to stand up, but Lean's bony talon of a hand pushed me right back down.

"You don't really got a choice," Stout said, his voice grown harsh and deep; his eyes narrowed to slits near hidden by folds of flesh. "It's that, or be dispatched to hell straightaway."

The tip of Lean's dagger found its way to the infant soft flesh beneath my chin. I drew in my breath, terrified to exhale, thinking of the instant when the Magician, in his guise as Ser Giovanni, had done the same with his stiletto. I wish he'd just killed me then.

So he was a traitor, the great Magician of Florence, swayed by the obscene wealth of Rome. And he thinking that I, a hungry thief, would be just as easily swayed by it, like Judas with his thirty pieces of silver.

Amazing, how fast the mind sprints when confronted with death: I could have agreed with the men, promised to work for Rome—and played along just long enough so that I could flee the city, but Ser Abramo had his magical claws in me. Going to warn Tommaso and Cecilia would only lead my enemies to them. Who knew what horrible things might happen to me, to them, as a result of the spell cast on me the night before? As a result of the new talisman hanging around my neck?

It could have been no accident, Ser Abramo kidnapping a potential courier who just happened to be talented with letters, with secret codes. What human—or spectral—eyes had been watching me, and for how long?

They knew about Tommaso and Cecilia. And if I quailed at any of their requests, what would become of my friends?

Not that I cared, mind you.

It all came down to the fact that I am loyal, and stupidly so. I could no more betray Florence and Lorenzo de' Medici than I could Tommaso or Cecilia. At least the latter two had the florin now and would get on fine without me. As for hell, if it existed, could it really be worse than living on the winter streets?

I slowly let go my breath. *"Palle, palle,"* I said softly; the Medici's rallying cry, referring to the family crest, five red balls—*palle*—and one blue upon a golden shield. "Long live Lorenzo and the Florentine Republic."

Six

I closed my eyes and tensed, waiting for my demise. They say that having one's throat cut is a quick and fairly painless way to go, but the thought of choking to death on my own blood was daunting.

Instead, Stout let go such a delighted chuckle that I dared open my eyes. At the same time, Lean nudged me off the stool. I stumbled forward and grabbed the edge of Stout's desk to keep from falling. I scrambled for the door, yanked it open, and ran, not bothering to wonder why neither man felt inclined to chase me.

"Tell His Magnificence this one's loyal enough," Stout shouted cheerfully. His voice echoed in the cavernous chamber beyond the door, where a white-haired but burly man awaited me. A burly man clad in a scarlet felt hat and matching cloak pushed to one side to reveal his hand resting on the pommel of a long sword.

I would have run past him had he not blocked my way. He did so firmly but politely, and—to my complete shock—put a gentle hand on my arm and led me forward in the direction I'd been running.

Stymied, I stared at our surroundings. Dirt filmed the high, small windows, which let in enough light to reveal a vast storehouse filled with at least a dozen square wooden looms, each as large as three men, their metal weights hanging high upon the chains without fabric to weigh them down. Nearby, rows of wooden tubs smelled of absent dye; tall shelves that had once borne piles of silk and wool lay bare, covered in dust—casualties, I thought, of the war. At the far end of the warehouse, near the huge, padlocked double doors stood a carriage, its arched, skeletal roof covered by a large red tarp to protect the occupants from winter winds and curious gazes. Two handsome geldings were harnessed to it in single file, the first white and the second black and bearing a servant with a crop.

As I paused in confusion, wondering whether to flee or stay, a man in his prime stepped from the carriage and turned to help an older woman down.

Gentleman and lady, I should have said, because both were dressed in heavy winter cloaks of the finest black wool which, like their regal bearing, marked them as persons of great importance.

They turned to face me as they lowered their cowls, revealing necks swathed in brown marten's fur, the mark of wealthy commoners, not royalty. The man wore a dark red hat of soft felt with a rolled brim, and an excess of fabric at the crown that was stylishly draped to one side. He scowled and gestured impatiently at the servant standing beside me.

I put my hand upon the servant's arm. I could do nothing else, because even at a distance, I recognized the man in the fine black cloak. Recognized the wavy dark hair, parted down the middle and hanging a few inches above his shoulders; recognized the slight underbite and mildly stocky, powerful build. Most of all—especially as I neared him—I recognized the exceptionally large nose. It wouldn't have made him particularly homely had it not been for the fact that at mid-bridge, it veered alarmingly to one side, as though someone had taken a pair of pincers to it and twisted hard. As if that weren't enough, the bridge of said nose was almost completely flattened, as if someone had taken not just pincers but a hammer to it. Lorenzo de' Medici was an eloquent speaker—he always addressed the crowds at carnival and holidays—but it was hard for children not to titter at his incredibly nasal voice, which sounded as though he was speaking with his nose pinched shut. I couldn't help wondering whether his appearance was the result of a clumsy midwife with strong hands.

I used to do a great impression of him for the other girls at the orphanage.

Beside him stood a matron wearing a sheer black veil wrapped around her plaited and coiled gray hair. Her face was oval in shape, and her lips thin and drawn downward at the corners; she lacked her son's underbite. It was hard not to recognize her, either, because of the nose, although the bridge was not flattened like her son's.

She had appeared in public only discreetly, in the shadow of her celebrated sons (one now before me, the other dead, the cause of the black mourning she now wore). But I recognized her all the same as Lucrezia Tornabuoni de' Medici, and her son as Lorenzo, politely called the Magnificent.

I was escorted up to them, and we three regarded each other a silent moment before I realized my mouth was gaping open and shut it. Lorenzo was scowling, his arms folded resolutely over his chest. He was clearly unhappy to be here, but Donna Lucrezia wore a faint smile.

"May I have a closer look at you, young man?" she said, in a voice not at all nasal, but low and liquid.

Before I could answer, she moved toward me and took my elbow before leading me over to a window. The servant hurried to unlatch and throw open the shutters, so that the two of us stood in a pane of winter light glittering with dust.

She took my chin gently in her hand, covered by the softest

leather ever to touch my skin, and studied my face intently. Her eyes were large, heavy-lidded, and hazel—quite beautiful, although worry and time had left purple crescents and wrinkles beneath them. The light struck her pupils, milky from age.

She drew back, gasping. "Your *eyes*," she said.

I lowered my gaze, wondering if such an educated woman believed the superstition that my having one green eye and one brown meant I was cursed, or a witch, or both.

But she seemed stunned, not frightened. She raised gloved fingers to her mouth in a successful effort to get control of herself. Her own eyes filled with indecipherable emotion, she lowered her hand and asked gently, "What's your name, dear?"

"Giuliano," I said, and felt a pang of guilt for taking the same name as her son, who had all too recently been stabbed repeatedly until he had bled to death in the great cathedral during Sunday mass.

But she didn't flinch. "A handsome name," she said. "And how old are you, Giuliano?"

"Seventeen," I said, then thought about it, and corrected myself. "Eighteen."

"And your family? Are they here, in Florence?"

"I'm from the orphanage," I answered.

She looked inward for a long time, as if still struggling for composure, and then turned away from me and walked back toward her son. "Go," she told him. "Look."

Lorenzo moved toward me and squinted hard into my eyes.

"Huh," he said. Something about me had struck him as odd—my eyes, I suppose—but, unlike his mother, he was unshaken. He went back over to her and began to whisper, though I could hear every word.

"Even if this lad is . . ." He cast a glance over his shoulder and scowled briefly in my direction. "Even if he *is* who Abramo thinks he is, it doesn't mean we can trust the boy. He's still a petty thief. We owe him nothing. He's not trustworthy."

"I want him," Lucrezia said firmly.

I gasped softly, thinking that my intelligence finally had been recognized; like my lucky tutor-friend from the orphanage, I was going to have a benefactor who would educate me.

But would the famous Lucrezia Tornabuoni de' Medici be willing to sponsor me if she knew the truth of my sex?

"He deserves that," she continued quietly. "And he has shown he can be trusted, regardless of what you say. He's bright, he has skills . . . It makes no sense to risk him. Find someone else, and let me take him."

Lorenzo's expression grew cold. "There's no time for that. Let's get him trained and get on with it. He'll be fine. He's been living on the streets all these years. And if he proves himself to Abramo, you can do whatever you want with him."

Donna Lucrezia looked on her son with sad affection and concern. "You've hardened, Lauro."

A faint ripple of grief passed over his features. "With good reason," he said tautly.

"So the loss of our loved one justifies risking *him*?" she countered, with a nod at me. "Despite the unmistakable resemblance?"

I found my breath and my tongue. "Resemblance?"

Both ignored me, each staring intently at the other. They knew who I was. They *knew*, and they were standing there discussing my fate as though I didn't matter.

I lost my composure, and with it, my habit of always keeping my voice in a lower register. In a perfectly girlish soprano, I cried out, "Donna Lucrezia, *please!*"

Lorenzo glanced over his shoulder at me, frowning at the interruption. But Donna Lucrezia pressed her hand to her heart and fastened her myopic gaze on mine.

She stepped past her son to stand in front of me and put her hands upon my shoulders. Once again, she stared searchingly into my face.

"My *dear*," she breathed. It was an address, not an interjection. She was a woman of keen perception and recognized another one, even if her distracted son did not. I struggled to keep the fear I felt from registering on my face. Would she tell her son? Would she tell Abramo?

Danger was one thing; the thought of being forced into skirts and married off was quite another.

She put a gloved, maternal hand to my cheek, as if I hadn't been a thief, an orphan, the lowest of the low. As if I mattered. I waited for her to divulge my secret to her son, but for some reason, she held back.

"You know who I am," I pleaded softly.

She shook her head—not in reply to the question, but to indicate that she was restrained from answering it, as if it had been too dangerous a thing to utter in front of all these men.

At last she said, "Giuliano." Her tone was pointed as she uttered the name, but so faintly that only I heard that she knew it wasn't my real one. "We are depending on you to help us and Abramo." She shot a sly sidewise glance at Lorenzo, who failed to note it. "For the time being. And then I will help you. As soon as I possibly can." She paused, and then with emphasis on each word asked, "Will you help us in our time of trouble?"

I'd heard of the Medici's legendary charm and scoffed at those weak enough to fall under its sway. But at that moment, I would have promised her my life.

"I swear, Madonna," I said solemnly. "And to you, Your Magnificence."

Lorenzo lifted his eyebrows. "Admirable patriotism," he remarked curtly. "See that you do." He gave me the briefest of nods, and gestured for his mother to return to the carriage.

"God keep you," Donna Lucrezia said simply.

Together, they turned away. The driver remounted the black horse while Lorenzo, grasping his mother's arm firmly, helped her back into the carriage.

Stout and Lean unlocked the padlock and pushed open the tall double doors to the warehouse, letting in the winter wind. The driver called to the horses, and they began to move.

I stood watching as the carriage rumbled off, wondering who the hell I was and what the hell I'd just sworn to do.

I returned to Ser Abramo the way I'd left: hidden beneath swaths of fabric in a rickety cart, this time unbound.

Eventually, the cart made its way through the city and over the bridge to the Oltrarno. I was let out in the forest a ways from Ser Abramo's hidden estate and had to use my memory to find my way back.

Ser Abramo was still waiting at the wall, his expression stoic, faintly guarded. "I apologize for scaring you twice now," he said matter-of-factly. "It was necessary."

In retrospect, I realize now how hard he was working to control his emotions. But at the time, I looked at him with disbelief. *Scaring* me? I had been kidnapped, terrified, threatened with death.

"You son of a bitch," I said, my voice low and trembling at the start, but escalating rapidly into a shout. "You let them take me. You *knew* all this time! Donna Lucrezia said—"

He cut me off with heat to match my own. "Don't *ever* use

names. Especially not that one. Not *ever*." He paused. "I assumed you passed the loyalty test, or they wouldn't have brought you back."

"Oh, I proved myself loyal enough," I responded bitterly. "But that's not what you're asking about, is it?"

He tilted his head, studying me intently, silently, waiting.

"You want to know how much *I* know! Well, I know *everything*!"

His expression changed only subtly: his lips parted, and his eyes widened a bit. In the charged silence, I could just hear him lightly draw in his breath. "Everything?"

"All this time, you've known who I am!" I shouted. "And Don—*she* knows, too. I have family somewhere. Tell me where they are, and who I am *now*, or I swear to God I'll cut you!" It was ridiculous bravado—I didn't even have my razor on me—but I didn't give a rotting fig.

He didn't react to my threat at all, but took a moment to parse what I'd said. His expression grew even more unreadable. Calmly, he responded, "We're certain of nothing, Giuliano, and even if we were, telling you now won't do you any good."

"Well, tell me anyway!" Like a child, I stamped my foot.

The act seemed to galvanize him. He turned the thunderous gaze of the Magician on me. "*No. The time isn't right.*" He drew in an angry breath and paused before letting loose an impassioned torrent.

"Has it occurred to you—assuming it's even true—that *maybe* we're actually trying to *protect* you? That it might hurt not only you, but others as well? You're going to have to trust someone for the first time in your life, urchin—me." He pulled the leather thong, heavy with keys, from his neck, singled one out, and thrust it at my face.

"Here," he snapped. "We haven't time to waste arguing; things have become critical and we have work to do. This key will actually open the gate."

"Please take me to them," I said, and made my lips quiver as if I'd been about to weep. I told myself I wasn't—that I was just playing him by pretending to be upset. "I've dreamed of knowing about my family for as long as I can remember. It's hard, not knowing where you belong . . ." My voice accidentally caught, which was perfect.

"You're telling me nothing I don't know well myself," he answered, unmoved. "Now, turn the key." He emphasized the last three words so that I'd see I had more chance of getting an answer from the stone wall beside us.

I swore under my breath and fiddled with the key until it turned in the lock. I had to use most of my strength to push the heavy gate open. I stalked through the opening and kept on going, refusing to push the gate closed, refusing even to look at the Magician as he did so.

His voice was soft behind me. "I couldn't tell you even if I wanted to. I don't have permission."

I didn't look at Ser Abramo as we walked across the estate and into his house. Leo greeted us enthusiastically, but I was too angry to respond in kind. Rage made eating out of the question, despite the delicious fragrance coming from the kitchen cauldron. Ser Abramo invited me to dine with him, but I walked past him and made my way up the staircase toward my bedchamber, where I closed the door, threw the bolt, and hurled myself facedown on the bed, too angry and frustrated even to cry.

I'd told myself all these years that the hardest thing was not knowing what had happened to my family. I'd been wrong. It was actually harder knowing that someone else knew and wouldn't tell me.

Night had fallen by the time Ser Abramo's tentative knock came at the door. At first I didn't answer, but he persisted until I grew annoyed and opened the door.

I intended to tell him to go away, but the man who stood there was the Magician, with a powerful gaze and voice, neither of which allowed for argument.

"Come," he said. For once, Leo wasn't with him; perhaps the dog had the good sense to stay out of his way when he transformed from mere Abramo to an omnipotent immortal.

"Where are we going?" I asked meekly, but he wasn't in the mood to answer. He had already turned and was moving down the stairs. I could do nothing but follow. We went through the map room to the storage room, where—every action brisk and forceful—he lit the lamp, threw back the carpet, opened the hatch, and crawled down to the cellar.

Reluctantly, I climbed down after him into the freezing blackness. He parted the velvet curtains, unlocked the arched door, and swung it open to reveal the cavernous workroom.

Without pausing, he strode up to the tall shelves and pulled a slender leather-bound book from the uppermost shelf. He set it down on the long worktable and opened it midway, where the centers of several pages had been cut away to create a groove. Ser Abramo picked up an iron key nestled inside.

"Remember where this is hid," he said pointedly. "Memorize the title."

I sounded out the Tuscan. "*Amarosa visione.*" *Visions of Love*, by the poet Boccaccio.

Meanwhile, he squatted down to clear away half of the dusty scrolls on the bottom shelf, exposing the wall behind them. The lamplight was too weak to dispel much dark, and he had to feel around with the iron key to find the groove. A door hidden in the wall popped open. Ser Abramo reached down and in and drew out a rectangular metal box.

He didn't rise, but instead held the dull key up to the lamp. "This opens the lockbox as well," he said, and to prove it, he put the iron key into a latch on the side of the box. The top was a bit rusted from the cellar damp and took effort to open.

Several pieces of paper lay inside the box. He drew out a yellowed one folded into quarters and set it on the table.

"Time to start your training," he said, very seriously.

"Yes, Ser Lorenzo said something about that."

"He meant something else. What *I* teach you—you're not to tell *anyone*. Do you understand? Not Ser Lorenzo, not Donna Lucrezia, not your friends. We never discuss it in anyone's presence. You must swear."

I hesitated. "I already swore allegiance to Ser Lorenzo—"

"Well and good. And now you have to swear allegiance to *me*, and the art I teach you."

I watched silently as he pulled out a colorful painted card just larger than my hand and set it down next to the paper.

He pushed the painted card across the table toward me and pulled out a small but exceedingly sharp dagger, the sort favored by brigands to slice people's throats.

"Hold out your finger," he said.

I recoiled.

"I suppose I should explain first." He pointed with the dagger's tip at the painted card. "Have you ever seen a card like this?"

I shook my head.

"They're very old, but in Italy they're new," he said. "Fortune cards. The way I see it, they're a means of learning God's will. Most people only talk to God. This is a way of listening to Him. There are many cards, of which this is the first: the Fool."

Lorenzo is the fool, I thought, remembering my opium-fueled dream.

"The Fool represents the start of a long journey," the Magician continued.

I stared down at a miniature painting of a village idiot with mouth agape and slightly crossed eyes looking out at the viewer. His thighs were completely naked; remnants of leggings covered him from knee to ankle, where they ended in shreds, leaving his feet bare. His tattered tunic barely covered his privates. A large club rested on his shoulder—no doubt protection from dogs and mockers who were probably responsible for the feathers stuck upright, like a crown, in his golden curls.

"The fool is an outcast," Ser Abramo said. "A guileless creature incapable of caring for himself. He's fallen so far in society that he cannot fall further." He paused. "You're far from stupid, Giuliano, but you've made yourself an outcast. You can continue alone on the solitary course you have chosen and remain ignorant—"

I was angry. I wanted to say, *I didn't* choose *this life. I'm an orphan, my parents abandoned me. I had no choice but to become an outcast. None of it's my fault.* I wanted to say, *I could fall further. I could become a whore.*

I wanted to say, *Don't call me ignorant.*

"Or you can take a blind leap of faith," Ser Abramo continued, "and walk a better path, if one with as many dangers. If you choose the latter, there are things I must reveal to you—secrets that you must swear upon your life to keep, at least for now. Secrets so deep they call for blood."

I tried to seem brave. "What dangers?"

"Enemies who want to find and destroy me," he said. "Who would destroy the Medici and Florence herself."

I hesitated. "Are you really a Magician, then, or just a—"

I don't know what I was going to say next, really. *Bodyguard* or *agent* or *spy* all came to mind, but before I could say it, Ser Abramo interrupted.

"I am the Magician," he said, in a way that left no doubt. "And I work, and always have worked, for Florence and for the Medici."

"I'm not afraid," I lied, and let go a gusting sigh to rid myself of nerves.

His expression softened at my bravado. "Swear you will die rather than reveal the secrets."

"Go ahead, prick my finger. I swear." I just wanted it all to be over with.

"Not just on your life," he pressed. "On the lives of your friends, too."

My heart skipped a beat. "You wouldn't hurt them, would you?" I thought of Tommaso and his missing front tooth.

He held my gaze without blinking. "*I* wouldn't have to."

For an instant, I considered running away. Living in comfort off that one amazing florin with Cecilia and Tommaso and forgetting that the Magician of Florence ever existed. Pretending there was no pope, no Roman army, no war.

"You're still paying me another florin afterward?" I asked, partly to break the tension. "I'd think more, since you're requiring so much more of me."

His thick coal brow lifted above his eyepatch. "Don't press your luck, urchin."

I thrust my hand in his, squeezed my eyes shut, and turned my face away. "Do it," I said. I was good with a razor and tried not to be squeamish, but blood wasn't one of my favorite sights. Particularly not my own.

The stiletto's edge was so sharp and Ser Abramo so quick that he had to tell me he was finished. It pinched only a little when he squeezed my finger in order to milk a fat, dark drop of blood from it, which spilled onto the heart of the Fool.

And then he pierced his own finger without flinching and let his own blood spill on top of mine. He offered me his handkerchief to stanch the flow from my finger, and put his own in his mouth and brought it out clean.

"We have a bargain now," he said. "I'll teach you all I know about magic. In return, I'll use it to protect you and your friends from danger for the rest of your lives."

"All you know?" I breathed, surprised.

"You're as intelligent as I am," he countered. "And I'm arrogant enough to say that's quite rare. When the time comes for me to retire, you'll be my replacement."

Ser Abramo reached for the lamp and took the cover off, exposing the wick and its yellow flame, which leapt on being freed. He picked up the painted card by one corner and fed it to the flame; it smoked when it found the blood and took a moment to catch, but when it did, the blaze jumped up toward his fingers. He rose, gesturing for me to follow, and together we went to the open pit of the little furnace.

Ser Abramo dropped the card inside the pit. We stared down at it as it burned. "There's your old life gone, and a new one beginning," he said softly. "Just as it was for me."

I looked down as the image on the card blackened and shriveled into ash. The last thing to disappear was the Fool's bare foot, stepping onto unknown ground before it finally darkened and transformed to gray-white cinder.

And that was how I became apprenticed to the Magician of Florence.

Seven

That evening, Ser Abramo and I settled in the sumptuous sitting room next to each other, while the great roaring fire in the hearth chased away the chill that had settled deep in my bones during the wagon ride. Leo slept on the floor at our feet, occasionally releasing a gusting snore that made his pendulous muzzle flap.

I sipped from a cup of mulled wine while Ser Abramo picked up the first parchment from the little table beside him and unfolded it. He held it in his lap and we both gazed down at the strange legends on it.

"You'll be good at this, you with your secret alphabet. This explains many magical symbols that you need to memorize right away." His tone grew relaxed, enthusiastic; the darkness that had come over him earlier vanished. "For example, here are the elements: air, fire, water, earth." He pointed at four little triangles, some upside-down, some with an extra line drawn parallel to the base. "And here are all the planets: Mercury, Mars, Venus, Jupiter, Saturn."

I recognized the symbols for Mars and Venus; they were the same symbols that represented male and female, respectively. Other symbols I recognized from both of my talismans, though I hadn't known before what they'd meant.

He set that parchment aside, picked up the other, and unfolded it. "This one shows the Tree of Life. It's a bit advanced, but I want you to see the colors associated with the gods."

He held it up for me to look at. The detailed diagram didn't look anything like a tree. Several lines connected seven circles, each of the latter painted a different color and bearing foreign letters and planetary symbols inside their diameters. It made no sense at all to me, but I nodded sagely.

Ser Abramo set the second parchment down and carefully lifted the piece of paper and handed it to me. It was so thin and its creases so deeply worn that I feared it would fall apart in my hands. I tried to read it upside down at first, until he righted it for me.

There were lines in some foreign language—Greek, I judged— at the top, with the translation in Tuscan beneath. Below were words and diagrams showing four five-pointed stars, each with arrows indicating how they were to be drawn. One star for the East, one for the South, one for West, one for North. And each had its own archangel to be summoned: Raphael, Michael, Gabriel, Uriel.

"How to cast a magical circle," I murmured, and felt a glimmer of fear. Although the ritual Ser Abramo did for my protection had felt holy, as if I'd been in church, the good Servants of Mary at the orphanage had drummed into me that all magic was the work of the devil, and right then I felt as though I was kissing his arse.

"I work godly magic," Ser Abramo said, lifting a brow at my apparently obvious fright. "It's not evil in well-meaning hands, and you shouldn't fear it, but you should show it the reverence you'd show God Himself in His temple. Because, quite honestly, that's Who you're communicating with."

"So magic really works?" I hadn't meant for my voice to drop to a whisper.

"If the magician believes in it," he answered promptly. "It helps if the recipient of the magic believes in it, too."

"And if the magician doesn't?"

"It won't work. At least, that's been my experience."

"So you can turn lead into gold," I asked, "and make dogs talk? Make people fall in love with each other? Create florins out of thin air?" It would certainly explain his generosity.

He gave a hearty laugh, thoroughly amused at the question. "Real magic isn't for that. It's for protection, health, and . . ." His voice trailed and he stared out into the distance, suddenly serious again. "For example," he said. "I asked to find—"

"You mean you did a spell," I interrupted.

"That's a crude way of putting it." He paused. "I did a *ritual* asking to find the right person." He glanced over at me; the muscles in his face relaxed, softening his expression. "And here you are."

That night, as I lay in my soft, sumptuous bed trying to fall asleep, I was torn between two opposing emotions. The first was . . . well, I'm not sure what it was, because I hadn't felt it before. It felt like coming in from bitter weather and feeling the heat from a well-stoked fire on my tingling cheeks.

The nuns at the orphanage, except one, had been adamant in their disapproval of me. I was an annoyance, a problem, a worthless creature who would come to no good. Yet here was Ser Abramo telling me I was wanted—so much so that he had used magic to find me. And someday, someday soon, he would tell me the truth about my family and who I really was.

This thought led to the second emotion, one I was all too familiar with: terror. I feared having something wonderful in my life, because God would take it from me all too soon.

.   .   .

The next morning, Ser Abramo and I were sitting over bowls of minestra in the kitchen, Leo drooling at our feet, when a stranger sailed into the kitchen unannounced, as if there'd been no locks, no walls to restrain him. He was a very handsome younger man, perhaps five years my senior, with short-cropped, shining black curls and the shadowy beginnings of a goatee. Too handsome, if you ask me—the better-looking a man, the likelier he is to be full of himself. That alone made me dislike him immediately.

Amazingly, he'd removed his winter cloak and hung it up in the outer room without anyone of us, including Leo, noticing.

"Bramo," he said, beaming, and held out his arms.

"Niccolo!" Ser Abramo jumped to his feet and the two men embraced, each thumping the other's back as if they'd been long-lost relatives seeing each other for the first time in years. Compared to the brawny Abramo, Niccolo seemed tall and willowy.

Ser Abramo drew back, holding the younger man's shoulders, and studied him. "You've put on a bit of weight," he said approvingly, then added in a lower, confidential tone, "How are things going for you?"

Niccolo's grin remained fixed on his mouth, but fled his eyes. "Fine," he asserted heartily. "Just fine."

Ser Abramo gestured at me. "And here is your pupil, Giuliano."

There was something vaguely familiar about Niccolo, something that made me dislike him even more.

"Giuliano." He nodded politely, his smile fainter, frostier, his gaze every bit as cold as mine.

I ignored him and looked questioningly at Ser Abramo. "I thought *you* were to teach me."

"I'll teach you my trade. And Niccolo will teach you his."

"Which is?" I asked sourly, even though I suspected I didn't want to hear the answer.

Niccolo's grin dissolved entirely. His pale green eyes, whose thick black lashes made them look as if they'd been lined with kohl, narrowed at me with outright contempt. "Swordsmanship." He turned to Abramo. "We'll have to use daggers, then. There's no way this tiny runt can lift a proper-sized weapon."

"Wait a minute!" I countered, talking over him. "I promised to be your apprentice, not get involved in violence! Much less trust *him* to teach me how to protect myself!"

"Me?" Niccolo's voice rose with indignance. "What's your problem trusting *me*? *I'm* the one who has the problem trusting *you*!"

Abramo's thunderous tone startled us. "You'll *both* do it," he commanded sternly. "And the two of you will get on nicely so long as you're in my house." His gaze was searing, disgusted, relentless. Niccolo and I withered silently beneath it.

Niccolo gave the curtest of nods, but his expression remained hostile.

"Giuliano," Ser Abramo ordered, his gaze pointedly holding Niccolo's, "go upstairs to the weapons room. It's on the floor above your chamber. You'll find it open. Go inside, and wait there."

"Yes, sir," I said politely, and headed out into the sitting room. I went so far as to open the door to the staircase and take a few steps up . . . and then tiptoed back soundlessly to the sitting room, my ear tilted toward the kitchen to better hear the men's conversation. Niccolo wasn't the only person who could steal soundlessly from room to room.

". . . disgusting little urchin," Niccolo was saying.

"Ho!" Ser Abramo responded, his tone now lighter and good-humored. "How quickly you forget what *you* were when you first entered this house!"

"You were lucky once, sir," Niccolo countered. "Very lucky

with me. But someday you're going to wind up with your throat cut. I have a bad feeling about this one—"

"Shall I tell you what that bad feeling is, young man? Jealousy. Pure and simple jealousy."

Niccolo sputtered, then managed a disgusted, "Please! I'm thinking of you, Abramo, not myself."

"Lorenzo and Lucrezia—and I—trust him, and that's all you need to know," Abramo replied firmly. "You have a job to do."

"But if he managed to fool them—"

Ser Abramo's tone turned dark. "These days, some would say I ought to distrust *you*. But I never will, because I know your heart." He paused. When he spoke again, he tried and failed to keep emotion from creeping into his voice. "Just as I know this lad's heart now. You must trust him."

"*Your* heart's too open, old man," Niccolo said, with a trace of sad affection. "I only pray it won't be your downfall."

"It won't," Abramo retorted confidently. "Don't worry, you'll only have to work with the boy this once. He'll stay in my care once this is over."

A long pause followed. I hurried silently back toward the stairs, but not without first hearing Niccolo say:

"I'll do as I'm told. Just don't expect me to like or trust him. And don't be surprised when he betrays us all."

The third floor of Ser Abramo's house was one massive, sunny room devoid of furniture or decoration save for large mirrors and weaponry hung on the walls. All manner of weaponry: daggers, long swords, short swords, staffs, scimitars, shields, belts, and mail vests. One corner held a small stack of wood cut into pieces the length and breadth of daggers and swords; another, padded floor mats and a man-sized dummy of stuffed burlap stuck on a pole.

I looked at them all with a sinking feeling. I was a small female—wiry and strong for my size, true, but as Niccolo had pointed out, barely capable of hefting a long sword. When it came to combat, my greatest talent was running.

This once, Ser Abramo had said. He wanted me to survive because he wanted a clever apprentice. But the original plan had been to use me in more violent work—me, a thoroughly expendable street thief. And the Medici were insisting on sticking with the original plan, at least this once, which meant I wasn't long for this world.

And Niccolo was on their side. Which made me hate him all the more.

He arrived less than a minute after I did, and like me, made no effort at pleasantries.

"Stand there," he ordered, pointing to a pane of sunlight in the middle of the bare sweep of wooden floor. He fetched a belt with a sheath from a hook on one of the walls and brought it back. I stood motionless while he went down on one knee and fastened the broad, heavy leather belt tightly around my waist. His movements were brisk and rough enough to make it clear that the last thing he wanted to do was touch me.

"God," he muttered with disgust. "You're as small as a girl. I don't see how this will work."

I stared at my reflection in a mirror on the opposite wall. The broad belt fell from mid-ribcage all the way to my hipbones. It was made for a man Ser Abramo's size. "How am I supposed to move?" I asked.

"Do your best," he answered curtly. "It's the smallest baldric we've got." He rose, took a step back, and caught sight of my expression. I'd been thinking about convincing Ser Abramo to take

Tommaso and Cecilia in after I died or at least make sure they got my earnings.

"Don't look so terrified," he said, irritated. "I'm not here to make a scrawny urchin like you into a master of the dagger. We're here to practice playacting, that's all. Your employer isn't so stupid as to rely on a weakling like you for real fighting or protection."

Insulted and relieved, I cast about for a proper retort, but was too slow.

"You and I are going to have a mock battle in front of an audience of sorts," he continued. "You need to look as though you've been formally trained—"

"Why?" I asked.

"Because if our audience doesn't believe our performance, they'll kill us."

"But why are we doing this in the first place?" I persisted. "Why are we trying to fool people?"

"To save my neck," Niccolo snapped. "Now stop asking stupid questions I'm never going to answer. You're in the business of secrecy now, and the fewer questions you ask, the safer we'll all be." He paused. "I hope you learn as quickly as Abramo says you can, because we haven't much time. So, the fighting stance is your first task." He took two steps back from me.

"Put your legs a hip's breadth apart. Now, left foot forward." He demonstrated; I aped him carefully. "Well done," he said. "Now the right foot goes back . . ." He pivoted on said foot until it was fully pointed to the right side. "And out from the body close to ninety degrees."

"Perpendicular?" I asked as I mimicked the stance, partly to show off my vocabulary, partly because I wasn't sure what ninety degrees looked like.

"Bend your knees, bend your knees." Impatient, he pointed at his own. "Don't ever lock them. Think loose, loose, loose." He bounced a bit on his feet to emphasize the point and put his hands out in front of his body as if preparing to wrestle with me.

I bent my knees and bounced a bit in imitation.

He nodded, content. "It's all about the feet. And the hips and shoulders, of course. But the feet come first. So your left foot is forward, but now shift the bulk of your weight onto your back foot. And lift the heel up . . ." He turned sideways to me so I could better see him demonstrate.

I did as ordered and realized that the move allowed me to spring forward quickly. I tested it with a lunge; Niccolo nodded again.

"You see?" he said. "You have more speed, more power moving forward. Now, back in position."

I practiced the stance for what seemed a thousand times. Halfway through the exercise, Niccolo began pushing against me to test my balance.

"Good," he said finally. "A strong foundation keeps you able to retaliate or move out of harm's way faster; you're less likely to fall from a blow. Once you lose your footing and fall, you're dead."

He moved over to the stacks of wooden blocks and picked up two. "Now a bit of practice with the dagger," he said, and threw a block at me. It was the same length and width as the weapon, about the length of my forearm.

Living on the street teaches good reflexes. I caught it easily— it was of lightweight cork oak—and returned promptly to my fighting stance.

He frowned. "Don't hold it underhanded, like a girl," he snapped. "It's not your pathetic little razor."

At the word *razor*, an image flashed in my mind: Niccolo's face, framed by long straight red hair.

"Officer Handsome," I blurted, and felt warmth rush from my heart to my cheeks.

At the words, he gave a quizzical half smile. "What?"

"You," I said. "You're from the Eight of the Watch."

"No, I'm not."

"Yes, you are. You were there outside the Buco Tavern when I nicked Ser Abramo's purse. But you must have been wearing a red wig."

His smile vanished. "You're insane," he said. "I have no idea what you're talking about."

"Yes, you do," I insisted. He was lying; I knew I was right. He and Ser Abramo had been playacting that night in order to trap me. Just as I was now playacting with Niccolo to fool some other poor sod.

"It doesn't matter," he said pointedly, in a manner that neither confirmed nor denied my assertion. "Now, hold the dagger over-handed, like this." He displayed the proper overhand grip on the hilt, then raised the stick above his head and whipped it up and down through the air, stabbing an invisible foe.

"Now I'm going to try to kill you," he said. "Stop me."

He raised the pretend knife and came at me. Although his motions were intentionally slow and mine fast, he'd landed several gentle killing blows by the time I realized I had to drop my own dagger in order to grab his weapon-wielding arm.

"So you see *that* doesn't work," Niccolo said cheerfully, forgetting his disdain for me in his enthusiasm for teaching. "Now you come at me, and I'll show you what does."

I raised my pretend dagger, intending to pelt him with less-than-tender blows, but before I could land even one, he reached out with his left hand and caught the inside of my forearm below the wrist so firmly that, try as I might, I couldn't plunge my weapon forward toward his chest, which remained a tantalizing hand's length out of reach.

As I struggled, he explained, "It's not so much the amount of strength you have—although that definitely helps—but the overhand grip. And if you keep trying to push forward, I can step backward while holding on to your arm so your dagger can't reach me."

We repeated this move in slow steps, with Niccolo explaining each. I assumed fighting stance—"Not quite Boar's Tooth," he said mysteriously—and lifted my dagger above my head. I began to bring it down, aiming for his heart, and Niccolo seized my forearm with his overhand grip and held my weapon at bay. I brought all my strength to bear, but couldn't push the mock dagger far enough to hurt him.

"Fiore de' Liberi was a master at hand-to-hand combat, particularly with the dagger. This is his first master of the dagger, first play. It's not my favorite defense, really—one clumsy move, or a Fiore-trained opponent who anticipated it, and my hand would be sliced to ribbons. But it's simple to learn, and with enough practice, you won't get hurt. Once more, now."

We repeated the move again—and again, until I grew frustrated over having my wrist caught and yearned to be able to swat Niccolo with my wooden knife until he pled for mercy.

Just as I felt myself losing patience, he stopped and said, "Now we reverse positions. Put your dagger in your belt and leave it there; you won't need it. I'll come at you, and you stop me."

Without pausing, he lifted his piece of oak and rushed me. For the first five tries, I was too late with my left hand, but managed to grab his right forearm on the sixth. It worked; although my strength was no match for his, when he pushed forward, I was able to step backward while keeping his weapon from touching my chest.

We practiced it over and over and over again, but this time, I enjoyed it even though I grew hot and thoroughly soaked with sweat, despite the chill.

On my last try, Niccolo twisted his wrist to move his blade to the outside of my forearm; in a blink, his weapon-bearing hand moved under my arm and pushed oak right against my heart. Our faces were close enough that mine could feel the heat of his, feel his breath, see the irises of his eyes: light, clear celery with one golden fleck, the whole ringed by evergreen. A sudden melting warmth stirred deep inside me, on my cheeks, on the flesh over my heart.

Too damned handsome. No good ever came of a pretty boy.

He stared steadily back into my eyes, his features slack with surprise at his own reaction, and his cheeks coloring like mine surely were.

"Fiore second play," he said softly, with faint embarrassment. "I win." He drew away.

I came to myself, cursing myself for my unwanted response, cursing him for his virile beauty. I hated him in that moment. I wanted to plant my piece of oak against *his* heart and pummel it to mash.

"But the grip is supposed to *work*," I protested hotly. "Why else did you teach it to me?"

"It does work," Niccolo agreed, "if your opponent doesn't know the countermove. Our audience has to believe I've killed you."

He regained his disinterested manner, and our session ended with his giving me a real dagger, if a blunted one, and demanding I unsheathe it a few dozen times. He shook his head at my clumsiness and made me promise that I'd draw it no fewer than one hundred times before he came again the next morning.

I followed him down the narrow stairs to the sitting room, where Ser Abramo sat in a chair close to the fire, the little table at his side bearing a jar of ink. He was bent over a folio, scribbling madly with his quill, so absorbed in his writing that he started when we entered.

His lips unsmiling, his thick dark brows raised in a question, he glanced up at Niccolo, who responded noncommittally:

"He'll do."

Ser Abramo nodded and returned to his papers. Niccolo hesitated where he stood for a moment, apparently awaiting a warmer dismissal; when it failed to come, his lips grew taut. He turned away from us and strode out of the room silently, without looking back.

I was glad to see the tension between them—glad that Ser Abramo had little to say to him, glad that Niccolo had been rude in not saying a proper good-bye to us—because it reminded me how very much I hated him.

After the morning's strenuous activities, Ser Abramo presented me with a roasted gamecock and demanded I eat my fill. I did, and then some, leaving nothing behind but a clean-picked skeleton.

"I don't want to become a street fighter," I said, and belched. "I knew there would be danger, but I never guessed that I would be crossing swords with an enemy. I don't like drawing blood." *Or having it drawn.*

"You won't have to," Abramo said softly. "You're just to give a little performance. Once it's done, I'll make sure you never have to do the like again."

I wanted to believe him, I really did—but he would have to do whatever the Medici told him to, just as he was doing now, and he knew it. Which meant he was lying.

Afterward, we sat together in front of the fire with the yellowed, falling-apart paper that contained the diagram of stars. As instructed, I'd begun memorizing how to make them for east, south, west, and north, but could make no sense of the words written below them. Ser Abramo stood and showed me how to carve the invisible stars with a finger—sweeping and large, almost the size of a man—and pronounced the four Holy Names, one for each quarter. It was the first time I'd ever heard the ancient Hebrew language. He repeated the names several times for me. I parroted them as best I could.

"Now," he said, "I'm going pretend to create a circle. Mark how I connect the stars, and how I vibrate the Names rather than speaking them. It comes from the very core of the chest; you should feel it with your whole body."

And he did so, facing east first. Once he made the great star, he stabbed its center while vibrating the Name for the eastern quarter. *Yod heh vav heh.*

His voice was very deep and low enough that someone standing in the next room might not have heard it, yet it rumbled like thunder. He drew each word out as long as possible, and when he finished, the very air itself seemed changed.

When he had finished the circle, he turned to me. "You must realize," he said, "that when you vibrate the Names, you're touching the hem of God's very garment."

"But you don't even pray before you eat," I said. "I've never seen you cross yourself."

"We've had this discussion before," he countered with faint weariness. "I don't believe in the dogma created by men. But I have experienced an interesting power in my life. And I know that for me, magic works when approached with reverence. Not the magic of telling God what to do, but the magic of opening a channel for His will. So if you want to be a magician someday, you have to find that place of reverence within you. It doesn't

come from anyone's teachings, not from a priest or pope or anyone, anything outside you. It comes from what you allow yourself to *know*. Fear kills it; trusting that there is something greater
than you, something good, fuels it."

I kept my mouth shut, trying to keep the fury I felt from showing. It was easy for him to believe in a kindly God. He was outrageously wealthy; he'd had a good life. He hadn't suffered as much
as I had. He'd had parents who loved him. He didn't know the
cruelty of the streets. That's why he could speak about fear and
compassion so easily; he didn't really know the former at all.

I decided then that *my* magic, if I lived long enough to become
good at it, would come from sheer will and street smarts.

Like Niccolo, Ser Abramo insisted I practice what he'd shown
me again, and again, and again, until I was sick of it.

When we finished, he must have been disappointed in my
performance, because he said, "For now, learning by rote will do.
But at some point, you'll need to find that place inside you in
order to vibrate the Names properly." He paused. "Take my seat,
and practice writing the symbols for the seven planets and the
four elements. Test tomorrow."

I spent the whole of the afternoon learning the magical symbols
for the planets. There were really only five to study, since I recognized the ones for Mars and Venus—the same used to represent
male and female. I learned the rest quickly, including their attributed metals: lead for Saturn, gold for the Sun, copper for Venus,
and so on. Triangles represented the alchemist's elements—earth,
air, fire, and water—the difference being whether the triangle
was upside down or not, and whether it had a line through it or
not. It was fun drawing them again and again; I'd always wished
for a life where I had ample time to take up a quill.

In the early evening, I practiced unsheathing my dagger, counting each draw until I reached one hundred. I'd thought that if I came to work for Ser Abramo, my life would become one of leisure, punctuated by an errand here and there, but I'd never been so busy in my life.

That night, I practiced drawing the circle and vibrating the Holy Names in the privacy of my bedroom. I didn't know how to do a proper magical spell, so I sent up an awkwardly agnostic prayer for God to protect Tommaso and Cecilia while I was gone.

Ser Abramo's test came first thing in the morning; I eagerly wrote out the symbols for him.

"You have an artist's hand," he remarked with faint amazement, looking on my scrawls with admiration, and promptly handed me the symbols of the zodiac to memorize. "You're already ripe for the furnace."

I didn't understand the last sentence. I only knew that I was terribly uncomfortable with his praise and terribly pleased. At the same time, it worried me. I was coming to care about my mentor, which was tempting Fate.

Niccolo arrived soon after. Once we were in the weapons room, he presented me with a handsome baldric of finely tooled leather. "We need to convince our audience you've been trained to fight," he said. His manner was still cool and detached, but not so terribly disapproving as it had been the day before. "Not that you found your belt in a trash pile somewhere." He paused. "It was nigh impossible finding one to fit a skinny child like you."

I ignored the insult and fastened it around my waist. It was new and the leather was stiff. But it fit much better than the old one and felt less clumsy.

"I rubbed the inside of the scabbard with oil," he said, as I stuck my blunted dagger inside it. "And tried to stretch it a bit. Now, show me how fast you can draw your weapon."

I pulled on the pommel. With the old baldric, the blade had slipped out easily. Now the sheath was much tighter, requiring me to pull harder, which cost an extra second or two. Niccolo shook his head in disgust.

"It's not fair," I protested heatedly. "You should have stretched it more. You came in here knowing this would slow me down."

He was unmoved, skeptical. "Did you practice one hundred times like I told you?"

"I did," I answered. "Do you think me so stupid and lazy as to put my life at risk?"

"Mind how you speak to your better!" he snapped.

"You're not my better!" I countered, with such surety that he drew back, surprised and a bit ashamed that I knew the truth. "I heard you speaking with Ser Abramo! You come from the same streets I do!" I waved the tip of my dagger at the new baldric to distract him from probing further. "Anyway, now I have to practice two hundred times with this stupid thing just to get as good as I was with the old one."

"Then you shall," he said.

I drew my dagger a few dozen times for Niccolo until he was finally convinced I had enough facility to begin our rehearsal. It now included Niccolo drawing his dagger, my grabbing his wrist with my left hand and drawing my weapon with my right. Before I could strike, Niccolo rotated his wrist to pull his blade to the outside of my left arm, and then up under it to tap his dagger to my chest.

We did this for what seemed like hours, until our mock battle grew faster, smoother, almost believable to an unenlightened viewer. My body began to remember the moves, so that my mind was freer to wander, and it focused on my rage that Niccolo and his masters did not value my life enough to spare me this. I should have been sitting inside the Palazzo Medici listening to a tutor, with Donna Lucrezia as my benefactor, but thanks to Ser Lorenzo, I was sweating in the weapons room, learning how to put my life at risk.

And so each time that Niccolo came at me, I fought harder, drawing my dulled blade and swiping at him in earnest, but his arms were longer than mine so he stayed beyond my reach. I bared my teeth in anger as I clutched his forearm with all my power and vainly sought a countermove to foil him.

He sensed my fury and retaliated with his own. His moves became rougher, stronger, his dagger's tap against my breastbone increasingly harder until it became a bruising thump.

On the last go, as Niccolo broke my hold and brought his dulled blade to my heart, he hissed in my ear:

"If you ever hurt Bramo, in any way, I'll do this to you in earnest with a sharpened blade."

I hissed back. "The same goes for you. Only mind you call him *Ser* Abramo, because he's by far your better."

My words struck him. He lowered his weapon and took a step back. "That's true," he said thoughtfully. "I ought."

"Then why don't you?" I demanded.

"He really loathes it, you know."

"Why? I call him that all the time."

His tone had warmed and grown familiar. "Because, my dear lad, he's one of us."

"Us?"

"An orphan rescued from the streets by the same benefactor and given a life." He paused. "He didn't tell you?"

I could only stare at him, stunned.

If such a good thing was happening to me, things would somehow go terribly wrong. They always did. Bad things happen on the streets, as I said. Not just to little boys like Tommaso, but also to young women like me, who find themselves in the wrong place at the wrong time with only a little razor to protect them.

In my mind, I was someplace very far away, because I jumped in my skin when Niccolo said in a loud, cheerful voice, "All right, one more go, and we're done for the day. Tomorrow, you practice the fall."

And a long, long fall it would be.

Eight

◦⟨⟩◦ The midday bells were chiming as I sat down to memorize the symbols and attributions for each sign of the zodiac and
to practice writing them: the sharp, stylized horns of Aries, the
upward arrow of Sagittarius, the underlined omega of Libra. I'd
always been too restless to sit still for long, but this was an entirely new alphabet, a code where each symbol held layers of
meaning. I studied and practiced forming the symbols for hours,
so joyously rapt that when Ser Abramo came to tell me it was
evening, I was astonished.

After supper, the Magician took me down to his cavern, where
wall torches illuminated the area surrounding his worktable.
The little furnace built into the dirt floor had been stoked until
the metal encasing it was glowing white, throwing off heat—an
agreeable heat, until one got too close.

He led me over to the table and pointed out a coin the size of
a talisman carved from yellow beeswax. I recognized the Latin
phrase *Confirmo O Deus potentissimus* in the outer ring, and the
stylized *4* for Jupiter in the center of the circle, but not some odd
lines and circles above it. The symbols were raised, just as they
would be on a real talisman. Two extremely thin steel dowels had
been inserted into the edge of the coin opposite each other.

The Magician turned the wax coin over; a square filled with
random numbers sat in the center, ringed by Hebrew letters.

"Obviously, there's more to learn than can be taught in a

week," he said, which puzzled me; I knew my playacting with Niccolo would only last seven days, but I'd thought that I had years in which to learn Ser Abramo's trade. "This is how the mold is created; it requires artistic skill, which your handwriting shows." He pointed at the wax coin. "This one is ready to be coated with wet clay in order to make a mold. But in the meantime, for purposes of demonstration . . ."

He picked up a hardened lump of clay and turned it in his hands so that I could see three small holes in the bottom of the mold and a larger one at the top. "This one is ready for the furnace."

"It's a love talisman, so we'll be working with . . . ?" He raised an expectant professorial brow at me.

"Venus," I said, proud that I had figured out the way the mold worked, proud that I had the right answer to his question. "And the metal copper."

He grinned at me with paternal delight. "My clever boy."

I would have killed to make him smile like that again.

"Copper has a high melting point, so the furnace is extremely hot. Respect it and keep your distance; it'll sear your flesh right off," he warned.

He rose and donned a thick leather apron with pockets and gloves that came to his elbows and took up a shiny copper ingot from a shelf and what looked to be a flattened spoon with a handle as long as I was tall. "Steel," he said of the spoon, "because it has a higher melting point than the other metals I work with." The hardened lump of clay and ingot went into his apron pocket. "Keep behind me," he said.

I obeyed as we walked back toward the little furnace in the ground, blindingly bright as the sun, its edges kissed by yellow and pale orange; it threw off so much heat that when we stood before it, rills of sweat began streaming down my chest and back, down my face.

I stood a half step behind Ser Abramo. He turned his head toward me, the perspiration on his brow and hollowed cheeks made dazzling by the hot white light, his profile glowing like a craggy angel's. "Lean in a bit closer," he said, "and look inside."

An iron contraption—a dowel inside the furnace, running across its width—had a small bowl hammered into its center; both dowel and bowl glowed a deep orange-red. A tall, perpendicular handle at the end of one dowel protruded up from the furnace, allowing Ser Abramo distance from the fire and the ability to manipulate the bowl side to side.

He produced the hardened lump of clay from his pocket and placed it carefully on the long-handed spoon; just as carefully, he set it down just beneath the iron bowl. The instant he did, the wax inside the clay melted and ran out the bottom of the mold, leaving it hollow.

"Now we cast the metal," he said.

He lifted the copper ingot from his apron pocket and set it on the flattened part of his steel spoon, then lowered it slowly into the fire, onto the iron bowl. "The copper's already been purified, so there should be little dross," he added.

The heat on my face had already grown unpleasant—I began to imagine how excruciating it would feel to burn my eyes—but I was far too curious to look away. After a time, the copper glowed first dull red, then orange, then yellow, then the white of pure sunlight. Ser Abramo took his steel spoon and used it to slide a hidden steel cover from one side of the furnace and a matching cover from the other side. They were made to meet at the center, producing a seam, but the Magician left them partially open, just enough so that we could see the ingot in the bowl.

"Behold the magic," he said.

At that instant, a beautiful pure green flame leapt up from the slit in the furnace; I gasped as Ser Abramo smiled and watched as the flame began to take on a bluish hue.

When it went from blue green to decidedly blue, he pulled on the protruding handle and tipped the little iron bowl so that the glowing white metal poured into the mold. Once it was full, he used his steel spoon to lift it up and out of the furnace, and set it some distance away, where the ground was cooler.

"In an hour or so, we'll break the mold. Copper cools quickly. And then our love talisman will be ready." He paused and gave a wry grin. "I ought to give you this one."

I made a disgusted face. "I want nothing to do with affection of any sort," I snapped.

His grin lessened to a faint mysterious smile. "I know. The spell I worked in the circle the night you arrived . . . it was for more than just your protection. Your heart's in a magical furnace now, Giuliano—one that will melt the dross away and leave the gold. The process has begun, and there's no stopping it now."

"You have no right to play with my feelings!" I shouted, furious. "How dare you!" I turned on my heel, thinking to pull an ancient scroll from the shelf and cast it on top of the little white-hot furnace before stomping out of the Magician's house for good.

"*Stop,*" he said, with just enough thunder to make me obey instantly and turn back to face him. "I said the process had begun. I didn't say that you had to cooperate. You're free to stay as miserable and cold as you like."

"I didn't ask to be abandoned!" I countered heatedly. "I didn't ask to be beaten or despised, or to live in poverty and filth. That's God's work! And it's stupid to think He doesn't hate me and every other homeless urchin! In winter, I see them frozen to death in alleyways. In summer, they're dying of plague on the cobblestones—" My voice broke.

"And what of the well-fed urchin living in luxury in my house?" he asked quietly. "Yes, people are dying, and it's tragic, horrible, more than enough to break anyone's heart a thousand times over. But you . . . You've been rescued from the streets. Why are you still there?"

"There are cruel—" I began, but he spoke over me.

"There are cruel people who are loveless because they are fearful. But for those of us who choose to be kind, we must find each other and treasure each other all the more. That is where I put my faith."

I sneered at him. "How can you be so old and still so gullible?"

He cocked his head gently. "It's taken me half a century to lose the anger born of loss and cruelty. I hope that it takes you less time."

On the third day of my training, I helped Niccolo drag a padded leather mat from a corner to the center of the weapons room. Thick gray clouds shrouded the sky outside; because of the gloom, the hearth was lit, and fine droplets of winter rain glistened in his black curls.

"Falling," he said, letting go of the edge of the mat, which thudded to the floor. "There's an art to it." He stepped onto the mat and gestured at me with both hands. "Come at me and watch carefully."

I drew my blunted dagger from my stiff new baldric with a bit more ease than the day before and ran at him.

This time, he didn't do the countermove, with the result that my dagger struck his breastbone with much more force than I'd intended. He fell backward to the floor, his eyes in a dead man's unfocused stare, his body so convincingly limp that I squatted down beside him and begged him to speak.

For long seconds, he didn't move, with the result that I grew anxious. Just as I was getting up to call for Ser Abramo, he sat up, arms propped behind him, a grin on his wicked lips.

"You *bastard*," I hissed, as we helped each other onto our feet.

He smiled at my irritation. "What I just did is exactly what I want you to do. It's even more convincing when one's wearing a cloak. Now I'll do it very slowly; mark the movement of my legs. Don't come at me this time; just watch."

I watched. He took a great step backward with his right leg, bending the knee slowly until he was low enough to let his rump drop to the floor without too much damage.

"The trick is to let your head strike last," he said as the small of his back, the blades of his shoulders, and then his skull hit the mat. "If we fix the hood of your cloak to stay up, you can fool them without having to smash it on the cobblestones."

I was to be pretend fighting on the streets, then.

He turned his profile to me so I could watch from the side and demonstrated the fall again. "It's easier to fall on your side, as you could fling out an arm and rest your head on it," he commented. "But I couldn't figure out a way to make that look realistic. So you're just going to have to risk banging your head a bit." He got up and dusted himself off. "Your turn."

I was awkward at first and afraid, but he demanded I do it again and again and again, until I finally relaxed and let my body flop realistically.

Pleased, Niccolo fetched a thickly padded vest from a wall hook.

"I'm going to start moving with real speed and don't want your chest to be bruised too badly if I can't rein my dagger quickly enough," he explained, as he held out the vest for me and I wormed my arms into it. "Now we'll do the whole performance, and you add the fall at the end."

I went into my fighting stance: he drew his blade, and I drew my dulled one in response. I was so focused on blocking his dagger with the proper overhand grip that I at first failed to notice that *its edges were sharpened, its tip fatally keen.*

I yelped, and gripped his wrist harder to stop it from rotating and breaking free of my grasp, but he was too strong, too fast. His dagger slipped under my wrist and past it, bringing his weapon into the undefended space over my chest. I took a huge step backward off the mat and pulled my upper body hard to one side, to no use; his wicked sharp dagger found its mark, and rather than pull it back from me at the last instant, he plunged it forward, into my heart.

I shrieked and fell clumsily onto my back against the hard wood—not the practiced fall, but one born of terror.

It took me two breaths to realized I was uninjured, and that Niccolo was laughing, the length of his weapon suddenly halved.

"Retractable blade," he said cheerfully, holding its tip skyward for my inspection. "We need to be as realistic as possible, after all." He pressed a knob on the hilt, and the blade shot up to its former length again with a click.

"Devil take you to hell," I gasped. "Take you to hell and make you his whore."

He offered a hand to help me to my feet, but I struck out with my fist, hard, and connected with his thigh. I knew it would leave a bruise, and I was glad for it.

The blow stopped the laughter; he winced, but soon returned to grinning as he moved out of range. "Surely you didn't believe

I would have hurt you. Have a sense of humor. It was a joke. You should have seen your face."

Furious, I clambered to my feet. "It wasn't funny. Not funny at all," I spat, with as much venom as I could muster.

I had thought, after he told me that he had been a child on the streets, that he would have retained some empathy for someone new to the notion of safety, of trust. I had almost come to like him, but wealth and comfort had made him forget his origins and look down on those who shared them. To him, I was only a pawn.

How did I know that he and Donna Lucrezia meant for me to survive our little performance? How could I be sure that, when the time came, the blade in his hand would be the retractable one?

I could trust only Ser Abramo. And even him, only so far.

The week of my training passed quickly, with my days divided among studying the basics of magic, working with Ser Abramo at the furnace, and mock fighting with Niccolo. Our little play had come to include my pretending to hand him a message and just beginning to turn away when Niccolo drew his dagger and the duel began.

The morning after Niccolo stabbed me in the chest with his retractable blade, he made a peace offering. One that brought me little peace, if any at all.

After we'd run through our moves several times, each one ending with my falling on the mat, he paused, and his tone grew serious.

"Look," he said, "there's a move I want to show you. One that might prove useful to you if anything goes wrong."

I scowled. "What do you mean, if anything goes wrong?"

"Nothing will," he said, less than convincingly. "But the time might come when you'll need more than knowing the simplest way to block a dagger and to fall. Go ahead. Come at me, slowly."

I was more than willing to lift my dagger overhead and rush at him, faster than requested. In the next instant, my knee buckled and I fell hard on my rump.

"How did you do that?" I gasped.

He extended a hand and pulled me onto my feet. "If you want to learn, you'll have to be more polite. *Slowly*, I said."

I wielded my blunted dagger overhead and took a step toward him. He didn't bother to draw his weapon. Instead, he grabbed my knife-wielding arm with the left-handed overhand grip we'd practiced so many times.

And then he turned his body slightly sidewise to mine, taking a broad step so that he now stood on the outside of my right leg. His bent right leg moved behind my left, with his heel catching the inside of mine.

"Now," he said, "watch what happens when I straighten my leg."

He straightened his leg—only a bit, thankfully, because the instant he did, my left knee began to buckle.

He grinned. "Even if you lose your weapon, you can make your opponent lose his balance and, with luck, fall."

"Then what?"

The corners of his mouth lifted up even more. "Then you run like hell."

It was my favorite move, making Niccolo fall, although he always recovered too quickly and gracefully to suit me.

"Just swear," he kept saying, "never to use it on me."

On the last day of practice, Niccolo and I ran through our performance from start to finish, which included his retractable dagger, my padded vest and dramatic fall, and—in order to make the rehearsal of my "death" complete—a bladder full of pig's blood hidden on top of my vest, beneath my tunic. The tip of Niccolo's dagger would pierce the bladder to make my gory end thoroughly convincing.

Ser Abramo insisted on coming up to the weapons room and watching our little drama in its entirety: my handing off an imaginary letter to Niccolo and beginning to turn away, my spinning around as he drew his dagger and I mine, and my skilled if vain efforts to stop his weapon from reaching my heart.

At its end—after my piercing shriek and skillful fall, and my perfect (I thought) death stare—I waited, hoping that the Magician would applaud, or offer words of approval, or both.

But he said nothing. Only stared, his expression faintly troubled and faintly accusatory, at Niccolo, who had ended our exhibition with an actor's sweeping stage bow, expecting, like me, to receive praise.

Instead, Ser Abramo's withering gaze stayed fixed on Niccolo as he responded grudgingly: "Simple enough. Fiore's dagger, first master, first and second plays. And I suppose you've taught him no alternative moves, in case something goes amiss?"

Niccolo's features hardened; stiffly, he said, "I taught him a defensive move."

Ser Abramo gave him the Magician's omniscient, piercing stare.

"The leg move," Niccolo prompted me, and I nodded.

We grappled again. This time, I moved my swift little pickpocket's feet to the outside of my opponent's right foot, and put my leg behind his, forcing his right knee to bend. Down he went, his dagger held carefully away from his body and from me as he fell onto the padding.

Ser Abramo finally spoke, though the heaviness in his voice remained. "I've never seen that one before. It's not Fiore, is it?"

Niccolo shook his head, unable to repress a self-satisfied grin. "I came up with it myself. Works like a . . . well, a talisman, I suppose."

Abramo didn't smile. I unstrapped my baldric and wiped my sweating face on my sleeve while Niccolo retrieved his cloak. As the latter moved past the Magician on his way toward the door, Ser Abramo spoke again, his tone challenging.

"What if the blade jams?"

Niccolo drew the dagger from his baldric. "This one's different," he replied coolly. "Better than the others; I worked with the smith myself to be sure the design was right. But to answer your question, if the blade jams, I'll take care not to pierce the vest. The sight of blood over his heart will convince them."

Ser Abramo gave the slightest shake of his head.

"We shouldn't be risking him," he said, so softly that he must have thought only Niccolo heard him.

Niccolo sighed—a sound of honest worry, not for me, but for his mentor. "Watch your heart, old man, and I'll take care of the lad's."

Before he left at the chiming of the midday bells, Niccolo made me repeat the location where our little play was to take place: The Oltrarno side of the entrance to the Ponte Vecchio, the Old Bridge, on the eastern side of the street beneath the guard tower, at the first peep of dawn the next day. After I saw him off, I found Leo settled by the kitchen door, his chin resting on his forelegs, his normally smooth brow furrowed with vague worry. I wandered through the rooms calling Abramo's name—even going so far as to lift the hatch and call down into the cellar—but there was no reply. The Magician had left the palazzo.

He'd never left before without telling me, but I shrugged it off and helped myself to the contents of the ever-simmering cauldron in the kitchen, then went upstairs to my chambers to study and rest.

The chambermaid had drawn me a bath—a luxury that happened on an astonishingly regular weekly basis. Leo followed me inside and lay politely down beside the tub as if he'd done so every day of his life. I let him stay, and since Ser Abramo was gone, I left the door unbolted and slightly ajar in case Leo had a mind to wander off again. Abramo always knocked anyway, and if I heard him coming up the stairs, I had plenty of time to cover myself and shut the door.

The drills with Niccolo had left me exhausted and sweating. When I'd eaten, I'd cooled off to the point of feeling chilled. The water in the tub was deliciously hot, and after soaping and rinsing myself, I lay sprawled in the round wooden tub, my legs hanging out one side, my head lolling out the other.

It was difficult enough to engage in swordplay at all, much less to engage in it with one's breasts tightly bound. Unwrapping them brought great relief, as did the warmth of the tub . . .

I must have dozed, because in the next instant, Ser Abramo was charging through the door as Leo sprang up to greet him, and I found myself thrashing in the water. I managed to reclaim my balance and clutch the nearby towel, which I pressed against my breasts and my decidedly un-male privates.

Ser Abramo and I gaped at each other. His lips were parted, and his gaze, though fixed on my unexpected breasts, held not a whiff of lasciviousness, but only the shock felt by a man warned to expect the impossible but who, upon discovering it, cannot fully believe it.

I bleated. He backed up to the doorway and flung an arm out as if to clutch the jamb to keep from falling. He failed and sank down to his knees at the threshold, then collapsed onto his rump. There he sat, dazed as a drunkard, his gaze unfocused, his chest heaving as he struggled to catch his breath.

By that time, I'd clawed my way out of the tub, wrapped the towel around my critical parts, and hurried over to him.

I thought that the shock had provoked a spell of apoplexy or some other dangerous fit. When I saw that his color was good and that he was merely startled out of his wits, I began to make my case.

"It doesn't matter if I'm female," I said urgently. "I'm still just as capable of working with Niccolo. I'm still just as smart, just as worthy of being your apprentice. I've survived two years on the streets, and I don't want to go back there ever again. And don't you dare try to marry me off to anyone!"

He seemed not to hear me at all. His jaw worked for a while until words finally came out, but he still didn't meet my gaze. "The silver talisman," he gasped. "Do you still have it?"

It wasn't the question I expected at all. It was still hanging around my neck; I held it up for him to see.

He shook his head. "No," he said. "Not that one."

There's an indescribable thrill—not the good kind—that comes when the body reacts to a shock before the mind can properly interpret what's going on. Like the unpleasant tingling jolt one experiences when stepping unawares on a hissing viper or looking up to find oneself directly in the path of a fast-approaching runaway carriage.

Not that one.

Thunderstruck, I sat down hard beside him on the floor, forgetting the fact that I was dripping wet and dressed only in a towel.

"The talisman," I whispered. "You remember my talisman. You really do know my parents."

"I thought Lucrezia was mistaken . . . but she was right about you. Your name . . . tell me your real name."

"I don't know," I said. "The nuns called me Giuliana."

He pushed himself to his feet and offered me a hand up; being a gentleman, he averted his gaze.

"Do you still have it? The talisman?"

"Yes." I began to shiver, and not just from the chill of water evaporating on my naked skin. "I mean, no. Not exactly. My friend—the little boy, Tommaso—I gave it to him to wear. It saved his life when—"

He waved me silent. His one eye was blinking rapidly; he opened his mouth to speak but closed it again, his expression one of agonized confusion. It took him a moment to regain his calm and state, with conviction, "We're going now to get it. I must see it. Others must, as well."

Stung, I lifted my brows. "You don't believe me? You think I would lie about this?"

He didn't take offense; he didn't respond to the questions. His mind was already elsewhere.

"Get dressed," he said crisply. "You're taking me to see your friend Tommaso."

With his white wig, skillfully hunched shoulders, and feigned reliance on his deadly cane, Ser Abramo walked slowly from the Oltrarno, over the bridge, and into the city proper. I walked beside him, my new dark blue mantello swathed around me, covering my head and my heretically short hair, my hand solicitously cupping his elbow as though I was supporting him. Any observer would have sworn we were grandfather and grandson taking an aimless stroll together. Grandfather and grandson from a wealthy banking family. I'd never worn such fine, soft clothing in my life.

The day was in fact unseasonably pleasant, perfect for a walk; the sky was cloudless, and the sun strong enough to feel pleasant on my face. The streets were crowded with pedestrians whose formerly pained expressions had eased into faint smiles.

Delicious though the weather was, it failed to cheer me. I was preoccupied with the image of Tommaso, who looked pleadingly up at me with a stricken expression, his blue-green eyes filling with tears as I was forced to leave him again. Yes, there was a man walking beside me with a stiletto that had come perilously close to the skin of my throat, and yes, I was worried that something would go wrong with Niccolo's retractable blade the next day. But I dreaded them far less than the encounter I was about to have with a six-year-old boy.

My uneasiness grew as we passed the Duomo and Baptistery and finally arrived at the potter's shop next door to the Porco Tavern, marked by a boar's head painted on the wooden sign hung over its entrance.

I paused in front of the shop, girding myself mentally, when Ser Abramo said, "One night."

"What?" The perplexing words drew me out of the near future into the present.

"Tell your little friend I only need the talisman for one night."

I nodded and pushed open the door; tinkling bells announced our arrival.

The balding potter, his face still red from the kiln, was haggling with a customer over the price of a large tureen near the back of the store; his grizzled wife stood beside him, reminding the would-be buyer of her husband's fame and skill. She glanced up as we entered and broke away to intercept Ser Abramo, clearly thinking he was a customer and that it had been coincidence that we'd come in together.

She never smiled at me. She hated me because she thought I'd made Cecilia pregnant with Ginevra, then refused to marry her. But Ser Abramo elicited her toothiest grin.

Ser Abramo played along. While I made for the stairs, he took a wobbling step toward her, forcing her to look at him instead. "I need a gift for my daughter-in-law, and I'd like to take a look at your merchandise." He gestured at the largest, most expensive vase in the store, painted with pastoral scenes in vivid blue and yellow. "That one."

Her face brightened; she clasped her hands over her heart in unintentionally comical delight. "Of course, signore. Let me show you."

She led him off. I bolted up the steps and passed through the first room into Cecilia's. The door was closed but she answered on the first knock and stood in the doorway, tall and buxom with her pale skin and hair, the latter done up in braids coiled beneath a linen veil. Her worn too-big gray kirtle was gone, replaced by a slightly used but better fitting one of heavier brown material. She was chewing, with her hand covering her mouth. An incredibly delicious smell permeated the room behind her.

"Giuli!" she whooped, spewing food in my face as she grabbed me and pressed me to her. Neither of us cared. She'd recently bathed and still smelled of soap, and when she finally eased her grip on me enough so that we could pull back and look at each other, I was pleased with what I saw. The sharp angle of her jaw-line had softened somewhat, and her cheeks had plumped. She'd put some of the florin to good use.

In the room behind her, the bed was now covered with a heavy blanket and two new pillows; nearby, a fat iron cauldron rested on a sturdy four-legged table, just large enough to serve as a small dining table. There were three solid chairs tucked next to it, one of which had clearly just been vacated. Tommaso sat in one of the chairs feeding himself and Ginevra, who sat on his lap sporting a new long dress, and when he caught sight of me, his face grew brighter than a flame at midnight.

"Tommaso!" Cecilia called, but she needn't have.

In a thrice, baby Ginevra was sitting bewildered on the bed and Tommaso was flinging himself at me with the speed of an arrow loosed from the quiver. Despite my feeling of heaviness, I laughed aloud with Cecilia at the fact that he'd nearly knocked me off my feet.

"I missed you!" Tommaso shouted over us. The faint accusatory note in his tone was overpowered by joy. "You were gone forever, but I knew you'd come back! I knew it! And you're getting fatter!"

"So are you," I said smiling. The once deep hollows beneath his cheekbones were almost gone; I could scarcely feel his ribs under his tunic, a brand-new one of bright green wool. His pale hair was still damp and neater than I'd ever seen it. Cecilia must have recently trimmed it.

"Look!" he commanded, and curled his lip to reveal his pink upper gum, and the emerging crescent slivers of white enamel where his front teeth used to be.

"Big man," I said approvingly. "Look at you, with grown-up teeth."

"They're coming in fast," Cecilia chirped.

I dug in the pocket of my cape until my fingers found four soldi Ser Abramo had recently given me as a reward for studying hard. "I brought you a present," I told Tommaso, and ceremoniously dropped one of the silver coins into his unusually clean, pink palm. Cecilia had even cleaned under his nails.

His mouth opened in awe, though not quite so wide as his eyes, as he stared down at it. I put the other three coins in

Cecilia's hand. "I've got another florin coming," I told her as an aside.

"Wonderful," she said automatically as I rose, gently extricating myself from Tommaso's grasp. "You'll come sit with us now, and have some soup. *Real* soup, with good sausage. The landlady is letting me use her kitchen hearth."

"Is that what I smelled?" I kept my smile fixed, even though I was unhappy about what I needed to say next. "I'm sure it's delicious. But I only came to give you the money, and to ask—"

"You're staying now, aren't you? You're not *leaving* again?" He stared up at me, his huge eyes already brimming with tears. The corners of his mouth were trembling.

"I have work to do," I said firmly. "I came by to give Cecilia the soldi and to ask a favor."

"What do you need, Giuli?" Cecilia's tone conveyed that whatever it was, I would get it.

"I need . . ." The words didn't want to come out of my throat. "I need the talisman, the one Tommaso is wearing. Just for a day. I'll return it tomorrow. I swear."

Tommaso let go a long wail, followed by great wracking sobs. There was no theater in them, no calculation as to what effect his performance might have on me or anyone else. He was brokenhearted; defeated, he staggered to the farthest corner of Cecilia's room—the farthest he could get from me—and sank to the floor, his face to the wall.

I followed and crouched behind him to put a hand on his shoulder; he pulled it away.

"I'm sorry this upsets you," I said, my tone brisk and nononsense, "but I'm not deserting you. I'm working so that you and I never have to play the Game again. We're going to be rich and have a fine house, and we'll never have to go hungry again, ever." I paused. "You'll see me tomorrow."

He sobbed silently all the while, shuddering, his lips pressed shut, until his face turned an alarming shade of red. Finally he sucked in a breath, and said, in a small, trembling voice, "You said you were coming back last time. But you're *not*. You *lied*."

Before I could answer him, he tore something from his neck, turned, and flung it over my head. I heard a faint clatter as it struck the floor on the other side of the room.

The silver talisman, the thong that held it now torn in two.

He turned his face back to the wall and wouldn't look at me. "I won't ever wear it again," he said, his voice still shaking but now grown cold. "Never. I hate it. I hate you. Go away."

He curled into a little ball on the floor and wept quietly.

I tried to pick him up, and he landed a punch square in my stomach. It took my breath away.

"Tommaso!" Cecilia snapped, but I waved her silent.

"I've got to get going," I said, my voice annoyingly husky. "I'll be back tomorrow."

She nodded, lips pressed unhappily but sympathetically together. "Can I talk to you in private for a moment?"

Reluctantly, I stepped outside and waited as she followed and shut the door on Tommaso and the perplexed baby Ginevra.

"I'm worried about you," she said. "You seem all right, but there's a lot you're hiding from me."

"Everything's okay," I countered. "I just . . . I need for you to do me a favor. I want you to go ahead and get that house, and clear out of this room. Offer your landlord a tip to serve as your escort and help you negotiate. Or tell him he can keep the rest of the rent I already paid him. But don't stay here anymore." I was thinking of how Ser Abramo had made me swear on the lives on my friends. I was thinking about what might happen to those friends if my performance went badly the following day.

She shrugged. "You saw all the new things I bought. We're comfortable enough. And we're eating well."

"You're not really safe here."

She shrugged. "I admit, living next to a tavern isn't the best situation, but nothing has happened so far—"

"Cecilia," I said emphatically. "You and Tommaso. *You're not safe.* I want you to move right away. Today. Or at least by tomorrow morning. You don't have to move everything, but I just don't want you staying here for the next few days."

She fell silent and lowered her pale chin to study me carefully. For a long moment she didn't speak.

"Giuli, what sort of business have you gotten yourself into?" she finally asked. "If Tommaso and I are in danger, what does that say about *you*?"

I glanced down at the tips of my well-polished boots and tried to think of a reassuring answer.

"Listen," Cecilia said urgently. "We'll buy a house. Somewhere where your so-called employer can't find you. I can't let you risk your life getting involved in God knows what sort of illegal business—"

"It's not illegal," I said without thinking. "Not . . . civilly, anyway."

"Whatever it is, it's bad. We don't ever want to lose you, Giuli. Stay with us. Let's go back inside." She caught hold of my wrist.

"I *can't*," I said.

The hardness in my tone made her turn back around and stare at me in silence, waiting.

"I'm his apprentice, Celia. He's teaching me everything. I'll be rich. And so will you, and Tommaso, don't you see? It's worth a little risk. What's the point of going on living this way?"

"At least we'll be living."

I took a deep breath. "I swore not to betray him. On my life. On yours."

Her eyes were already large and round; they got even larger and rounder. "So you're involved with a murderer, then. An assassin. Giuli, is he training you to kill people?"

"It's worse than that," I said. "He's a magician."

I meant it as a sort of joke, but Cecilia didn't take it that way. She took a step back and touched the little cross at her bosom.

"Witchcraft?" she whispered.

"Hebrew magic," I said. "God and archangels. It can't be bad if there are angels, Cecilia. But it's secret. You can't tell anyone. You can't ever tell Tommaso."

She was no less aghast. "You lied," she said, her voice still low. "You said it wasn't illegal."

"It's not."

"Well, it's against canon law. Heresy. The Church punishes that sort of thing."

I shrugged. "The Church is in Rome. This is Florence. Besides, the Church only has jurisdiction over Christians."

"So now I have to worry about your immortal soul as well as your life?"

On the other side of the closed door, baby Ginevra let go a gusty wail. Cecilia instinctively put a hand on the leather door pull.

"Cecilia," I said, stopping her in midstep.

"If you knew the man I worked for, you'd know he's as good a person as anyone," I said as earnestly as I knew how, even though I still wasn't completely sure of it. "Better than most, I think. This job, it's a gift." My tone grew businesslike. "I'm going to leave now. Go and find somewhere else to stay for a few days. I just have to prove myself to him, that's all, and I'll be back."

I turned to leave. Behind me, Cecilia said, her tone conciliatory, "I'll pray for you to be safe."

God doesn't hear you, I wanted to retort. *And if He does hear you, He doesn't care.*

Instead, I left without looking back.

As I went down into the shop, I worked hard to erase all emotion from my face. Ser Abramo was standing in front of the large, lovely blue and yellow vase putting a gold coin into the open palm of the beaming potter's wife. She slipped it into her apron and listened, nodding and rapt, to his instructions for delivery, to the house of one Giovanni de' Benci in the wealthy banking district. She appeared not to see me at all, but instead focused entirely on Ser Abramo as, fawning and excessively grateful, she took his arm and helped him out the door. I followed closely, trying to make it look like sheer coincidence that I happened to be going out the door at the same time.

The encounter with Tommaso had left an ache at the back of my throat, just behind the roof of my mouth, as if a string were attached there and someone was pulling hard in an effort to bring tears to my eyes. I cursed myself for such silly weakness and shook off the reaction. But I couldn't quite shake off the unbearable sense of anxiety as I slipped my unsteady hand into my pocket.

"Do you have it?" Ser Abramo asked beside me.

I nodded and reached into my cloak pocket to pull out the talisman, but he immediately laid a restraining hand on my forearm.

I glanced up, surprised. His expression was cold and utterly unreadable.

"Not here," he said flatly. "Not in public."

"But my friend," I protested. "He's crying. Can't you look at it now so I can give it back to him?"

He wouldn't look at me. "Keep it in your pocket and don't speak another word. Come."

He leaned heavily upon his cane and I took his elbow like the dutiful grandson I was not. Without a further word, we walked the length of the city and crossed the crowded bridge into the Oltrarno, me carrying the burden of Tommaso and my unknown heritage all the way.

Nine

During the long walk home, Ser Abramo's hardened stare remained steadfastly fixed on the road ahead; not once did he glance at me. The afternoon sun illuminated his craggy profile, showing every line etched by age; the dark intensity in his exposed eye unnerved me. The presence of the talisman had changed him into someone I didn't recognize.

When we finally arrived back at the Magician's lair and entered the dark room outside the kitchen, I pulled the talisman from my pocket and hung my cloak up.

The minute I turned toward him and opened my palm, he snatched the talisman and closed his fist over it without a glance. Still in his cloak, he unlocked the door and strode into the kitchen, his expression remaining that of a grim stranger—one who could see anything but me.

I followed and bent down to greet Leo properly with a pat, but Ser Abramo hurried past us, through the kitchen and the sitting room with such long strides and speed that I couldn't keep up. Leo and I made it into the storage room just as the wooden hatch to the cellar closed over him with a thump.

I ran to the hatch despite the sound of wood sliding against wood beneath it. Tugging on the big leather strap did no good.

He had locked me out.

.   .   .

For an hour, perhaps more, Leo and I sat beside the hatch, my arm flung over the mastiff's broad back as we waited for Ser Abramo to emerge. He would appear soon, I told myself, and apologize for his coldness. He would explain the powers of the talisman, why it had been made, and—most importantly—who had asked for it to be made. It had been eighteen years, but he was the Magician; he surely could remember everything. A name, that's all I wanted. The name of a father. A mother.

But he never came out that long afternoon.

And that was when I began to worry: Was the talisman all they had ever wanted from me? Was there some significance to it that went beyond me and my true identity, one so important that everything, including the lessons with Niccolo and my apprenticeship to Ser Abramo had all been part of an elaborate charade?

Staring at the hatch, I finally realized that sitting only encouraged my imagination to move toward the sad and fearful. The path to sanity was to busy myself. I checked the kitchen to make sure the bag of fresh pig's blood was kept cool in a bucket of cold water and then went up to the weapons room to practice my role in the next morning's drama. I drew my dagger a hundred times, counting each the better to distract myself. A hundred times, I did the fatal dance Niccolo and I had practiced; a hundred times, I feigned the look of horror as an imaginary blade pierced my heart and, a hundred times, fell down with the abandon of the dead.

Fell down wondering whether Niccolo's blade might not stop at the pig's bladder, now that I'd been relieved of the talisman.

Which was why I practiced a different dance a hundred times: My left hand gripping the imaginary wrist of Niccolo's dagger-wielding arm, my left leg moving blink-swift behind his right, forcing that knee to bend and him to fall before his blade had the chance to break my grip and kill me. If he meant harm, I'd use his own trick against him and wouldn't blanch at drawing blood once he was down.

Well, not much.

I worked until the sun began to set. Sweating, I kept my baldric on and switched my dulled dagger for a keen new blade. I went downstairs hoping that Ser Abramo would be waiting for me with a happy tale to tell.

But the lamps were unlit, and the sitting room and kitchen were empty, as was his bedchamber. Disheartened, I went back downstairs and tried the cellar hatch again; it was still bolted fast.

I stirred the fire in the sitting room and lit a lamp in the kitchen, where I pulled off the leg of a roast capon on the spit and ladled a bowl of pasta with broth from the cauldron. I poured a generous cup from the wine carafe left on the table. I ate solely for strength, but food tasted unappealing and drink bitter. With the lamp in my hand and Leo in tow, I went to the storage room and gave the cellar hatch one last try, to no use.

There was nothing more to do but go ahead with the rehearsed plan in the morning and try to protect myself as best I could, whoever the enemy. I shut my bedchamber door and set my baldric and dagger on the table next to the bed, less than an arm's reach away.

I told myself, as my head found the pillow, that Ser Abramo would be downstairs when I woke the next morning and everything would be all right.

Everything all right. Remember to repeat this a hundred times, I told myself, until you believe it.

Everything all right, I said silently. One.

Everything all right. Two.

And then I remembered nothing.

. . .

At some point I fell into a nightmare of being drowned or smoth-ered or both; my arms thrashed as I fought a hulking giant to free my face, to get air.

I opened my eyes just as the tip of Leo's wet tongue found the inside of my nostril. I groaned in disgust and moved to wipe my nose, but my arm felt heavy, the effort great. I let it drop and shut my eyes, wanting only to sink back into the bliss of sleep.

But his kisses were insistent, like that of a mother cat clean-ing its newborn kitten; drool dribbled down my nose and made me cough until I reluctantly sat up. The fire in the hearth had died to glowing cinders, but even in the gloom, Leo's massive bulk was unmistakable.

"Okay, dog," I murmured. "Enough." I sat up languidly against the pillows and drew the back of my forearm across my dripping face. Immediately, my arm dropped and my eyes closed of their own accord. I could easily have fallen asleep again right there until Leo whined.

It was an unhappy sound full of urgency. That whine brought me to my senses, enough to realize that I had been dosed with the poppy, that Ser Abramo must have emerged from the cellar with news, and—most fog-dispersing of all—that this was the morning that I was to meet Niccolo for our scripted duel at the instant of daybreak.

"Do you need to go outside, boy? Are you hungry?" I mum-bled. It wasn't like his owner to neglect the dog's needs, but Leo responded to neither suggestion. "Where's your master? Where's Abramo?"

At the last question, the mastiff jumped off the bed and sat, expectant.

I reached for the baldric and dagger I'd left on the night table. Gone.

Gone, and my chamber door wide open. At that instant, I remembered, as if in a dream, hearing the muted bells of the cathedral Santo Spirito in the Oltrarno greet matins, the first hour of the morning. Dawn would have been ninety minutes away then. Had I overslept?

I scrambled gracelessly out of bed. While Leo panted and paced anxiously, I pulled on my undershirt and leggings as fast as my wooziness allowed and opened the shutters.

Outside, it was still black, but despite the poppy-induced lethargy, my body knew dawn wasn't that far away.

I called for Ser Abramo. At the name, Leo let go another whine filled with such pathos that I half ran, half stumbled to the Magician's bedchamber, convinced something horrible had befallen him.

The bed curtains were parted, the bed itself empty and undisturbed. Leo at my side, I staggered full tilt up to the third floor, to the weapons room, thinking to arm myself again in case the Magician was in danger. And even if I'd read Leo falsely and Ser Abramo was fine, I still intended to show up for my pretend duel with Niccolo, just in case it really was the patriotic thing to do for Florence.

I yanked on the door to the weapons room and swore when it failed to yield. It was bolted. I pressed my ear to the door and heard nothing but silence.

I ran down to the storage room to find the wooden hatch to the dungeon unbolted at last. I lifted it and shouted for Abramo, but there was no reply, only blackness. I hurried to the sitting room, where the hearth was freshly lit, and then into the kitchen, where a simmering kettle of stew hung from a hook above the fire.

A piece of thrice-folded paper sat on the long table across

from the cupboard—the note I was to hand to Niccolo before our mock battle began. On top of it lay my old silver talisman, strung on a new leather thong.

I slipped the talisman over my neck and picked up the note. Niccolo had told me there was no point in reading it—that it would make no sense to me—but to my surprise, my name was written on the outside in bold handsome script. I unfolded it and read.

> *Dearest Giuliana,*
>
> *I apologize for yesterday's aloofness and for seasoning your supper with a bit of the poppy. I had good reason for both, and much I need to tell you when I return.*
>
> *I forbid you to rendezvous with Niccolo this morning. Remain here for your own safety. Keep Leo by your side; he can protect you far better than any blade. Let no one enter the house—except Niccolo, and then only if you are certain he is alone.*
>
> *There is food enough for you and the dog, and you have your studies to entertain you.*
>
> *If I do not return by midday, find the key to the lockbox I showed you. You will find further instructions there. Know this: Death can never separate us. I am with you always.*
>
> *Be well.*
>
> *With sincere affection,*
> *Abramo*

A horrible feeling settled over me heavily, relentlessly. Somehow, everything good that had happened to me had just gone horribly wrong.

Don't panic, I told myself: Ser Abramo had simply gone to tell Niccolo that our little drama had to be postponed until a substitute could be found. Perhaps, after I had gone to bed and Ser Abramo had finally emerged from the cellar realizing that he couldn't trust a mere girl to pull off the performance with Niccolo, he had left the estate and gone to search the streets in the wee hours to find a substitute to play my part.

An expendable urchin like me, one bright enough that he could learn all the fighting moves in one night. One that they could trust, one that trusted them enough, one that was thoroughly loyal to Florence and the Medici.

Right. I was good at lying to myself, but that was one I couldn't swallow. It had taken weeks to ascertain my loyalty and train me; someone fresh off the streets wouldn't do. They needed someone with basic swordsmanship skills who could work with Niccolo, someone Niccolo and Abramo and Lorenzo could trust completely.

There was only one other person who filled those requirements.

On impulse, I moved to the part of the kitchen farthest from the hearth, where the day before Niccolo had left a bladder full of fresh pig's blood in a metal bucket filled with freezing cold water from the Arno. I was to set the bladder on top of my padded vest under my tunic that morning.

I stared down into the bucket, empty now save for murky river water, and recalled Niccolo's words to Abramo.

Watch your heart, old man.

It was too good to be true, of course, that Ser Abramo really cared about me.

My clever boy.

Cared enough to protect me from risk, from danger. Cared

enough to hide my weapons and the pig's blood from me, to make it impossible for me to play my perilous role.

Leo sat down and stared intently at the door leading out to the dark cloakroom.

I followed his gaze and stood thinking, the note in my hand. *Watch your heart.*

Leo looked up at me, gave a low, throaty whine, and looked back at the door.

I drew a deep breath and set the note down. It seemed impossible. How could someone care enough to place himself in the danger meant for me?

Who was Ser Abramo to me, and who was I to him, that he would do such a thing?

It was too good to be true, and too awful, and I couldn't let it happen.

Because I didn't want to give up a life of luxury, I tried to convince myself. Because the last thing I needed was the Medici family angry with me.

Another lie that was hard to swallow. The simple truth was that Ser Abramo had done a spell to bring me to him. Someone, finally, had *wanted* me, cared about me, and I could let no harm come to him.

I fetched my cloak from the outer room, then rummaged about the kitchen and found the freshly sharpened carving knife I'd used on the roast capon the night before. I had no baldric in which to sheathe it, but I wrapped the blade in some rags and fixed it so the metal handle was upright in my cloak pocket.

There was no time to bind my breasts or worry with stuffing my leggings so I looked male. My mantle alone would have to serve to hide my femininity.

I bent down and petted Leo's soft furrowed head. "I'll be back soon," I promised, though the dog looked less than reassured. "We'll both be back."

The doors to the house were easily unlocked. I hurried out into the night and felt a chill mist settle on my face. The moon had set and a heavy fog made it impossible for me to see beyond my next two steps. Even so, I made unerring haste to the gate in the first stone wall. It was unlocked, but somehow blocked. I put a shoulder to it and strained against it with all my weight. It wouldn't budge.

I cursed and grabbed the tangle of thick woody vines. They were strong enough so that I could have pulled myself up, but the soles of my boots slipped off the damp stone and I fell back to earth. The gracelessness caused by the poppy wasn't the only problem; my arms simply weren't strong enough. I needed the strength of my legs to boost me over.

The cold air stinging my face, I turned about thinking to find some stones to pile up, but with the fog limiting my vision, I would have had to slowly wander the grounds. There wasn't time.

And then I remembered the stools in the kitchen. I ran back and dragged one out to the wall. My plan: to get to the top of the wall, then reach down and retrieve the stool so that I could use it to get over the second wall. The plan worked only partially. The final push with my legs that boosted me to the top knocked the stool over, and I slipped, right over the edge onto the other side.

I landed hard on my back, the air knocked from my lungs. As soon as I could draw a breath, I exhaled a whispery laugh. I'd fallen onto the bed of the cart that Ser Abramo had used to block the gate. It solved the problem of getting over the second wall, but the wagon was damnably heavy and difficult to maneuver. I spent too much time pushing, pulling, and cursing while the fog lightened from charcoal to dove gray.

Dawn was coming. Too soon, the Magician would be drawing his dagger, risking his neck. I pushed with more force than I was able, until I felt my howling sinews tear, and then I pushed harder. Dangerous minutes passed. By the time I had the wagon aligned with the second wall and hurled myself to freedom, the trees in the forest were no longer black silhouettes, but objects painted in varying shades of gray in the colorless hour before dawn.

The minute my feet found earth, I went flying through the countryside in search of the Magician, with the same desperate speed I'd once used to flee him.

Ten

My feet finally hit city cobblestone a quarter-hour walk from my rendezvous point with Niccolo. I'd never run so fast— faster than I'd ever run from the police or an angry mark—down side streets, through alleys, using every shortcut I knew to get to the Ponte Vecchio. I hurled myself half blind into the fog, able to see only a stride ahead but never slowing, swathed in brume that muted outer sounds but magnified the drum of my every step, the gasp of each breath.

The Magician was stronger, faster, more experienced with a sword than I could ever hope to be. He'd trained Niccolo in the art of the dagger and could work better with him than I could. Except that he didn't understand that I was cursed: everyone I'd cared about had abandoned me or died. Which meant something was going to go wrong.

I finally turned right onto the Borgo di San Iacopo, the broad boulevard running alongside the River Arno, blocked from my view by waist-high walls built up along the steep embankment. Niccolo and I were to "fight" near the archway spanning the entrance to the bridge, where the Borgo intersected with the ancient Via Romana, the Oltrarno's main thoroughfare. The fog should have been thicker near the water, but the lack of houses on the embankment had allowed the rays of the rising sun behind me to penetrate the street and reduce the thick brume to a light, swirling mist; the feel of the sun on my back spurred me on.

I could see farther, but the dawn's colors were still paled and the edges of the visible world as indistinct as a dream. On the other side of the river, feathery streaks of fog drifted downward, thinning to expose a sea of slightly peaked orange-red roofs atop pale stone: Florence proper, her buildings dwarfed by the massive orange dome of the city cathedral and the gray slender tower atop the government fortress called the Palace of Lords, the Palazzo della Signoria.

A block from my destination, the orange roofs of twin square watchtowers appeared out of the silent white fog, positioned on opposite sides of the archway over the entrance to the Old Bridge. The windows of the western watchtower were dark, but those of the eastern—the one under which the play would unfold—were lit. In the near distance, a dark huddle of monks ambled ahead of me.

I slowed to a rapid walk and raised my cowl, hanging close to the southern side of the street opposite the riverbank and watchtower. The smell of rising yeast and the yellow glow from every window meant the city was coming to life. At any second, the boulevard would begin to fill. I wanted to attract no attention, and if I was too late, I didn't want to endanger Ser Abramo with a distraction. And if I wasn't . . .

Several close-pressed buildings away from the watchtower, I stopped, squinting through remnants of the lifting mist looking for both men. They would be cloaked, of course, but I knew their builds, their movements.

No one lingered near the bridge's gate. I stood motionless for at least a full minute scanning the area, feeling the cold sweat run down my back and chest, and began to shiver.

The sun had definitely risen; the mist was burning off rapidly. No sign of either man.

I inched closer to the gate, looking at everything about me, hanging close to the buildings opposite, until I had a clear view of the appointed place, until I was close enough to intercept Niccolo the instant he appeared. A donkey and cart on the Via Romana rattled onto the Ponte Vecchio. A brown flock of Franciscan monks moved past me and turned to the right, away from the bridge, onto the even broader Via Romana.

I waited another full minute, glancing behind me at the Borgo di San Iacopo, to my left at the entrance to the bridge, to my right at a few sleepy pedestrians ambling down the Via Romana. But I saw no Niccolo, no Abramo, and the moment of sunrise was past.

At last, I let go a soft, profoundly relaxing sigh. I'd been wrong; the performance had been called off. Ser Abramo was safe and probably already back at his estate, wondering what had become of me.

As I began to turn to head back down the Borgo, I caught a blur of black in the corner of my eye and pivoted around. A cloaked figure darted from shadows beneath the arch over the gate to the street immediately beneath the guard tower.

Niccolo.

Before I could take a single step toward him, a hooded Franciscan friar—one from the huddle that had all presumably already passed by—appeared out of a sliver of shadow and brushed elbows with Niccolo. The friar slyly palmed Niccolo a folded paper—the note that should have been waiting on the kitchen table for me that morning.

I suppressed the urge to cry out or intervene, to avoid putting both men and myself in even more danger, and closed my mouth. The Medici's—and the Magician's—enemies were somewhere, watching, and soldiers were minding the eastern tower, soldiers who could easily intervene if alerted to the coming violence.

The cloaked Niccolo slipped the note into his pocket. Just as

the Franciscan friar began to move away, Niccolo unsheathed his
dagger, the friar unsheathed his, and the dance began.

Fiore, first master, first play.

Niccolo raised the dagger in a high arc; as it came down relentlessly aimed at his victim's chest, the friar caught his wrist
perfectly, skillfully, stopping the blade in midair as he drew his
own weapon with his free hand. The quick movements caused
Niccolo's cowl to slip back, revealing his face: the lips drawn back
over gritted teeth, the dark brows colliding to form an extreme
vee, the narrowed eyes full of such venom, such deep contempt
that I was tempted to scream a warning to his victim.

Second play.

But I stopped myself. Playacting; it was only playacting, even
though Niccolo was unnervingly convincing.

With his right hand, the Franciscan swiped at Niccolo with
his dagger. Unlike mine, the friar's arms were long enough to
reach his foe, and the tip of his blade sliced through Niccolo's
cloak at the level of his thigh and made him cry out in startled
indignance: a surprise defensive move, one that the friar repeated
to the effect that Niccolo cried out in pain again. The friar took
another step closer, moving in for the kill.

This was not what we had practiced; this was not part of the
plan. This was *real*.

I pulled my kitchen knife from my pocket and clumsily freed
it from its wrappings, ready to enter the fray, ready to protect
Niccolo.

As I began to move, Niccolo rotated his opponent's imprisoned
wrist, slipping the dagger to the outside of the friar's arm and then
under it, moving the blade back into the vulnerable area above his
victim's heart. His movements were vehement, vicious, the look
in his eyes terrifying as he gave his blade the final brutal thrust.

The dagger struck just to the left of the breastbone. The friar let go a strangled, mortal cry and began to fall straight back, as I should have, onto rough cobblestone instead of padded leather. In mid-fall, the friar's cowl slipped back.

Abramo the Magician fell limp against the stone, his exposed face utterly slack.

Shouts reverberated in my ears, but I could not have told you whether they were near or far, masculine or feminine. I ran to Abramo's side, no longer caring about whatever enemies might have been watching. I knelt on the stones beside him, pulled away his cloak and watched blood well above his heart, an irregular darkness slowly consuming the worn brown wool of a Franciscan habit.

During the fall, the patch over his right eye had been pushed up onto his brow. For the first time, both his eyes were exposed and open, staring sightlessly at a point far distant, one only the dead could see.

I leaned down, letting my mantle fall around us both, shielding our faces from the crowd. What I saw hurled the breath violently from me.

His left eye, of course, was brown like mine.

His right eye—the one hidden from me all this time by the silk patch—was whole and unblemished. I'd assumed the eye had been missing or blind, but realized that he'd worn the patch for me. His right eye, like mine, was green.

No wonder Lucrezia de' Medici had gasped at the sight of me.

Of course he had made a talisman for me when I was born. Of course he had.

Of course he had.

In that thunderous instant, I saw every second of time I had spent with him, from first encounter to last, in this new, fresh, glorious and terrible light.

"Just blink," I sobbed. "Please. They can't see. Just please, be alive. You *can't* die. Not now!"

But the dreadful absence in his gaze remained; his body drew no breath.

I pressed my fingers against the bloody spot on his chest, felt the empty pig's bladder and beneath it, a padded vest. Perhaps this was a trick after all; perhaps Niccolo's dagger had gone no further. Shielding my movements with my cloak, I cut his robe open with the kitchen knife, exposing the bladder.

It had been pierced clean through. The vest was soaked with blood—pig's blood, of course, reassuringly dark because it was old.

Perhaps the play had gone exactly as Niccolo and I had practiced.

My mind raced to reassure me: The blade had retracted, the knife hadn't gone that far through, I would see that Abramo wasn't really dead. It all came clear: Niccolo was proving himself to the enemy, he was a double spy of some sort for the Magician and the Medici, and I didn't dare ruin things for him. I would quickly retreat or, better, could stay and wail that Abramo was dead, murdered.

I lifted up the bladder ever so slightly, careful that no outsider could see my movements. The protective vest beneath was stained with the same dark blood, but it had been slit through, leaving a tear broad enough for my entire hand to slip through the padded fabric. I parted the slit enough to expose the skin beneath, and a sickening chill coursed through me.

The flesh over the Magician's heart was covered with fresh blood, bright red and warm.

I lifted my contorted face to scan the growing crowd of on-lookers for Niccolo, intending to scream after him that he was a traitor, that he had betrayed the Medici, so that the guards would pursue him.

Before I could open my mouth, someone knocked me off balance and straddled Ser Abramo's still form. He was huge, broad—a giant compared to those around him, even to the Magician.

As I scrambled to push myself up off my backside, I glimpsed the man inside the cowl: flame-bearded and grinning, with ice pale eyes full of madness. He reached inside his cloak for a hidden weapon: a stiletto, shorter than the one Abramo carried in his cane, but no less deadly. "We'll find out now who's really dead," he said cheerfully to the fallen Magician, and lifted his blade above his shoulder, its tip aimed directly at Abramo's heart.

"No!" I screamed. I struggled onto my knees and grasped his wrist—twice the breadth of mine—but I couldn't slow him even a whit. Desperate, I lifted my eyes and screamed for the police, only to see Niccolo several steps distant, calling for the lunatic to come away, to hurry, that the police were running down from the guard tower. A second cloaked form appeared beside Niccolo, both of them calling for their fellow to flee.

I stared gape-mouthed at Niccolo. He stared back, his eyes afire with a rage that teetered on insanity; a rage that would have seen me dead, had he been close enough to wield his weapon. Teeth bared, his face a tortured rictus, he shouted at his comrade, "*Run!*"

The red-bearded madman ignored him and plunged his blade into the lifeless Magician's chest again, again, while I scrambled screaming for my kitchen knife. Abramo's body shuddered lifelessly with each strike, but made no sound, no other movement.

"All good," the monster said to himself, smiling. "If he wasn't already dead, he is now."

I sank my kitchen knife deep into Red Beard's forearm, the one that held the stiletto. Yowling, he dropped his stiletto in order to pull out my offending weapon. I braced for the blow—

I was ready to die alongside my father rather than abandon him—but the red-haired devil hurled the kitchen knife to the cobblestone and fled to join his cohorts.

I took up the murder weapon, thinking to flay anyone who came near us, and bent over the Magician. I put my free hand over his wound, as if I could stop the bleeding, and realized that his golden talisman was gone, missing. All that remained around his neck was the leather thong heavy with keys.

"Breathe," I whispered hoarsely, and bent over him. My back was to the east; my head cast a shadow over his, making his eyes look dark and sunken, the strong bones of his face skeletal. "Please, breathe . . ."

But he didn't, and I couldn't. I looked up wanting to cry out for help, but my voice had fled with my breath, and my sight was blurred: the entire street was alive now, a dizzying swirl of dark red and blue and drab mantellos, of blank winter-white faces staring down at me, the air filled with babbling. A quartet of black-clad bodies surged toward me, too fast.

All too fast, and all too real.

The four guards' short swords were drawn. They elbowed their way through the gathering crowd.

Shouts came from passersby, and screams.

That way! They went that way!

Too late, they're gone! We'll never catch them!

He's dying, he's dead, get him upstairs! Get him out of here!

Get the boy! He's got a dagger! He's one of them!

I pulled the thong from Abramo's neck with a silent apology as the keys, still warm from his flesh, jangled. Boot soles pounded against stone, eclipsing other sounds. A dark wool-swathed arm reached for me, an all-too-nearby blade flashed with morning light. I jumped up, yanking the edges of my short mantello out of reach of grasping fingers.

Three of the guards swiftly surrounded Abramo's body—one at his head, one at his waist, the third at his feet. They crouched, their knees bent directly beneath their hips.

"Don't take him," I cried, my voice breaking. "Don't take him away!"

The fourth guard—dark-haired, with pale skin and a black mantello and cap, the whole utterly colorless—grasped my wrist while I was thus terribly distracted. "I've seen you—you're a pickpocket! You helped kill him to get his purse! You little bastard!" He sprayed spittle, his face contorted by indignance. When I pulled away, he aimed the tip of his short sword at me. He seemed unaware of the stiletto in my other hand.

I'm his friend! I wanted to shout. *Niccolo did it! And a lunatic with a red beard! And they're getting away, you idiot son of a whore!*

There wasn't time.

It all happened so fast in one stunning, mindless moment: The three guards counted to three and grunted as they jerked Abramo's bloodied body up. I sank the tip of the stiletto into the shoulder of the guard holding me. It was so sharp it slid in deep without effort.

At the sight of his own blood, my enemy roared and moved to plunge me through with his sword.

I knew exactly what to do.

I gripped his right wrist with my left hand, overhanded.

At the same time I took the very long sidewise step, placing my right leg behind his, my knee deeply bent. And then I straightened my leg.

Some downward pressure on his left shoulder, and down he went, roaring.

Rage pressured me to kill him while he was off his feet, as if that would have somehow avenged Ser Abramo. But as the other guards staggered back to the tower with the Magician's body, pedestrians were starting to circle around, most of them pointing at me. The guard on the ground howled, "Get him!"

He meant me. Stupidly, I dropped the stiletto. And I ran.

As fast as I could, faster than I ever had, not so much to get away from the crowd and the guard as from what had just happened.

Back down the Borgo di San Iacopo, my breath coming out as wrenched, strangled noises, growing higher in pitch with each frantic strike of my boots against cobblestone. The city streets appeared as if underwater: blurred one instant, impossibly clear the next, as if I'd been swimming with eyes open beneath the River Arno.

I flew over the street, over horse dung and human piss, over puddles of dirty water thrown from upstairs windows. There were buildings, landmarks, people, but I saw none of them: I saw only Ser Abramo's torn vest pulled open, saw the blood covering his flesh, saw the terrible unfocused look in his eyes, different-colored like my own. I felt the lightning shock of knowing. There was no room in the world for anything but those sights, that feeling.

I ran through the entire citified Oltrarno. As I finally stepped from paved ground onto soft earth where the city faded into forest, I heard the sound of another pair of boots thudding fast against the ground. I glanced over my shoulder to see the red-bearded giant, the second of Abramo's murderers, several strides behind me. His cowl was thrown back, his yellow teeth bared above his cinnamon beard, his thick arms pumping as his long stride made short work of the distance between us.

I thought it impossible for me to run any faster, but I did, ducking into a thicket of tall evergreen cyprus and coming out into an ancient olive grove with silvered leaves, the gnarled low-hanging limbs forcing my enemy to crouch and slow.

I was in such agony already that his pursuit barely added to it. Part of me wanted to slow down, to let him catch and kill me, to be done with my painful life. But my thief's instincts were too strong, and so I ran.

I remembered little else of the chase—a glimpse of Red Beard the killer, and the rest of it, that final sight of Abramo dead, always before my eyes.

But the moment finally came when I found myself gasping in front of the thick woody tangle of dead vines covering the secret gate in front of Abramo's hideaway. I reached for the long necklace of keys around my neck and fumbled for the right one. My fingers trembled so badly that I dropped the ring once, so that the keys chimed against my chest, but I recovered them quickly and found the correct key.

My hands shook violently as I scrambled to find the lock and mate it with the key. Behind me came the muted thud of leather boots against uneven earth.

I dared not look back. I turned the key hard in the lock, heard the muffled click, and pushed against the wall.

It barely moved. The cart that I'd used to scale the wall after Ser Abramo had locked me inside was blocking it. I braced my legs and feet and put my shoulder into it; on the other side, the cart's wheels groaned and moved back slightly.

It was enough of an opening for diminutive me to sidle into, but my forward progress was still blocked by the cart. I pushed again, gritting my teeth, straining every muscle until I involuntarily cried out with the effort.

The cart rolled backward a bit, leaving just enough opening for me to squeeze through—but not before I felt a thick hand swiping at my shoulder. I turned to see the giant's arm reaching through the slit in the gate, less than a finger's length from catching me and pulling me back.

I yelped and shot forward, the keys jangling sharply against my heart, stunned that the red-bearded monster hadn't simply run me through with a blade and killed me on the spot.

It was too late to protect Abramo's lair from the Roman enemy, too late for me to escape him, too late for me to concoct a proper plan. I darted across the outer estate to the inner wall, reached again for the keys, unlocked it, and glanced back only long enough to see that the towering Red Beard had pushed the heavy cart entirely out of his way and was only four or five paces behind.

I pushed the inner gate open. There was no time to stop and close it. My enemy was on my heels, gasping with increasing aggravation, "Stop! Stop! *Stop!*"

I sprinted toward the house, the key held ready in my hand. I unlocked the door, stepped into the cloakroom with its black curtains, and pivoted to shut the door. In my haste to leave, I'd left the kitchen door open and the curtains parted; the hearth fire eased the room's darkness. As I moved to slide the bolt, the door pushed back against me with unassailable force. In the shadows, I saw my enemy's foot planted in the doorway.

I cried out as he thundered over the threshold, letting in the cold. I headed for the kitchen door, but he clutched my shoulder with a huge paw and pulled me backward. I lost my footing and fell.

I closed my eyes to await my end. But the end was not to be so simple.

Eleven

Something low, massive, and roaring clawed me with its bruising talons as it scrambled over me. Disoriented, I fought to cover my head with my arms and cried out when the beast crouched atop me and pushed against my body with crushing power as it lunged upward. But my cry could not compare to the shrill scream that emerged from the red-bearded giant or the savage, vicious growl from his attacker. Both of them now trampled me as they engaged in shadowy battle.

I rolled onto my stomach and dragged myself clear of the fight using my elbows. Once clear, I propped myself up and looked behind me. The struggle had pushed the doorway open, letting in even more light.

Less than an arm's length away, the red giant lay supine, the backs of his boots pummeling the cold floor, his elbows bent and his hands gripping the neck of the Neapolitan mastiff who stood atop him, its jaws fastened firmly around his throat.

The mastiff pressed its head downward until its jowls and head thoroughly obliterated the face of its enemy. Red Beard let go a horrible, feral howl, cut short by a dull, sickening crunch. His legs went still and slowly rolled outward.

Leo lifted his face, his eyes bright and wild, his pale gray muzzle bloody, his teeth and tongue frothing with fine red bubbles. His stump wagged madly and his whole body trembled with a dark gladness, a primal satisfaction. In such a state, he turned his gaze on me, half-sitting as I was, my legs stretched out in front of me, my elbows propped behind.

For a dangerous instant, his eyes burned with that bright madness that showed no recognition; I held my breath, then eased it out slowly and whispered,

"Leo . . ."

The dog shook his entire body from head to tail, his flapping jowls spewing Red Beard's blood mixed with thick spittle. It struck my cheeks, my lips, and I hurriedly wiped it away.

He stepped toward me, his great square head a hand's span from mine, and grinned sheepishly.

"Oh, Leo," I said, my voice unsteady.

Leo licked my face gently, comfortingly; his breath smelled of iron. Despite the blood, I threw my arms around his neck and made a noise that sounded very much like weeping, but no tears came.

I wanted to drag the giant's corpse outside, but I was too squeamish and the body too heavy. I left it where it was and locked the door to the cloak room, then went inside, Leo padding beside me.

The note Ser Abramo had left still sat on the kitchen table. My memory of trivial things had been undone by horror; Abramo had instructed me to do something, but I couldn't remember what. As I unfolded the note, I felt a sharp pain just below the well of my collarbone at the realization that his hand had touched the paper only hours ago. Still, I kept from crying and stared at it again. One line popped out at me:

Keep Leo by your side; he can protect you better than any blade.

My face twisted at that. I petted the dog's head with a mixture of gratitude and revulsion.

Let no one enter the house, Abramo had written, *except Niccolo, and then only if you are certain that he is alone.*

Niccolo was a murderer, and traitor, and while Leo would be no defense against him, if he came anywhere near me, I would chop him into little pieces or die trying. And Niccolo and his gang knew where I was—so whatever Abramo wanted me to do, I had to do it quickly and leave.

If I do not return by midday, find the key to the lockbox I showed you. You will find further instructions there.

"The key to the lockbox," I said aloud to the dog. I had to get to Ser Abramo's message before Niccolo did.

In my state of shock, I could remember only that the Magician had told me about the key while we were down in the dungeon. I hurried down there with a lamp and moved to where I remembered him standing—near the bookshelves, by the entrance, just past the black velvet curtains.

I closed my eyes and pushed aside the painful sight of the dead Magician, and instead imagined him alive and standing there in front of me. He'd been holding a book in his hands; the pages had been cut out to hide a key—the key to the lockbox—inside the book. A slender book, leatherbound . . .

I ran my fingers over the books within my reach until I finally came across it: *Amarosa visione*, Visions of Love, by Boccaccio.

The key was inside. I remembered to move the scrolls on the bottom shelf and found the groove hidden in the wall behind them. I jiggled the key in the groove until it found the lock and the tiny hidden door popped open.

I pulled out the lockbox, set it on the worktable, and opened it.

The folded, yellowed pieces of paper that had been there before hadn't been moved, but a brand-new folded piece of paper—with my name written on it—had been placed atop them.

I picked it up and opened it; a key clattered out onto the table. I held the note to the lamp and read:

Dearest Giuliana,

If I have not returned by now, chances are I will never do so. Therefore, I must task you with a grave responsibility. This key opens a sliding panel on the wall of my bedchamber opposite the door. I need you to go inside the secret compartment there and take the wheel.

You are my daughter; it was indeed my hand that cast the silver talisman for you. I was told you had died, else I would have spent my life looking for you. Suffice it to say you are heir to all of my properties and belongings.

Assuming I am dead, you are now in dire danger. Leave all else behind, but take the wheel at once to Lorenzo de' Medici, taking extreme care that you are not followed. I ask that you take Leo with you, if at all possible, and see that he is well cared for.

I am sad that I am not here to help you in this perilous hour. But mark this: Death cannot separate us. I am indeed the Magician, and my reach extends beyond the grave.

Be well, and for your own safety, burn this note at once.

With deepest affection,
Abramo

My mind couldn't accept what I'd just read. I went numb. Words on paper, that's all they were, and all the horror of that day a dream from which I'd soon wake. Breathing ceased being a natural act and required my full attention. I watched myself move as if I were an outside observer. Watched as my body moved mechanically, without my conscious participation, as it picked up the key. Slipped it and the letter into my pocket. Replaced the lockbox. Climbed up out of the dungeon and, as an anxious Leo padded alongside, walked up the stairs to Ser Abramo's bedchamber.

I pulled back open heavy black curtains over a high solitary window to let in the morning light; it fell upon the busy wooden walls opposite the bed in great detail. They were golden brown with built-in cabinets covered by lattice doors and bas-relief panels of busy geometric designs set alongside them. In the corner farthest from the door, a prayer bench built into the wall had been unfolded; above it, a large bas-relief seraph lifted one hand in benediction, the other hand pointing downward as if to draw the viewer's eye to something holy—an absent Christ child, perhaps, that the artisan had failed to add for want of space.

The reminder of God provoked a spasm of bitterness in me. I spat on the angel. My spittle struck its waist and trickled down until a single shining bead dripped from its finger.

It landed like a fallen tear upon a thumb-sized repair in the wood—a tiny square set in so perfectly that its seams were barely visible.

And the angel's finger pointed directly at it.

I fingered the square, applying pressure in various corners until a little hatch popped open. Inside was the keyhole, and I hastily applied the key. I heard the successful click, but nothing happened until, in desperation, I pushed with all my strength against the angel.

The entire section of wall groaned and slid backward, like a door.

Inside was darkness. I took the lamp from Abramo's night table and lit it. The room was the size of a generous closet, just large enough to hold a table and stool with a map of Italy on the wall above them. Upon the table rested pages of text in the tiny, cramped script I knew as the Magician's. Atop them all was a cheap, thin talisman made of zinc and silver, with inferior engravings and no mark signifying its creator. It certainly wasn't the work of the Magician of Florence.

Moreover, the legends on it were a nonsensical hodgepodge of planetary, elemental, and zodiacal symbols, all mixed together so that I could discern no clear magical purpose. The numbers on the back were in a sequence that matched no known planet. Whoever created it had to have been completely ignorant in the subject of magic and the creation of talismans.

More intriguingly, a square slab of wood the size of a small platter rested beside the stack of papers; it looked rather like a clockface without hands, but far stranger. Three concentric rings had been carved into the wood around a central circle. I set the lamp down beside it and peered more closely.

Twenty-two symbols had been painted along the outer ring, symbols I knew well: those for the signs of the zodiac, the planets, and the four elements. The ring just inside it contained the twenty-two letters of the Tuscan alphabet.

I pressed my finger against the outer ring; as I'd suspected, it slid easily, as if well-oiled, so that any magical symbol could be made to correspond to any letter of the alphabet. The third interior ring contained abbreviations of the names of cities and towns: Rome, Florence, Milan, Viterbo, Pisa, and so on. The immovable center circle contained numbers in random order: 1124, 7, 20, 325, 60, on so on: the apparently random numbers that appeared on the back of magical talismans, associated with different planets. I slid the outer ring back to its original configuration.

A code generator. A sort of cipher wheel, using a magician's alphabet.

I thought of the secret alphabet I'd created as a child; I remembered how Ser Abramo had made me write it in the freezing mud.

How he'd accused me of being a spy.

Breathless, I put the cheap talisman in my palm. The writing on the front began with the Hebrew letter aleph and the number 0, neither of which appeared on the wheel. These were followed by the alchemical symbol for air, an upward-pointing triangle bisected by a horizontal line.

I looked down at the cipher wheel, wondering where to begin—and realized that the symbol for air had been aligned with the letter L.

Air. I stared at it as my memory stirred. Air, aleph, 0. They were all connected, all part of an attribution to a particular Tarot card, one of the few Ser Abramo had insisted I memorize.

Air, aleph, 0.

They were associated with the Tarot card Ser Abramo had used when I swore lifelong fealty to him.

Air, aleph, 0 equal the Fool. Air equals *L.*

The words I thought I had imagined, emanating from the wall of Abramo's bedchamber—intentionally for me, or not? *Lorenzo is the fool.*

The hairs on my forearms and the nape of my neck lifted; my fingers found the silver disk over my heart and closed around it. In my mind, Abramo spoke.

"*. . . there are things I must reveal to you—secrets that you must swear upon your life to keep. Secrets so dark, they call for blood.*"

His blood and mine, mingled upon the image of the Fool.

Upon Lorenzo. Here in front of me were the secrets the Magician would have revealed to me in time, had he lived.

Florence was at war. Despite the fact that our city was virtually surrounded by armies, Lorenzo had courted Milan, to no avail, and was now courting Venice, whose army was less impressive but no less desperately needed. But getting a professional courier with an encoded letter past the troops—*any* letter, no matter how innocent—was close to impossible.

But a poor, superstitious soul wearing the world's cheapest charm just might get through. All manner of folk wore talismans—travelers especially, for safety. No one would think twice.

Had Ser Abramo been a true magician? *The* Magician? Or had it all been deceit?

I thought of his manner when he was in the magical tent, of his voice when he was chanting before the altar. I remembered the way he spoke of God and magic. He had meant what he said with his whole heart; I trusted him as much as I trusted Tommaso, as much as I trusted Cecilia.

But magical talismans hadn't been his only stock in trade.

He had spoken of danger, of enemies who wanted to find and destroy him, and I'd foolishly thought he'd been referring to magical foes.

But it was Niccolo, his own protégé, the boy who had grown into a man in Abramo's house, who had betrayed him. Betrayed Lorenzo and all Florence to the Romans. Had killed his own mentor, because the latter was encoding messages for Lorenzo, for Florence, to send to Milan, to Rome, to Venice, to all the cities listed on the cipher wheel where he had agents.

I hadn't much time, but Abramo had known that I would be able to decipher the talisman quickly. I was born with the knack, and in a minute—using the cipher wheel with the symbol for air set to *L*, I managed to break the code.

> THE FOOL 30 NOV S TO GROSETTO, TO SHORE,
> TO GENOA, MARSEILLES.

Even being female and therefore intellectually impaired according to most, I found the message obvious.

Lorenzo was abandoning Florence, sailing via the northern port of Genoa to Marseilles, France. The rumors were true: he was saving his own neck and leaving the rest of us to the mercy of Rome and Naples' armies.

Get the wheel to Lorenzo, the Magician had said. I supposed I was to deliver the encoded talisman to Lorenzo as well, so that those responsible for helping him escape Italy could prepare his way.

Damned if I was going to help the coward. I couldn't stop him from leaving, but damned if I was going to give him his talisman or the wheel. But I couldn't leave them here. It was only a matter of time before Niccolo or his cohorts would come looking for me.

I had to get to Tommaso and Cecilia as fast as I could, and somehow, *somehow*, we would need to flee north past the armies and away from the fighting. But we couldn't leave without means to survive. The sense of purpose got me moving despite my shock and sorrow.

I'd sewn large pockets into my new dark blue mantello shortly after Ser Abramo had given it to me, when I was still planning on nicking his treasures; I am, after all, a thief at heart. In went the wheel, the papers; I didn't have time to destroy them now. I climbed down to the magical dungeon and took what small bars of gold I could carry.

Leo was waiting for me when I crawled back up. "You have to come with me," I told him. "You just have to." His soft gray brow was deeply furrowed, and his pale eyes somber, but he seemed to understand.

I added the pillaged gold to my pockets, which were getting very heavy. Leo shadowed me as I hurried into the sitting room. I meant to keep on going, but the goblets carved from gems glinted in the firelight, catching my eye.

They were priceless, but I had little room in my pockets. I made a quick calculation and went for the ruby one. Somewhere between my hand grasping the goblet and putting it in my pocket, my mind went blank. Suddenly all the goblets were lying in front of me on the hearthstone—glittering faceted ruby, sapphire, emerald, and amethyst, all deep and clear—and me standing over them all, the iron poker held high in my hand, ready to strike.

All the rage, all the hatred, all the grief I had ever swallowed rushed over me like ruthless floodwaters. I roared and brought the poker down with all my strength, smiting the crystalline colors, purple and green, dark blue and blood red lying against the hearthstone. Up again and down again, cursing God for giving me everything I'd thought I wanted and taking away the one thing I truly did. I could have wept with fury, but I would not give God the satisfaction, as if He'd been real, as if He'd been standing there in human form, mocking me.

To have been in the presence of my father all this time and to have lost him before I knew it . . .

"You bastard!" I screamed. "How dare you die? How dare you die without telling me who my mother was!"

Shrieking, I kept pounding against the gems until Leo slunk away to cringe in a corner, until sweat streamed down my flushed cheeks, but the act brought no relief, only frustration. I could only put a solitary crack in the grape-colored amethyst, the faintest nick in the emerald, and not a scratch on the ruby or the sapphire.

I lost all reason and sense of time until I glanced up to see Niccolo, his eyes murderous and wild, coming at me with a dagger.

"You bastard!" he snarled, echoing me. "You vile lying little thief!"

"Leo!" I shouted. "Get him!"

The mastiff whined and stayed fast in his corner.

Niccolo swiped at me with the dagger. He would have sliced me, too, but he'd taught me how to leap back gracefully from an oncoming attack. Luckily, the fireplace poker was near thrice as long as the dagger. I wielded it like a scythe cutting grain, and felt darkly gratified when it hit his hipbone with a solid thud. He staggered to one side and almost fell, but pressed his hand against a chaise longue and regained his balance.

"Murderer!" he hissed.

"Traitor!" I howled.

Leo started barking, a confused entreaty for the violence to end.

Niccolo advanced again, his dagger raised overhand. I turned the poker sideways, one hand at either end, and raised it to meet the sharp slender blade whistling toward my heart. The poker was thick, the blade not; its edge chipped when it struck the poker, with such force that the weapon went flying from Niccolo's grip.

He dove for it as I moved in; he rolled swiftly toward my feet and knocked me down. I scrambled for the poker on my belly, reaching for my weapon, when he pressed a foot firmly on my hand, and leaned down for the kill.

I glared at him. I wouldn't shrink from death or hell, wouldn't close my eyes. Defiant to the end.

Niccolo straightened and lowered his blade. He bent down and, lifting his foot off my hand, grasped my upper arm, and pulled.

I used all my weight to resist.

"Get up," he said. His tone was no longer murderous, but implacable and very, very dark. His black hair fell forward, dripping sweat; he unconsciously wiped it away.

"Kiss the devil's arse," I said.

He saw I meant business, but didn't let go of my arm. He pressed the tip of the chipped blade against my throat, and I shrugged. *Kill me.*

His eyes narrowed. He was mightily tempted to oblige.

"Bloody traitor!" I spat on him, goading him. "Murderer! Liar!"

His lips drew back and he showed me his teeth, but he said nothing. Instead, he yanked my arm and half pulled me to my feet. I was kicking, mindless of his blade.

"Leo!" I screamed, as if Niccolo was murdering me. "Leo, *help!*"

Leo sprang from his corner and, barking, threw his powerful bulk against both of us.

We both fell onto our backs. Niccolo rolled to his side and grabbed me. His fingers found my soft breast, and he drew his hands back as if he'd been stung; his face bloomed red and he gaped at me in shock for only an instant, but it was enough. I had the poker and was on my feet.

He snatched his dagger, but didn't wield it. Instead, he sat staring up at me, suddenly unwilling to fight.

"You're a girl," he said, marveling to himself.

"And you're an ass!" I snapped, abruptly afire at his touch despite all my sorrow, all my rage, and bent down to kiss him full on the lips. He pushed himself toward me, toward the embrace, and slipped his arm around my ribs, drawing me gently, urgently to him. I melted only an instant. With a start, I came to myself, pulled away, and struck him with the poker. It made contact with his skull, though not with as much strength as I'd intended because Leo had wormed his huge bulk between us.

Niccolo fell back, stunned. I should have kept hitting him until he fell unconscious, until I saw blood and brains, but I couldn't make myself. Even if I'd wanted to, Leo pushed me back and, like my victim, showed me his teeth. His body became still and taut; he let go the low, threatening growl that I'd prayed never to hear.

"Leo," I said softly, not daring to move a muscle. "You have to come with me, boy."

The mastiff sank onto his haunches beside Niccolo's still form, his amber eyes gone feral, his stark gaze focused intently on mine.

"Leo," I said. There were tears in my voice, but I wouldn't shed them. "I can't leave you here with him. Please, come." I reach gently toward him.

Leo snarled, the twitching muzzle beneath his nose lifting fully to expose his upper teeth.

I put my face in my hands, stricken. Ser Abramo wanted me to take care of the dog, but I couldn't even do that. Defeated, I walked out of the sitting room toward the kitchen and then outside. I left the goblets where they were; I didn't ever want to see them again.

I wasn't sure where I was ultimately headed, not sure what to do with the cipher wheel and talisman. I staggered over the Magician's threshold and out into the blinding day.

Twelve

I ran off the estate, the cipher wheel and heavy gold bars in my deep pockets banging against my thighs and knees, the keys jangling wildly against my chest. Pain and outrage propelled me; if the weight slowed me down, I did not notice. The two hidden gates to Ser Abramo's house were unlocked, and I paused at each one just long enough to lock them behind me. I pushed the wagon next to the outer gate, hoping to prevent my guilty victim from escaping.

I cursed the whole way, furious at Niccolo's betrayal of his mentor, furious at Ser Abramo for taking my place and dying, furious at him for being my father. Most of all, I was furious because I hadn't killed Niccolo. I was determined to remedy that as soon as possible, when Leo was out of the picture.

At the same time, I felt I finally understood why God had abandoned me, why He had singled me out to become a miserable thief and murderer.

Someone had to kill Niccolo, to avenge Abramo's death. And it might as well be someone who was already bound for hell. At least I could go there knowing that my eternal suffering would now be for a noble cause.

For now, though, I'd managed to inflict a wound that gave me a good head start over Niccolo. My job was to live long enough to seek revenge.

As I careened, gasping, twisting my ankle once, twice on the uneven hole-pocked ground in the forest, my reason returned. I began to realize I was doing more than just running away from Niccolo until I could figure out how to lure Leo away from him. I was running toward the city—toward Tommaso and Cecilia. If I were killed or captured, they would have no one to provide for them. Cecilia would have to work the streets again, and Tommaso . . . he'd never last long, playing the Game alone.

And they'd be alone in a city abandoned by its first citizen and de facto ruler, Lorenzo de' Medici, to the mercy of Roman and Neapolitan invaders. Florence didn't stand a chance.

I was so obsessed by all that I needed to accomplish in the next few hours that my feet hit paved ground before I knew it. I pulled up my mantello to hide my face and slowed to a trot in order to blend in with others milling in the street. The busy Oltrarno looked disquietingly normal: everyone was going about their business, as if nothing terrible had happened. People were laughing, drivers cursing at horses and donkeys, street merchants were singing of their wares. Even as I made my way to the archway over the entrance to the Old Bridge and arrived at the place where Ser Abramo had died, there were no guards standing watch, no blood staining the street, nothing to mark the solemnity of what had transpired here. Pedestrians and animals casually trampled over the very spot, desecrating it in their ignorance.

I couldn't bear to stay. I sidled quickly through the crowd, desperate to escape the pain of the fact that Ser Abramo had died and none of it mattered. Soon I was pulled along with the tide of people crossing the Old Bridge.

I don't remember moving down the broad Via de' Calzaiuoli, don't remember seeing the landmarks of the tower of the Palazzo della Signoria, or the great orange-brick cupola of the Duomo. I don't remember turning down the little side street or opening the door to the pottery shop, or moving past the potter and his wife to take the narrow creaking stairs to Cecilia's door.

I do remember the door opening, and Cecilia's fleeting smile, which turned immediately to a deeply worried frown. I remember Tommaso's face—so clean and pink beneath white-gold hair that had grown a bit longer during our time apart, his eyes so bright and blue. Without a sound, he threw himself against me, all anger forgotten, burying his face hard into my waist and wrapping his arms tightly around my upper thighs, so that I rocked, trying to keep my balance. I put my madly trembling hand upon his head—his hair was so clean and so soft—and the warmth and realness of his presence brought me back to myself.

Back to the pain, and I had to swallow mightily to hold back tears. It was weak and maudlin of me, but I felt a pang at the thought I might never see him, or Cecilia, again.

I looked up at Cecilia's pale face, at her golden eyebrows and lashes and her too-small nose on her beautiful face.

That face reflected such alarm that I wondered what my own looked like—but I was in such a state that I couldn't have feigned cheer or normalcy if I'd tried; the weight of all that had happened had made my features feel heavy, immobile.

She said nothing, simply took my hand gently and drew me inside, Tommaso still clinging to me so that walking was awkward, and closed the door behind us. And then she waited.

For the longest moment, I couldn't make a sound, could only stand with my hand still resting on Tommaso's crown. I knew that once I opened my mouth, everything would be different from that moment on; the wheel of fate would turn, and there would be nothing I could do to hold it back.

But I couldn't stand there forever pretending things hadn't inexorably changed.

"You have to pack," I said. "Everything. We have to leave Florence. Today. Now."

Tommaso released his grip on me. Normally, he would have started whining and arguing and finally crying at this point, but this time, he took a step back and stared up at my face, his eyes owlish, his pink cherub's lips parted in surprise.

"Why?" he piped.

I didn't answer.

Cecilia said nothing. She half turned to look back at baby Ginevra, so heavily asleep on the bed beside us that she hadn't stirred at our entrance. And then Cecilia turned back and gazed solemnly at me.

"I have more than enough money for us," I said. "We could head north, find a little town, buy a house and property. Away from the war. Away from the fighting." Even as I said it, I realized what shock had caused me to forget: Cecilia would be suspect the minute she tried to buy anything with a pure gold bar, which would immediately make her prey to robbers. I'd forgotten to exchange the bars for coins—something I needed to do fast.

"You pack now," I repeated. "I have some errands to run, and then I'll be back. Right back."

But I knew, once I had given them the coins, we'd have to part; I couldn't go with them. I had things to do, things that would put them in danger if they were seen with me.

"Why do we have to go?" Tommaso asked again. He didn't whine; he didn't try to play on my sympathy, but his little voice was pitiful all the same, and honest, unshed tears shone in his eyes.

"Because Florence isn't safe for us anymore."

"Stay here, Tommaso," Cecilia told him gently. She glanced at me, then nodded at the door, her expression troubled but set.

We stepped outside, and she closed the door over the two children.

And then Cecilia folded her arms over her chest; I knew the gesture. I've never seen her angry, but I have seen her grow stubborn, so amazingly so that my thick-skulled determination couldn't match hers.

"What's in your pockets?" she asked, with a vehemence I'd never heard coming from her lips. Her tone left me unable to do anything except comply.

It wasn't the question I'd expected at all, but I reached deep into one pocket and produced one of the bright gold bars. "It's not the only one."

She stared at it a long moment without reacting a whit. When she finally looked up at me, she whispered, "Giuli, tell me the truth. Did you kill someone to get this?"

I shook my head, even though Niccolo might well have died. "Not yet," I said. Because I wanted to do more than ensure Niccolo was indeed well and murdered; I wanted to find the men who'd been with him, dangerous spies or not, and kill them, too.

"You can't do it," she answered. "I beg you . . . Just come with us."

I knew what she thought; that I'd decided to risk my life by stealing from my kind mentor.

"They killed him," I said, my voice catching despite myself. I couldn't explain everything. I knew if I began to talk, I'd break down, and I didn't have time for that. "He was a good man. He . . . trusted someone, someone who killed him. The money is rightfully mine, Celia. He gave it to me."

She paled. "Is this person after you, too?"

I nodded even though I wasn't sure it was true . . . yet. But it was only a matter of time before someone discovered what I'd done.

"It's not just that. It's the war. The city's being abandoned to the enemy. You and Tommaso can't be here when that happens."

She unfolded her arms and put a hand upon my forearm. "Don't leave, Giuli. Please. Worry about the coins later, and come with us now."

"I . . . I have to do this . . . and one other thing. I'll be quick. I promise." I turned and walked away as quickly as I could, half running down the stairs so she, in her skirts, couldn't catch me.

As I left, she called my name, so plaintively that it echoed in my ears for days.

It was all I could do to keep from breaking into my fastest run, but it would have aroused suspicion; I held myself to a steady jog instead and headed south of the Duomo, then swung to the east, ignoring the grim toothy tower of the Bargello to my right. I ran down the busy Via Ghibellina to the bells of Santa Croce, the church supposedly founded by Saint Francis. One block north, and I was on the Via dell'Agnolo, peppered with all manner of shops, including the famed workshop of one of the finest painters, sculptors, goldsmiths, and all-around artisans of Florence.

Verrocchio wasn't his real name, of course, but people had called him that for so long that they'd forgotten what the real one was. As a boy, he'd been apprenticed to a goldsmith who had been dubbed *Verrocchio*—true eye—because of his incredible talent. The boy grew to be the equal of his teacher, even greater, according to some, and out of respect, he'd taken on his master's name as his own. Everyone in town used it, because there were few eyes as keen and perceptive as Andrea del Verrocchio's.

His bottega stood on a prominent corner; like so many Florentine buildings, it was an unimpressive rectangle of whitewashed stone. In warmer weather, its front portico was open to street so that all passersby, including pigs and chickens, were free to wander up and see what the students were working on that day—the best form of advertisement, aimed at common folk, because Verrocchio was not too proud to accept the humblest commission, be it adding a bit of gilt to a frame or decorating a teapot. But today, in recognition of the cold, the portico was draped in heavy awning, to which a few less expensive paintings had been fastened, a hint as to what lay inside.

I pushed through the open seam in the awning and walked through the chilly portico to the front door. The minute I opened it, warmth and the fragrance of oil and solvent and heated metal rushed out. Inside, the single large room, comprising the entire ground floor, was crammed to capacity. The walls were covered with the equipment of the artisan's trade: engraving tools, blank strips of unmounted canvas scented with bleach beside willow sticks, chisels, feathers, bundles of various types of animal fur. Near the large hearth stood a small kiln and a grindstone.

Besides the twenty-odd preoccupied bodies, the quarters contained as many worktables set side by side, each occupied by works in progress: gleaming pieces of partially engraved fine armor, half-gilded candelabra, unfinished headboards and china and a thousand other things. Painters worked on a dozen canvases— sometimes two or more lads worked on a painting at a time, conferring with their elders; so it was with the large sculptures set on turntables, where I saw no fewer than four lads chiseling away on a statue of an ancient goddess. Nearby, three young boys sat on the floor, large mortars between their knees, stone pestles in their hands as they furiously grinded away beneath a large shelf bearing labeled glass jars of semi-precious stones and various colors of earth.

The oldest student in the lot was in his twenties, the youngest around ten years old. Verrocchio, by far the eldest of them all, had survived his fourth decade, though he hadn't a single white hair. He stood with his arms crossed, one hand bracing his chin, squinting at the sculpture of the goddess and giving verbal direction to his students. He had to raise his voice above the singing of the chisels, the pounding of the pestles, and the din of conversation.

I headed toward him, the gold bars in my pockets suddenly unbearably heavy. I'd done business with Verrocchio on several occasions. He was stocky, but not fat, as his work required a great deal of muscle, but his face was broad and pudgy. Even at rest, his features were stern; his forehead was perpetually furrowed, his large dark eyes solemn beneath scant eyebrows, his nearly invisible lips turned downward at the corners above a small womanish chin. That day, his felt cap was pulled down tightly but couldn't repress his indefatigable curls, which bloomed around his face and neck like a soft black cloud.

Despite his rather intimidating expression, he wasn't cruel to his students, but he wasn't kind to them, either. Although he wasn't married, he was the sole support of his family, including a bevy of nieces and nephews. His desire to take proper care of them had led to him taking his work very, very seriously.

Yet when he caught sight of me heading toward him, his gaze softened, and the downturned corners of his mouth lifted a bit. He said a bit more to his student, then came over to meet me.

"Ser Andrea," I said mechanically; he always chuckled a bit at the fact that I would address a commoner like himself with such an honorific. But today he studied my stricken face and, rather than speak, jerked his head in the direction of the stairs that led up to the artists' living quarters.

We went up to the kitchen. It was empty, save for a pot of simmering minestra in the hearth. He gestured for me to sit at the wobbly, paint-stained table across from him and held me with those great serious eyes. I struggled to make my expression appear as normal as possible, but he wasn't fooled. Not someone with such a keen eye.

"What happened?" he asked quietly. "Do you need money?"

I had to bite my lip at his kindness. I shook my head and leaned down to pull one of the gold bars from my pocket. I set it on the table and pushed it toward him.

He let go a sharp, audible breath.

"I want to exchange it for coins. I can't go to a bank."

He raised thin, sparse eyebrows; his gaze remained on the gold bar. "No, I imagine you couldn't." He paused. "Where did you get this?"

"If I told you it was mine, would you believe me?"

"No," he answered honestly.

He stared at the gold bar for a long minute. I knew he wanted it for his workshop, but was weighing the risk. It was one thing to buy the few trinkets I brought him from time to time and melt them down; it was a far different thing buying such a huge amount of gold. Such a theft would undoubtedly be reported, and one of his students might remark to the wrong person about the master's sudden unexpected acquisition.

I jiggled my legs, trying not to tremble, but finally he rose and said, "I don't have enough money on me. I'll have to go to the bank"—he meant the Medici bank, of course, since the family was his major patron—"to get more."

I took a chance, perhaps a stupid one. "If I had two . . . would you be willing to buy them both?" If he answered enthusiastically, I would try to sell him the third.

Ser Andrea was calm by nature, but even he managed a slight double take at my question.

"One at a time," he said. "It's safest for both of us. Only one is a lot of money."

I nodded in reluctant agreement, but I was relieved that he

was willing to do the exchange, that he was willing to take precautions. Cecilia and Tommaso would simply have to find a way to exchange the others at a later time, but this would give them enough cash to get well situated elsewhere.

He went into a back room. When he came out, he was dressed in his winter cloak. He pocketed the gold.

"I'll ride instead of walk," he said, "but it still might take a while. Wait here. Help yourself to some soup if you like."

I couldn't eat, of course. I was upset to the point that the smell of the minestra nauseated me, and the fact that I was finally alone and sitting with time to think made me fold my arms atop the table and set my head down on them.

Had I been thinking clearly, I would have thrown the cipher wheel and the talisman bearing a message from Lorenzo into the Arno before I set foot on the Old Bridge. By the Medici's calculations, that would have branded me a traitor—all the more reason for me to flee the city—but I had no intention of physically harming Lorenzo, especially since I couldn't have if I'd tried, given his bodyguards. But I wouldn't help a traitor. I'd get to Cecilia and Tommaso with the money, then immediately head for the nearest riverbank and throw the wheel in the drink.

Then it was a matter of getting Leo safely away. And of course, killing Niccolo, if he wasn't dead already.

No matter what, killing Niccolo. Even if it meant dying myself.

The plan raced through my mind a hundred times; a hundred times, I told myself that Verrocchio wasn't late, that it was only my imagination, that he surely wouldn't turn me in, but would return soon, very soon, with the coins.

The nearby bells of Santa Croce marked the half hour. I hadn't been given permission, but I went from the kitchen to one of the bedchambers—the floor covered by a jumble of cheap mattresses and students' dirty, paint-stained clothing—and looked out the west-facing window down the street. Just the usual: pedestrians, carts, street vendors, chickens and whores and priests. I listened carefully for signs of anyone coming up the stairs, but except for the normal din, all was quiet.

I began to pace; I began to sweat. I grew anxious enough to vomit, but refused to give in to the cowardly urge.

The brightness of midday eased. I judged an hour had passed, and then a few minutes more. Ser Andrea had ridden a horse. He should have returned half an hour earlier.

Something had gone wrong.

On impulse, I ran down the stairs, past the mildly curious artisans, and out onto the street.

They were coming from the east, less than a block away: gendarmes in cowled, belted black cloaks with the hilts on the outside, the better to grasp their long swords, the militia and police's weapon of choice.

I ran as though the devil himself breathed down my neck—gold bars and wooden wheel striking my legs, bruising my flesh mercilessly while I prayed that the men's appearance was simple coincidence.

Until one of them shouted, "There he is!"

I should have known. The Medici had always been Verrocchio's bread and butter, and he would have reported anything unusual to them, to avoid being suspected himself.

I cursed his name, cursed his mother and father and all his nephews and nieces, because his betrayal hadn't hurt only me. Tommaso and Cecilia would now suffer, if I couldn't get the money to them.

I've always been fast, almost as fast as Tommaso, even though my legs were always shorter than my pursuer's. But the Magician's gold and cipher wheel weighed me down far more than I'd realized. The city became a blur as I raced south toward the Arno River, down piss-scented, garbage-filled alleys, past the simple façade of the Franciscan cathedral. When I glanced over my shoulder, I saw that the faceless, hooded men were gaining on me, scrambling down the alleyways with ease.

Soon they were half a block away, then a stone's throw. I pushed myself impossibly faster, till I felt I couldn't breathe, till I was dizzy and gasping, but still they came closer. At last the cobblestone gave way to spongy, uninhabited marshland on the riverbank, and I propelled myself to the stone barrier that kept the Arno's floodwaters at bay.

I dared not look back again. I knew, in that terrible instant, that my enemies were at my heels, almost an arm's length away. Bitter, I yanked both talismans from my neck—the silver one I'd had since childhood and the cheap one hidden in the secret room—not even feeling the pain as the leather thongs broke. I gave them an overhand swing and hurled them past the barricade and into the river; neither could help me anymore. Cecilia and Tommaso would never get the money to make a better life; I could never be certain that Ser Abramo had been avenged. The whole of my life had been meaningless. There was only one last useful act I could perform: to leap into the freezing waters taking the cipher wheel with me, and let Abramo's gold pull me down.

I scrambled atop the barrier and, out of instinct, spread my arms to keep my precarious balance. I contemplated the deep for less than a breath; I emptied my lungs and pushed off . . .

Just as my boot heels left the platform, a stone hard arm clamped around my waist, squeezing the air out of me so hard I saw a bolt of blue pain as my rib cracked. I was swept off the barrier, pulled back, and cradled in those stony arms like a child. I was paralyzed, unable to draw a breath. Helpless, I stared up at the face of my captor, whose cowl had been pushed back by the wind and the chase.

"Hello," Niccolo said.

Thirteen

He dropped me immediately onto the damp soft ground, and fell, retching, onto his knees. I pushed myself up to sitting and was immediately yanked to my unsteady feet by two of the gendarmes; the third rested his hand on his hilt and glared menacingly at me. I spat at him. They were all Roman spies in costume, I knew, come to steal the key to breaking the Medici code.

"Damn," Niccolo gasped, as he pushed himself to his feet; a gratifyingly bright cherry bruise above his right eye. He nearly lost his balance, and the third spy seized his arm and gently helped him up.

I wanted to scream curses at him, at the armed men, at God, but what came out of my mouth first startled us all.

"Leo," I blurted. "What have you done with Leo?"

Pale and swaying, Niccolo blinked. He spoke in a calm, puzzled tone, as if we hadn't just been trying to kill each other. "He's fine," he said. "The dog's fine. Someone will go fetch him and take care of him."

It was what I wanted to hear, even though I knew it couldn't be true.

Niccolo kept looking at me strangely—reinterpreting everything I did, I assumed, now that he knew I was female—but he said not a word about it to his cohorts.

As we turned and started walking back toward the city, I wanted to kick my captors. I wanted to shout curses and scream for help, but no one would believe a lad, however finely dressed, who was being dragged to prison by gendarmes. I should have fought, so I'd be killed right away and wouldn't have to suffer, but everything I had gained and lost over the past several hours struck like an avalanche crushing my body, my heart. I froze. My legs went out from under me; I stopped fighting God and fate altogether. Like Niccolo, who was still unsteady on his feet, I had to be dragged the entire way back to the city.

I was taken to the guardhouse at the intersection of the Borgo di San Iacopo and the Old Bridge—the very guardhouse in front of the street where Ser Abramo had died, and I began to realize that my captors were the very gendarmes that had rushed onto the street and carried the body away. Niccolo disappeared at that point, supposedly carted off by one of the guards to see a doctor. I was forced to stagger up narrow stone stairs to a small windowless room, hot and stuffy because of a large snapping fire in the hearth.

There was a stool near the hearth, where the two guards flanking me obliged me to sit. The only other object in the room, besides the poker and broom, was a small square table, occupied by a very thin, keen stiletto, a pair of sturdy pincers, a flagon full of red wine, and a ceramic cup. The guards relieved me of my heavy cloak and retreated. Under normal circumstances, I would have considered lunging from the stool to take up the stiletto or the poker, but I hadn't the heart. It wouldn't have mattered, anyway.

"And here we is again!" a familiar baritone growled cheerfully, accompanied by heavy tread. The man I'd come to think of as Stout—with his ample belly and heavy red cheeks that almost eclipsed his tiny eyes—stepped into the room and took his place between the table and me. "I hear you've been quite the busy lad today."

I didn't answer. I propped my head against my hand, confused. Stout worked for Lorenzo—at least, I had seen him with Lorenzo when both were testing my loyalties. But was Stout loyal? Niccolo was definitely not. Should I lie or tell the truth?

"You look to be a bundle of nerves. I just come to make some nice conversation; nothin' to worry about." He unstopped the flagon, poured some wine in the ceramic cup, and handed it to me.

I didn't care if it was poisoned; I hoped it was. I took the cup and threw the wine back in two gulps, and then grimaced. I'd become used to Ser Abramo's fine wine, and the taste of cheap sour swill made me shudder.

"Ooh, ain't we the fine one now," he teased, grinning, exposing that missing front tooth and making me inhale sharply at the thought of Tommaso, waiting for me. He gestured for the empty cup. I handed it to him and he filled it again.

"Here," he said, handing it back to me. "Drink up. And while you're drinking, answer me one question. Why'd you run off with things as din' belong to you? Some says as you're only a thief. Some says as you're a traitor."

I swallowed more wine before answering, "I'm a thief. But I'm no traitor. Maybe I took things because they belonged to me. Maybe I took things to keep them from getting into the wrong hands."

He tilted his head. "Some says as you were just using the old man. That you were learning things just to sell 'em off to the highest bidder."

"Bastard!" I snapped, but I was too weak to say it with the vehemence I felt. "Don't you dare call him the 'old man'! You speak of him with respect! His name is Ser Abramo!"

He widened his eyes and raised his hands in mocking apology. "No need to get huffy with me, miladdo! I'll call 'im whatever you like!"

Mollified, I drained my cup again. As grief-stricken and anxious as I was, I expected the wine to have little effect. But the muscles in my back and legs abruptly unwound, and I found myself slouching on the stool. I had been running in a panic for so very long and was so very tired . . . I suddenly wanted to get very, very drunk, past feeling anything. Past caring that I was about to die.

"It's a lie," I said, as I passed my cup back to Stout, who promptly refilled it and set it in my hand. "A lie. I . . ."

My voice trailed off; I turned my face toward the fire.

"Was it?" Stout asked curiously. He took one of the items from the table and stirred the fire with it. "Was it really a lie? You told me once you was loyal to Florence. To the Medici. But what if you knew the Medici was comin' t' see us that day?"

"How could I ever know that?" I said, to myself more than to Stout. I watched the fire flicker as he stirred the logs; there were small sparks of blue and green in the orange-red flames. He held the poker in them until its tip began to glow a dull red.

"Maybe Niccolo knew," he said, staring down at the poker. "Maybe Niccolo knew, and he told you."

"Niccolo is a spy for Rome," I slurred, aware that I was doing so, and pleased that the wine was having an effect. I drained my cup again and felt the warmth from the hearth permeate my bones and muscles, which seemed to be melting, relaxing into a warm pool. My breathing slowed.

"An' you're not?" he asked. He lifted the glowing poker—no, not poker, *pincers*, out of the fire and pointed them at me.

I stared at them. Somewhere deep beneath a curtain of warmth and calm, I felt fear.

"You drugged me," I said sleepily. "And that's fine by me. You can use the pincers or not, but I'll tell you the truth either way."

"Do you work for Rome?" he asked, his grammar dramatically improved.

"No," I said. "I serve Ser Abramo."

He grabbed my arm with his left and caught what little flesh on my upper arm he could with the pincers. The pain was visceral, animal; drugged or not, I couldn't have stifled my screams if I'd wanted to. The room filled with the smell of scorched flesh and wool. The cup in my hand fell to the floor and cracked. Stout ignored it.

"Ser Abramo's dead," he said harshly as I moaned, rocking on the stool at the pain. "He don't count. Where's your loyalty *now*?"

"Ser Abramo," I said, still rocking, still in horrible pain, and wishing I could fall off the stool to the ground and sleep. I closed my eyes; my head began to nod. "Everyone betrayed him. Everyone except me—"

"And the Medici? Lorenzo?"

His voice seemed distant, as if I were hearing it in a dream.

"I have a bone to pick with him," I said, and promptly fell asleep.

The earth was rumbling and rattling beneath me. I was vibrating all over as I opened my eyes to a small enclosure with a ceiling of wooden ribs, as though I were inside the belly of a whale made of oak, not bone. A dark red tarp had been fastened atop the ribs like skin covering flesh. Wheels rumbled over cobblestone, accompanied by the clop of hooves. I sat propped up on a bench covered by cushioned velvet, my spine pressed against the back, my head tilted upward, my mouth agape, my lap and knees covered by a magnificent fur blanket. Even so, I was shivering. They'd taken my cloak, and there was only a wool tunic between me and the cold.

And then there was the throbbing ache in my upper arm, the dreadful burn from Stout's pincers. I looked down at it. Interestingly enough, someone had bandaged it beneath my scorched sleeve. There'd been a fair amount of poppy in Stout's wine, no doubt, or the pain would have been much worse.

I closed my mouth and lowered my head to look about.

"I hear you have a bone to pick with me," someone said.

I turned my head toward the man sitting next to me—sharing the same blanket, in fact, the two of us so close together, facing the same way in a two-seater carriage, that our hips were less than two fingers' breadth apart. I could have easily throttled him, but he was strong and would have been the winner.

There he was, first citizen of Florence, his great twisted nose barely noticeable given the intensity in his dark eyes and the grim set of his lips. He had not yet reached middle age, but any sign of youth in his face, in his expression, had died when his younger brother had been murdered six months ago. The gravity of his presence—like that of a king, a pope, a god—the horrific weight upon his shoulders, the burning determination to get revenge on those who had killed his beloved Giuliano—all of that had left him a physically young man with ancient, ravaged eyes. The day I had seen him with his mother, Donna Lucrezia, had found him irritable and distracted. He hadn't wanted to be bothered with me.

But now, I was his sole focus, and the barely contained rage and contempt behind those powerful, fearless eyes terrified me into breathlessness, made me shrink. But only for a moment—until the image of Ser Abramo bleeding in the street reminded me that Lorenzo was not the only one who had lost someone to murder, not the only one consumed by the desire for revenge. I straightened and ran a cold hand across my forehead wiping all fears away and staring back with the same cold contempt.

"You say you have a bone to pick with me," Lorenzo repeated.

"Yes," I said, but before I could say more, he interrupted, his tone icier than my hand, and dark.

"You say you have a bone to pick, yet my best man is dead because you manipulated him into taking *your* place in a dangerous situation. Worse, you stole his gold—and with incredible brazenness, tried to exchange it with one of my most loyal protégés. Worst of all—Abramo trusted you enough to make you my agent, yet you betrayed him and me by flinging a sorely needed item into the Arno and stealing an incredibly invaluable item, an item that in the wrong hands could destroy years of careful work and put Florence in grave danger!"

I tried to interrupt, angry with him and furious with myself for feeling intimidated, but he raised his voice and lifted his gloved hand for silence.

"And these are not the least of your crimes—you murdered one of my agents and tried your best to kill a second one. So explain to me why we should not travel together to the Bargello this very instant, where I shall personally see you hanged from the highest window."

I stepped in the second he paused to take a breath and countered angrily, "I would never betray Ser Abramo! *Never!* I didn't force him to take my place—he wanted to. I tried to stop him. I tried to . . ." I trailed off at the sound of increasing anguish in my voice.

"Why would he feel moved to do that?" Lorenzo demanded. "He knew his life was more valuable to me than any item under discussion. He was irreplaceable." He lowered his voice. "He was my friend."

I looked into that regal, homely face, with its jutting chin and twisted nose. His eyes were a soft brown, but try as he might, he could not quite hide the hard calculation that lurked behind his feigned sadness. His words were designed to make me think he shared my grief, to soften me up so that I would tell the truth.

I wouldn't say, *Because he was my father.* Lorenzo already

knew that and was apparently testing me to see whether I knew it, too. I shrugged. "Search his estate. The reason is there, written in his own hand, the very reason I would never cause him harm."

His Magnificence paused at that.

Uncanny, Donna Lucrezia had whispered as she'd studied my face. And Lorenzo replied, in the most scathing of tones, *An instant of patriotism doesn't mean he can be trusted*. His point had been that even if I had been Ser Abramo's child, I was still a criminal fresh off the streets. They'd probably thought then, all of them, that I was a son Abramo hadn't known about.

Ser Lorenzo knew that I was Abramo's child the moment he looked into my eyes. Yet he had been willing to sacrifice me. Abramo hadn't.

"It doesn't explain why you killed one of my men," he said suddenly.

"How many times must I say I didn't kill Ser Abramo? The only man I *tried* to kill was his murderer."

"The evidence says"—he began, then abruptly caught himself, in a way that made me think he'd just realized he'd said too much. "The evidence says you're a murderer. There was a body on the estate—a very mangled, bloody body."

"Why are you doing this?" I blurted. "Why are you even bothering to question a cur like me? Why not simply hang me, if you really believe I'm guilty of all these crimes?"

"You killed a man. A man who pursued you onto the estate."

"I didn't kill the man. I wish I had—he was a damned Roman spy, the one who finished the job Niccolo started. He made sure Ser Abramo was dead."

"Then pray tell who killed him."

"Leo."

"Who?"

"The mastiff. The dog. He was trying to protect me. You only need look at the body. Why are you asking me? These are things your people can report to you. And, as for trying to kill Niccolo—Niccolo deserves killing, and I'm sorry I wasn't able to finish the job. He's your spy, not me. He's with the Romans, he's only pretending to work for you. I saw him with a gang of men with Roman accents. He stabbed Ser Abramo. He hurt him and was going to run off, but one of the spies with him came back and . . ."

My voice broke. Ser Lorenzo was motionless, listening. I recovered myself and added, "Made sure that he was dead. If you're looking for murderers—look to Niccolo. Ask *him* questions."

"What makes you think they were spies?" Lorenzo leaned forward, putting his face so close to mine I could feel his breath, warm against my icy cheeks.

"The . . . the cipher wheel. The talisman. I decoded it . . ." My outrage flared in earnest. "It said that you were leaving for France!"

"Indeed?" His tone was flat. "So you are every bit as clever as they say, then."

I couldn't keep my own tone from rising. "Clever enough to know that Ser Abramo worked for you and that you failed to protect him! Clever enough to know that you're going to abandon your native city, flee to France, and leave us all at the mercy of the Romans. Coward!"

He eased back against his seat; his brows lifted high, and an odd light came into his eyes. I braced myself for another burst of rage, but instead, he laughed softly. It wasn't a happy sound.

"And this," he said finally, "is why you decided it would be best to throw the talisman and wheel into the river."

"Why I was willing to jump into the river with it," I corrected him harshly. My arm began to hurt and I scratched it unconsciously and winced at the resulting agony. "The gold would have pulled me down. No one could get to it. Not you, not the Romans."

"You jumped to the conclusion I was a traitor." His voice was calm, but his lips grew tauter; his eyes grew hard and unreadable. "Because the talisman said I was going to France. You assumed I would not return."

"There's no help for us in France. The king supports the pope. What else would you be doing?"

He turned his head away to stare straight ahead, at the curtain of wool that separated us from the driver and the gazes of passersby. "You need to trust me," he said, as the carriage encountered a pothole and we were jostled together. "I would never desert Florence."

"Why do I need to trust you? Just kill me and be done with it."

"No," he said. "I need you now. My cryptographer has been murdered. The wheel, however, has been recovered and is safe. No enemy knows of our method of communication."

"I doubt that, seeing as how Niccolo came to the estate every day," I countered. "And I won't work for you."

"You will," he said as he turned toward me again, his expression frighteningly intense. "Because in return for your services, I will keep . . . oh, what are their names? Your friends."

Aghast, I stared at him. I dared not speak.

"Tommaso, yes? The little boy. And the baby girl, Ginevra. And your friend—don't tell me. Cecilia, yes, a lovely and admirably loyal young woman. In return, I will keep Tommaso and Ginevra and Cecilia safe from harm." Solemnly, steadily, he held my gaze. "They're all quite worried about you. God knows what would happen to them if they fell into the wrong hands."

I would have been happier if they'd taken me to a proper prison, with darkness and rats and iron bars, so that my surroundings matched my insides, an appropriate place for a thief to die.

Instead, an hour after the carriage ride, I found myself inside the bedchamber I'd slept in the previous night—a thousand years ago, a lifetime ago, in a different era. There was the hearth, still carefully tended by an invisible charwoman, and the large, soft luxurious bed with its feather mattress and fur coverlets.

I'd known where I was by the smells even before they removed my hood and bolted me inside the chamber: Leo's earthy animal scent, Ser Abramo's faint haunting trail of rosemary. I would have struggled, fought, and tried to make them kill me because I could not bear to be there, of all places on earth.

When they pushed me into my old bedchamber and bolted the door from the outside, I couldn't bring myself to lie in the cloud-soft bed, couldn't bear to sit upon it; instead, I settled cross-legged on the floor in front of the fireplace. The poker had been removed—I suppose so that I couldn't kill myself, but it did occur to me that I could easily have destroyed the place by setting the bedding on fire.

But I couldn't do even that, for Tommaso and Cecilia's sakes, even though I had failed them and Ser Abramo abysmally, even though I wanted desperately to die and be done with suffering. Their lives depended on mine now in a new and terrible way.

There came the sound of the bolt sliding in the door, and a burly golden-haired man appeared alongside a tall, wiry Nubian lad who set a tray of food with a flagon of wine on my bed. The lad was no ordinary kitchen servant; he wore a baldric with the hilt of a fighting-sized dagger emerging from the sleeve, like his pale fellow, who was dressed in black. The latter was one of the men who had pursued me the day before—and, I decided, had also come rushing out of the guardhouse to whisk Ser Abramo's body away.

Still on the floor, I glanced up at them but did not rise, instead turning my hopeless gaze to the fire. I could smell the stew and the fresh-baked bread, but the thought of eating made my throat tighten with sadness; the food seemed an affront, a sign of disrespect to Ser Abramo. When it became clear I was going to leave it untouched on the bed, the golden guard drew his dagger.

"You must eat," he said.

I shook my head without looking at him. He wouldn't kill me, after all. His master needed me now that the Magician was gone.

The Nubian squatted beside me and said, in a voice like velvet, "At least drink the wine. It has poppy in it. You're in pain. And you must rest if you're to work."

I looked at him, into his heavy-lidded dark eyes and saw something surprisingly like sympathy in them. I nodded in revelation—yes, I was still in physical pain from the terrible burn, but it had paled in the presence of a different sort of suffering. It seemed wrong not to suffer, but the coward in me wanted nothing more than to blot out memory and truth.

Rather than drag me to the wine he brought it to me, squatting down again and handing me the glass with long, delicate fingers.

"Drink," he said firmly, but not unkindly, and I drank. It was fine wine, not the swill proffered by Stout. He waited for a moment to be sure I'd taken enough sips, then he rose.

"Finish it," he said, and he and his companion left and bolted the door from the outside.

I left the food untouched upon the bed and sat drinking in my glamorous prison, until at last I sank sideways onto the floor, numb and staring at the glittering flames.

Day turned to night and at some point the flames ebbed and in their place appeared the face of the Magician, uncloaked and looking very much as he had when I had last seen him alive, before he disappeared into his magical dungeon with my silver talisman.

I am the Magician, he said, *and I will never die nor forsake you. It was only a play, after all. It was all ever only a play.*

His voice still fresh in my ears, I awoke with a start and deep joy at the knowledge that Ser Abramo was alive—a joy that turned quickly to despair at the realization that I'd been dreaming.

The sound of the bolt being slid had wakened me and the golden-haired guard, his beard glinting as it caught the light from the fading embers, took hold of my arm and lifted me to my feet. He urged me to attend to my toilet—I found the chamber pot under the bed, used it, and washed my face with the ewer and bowl provided while he stood with his back to me, confirming that mine was a prison for fine ladies and gentlemen. Ragged and exhausted as I was, I neither spoke nor resisted as he, equally silent, led me by my arm, adjusting his grip only when I yelped when he inadvertently touched the small burn left by Stout's pincers.

He took me to the open hatch leading down to the magical dungeon and indicated that I should crawl down ahead of him. The memory of the weapons propped against the wall near the magical tent returned to me. If I were fast enough, I could be waiting for him with a scimitar. But my hopes were dashed when I discovered that the Nubian, an oil lamp in one hand and a drawn short sword in the other, waited at the bottom for me.

The curtains were pulled back and the arched doorway opened. The lad gestured for me to walk ahead of him. My destination was clear: Past the narrow apothecary's cabinet, past the shelves of books and scrolls, and the furnace built into the ground, a lamp burned on the worktable next to an ink well and quill and a stack of blank paper. The wooden cipher wheel had been set upon it, alongside a letter.

The silent Nubian sat in an armchair off to one side, watching solemnly as I sat on the stool—too low for me, so that the edge of the table hit just under my breasts—and read the message. It was written in a careful, definitely feminine hand.

Four talismans of appropriate but inexpensive metal, made in the following order:

One shall hold the new key.

One shall say: 4 Dec sunset, arriving Livorno 16 Dec dawn, (signed) the Fool.

One shall say: 9 Dec dawn, arriving Ancona 19 Dec sunset, (signed) the Fool.

One shall say: 30 Nov sunset, arriving Grosetto 4 Dec midday.

All with the insignia. All appropriately magically charged to ensure the message and its wearer arrive without mishap at their destination.

Three days, without fail.

Livorno, Ancona, Grosetto. These were all small towns, hardly refuges, as it would be hard for a man like Lorenzo to go unrecognized for very long, and all close enough to the fighting that they were poor choices for an indefinite stay. Nor were they good choices for someone trying to escape by land; anyone headed south or north would eventually run into a Roman or Neapolitan army.

But they were all on the coast—good places to meet a ship and sail off to a safer destination.

France, I thought at first, and then stopped myself. Lorenzo was highly devious, if nothing else. Had the talisman that Ser Abramo left behind included Lorenzo's *real* destination? Or had it been left there to confound me, in case I was a Roman spy?

Very clever, all of it. And even if the Romans learned that the talismans held code, and managed to decipher them all, no one except Lorenzo and his inner circle knew his ultimate destination, or even the person he was communicating with.

Of course, Lorenzo couldn't be in all these different places at once. Only one message was true, which meant that even if I, the cryptographer, were captured and interrogated, I could give only contradictory information.

But *three days* . . .

I scowled up at my captor, who was watching me with a benignly curious expression, his long fine hands steepled beneath his chin, the lamp on the ground beside him, painting him half in light, half in shadow, sculpting his flawless skin, neither dark nor pale, but the light ash brown of a walnut's shell.

"It's impossible!" I said. "It says I'm to make four talismans in three days!"

"I know what it says," he responded agreeably. "I can read."

"But I'll need help! I can't do this alone in three days!"

"I'm not your assistant," he said, just as pleasantly. "I'm not a slave. I'm as Tuscan as you are, here of my own volition—while you are not. I suggest you do as you're instructed."

"They trust a guard enough to let him read this?"

His lips curved slightly upward; he lowered his hands. "They would if he was a Medici, raised in the same household as the one who wrote this. I have a great interest in making sure that you do exactly as you've been ordered to."

I looked down at the message again and swore softly. And then I thought of Tommaso and Cecilia and got right to work.

One shall hold a new key.

I studied the cipher wheel. The inner wheels had shifted a bit during the run, so that the *L* no longer lined up with the symbol for Air. I could easily have set it back, but obviously, the great Lorenzo and his mother were being cautious. So I thought a bit: Lorenzo was represented by aleph, 0, air, the Hebrew and alchemical symbols for The Fool. I did something extremely simple: I shifted the *L* on the cipher wheel until it lined up not with air, but with the symbol for aleph.

The talisman wasn't as complicated as it might have sounded. Obviously, the recipient was either using a similar wheel—at least, I hoped so, as deciphering the messages the old-fashioned way would be ridiculously complex. All they needed to know was which letter of the alphabet lined up with a particular magical symbol.

I turned behind me to the large shelf that held all the contents of the jeweler's trade and took up a slab of creamy honey-colored beeswax. It was cold in the cellar; so cold, I'd been shivering without realizing it, and the beeswax was so hard that any attempt to carve it would have cracked it.

I went at once to the furnace, realizing that it would take hours for it to reach a good temperature, stoked it with coal, sparked the flint, and got a fire going. I didn't have the luxury of waiting for the air to warm, so I held my achingly cold hands over the fire until they grew heated.

Then I turned my attention to the wax. Ser Abramo's writings—the ones I had studied so carefully—had been laid upon the desk, so I had all the references I needed. I scribbled out a design for the talisman. I would use copper for Venus, the ruling symbol for Taurus—in honor of Lorenzo's murdered brother Giuliano, who had died in late April. I painstakingly carved the back of the talisman first—the square of numbers that represented Venus. It would be a love charm, the better to help along any diplomacy, if that was its purpose, and it would look like a real love charm, with the symbol for Venus on the front. There were an infinite number of phrases that could be written around the edge of the coin, surrounding the central symbols, depending on the planet and the talisman's purpose. I chose one from Virgil, from my days secretly studying Latin: *Omnia vincit amor,* love conquers all. But at the end of the phrase, I added an extra *L,* followed by the Hebrew aleph. Even an apprentice magician would notice the odd addition, and even a slow cryptographer would pick up the hint.

It took hours just to finish the back of the talisman to my satisfaction—during which, food, water, and wine were lowered down to us in a basket. I scarcely touched either. By the time food was lowered down a second time, it must have been evening. I suspect it was midnight by the time I finished carving the front of the wax talisman. I was just about to sink the little steel dowels into its edges to prepare the mold when I realized an image was missing. There were no notes from Ser Abramo to guide me, but it was a symbol I could never forget.

See there? Sister Anna Maria had told me, her finger pointing to an inconspicuous letter *M* on the silver talisman my parents had given me. The third leg of the *M* had the letter *F* growing out of it, and the center point of the *M* gave birth to a circle. *That little sun and moon conjoined? See the tiny crescent moon embracing the sun—that circle with a dot in it . . ."*

The symbol of the Magician of Florence.

I drew in an uncertain breath. I hadn't the right to make such a symbol; it seemed disrespectful, somehow profane. But the talisman would not be complete without it. I had no choice. I used the fine engraving tool to carefully scoop out the tiny bit of wax whose absence would create the powerful symbol, biting my lip until it hurt to keep my mind from straying to memory.

And blinking down at the legend I had just carved, a sense of infinite weight and inexpressible awe settled over me at the realization of who I had just become.

I was now the Magician of Florence.

Fourteen

I sat and stared at what I had just created. No wonder I was still alive—Ser Abramo had trained me to be his replacement. I was his child, with the same exceptional skill for language, for symbols, for understanding and creating secret codes. Lorenzo would be hard-pressed to find another urchin quite like me.

I was motionless for so long that the half-blood Medici, whose heavy lids had grown even heavier, rose and stretched long thin arms as he let go an emphatic yawn and ran a hand over his cloud of black-brown hair. "It's very late now," he said. "You must sleep—you've grown tired."

I stared up at him and stood myself, to turn toward the shelves behind me and reached for four tiny steel dowels and the large jar of white powder. "You speak for yourself," I said. "Three more talismans in two days. I worked all day on one, and it's nowhere near finished. I won't be sleeping anytime soon."

I stuck the four dowels at equidistant intervals along the thin edge of the talisman, then took a flagon of water from the food tray. I went to the far corner of the long worktable, where I poured the powder out in a little mound and made a depression in it, the way I'd seen Ser Abramo do. It was sloppy work, but soon I had malleable plaster and covered the talisman thickly with it, taking care that every dowel was exposed. I set the damp ball of plaster on a shelf for drying. With luck, it would be ready by morning, and so would the furnace.

To be honest, I was grateful to be sorely pressed for time, and strangely grateful that Tommaso and Cecilia's lives depended on my success. Otherwise, being in Ser Abramo's house, looking at notes written in his hand, creating the items as he had taught me . . . It would have been unbearable if I hadn't been impossibly busy.

Ignoring the Nubian, who didn't press, I sat down again, took up ink and quill and the blank backside of my captor's message, ready to design the next talisman.

The remaining three were to be for protection. Saturn was the best choice, lead the best metal. I rifled through Ser Abramo's notes, found guidance, and began to scratch out the talisman's basic design.

By morning, the young Nubian was bleary-eyed and I was still busy. The plaster had hardened during the night on the first mold, and I had shoved it into the furnace and watched the wax melt away, leaving a suitable cast. Using Ser Abramo's clever levers, I melted the copper—watching the fire change color until it finally flared green, then deepened to a beautiful blue—and poured the molten metal into my plaster cast. The metal had cooled fairly quickly, and I had broken the mold to stare down at the fine copper talisman with bittersweet pride.

That pride was quickly tempered by trepidation. It was time to magically charge the charm while I waited for the second mold to dry. I went to the apothecary cabinet and found the tiny drawers with yellowed labels written in Abramo's predecessor's hand. Several drawers were marked with the symbol for Venus, but I chose only two of them: rose petals and benzoin, as I hadn't time to grind a special incense. With these in hand, I went toward the magical tent. The Nubian, despite his weariness, was quick to follow. It was painful, seeing the Magician's robe hanging on the earthen wall, and painful to put on the shorter one that I'd worn before. The Nubian left his lamp burning on the floor by his chair, while I took the one from the worktable.

Hands trembling, I pulled back the black velvet flap leading inside, and gestured for the Nubian to go in.

He balked and shook his head.

"What are you afraid of?" I asked, with no small amount of superiority.

"Magic," he said.

"You believe in it?" I was a bit skeptical. If he'd been truthful about being a Medici, he had been educated by the finest minds in Italy.

He nodded, suddenly seeming like a child.

"Really?" I said, my tone faintly snide. "Have you seen birds talk or objects drawn from thin air, because I haven't. Shall I produce snakes to bite you or a weapon so that I can escape?"

"Don't be silly," he said. "There's no such thing as that kind of magic. But the kind that changes people—that's the most powerful kind."

The Magician's words resonated so loudly in my head I was tempted to cover my ears. *The spell I worked . . . was for more than just your protection. Your heart's in a magical furnace now . . . there's no stopping it.*

I drew in a breath of pure resolve and stepped inside a room darker than night, while my cautious and willowy companion hovered on the threshold, velvet flap in hand, unwilling to take another step.

I put the rose and resin in the thurible and held the lamp to it until it began to smoke. Then I lit the candles at each quarter, in the proper sequence—clockwise, starting with the east—and finished at the altar, where I lit the white candle representing the element of fire. All was in its place: the candle representing the element of fire, the goblet representing water, the pentacle representing Earth. But the element of air was missing.

"The dagger," I said. "Someone moved the dagger."

"A good thing, too," my owl-eyed guard said, his tone hushed. "You'll have to do without."

I considered arguing, but realized it would simply waste time. I chanted the prayer Ser Abramo had taught me, then used my finger to draw the star of the east, almost as large as me, in front of the altar.

It worked just the same: dagger or no, I felt the strange shift within me, the same as I'd felt when Abramo had first cast the circle about us. The air seemed to shimmer faintly, to vibrate, just as if he'd been standing there beside me. Spy or not, he had truly been a magician—*the* Magician—and the power of his talisman had reunited us at last.

A sense of fate and reverence overtook me. I felt the power as I cast the circle, called upon the archangels' protection, and invoked Almighty God and the essence of Venus to bless the talisman so it would fulfill its purpose.

At last the ceremony was over, the circle closed. I was glad that the Nubian had remained outside, because when I took the charged talisman off the altar, I noticed a folded piece of paper off to one side, easy to miss in the flickering lamplight if one wasn't looking for it. Some magical note of Ser Abramo's, I assumed, and eagerly snatched it up while at the same time telling myself that it would do no good to read it, as it would only bring pain.

I unfolded it. It was indeed written in the Magician's hand, and I quickly read:

What happened was entirely my fault, due to my inability to control my heart. I was blind to the pain I was causing those who loved me most.

I was a young, unmarried man, and my heart belonged—and had, for years, to a married woman whose name I shall not mention here, out of respect for her reputation and privacy. Let us call her A, for want of a better name. A and I resisted our mutual attraction for years, although the fact that I worked for her father-in-law and later, her husband, put us in daily proximity. For years, A and I worked together without speaking of or acting upon the love we bore for each other, out of respect for her husband, who nonetheless openly had numerous affairs.

But the day finally came when—after years of chaste behavior— our resistance broke, and we fell into each other's arms. This continued some months until the lady put a stop to the affair.

There was a beautiful young woman named Flora in A's employ. I did not love Flora, but at A's insistence, I wed her. A and I both hoped that my new wife would capture my heart, so that A and I would never again be tempted to sin.

It failed to work, though sweet Flora loved me well enough. But I had long ago given my heart to A, and there it steadfastly remained.

The time came when both Flora and A became with child. Flora and I rejoiced at her news, but A was filled with trepidation. By that time, her husband was in poor health, so a pregnancy by him, while possible, was unlikely. A was convinced the child was mine, and her greatest fear was that the baby would resemble me more than her husband.

We waited anxious months. By chance, the babes were born a day apart. Sadly, Flora's child—a boy, my son—died before drawing his first breath. A gave birth to a strong, healthy daughter, but—as she told me later—the child opened her eyes almost immediately, revealing the truth of her heritage at once. For just like mine, her right eye was green and her left brown.

The innocent babe could not remain under the cuckolded husband's roof an instant, or the truth would be known and A's reputation permanently sullied. With the midwife's help, A told her husband the girl died—and because I was a selfish fool, I convinced Flora, without telling her who the real mother was, to take my infant daughter as her own, because I could not bear to let the child be raised by anyone other than myself or A. I made the baby a special talisman, one that would protect her and bring her good fortune in life.

My incredible selfishness led to death and despair. Poor Flora, despite being heartbroken over my infidelity, agreed to raise the girl out of the goodness of her heart. But over the next weeks, the loss of her own child and my faithlessness caused her to fall into such deep despair that one night, she crept from her bed and, taking the child with her, ran to the nearest bridge and flung herself into the Arno.

Or so witnesses told us—but now I see that even though she was clutching the child's blanket when she leapt, her innate kindness caused her to leave the babe in a place of safety.

For many years, I did not want to live, but my obligation to others was too great. My grief and guilt faded during days of work, but awaited me in full fury at the fall of night.

There is a love that can never be quelled—a love that transcends mortality. Therein is the highest magic, the magic I poured from my heart into that infant's talisman. And at last it has repaid me a thousandfold: Our child has returned to me, and I will let nothing take her from me again.

Not even death.

You do not see me, but I am here, Giuliana.

The hairs on my forearms, on the nape of my neck, rose. *I am indeed the Magician, and my reach extends beyond the grave.*

My mind reeled. Everything I had believed about my past, about my parents, had been untrue; all the anger I had felt toward them, unwarranted.

I had been wanted, and desperately so. My supposed death had brought others years of grief.

I sank to my knees in front of the altar. My heart swelled at the thought—and shrank again with the very next breath. God was crueler than I'd imagined. He'd hurt not just me, but had broken my mother and father's hearts. He'd given me my father back only to cruelly murder him before I could even acknowledge him. To think that Ser Abramo and I had lived together in the same city our entire lives, each unaware of the other . . .

And I had a mother—but if she was still alive, how could I ever find her? Ser Abramo had taken her name with him to his grave. And even if I did manage to find her, would she, could she acknowledge me?

"Please," I whispered, beginning to rock myself out of grief. "Please, come back. Help me . . ."

"What are you mumbling? You're done, aren't you?" the Nubian asked. "Get up. What is that you're reading?"

"It—it was nothing."

I rose and folded the letter up, meaning to put it in the waist of my leggings; as I reached the tent opening, he took it, and after a cursory glance, decided it wasn't a secret message.

"Give it back," I said, and he did.

"That was sad about Ser Abramo," the Nubian said respectfully as we left the tent, and I pulled off the too-large magical robe and hung it back on its peg.

I felt raw. I spat on the ground. "You don't deserve to speak his name!"

He seemed confused. "Why not? He was much esteemed in our household."

"In the Medici household?" My voice broke, and all my rage tumbled out in a rush. "Is that why Lorenzo let him be killed? Is that why no one protected him? Lorenzo questioned me right after it happened—do you know what he felt? Irritation! Suspicion! If he felt any grief over the loss of a family member, he did a good job of hiding it!"

I moved forward so aggressively as I shouted that the Nubian drew back and his hand instinctively went to the hilt of his dagger.

"You're a liar," he said calmly. "And if you'd ever spoken with Lorenzo, you'd know just how preposterous that lie sounds."

"Preposterous?" I was angry, aghast. We certainly couldn't be talking about the same man; out of grief, Lorenzo had executed not just the men responsible for his brother's death, he had executed many of their family members and had in essence destroyed the name and torn away all rightful privileges and properties of one of the oldest and most respected clans in Florence, the Pazzi. "Lorenzo is holding my friends—he'll kill them if I don't perform for him!"

The Nubian's great heavy-lidded eyes narrowed with suspicion; he shook his head, indicating that he wouldn't deign to respond to such an outrageous charge.

"Lorenzo is a disgrace!" I pressed. "He's going to abandon Florence—I suppose all you Medici are—and leave us common folk to be killed!"

"*What*," the Nubian countered, his own temper flaring, "would make you say such a thing?"

"The talisman," I said. "The one I . . . threw in the river. It said Lorenzo was going to go to France. The French are loyal to the pope; he wouldn't be going there to try to enlist help, only to escape . . ." I trailed off, realizing the very thing that the young guard would say next.

"You say a talisman told you this," he said wryly. "And yet . . ." He gestured at the worktable as we began to head toward it. "Here are three different messages. Has it occurred to you why?"

I lowered my gaze, silenced by my own stupidity. Because Lorenzo didn't trust me, for one thing, to be sure which course he was taking; for another, if the Romans ever did break the code, they wouldn't know, either.

"Because the less you know—and the less I know—the better for us, for everyone. Your temper makes you jump to some very silly, nasty conclusions," he said. "Lorenzo de' Medici would never abandon Florence. He's been seriously considering surrendering himself to the pope in order to stop the war. They'd draw and quarter him in St. Peter's square! They'd impale his head on the city gates and leave it there to rot!"

I lifted my chin at his vehemence. "That may be so, but he's still holding my friends and has threatened to kill them."

It was the Nubian's turn to spit on the floor. "It's a shame he's thinking of putting his neck on the line for an ingrate like you!" He lowered his voice. "He'll die before any of us will." He paused. "If he's holding your friends, then there's very good reason for it."

"It makes no sense," I said, "that he should need me of all people. The Magician was too important to risk—he should have broken in another apprentice years ago, in case anything happened to him. That he should have chosen me, and only after things had become so dangerous because of the war—"

"He did have another," The Nubian said, and retook his chair as I settled on the stool in front of a completed wax mold and stuck dowels in it. "He died of fever five years ago."

"Why not Niccolo, then? Ser Abramo raised him."

The Nubian tilted his head as he decided whether it was safe to reveal such information. "Niccolo can't read."

I frowned as I reached for the plaster powder. "Abramo never taught him?"

He shook his head. "It wasn't that. Abramo tried. But the letters always appeared jumbled to Niccolo. And he hadn't an artist's hand. He made a far better fighter . . ." He trailed off, unwilling to say more about Niccolo, but decided to add: "Abramo's talent is amazing." He blinked rapidly, trying to disperse sudden tears, to contain the sudden well of emotion. "*Was* amazing. His apprentice was skilled enough, but not enough to approach the quality of his master's work. Abramo had given up hope of finding a talent like himself to fill his shoes one day. And then, *you* . . ."

He said no more; he didn't have to. Perhaps he knew that I was Abramo's child; perhaps not. But he had real feelings for the Magician, at least, feelings that might sway him to my side if I was skillful. Feelings that might eventually convince him to release me to take revenge.

Instead, I said, "Niccolo kills his own mentor, the man who raised him. Yet here *I* am, a prisoner, only because I tried to avenge Ser Abramo."

He let go a short laugh of disbelief. "Niccolo? Now you *are* lying."

"Niccolo," I said, my tone heavy and venomous, "is a spy for Rome. And he killed Ser Abramo. I saw it with my own eyes. I saw . . ." I suddenly couldn't speak. I closed my eyes, and the image of Abramo bleeding to death in the cold street stole my breath.

When I opened them again, the Nubian's expression was cold and guarded. "Ser Abramo was murdered by brigands," he said flatly.

"That's what you were told," I said softly, struggling to regain control of myself. I wasn't going to let myself break down, especially not in front of someone who would think I was playacting. "Believe whatever you want. I was there. And if I survive—I will kill Niccolo with my own hands."

Something in what I said, or the way I said it, gave him pause; the tiniest glimmer of doubt passed over his features.

"I speak the truth," I pressed, my voice calm and low. "Ser Abramo must be avenged. You could help me do that."

He frosted immediately at that and narrowed his eyes at me. I had gone too far, of course.

"You fool," he said slowly, deliberately. "You total and utter fool. Your morals have been so twisted, you can't imagine anyone could be trying to help you. I'm not here as your jailor. I'm here to *protect* you."

He may have been right about my morals, but I was offended all the same—as was he, and so we gave up our efforts at conversation. We remained silent as I set to work on creating a plaster mold around the second talisman and said no good-byes as the golden-haired guard came to relieve him.

His replacement was a burly lad named Albrecht, in whose pink plump palm rested what looked to be a coin but was not. It was a brass talisman, clearly not from Ser Abramo's hand: the planetary symbol for Venus was crudely wrought, and the choice of metal was cheap, the more powerful and expensive copper compromised by the presence of zinc. The magician who made it (if indeed a magician at all) had left no identifying mark, but I recognized the out-of-place symbols and letters at once. Code.

"They told me to say that the mistress of the house wanted you to have this," Albrecht said, with a hint of a German accent.

"They want me to translate it for them?" I asked, frowning down at it.

Albrecht looked a bit bewildered by the question. "No. They only said that she wanted you to have it."

I should have eaten and drunk, and returned swiftly to my assignment, but the cheap charm and its hidden message were impossible to resist. I went at once to the cipher wheel, and slid the wheels within wheels so that the letter *L* corresponded with the element for air—the setting on the day I'd discovered it in Ser Abramo's secret chamber.

The numbers on the back of the talisman slowly began to spell out a message:

Via . . . our royal vessel . . . La Perla . . . to Resina. Date . . . point of rendezvous.

Date and point of rendezvous. A request for information, which I was at the moment encoding into other talismans.

4 Dec sunset, arriving Livorno 16 Dec dawn, (signed) the Fool.
9 Dec dawn, arriving Ancona 19 Dec sunset, (signed) the Fool.
30 Nov sunset, arriving Grosetto 4 Dec midday.

Grosetto was in Tuscany, inland and dangerously close to the fighting, a poor choice for a rendezvous. Ancona was on the eastern coast and made sense if Lorenzo had been going to meet with Venice. But Venice was a republic; any vessel they sent would never be referred to as royal. But Livorno . . . Livorno was on the west coast, as was Resina. And Resina was nestled on the shore immediately next to the city of Naples.

Naples, our sworn enemy, ruled by King Ferrante, whose mighty army had joined with Rome's, making the defeat of

Florence's pitiful handful of mercenaries inevitable. Crazy King Ferrante, who mummified his dead enemies so that he could visit them and lord his victories over them. But his rumored insanity was tempered by political shrewdness, which had caused him to throw his lot in with Rome in an uneasy alliance.

Via our royal vessel . . . Lorenzo was going to visit the king. Lorenzo was going to risk his neck to try to charm Ferrante into becoming our ally. With Naples on our side, Rome could not win. True, Lorenzo was a silver-tongued charmer, a diplomat of considerable skill—but all King Ferrante had to do was lop off Lorenzo's head the moment he arrived.

The pope had never wanted to rule Florence; all he'd ever wanted was vengeance on Lorenzo for killing off his brother's assassins (who happened to be the pope's bankers) and for imprisoning and scaring the piss out of his nephew (read: the pope's son). With Lorenzo dead, the war would instantly be over.

Which meant that whether Lorenzo lived or died, Florence would be saved by his taking the bold risk of going to Naples.

I looked down at the surface of the worktable without seeing it. Lorenzo was anything but a traitor—far from it. He was risking his neck by committing an act so audacious that even if our Roman enemies got wind of it, they'd never believe it.

"What's wrong?" Albrecht asked. He had taken the Nubian's chair and was leaning forward, his chubby hands on his thighs, oddly concerned. "Does it mean something?"

I realized my mouth was gaping open and closed it. "Nothing," I said lamely. "It's . . . nothing."

Donna Lucrezia had sent this to me, entrusted me to deduce the explosive secret that Lorenzo was going to meet with the King of Naples. Surely she had done so without Lorenzo's approval or even knowledge.

Obviously, she had wanted to unquestionably secure my

undying loyalty. Perhaps she had wanted me to be willing to risk my life in order to keep this information from the enemy.

If that had been her plan, she had succeeded a thousandfold. I launched into my work with new dedication and zeal. I now believed what the Nubian had told me about Lorenzo's character; I was being protected. Which meant that wherever they were, Tommaso and Cecilia and little Ginevra were safe.

By the time another food tray appeared (at midmorning the second day, I presumed), I was shaking with hunger; unfortunately, Albrecht devoured most of it. I had to fight for a bit of bread and tiny chunk of cheese. I took only small sips of wine, as it added to the tears prompted by exhaustion and unreleased grief—tears that forced me to grit my teeth, lest they spill. I had arrived at that uncertain state of mind that left me wondering if I was half dreaming, even though my eyes were open, my body awake. I couldn't have drunk more if I'd wanted it. Albrecht drained the flagon in short order and called up for another to be lowered. As a result, he was no stranger to the open privy at the farthest corner of the cellar. Modesty compelled him to turn his back to me, but each time, he would draw his sword with his free hand, and bellow, "I have eyes in the back of my head! Mind you behave yourself!"

By then, another talisman had been cast in the furnace and was cool enough for magical charging. A second was freshly plastered, and the front of the last beeswax mold had been partially carved. Too tired to announce my intention, I stood, the warm lead talisman of Saturn in my hand, and walked over to procure a small lump of frankincense from the apothecary. The resin would burn more evenly if ground into powder, but there was no time for perfection. Talisman and incense in one hand, the lamp in the other, I headed for the magical tent.

Albrecht, his already-pink face flushed cherry from the wine, set down his goblet. "Here now!" he growled. "Where do you think you're going?"

"To work magic," I said over my shoulder, too busy trying to concentrate on the task at hand to worry about whether my captor might take alarm and skewer me.

He rose, drew his short sword, and followed me hurriedly. I opened the flap of the tent and proffered the corner of the velvet to him. Just as the Nubian had, he balked; unlike the Nubian, he held his hands chest level, palms out, and waved them at the fabric.

"I'll not touch that!" he exclaimed, his blue eyes wide. "It's accursed." Apparently no one had told him about the occult aspect of my task.

I was so tired I didn't understand at first. "You're not coming in?"

He shuddered at the thought. "The devil's in there. One look at him, and I'll die."

Unlike the Nubian, he was entirely uneducated and amusingly superstitious, probably the son of one of the poor German weavers who made the Florentine silk trade so lucrative for its Italian masters. Despite my despair, I gave a feeble laugh. Albrecht took no offense at my mirth. Indeed, he still looked terrified.

"Then keep the flap closed while I'm in there, because I'm going to be talking to him," I said cheerfully. "And no peeking, else I'll cast a spell on you."

He leaned forward, squinting at my face and started as if suddenly seeing me for the first time.

"Your eyes!" he blurted. "You have a witch's eyes!" He crossed himself and stepped back as I entered the tent and let the curtain fall behind me.

"I'll be right outside," he said, with forced bravado. "No funny business."

I went to the altar, set the frankincense in the thurible and ignited it; a camphorous churchly smell filled the air, as did a light film of smoke. I then lit the white altar candle, sad at the sight of Ser Abramo's final missive to me.

Despite my exhaustion, despite the weakness in my voice, the holy words vibrated so strongly in my chest that the circle I cast seemed the most powerful ever, the very air the most alive, as if the towering theoretical archangels surrounding me were not theoretical at all, but tangible if only I dared reach out with trembling fingers, as if the sewn thread-of-gold stars were real ones, and I stood not on earth, but in the starry heavens. Albrecht and my imprisonment disappeared, as did all terrible events in recent memory. There was only the power that emanated from within me and without, from every atom, from every pore.

And after the holiest powers had been invoked, I knew that the talisman was true, that no harm would come to him who wore it.

When I opened the circle and returned to the altar, a pang of pure emotion struck me as I thought of Abramo writing how he had poured his love into the talisman he'd made me as a babe. Moved, I closed my eyes and set my hand down upon the black silk where the message had lain.

And touched not soft cool silk, but paper.

I opened my eyes. The altar had been completely bare save for the chalice, pentacle, and lamp. The folded letter that lay beneath my palm *had not been there* when I had entered. In disbelief, I examined the area around and behind the altar, searching for an opening in the tent's velvet wall that Albrecht could have used to slip the letter in while I was distracted or a secret compartment that might have sprung open. I found nothing that could have explained the letter's sudden appearance.

Yet here it was. I lifted it with hands that shook so badly, it dropped upon the carpet in front of the altar. I sank down and sat, choking back curses at unsteady fingers that fumbled several times until they finally unfolded the paper, revealing the Magician's unmistakable script:

Trust Lorenzo with your life, and you and yours will encounter no danger. Keep silent regarding Niccolo.

I cannot say how long I sat staring at the paper, too stunned to feel, to think—to do anything but believe.

At some point, my weary mind grew skeptical: An extremely convincing forgery—this letter, and the one from the day before. Some shrewd plot by Lorenzo to win my trust, some cruel joke of the guards.

But my eye for words and alphabets was keen. The forger's talent would have to be as remarkable as Ser Abramo's, and such men are rare. And tired as I was, I had been alone in the tent and the letter had definitely not been on the altar when I arrived.

Against every instinct of mind and heart, I let myself believe, just long enough to whisper:

"Help me, then. Help me to escape. Help me to avenge your death."

I sat there for a time, shivering, though not from the cold. I refolded the message and slid it inside my undergarment, next to the bare skin at my waist.

When I pushed myself up to my feet, my fingers pressed against the carpeted floor along the very edge of the altar.

Everywhere I had stood inside the tent, I had experienced the sensation of carpet set over bare earth—the same earth that formed the floor of the rest of the cellar. But at that moment, my fingers found a fingernail thin depression in the ground, where earth gave way to something harder.

I stooped down and ran my fingertips along the bottom edge of the cube-shaped altar where it met the carpet. There was definitely a fine seam there, a depression in the rug. I pushed the altar back a thumb's breadth, sliding it quietly so that Albrecht would not hear.

I ran my palm over the exposed area. It felt not like earth, but hard wood. I grew bold, and pushed the altar farther back, and touched what felt very much like a leather handle.

No sound came from Albrecht outside, so I pushed the altar as far back as I could, and rolled back the carpet to expose a wooden hatch smaller but very similar to the one that led down to the cellar.

Mind reeling, I quickly covered the hatch with the carpet again, and slid the altar back over it as quietly as I could. After snuffing the incense and candles, I returned to find Albrecht waiting a respectful distance away. He accompanied me back over to the worktable, keeping sufficient space between us, as though afraid my very touch was dangerously devilish.

Perhaps it was, for him, as I had already begun to hatch a plan, one simple enough for my sleep-deprived brain to grasp.

Sitting at Ser Abramo's worktable—*my* worktable, now—I must have looked ghoulish, the flickering lamp illuminating my wan, weary face and casting faint, wavering panes of light upon the earthen walls, broken only by my sharp, larger-than-life shadow. The cellar was vast, and the light from our lamps too feeble to illuminate anything save the little circle wherein I worked and Albrecht sat, cup in hand. The magical tent and corners of the room had disappeared into blackness.

When my touch revealed that the second talisman of Saturn had cooled sufficiently, I turned from the shelf to smile crookedly at Albrecht. "Another one ready to be charged. Time to go to the tent."

I immediately moved to the apothecary. Albrecht did not know that I had left enough frankincense in the thurible to

charge the remaining talismans, and, giddy from extended wakefulness, I fumbled with the drawers until I found the one marked,
not with the word *poppy*, which would make it too tempting for
uninvited visitors and myself, but with a single *P*.

I took a pinch and pressed it against the back of the talisman;
the warmth allowed it to stick. Then it was simply a matter of
charging the talisman again while Albrecht waited nervously
outside the tent—and then a matter of waiting until he drank sufficient wine to force him to the privy again. As he waved his
sword, roaring warnings with his back to me, I slipped the poppy
into the half-finished flagon of wine and stirred it well with a
long engraving tool.

He was quick, but I was too, and forced myself to keep my
eyes focused on my work—that of administering the final touches
to the beeswax mold of the fourth and final talisman—as he returned to his chair and refilled his empty cup. As the furnace had
been well-stoked for more than a day, the worst of the chill had
eased in the work area, though it was still far too cold for me to
be sweating as I was. By the time I was patting the cold, mixed
plaster around the last mold, Albrecht had finally begun to nod,
but each time I stirred, he would pull his head back up and stare
at me with squinting pale eyes.

He was still drowsing as I rose and melted lead in the little
doweled pot on the furnace floor, half closing my own eyes at the
near-painful heat. Lead melts faster than most of the other metals, and by the fourth medallion, I'd grown quite efficient at casting. I watched the beeswax spill like water out of the holes in the
bone-white plaster, then used the levers extending out of the furnace to tip the little pot over so that the lead poured, dark quick-
silver, into the plaster orb.

I sat listening to Albrecht's blatant snores and the ringing in
my tired ears as I waited for the mold to cool. A quarter-hour was

obligatory if I wanted the medallion to set properly. Enough time
to notice, with the odd detachment of the sleepless, that I could
feel the strong, too-rapid beating of my heart: apparently I was
frightened. There were things I hadn't thought through—things
I couldn't clearly think through, given my stunned and foggy
mental state—such as what I'd do if the hatch was simply a storage closet and not, as I'd assumed, a tunnel leading to escape, or
what I'd do if Albrecht woke up, or another guard came to replace
him and realized that he'd been drugged.

Or, and this was the most troubling thought of all, what I'd
do if I couldn't find Tommaso and Cecilia once I got free.

I sat in the circle of feeble light surrounded by gloom, staring
fixedly at Albrecht and the way his lips puckered and blew gusts
of air at slowly increasing intervals.

I'm not here as your jailor, the Nubian had said. *I'm here to
protect you.*

Trust Lorenzo, the Magician had said, *and you and yours will
come to no harm.*

No problem.

Keep silent regarding Niccolo.

Oh, I'd keep silent, all right. But now that I knew, thanks to
the Magician, that Tommaso and Cecilia would be well looked
after if anything happened to me, nothing could stop me from
having my revenge.

The time came. I broke the plaster mold as quietly as possible and
left the talisman on the worktable without charging it. Leaving
one courier magically unprotected was surely a small price to pay
compared to justice for Ser Abramo—and a chance to see Tommaso and Cecilia safe before that justice was administered.

Albrecht's round head was thrown back against the top of the

chair, and his uptilted mouth wide agape. His snores, now infre-
quent as the poppy weighed on his lungs, were so loud I feared it
might alert anyone upstairs.

I took up the lamp and stealthily made my way to the magical tent. Once inside, I set the lamp down in a far corner, close
enough so that its spherical glow encompassed the altar. I had
decided in advance to leave the lamp behind and brave whatever
I found in darkness, as Albrecht might wake—in which case, he
would see the lamp in the tent and be loath to investigate.

I stood flush against the low altar and pushed against it with
my hips, my hands clutching the smooth right and left sides as
best I could. It slid backward with a muted hiss over the fine
Persian carpet, then a duller scraping sound as it found earth. I
flung the edge of the carpet back to reveal the wood and pulled
on the thick leather handle with both hands, praying that the
wooden hatch's undoubtedly loud groan would not disturb my
captor.

It made only the slightest creak. I carefully swung it open and
set the wooden door softly down upon the furled carpet.

I stared disappointed at what looked to be nothing more
than a shallow pit, the width of two men and the height of one.
But appearances can deceive, so I sat down upon the edge of the
pit and pushed off with my hands. I landed feet-first in the pit,
which smelled moldy and dank, and then, beyond the light's
scope, I patted the invisible soft earthen walls surrounding me.
With palms and fingers, I discovered the short wooden ladder
that would have allowed me to climb down rather than jump,
and after a short search, came upon a low crawlspace tunneling
east, headed directly beneath the altar.

I dropped to my hands and knees and had just stuck my head
into the opening when I heard men's voices and froze. My worst
fear had just materialized: Albrecht's replacement had come. For

an instant I considered crawling to my escape, but I had no idea where the tunnel led or if indeed it led anywhere at all.

I quickly crawled up the ladder and replaced the carpet and altar. As I did, a piece of paper fell from the altar to the floor—a message that *had not been there before.*

My weary heart quickened its beat; my breath escaped me and for a few seconds, would not return. I squatted on the floor and unfolded the note.

Should trouble come, go at once to Lorenzo, the invisible Magician said.

I felt drunk, wondering whether the note was real, whether I was dreaming. I hid the magical message inside the waist of my undergarment and rose. Outside the tent, male voices began to rise in volume—to be expected, since Albrecht had been sleeping on the job, and his stupor would be attributed to drink, at least by the other guard. A new one, judging from his voice, which was familiar. I took up the lamp.

But as I opened the velvet flap to emerge, the heated exchange escalated to shouting of a dangerous kind. I hung back and lowered the velvet to watch through a sliver.

The replacement was not the Nubian, but a decidedly corpulent man of average height whose back was turned to me. In his raised hand was a long sword, and Albrecht—slow and sluggish, his red face and straw curls visible—held the same.

An impasse, one that boded ill. I blew out the lamp, hoping the stranger hadn't noticed that the light had been lit when he'd entered.

"Is it money you want?" the intruder growled. "I got money. Stand back, shut up, and you live. Otherwise . . ." He swiped his blade in the air.

Albrecht shouted something incomprehensible and lunged clumsily with his own sword, stumbling in the process. The stranger was obliged to catch him before he fell and dropped his sword, as a result turning his pink, puffy, vaguely familiar profile toward me.

It was the man I'd come to think of as Stout, the one who'd questioned me about my loyalty to Lorenzo by tricking me into believing he was a Roman spy. I drew back instinctively and narrowed the slit I was peering through.

Stout, graceful in motion, wrapped one strong arm around Albrecht's shoulders and pressed the German's back against his, Stout's, chest, supporting him on his feet while causing his head to loll back. As a skilled musician would draw a bow across a stringed instrument, so Stout drew the edge of his sword smoothly, deeply across the tender flesh beneath Albrecht's left ear to his right, renewing his grip on his victim when Albrecht struggled, with only a slight staccato when the blade found the windpipe. A rush of burgundy cascaded from the dying man's wound; vermilion spewed straight up from the slit, spraying Stout's face and clothes and the very air with a bright red mist. My gasp proved inaudible against the splash of blood spilling to earth, of the horrid gurgling as Albrecht drowned, red foam bubbling at his neck, as he struggled to draw a final breath.

All of which explained, in vivid, gruesome terms, why Stout had earlier convinced me of his dedication to Pope Sixtus, of his loyalty to Rome.

I meant to step back. I meant to crawl into the tunnel and run away. Instead, I dropped to all fours and retched, as quietly as possible, while Stout dropped Albrecht's motionless form, still gushing, to the floor.

"Bloody 'eretic," he said, giving the body a kick, and headed to the worktable in the light from Albrecht's still-burning lamp on the floor by the chair, his portly shadow a dark looming giant behind him.

I got to my unsteady feet and wiped my mouth and streaming eyes while Stout squinted down at the items scattered on the
table. All but one of the talismans were gone, delivered dutifully
to other hands by the guards once they were magically charged.
Stout showed no interest whatsoever in the remaining one. I held
my breath as he peered at the cipher wheel, but he skipped over
it just as he did the talisman, apparently thinking it strictly
related to magic. He snubbed the ink and quill, the engraving
tools, the smudges of unused plaster hardening on the wood,
and instead put his thick hands upon the stack of papers set aside
to one corner. His lips curved in grim satisfaction. He took the
papers, glanced at them in illiterate confusion, and stuffed them
inside his cloak. Then he stepped into his own shadow, to the
shelves behind him, and began to examine their contents.

I moved toward the tunnel to flee.

But then my dulled mind realized that the dates and locations
for Lorenzo's supposed departures were all written—unencrypted,
for any educated eye to decipher—on one of the pages in Stout's
cloak. I turned back toward the flap.

It didn't matter, I reassured myself. Lorenzo could change the
times and dates. The important thing was that the Romans would
still be unable to break the Medici's ingenious code.

Drawn suddenly by an invisible force, Stout turned away from
the shelves and moved back to the cipher wheel.

And tucked it beneath his arm.

A good thief would have run away. A good thief would have
said, *Lorenzo and Florence be damned* and would have fled north
with her cronies.

Apparently, I was not the consummate professional I believed
myself to be.

Apparently, I was an idiot *extraordinaire,* because I slipped crouching from the tent and—grimacing and careful not to slip on Albrecht's faintly steaming blood—took up his wet sword.

There's no way this tiny creature can lift a proper-sized weapon, Niccolo had said long ago, but I was bound to try. *And don't hold it underhanded, like a girl. It's not your pathetic little razor.*

I changed my grip to overhand.

Still crouching, the tip of the blade preceding me, I moved quickly toward Stout, who had turned back toward the shelves for a final look. His position was providential—I could easily have run him through. But my exhaustion caused me to misjudge the distance. I lurched forward with Albrecht's bloodied sword and plunged it as far as I could into his thick cloak, aiming for his left kidney. The cipher wheel tucked beneath his left arm clattered to the floor.

But while I felt the tip pierce flesh, I was half a step too far from my target, and the wound was less than lethal. Not even crippling: Stout wheeled about roaring, fumbling for his weapon. I used all my strength to hold on to mine as he turned, my blade slicing through the side of his cloak and biting into the belt beneath. The pocket was slit, along with the papers it held; pieces of them fluttered to earth.

It's all about the feet, Niccolo said. *Left foot forward, knees bent, all the weight on your back foot. You're less likely to fall from a blow. Once you lose your footing, you're dead.*

In a heartbeat, I shifted my feet into position. A strong position.

"You little bastard!" he snarled. He hefted his short sword overhead and brought it down hard, going for my head as if to split it.

I blocked him with the flat of Albrecht's sword, but my strength was no match for Stout's. The momentum caused my flat to strike my crown with deafening force. The pain was breathtaking, the force enough to knock me from my feet but for Niccolo's timely advice. I managed to block another blow and launch one of my own, directed at Stout's ample gut. It landed and he howled, but his girth protected him from a mortal wound. He struck again, I defended and struck again, and suddenly saw Niccolo standing in my opponent's place.

He was dressed in the same garb as when we'd practiced in Ser Abramo's weapons room. He was half smiling, far too cheerful given the circumstance.

"I've gone insane," I said aloud. Either that, or I was dead, and this was someone's idea of my perfect hell.

You've always been, Niccolo retorted. *Are you still hell-bent on murdering me?*

"No time to argue. He's going to kill me," I said earnestly of Stout. "You're right, I can't heft a man's sword very well."

So the time has come, said Niccolo, with smug relish, *when you need more than knowing the simplest way to block a dagger and to fall.*

"Hurry," I begged. Stout should have killed me a thousand times over by then. Or maybe this was magic, all happening outside time.

Niccolo shook his unreal head, mocking my desperation. *Why do you think I showed you an extra move, one that could save you in a time of trouble? Because I wanted to hurt you? And if I didn't want to hurt you—and God knows, a little thief like you deserves hurting—why in heaven's name would I ever hurt Abramo?*

"I don't know," I said.

He lifted a brow archly. *Ironic, don't you think, that I should save your life when your greatest aim is to end mine?*

"I was mistaken," I said desperately. At that point, I would have told him I loved him if it made him save my life. Or maybe I believed what I was saying; I couldn't be sure. "I was wrong."

Apology accepted, he said, mollified. *Come at me, then. Remember? Sidewise to me. A giant step so you're standing outside of my right leg.*

"He's too big," I said, panicked, but I did it.

Now your bend your right leg and slip it behind my left one. Good. Now watch what happens when you straighten your leg.

Niccolo vanished, replaced by Stout—so close I could smell his sweat and the iron tang of Albrecht's blood. Thick arms flailing for balance, he fell back against the supply shelf, hitting it so hard that it gave a great shudder before toppling forward. I ran in the opposite direction, the top shelf grazing my shoulder as it came down. The center of the great shelf struck the worktable with a deafening thud, a thousand clatters, and an enveloping cloud of thick white plaster dust.

I closed my eyes, turned my head, and held my breath as the plume of white slowly settled. When the soft rain of dust upon my cheeks stopped, I drew a sleeve across my eyes and dared to open them again.

The midpoint of the shelf had slammed against the worktable, so that its upper levels hung over the latter's surface; the bottom levels had lifted up slightly over the ground beneath table and shelf. Heavy lead and gold bars on the bottom shelves had fallen forward in a heap on the ground; the middle and upper shelves had loosed quills, pots of ink, metal files, engraving tools, honey-colored slabs of beeswax, and paper notes onto the table, between the rungs.

Somewhere beneath the powdery mess, beneath bright silver and pink copper and heavy wood, Stout's portly form had been pinned facedown against the worktable's surface. So had his weapon. Through some miracle, I had managed to hold on to my own; I used my sword to push away the detritus, enough to reveal the location of his head and cloak-covered torso.

"Who sent you?" I said, meaning to sound harsh and disappointed that my voice was weak and shaking. Between a pair of shelves, I found the damp spot where I had dealt him a shallow wound, and I pressed the tip of my blade there.

"Who sent you?" I said, trying to imitate Stout's growl.

No answer came. I pushed against his body with the flat of my weapon: no movement. I decided he was dead, or at the very least, so wounded as to no longer present a danger. I dropped down to my knees and scrabbled about through the debris on the floor, clawing at it until I found, with a relief that brought me near tears, the cipher wheel. Its surface bore a few shallow dents, but it was otherwise intact.

The remaining talisman, however, was trapped beneath the shelves and table somewhere with Stout—and the papers with the dates of Lorenzo's rendezvous were still inside his cloak pockets. Unfortunately, his heavy motionless torso rested upon those pockets, and the shelves that held his body fast in place were too heavy for me to lift.

I took my cloak off the peg and pushed the cipher wheel—it barely fit—into one pocket, then I headed to the ladder leading up to the ground floor. I meant to call upstairs, hoping that the Nubian or the chambermaid would be nearby, but Stout had closed the hatch behind him.

I crawled up the ladder, calling the entire way, and when I pulled myself up into the storage room, I found it curiously empty, as there had always been a second guard posted there.

I was calling for the Nubian when I found him in the adjacent map room. He lay on his back, large dark eyes wide, mouth slack and open, run through at the level of his heart. A bloody pool had spread out on the floor beneath him, extending from each shoulder like dark wings. I turned my face away as quickly as I could, in the vain hope that I could avoid remembering the sight.

The body of an aproned woman—the one who had lit the fire in my hearth the night of my arrival—lay near the kitchen hearth, and the body of an armed man lay just inside the side entrance. I did not stop to examine them, but stepped outside into cold bracing air and blinding sunlight.

Sightless, I stumbled out into the day, in search of Lorenzo.

Fifteen

I crossed the Old Bridge and loped northeast along the city's cobblestone streets, squinting beneath the unoccluded sun. Florence was a blur of endless orange tile roofs against white-washed stone, of horses, carts and asses, of men and women, nuns and monks, clad and veiled and hatted in dark blues, greens, reds, browns, and black. Florence was a cacophony of neighs and brays and clattering wheels, of human chatter, of shouts and street vendors' songs, all scented with roasting meat, yeasty rising dough, dung, and sweat. The Duomo tolled a dirge, its bells so loud my teeth vibrated.

It was a warmer day than most, and every cheerful citizen, it seemed, had surged forth into the streets, streaming shoulder to shoulder past me in a mighty tide. I pushed exhausted against the current, not just of human flesh but of the intermittent visions that eclipsed the world around me: Albrecht's blood a geyser in midair, the Nubian's blank stare. Again and again, Ser Abramo's sightless bicolored gaze toward heaven.

I gasped in cool air and drew myself anew into reality: I had trotted so fast and so far that I had covered the many *braccia* between the Oltrarno and the western end of the Via Larga, lined with the palaces of the city's oldest and wealthiest clans. None of Rome's ostentation here: these were solemn, earnest structures of stone—rusticated or smooth, decorated at most with plaster family crests—all, like most homes in Florence, three stories high

with flat roofs. Even so, the Medici palazzo was a monolith, so
deep and wide it consumed an entire city block. On one less frantic visit to the neighborhood, Tommaso and I had counted the
windows on the second floor: sixteen across, just on the north
side facing the Via Larga.

One corner of the palazzo's ground floor was an open loggia, its
wide stone arches admitting the Medici bank's many customers.
Businessmen in fine wools and silks swarmed the loggia like a hive,
and the queues in front of the bankers' desks reached all the
way out into the street. Haggardly, I elbowed my way inside. Even
though I was dressed quite respectably, my thief's skill at sidling
swiftly through a crowd made the gentlemen recoil and blatantly
clutch their purses lest I nick them. Ignoring the chorus of *tsks* and
the withering glances, I made my way to the front of one line.

Apparently, a lot of gentlemen were armed these days; a half
dozen of them emerged from nowhere, pushing their mantles
aside to reveal short swords and daggers in their hilts. And then
I realized: Those were not customers, but guards.

The banker behind the desk—a man whose curling white hair,
peeking out from beneath a new but decades-outdated black
toque, just covered his ears—had just finished joking with one
customer and was waving the next forward as if he were a friend
(which he likely was). At the sight of me blocking the customer's
way, he lowered the spectacles on his nose and looked up at me,
the insolent unfamiliar youth, over the top of his lenses.

"What is the cause of such rudeness?" he demanded.

I said: "Life or death. I must speak to Ser Lorenzo. Immediately."

My exhaustion, my trembling, the sheer sincerity and agony
in my tone made him straighten in his seat, all disapproval gone,
and blink at me. By then, I was unsteady on my feet. I wondered
if I looked as drunk and near madness as I felt.

"On what account?" he asked softly.

My legs began to give way beneath me. Dizzied, I set a palm upon his desk and sank onto my haunches; he rose.

"I can't speak about it here," I whispered. "Please ... would you tell him or Donna Lucrezia, if he isn't available, that Giuliana is here." In my distress, I gave my real name, not realizing how incongruous it seemed with me dressed as a man. "I have something extremely valuable that I can give only to them. No servant, no one else, but them."

The banker's expression divulged that his first impulse was to dismiss me outright, but a second long glance at me apparently changed his mind. He came around his desk and extended a hand. I took it and let myself be pulled to my feet, surprised at his strength and my own weakness. He led me over to a cold, shadowed corner near a thick wooden door leading into the estate.

Four guards in red-and-white livery stood by the door, a pair on either side. They nodded to one of the incognito guards among the customers, who came over and patted me down thoroughly. I'd bound my breasts so tightly that they couldn't be felt beneath my thick tunic. They found the cipher wheel in my pocket, drew it out, and examined it. Convinced it was harmless, they handed it back to me, and I clutched it possessively, as a child would a doll. "This is for Ser Lorenzo's eyes only!" I exclaimed, huffily stuffing it back into my cloak as best I could.

The guard nodded to the banker. The banker directed his words to me.

"Wait here," he said, and disappeared inside. I leaned inside the cold stone wall, pressed my hands to my eyes, and saw Ser Abramo's face.

Trouble came, I told him silently, *and I've gone to Ser Lorenzo.*

I lowered my hands as the door opened again. The banker came out too quickly, without Lorenzo, without Donna Lucrezia, without so much as an assistant.

"Please . . ." I began. He lifted a kindly hand for silence.

"Someone will be out shortly to tend to you."

I waited a minute, then two, then three, and wondered blearily whether I should leave, whether I would be believed or blamed, whether it would be wiser simply to shove the cipher wheel inside the door and flee.

I stayed only because of the Magician's most recent message.

In time, the door opened a third time. To my utter disappointment, it was neither Lorenzo nor Lucrezia, but a middle-aged woman with iron hair tightly plaited and wound beneath a veil of black gossamer. Her severe brows were just as tightly knitted and the corners of her lips drawn tautly downward. She was well-dressed, a household servant with great authority, judging by her bearing, but a household servant nonetheless. She held the door open without stepping out of the palazzo; a wave of warm air accompanied her.

Beside her was a large brute of a man dressed in black, with a neck as thick as his head. He motioned for me to stand still—I obliged quickly—and I was again patted down. The brute frowned when he felt the square wooden object tucked into my cloak. I shook my head when he motioned for me to take it out. "It's too precious," I said. "I'm carrying it for Ser Lorenzo, with orders that only he is to see it."

"It's harmless," one of the guards at the door reassured him. He shrugged.

The woman servant gestured sharply with her chin for the bodyguard to step back.

"Ser Lorenzo, of course, cannot see you," she told me dismissively. "And Donna Lucrezia is far too busy to be bothered by the likes of—"

"Simona!" A familiar voice called behind her. "Simona, let him in at once!"

Simona looked over her shoulder at her mistress with a look of disbelief and poorly hidden disapproval. She held the door open and flattened herself against the wall lest I brush against her when I entered. Wobbly, I stepped over the threshold and found myself in the presence of Donna Lucrezia—flanked by a pair of armed, disagreeable-looking men.

Her gray hair, like her underling's, was plaited and wound and topped by a sheer black veil; her unfitted shift was of plain black wool, her overdress of black silk, her old-fashioned bell-shaped sleeves without slits. Her homely face was worn and her dark eyes deeply shadowed; at the sight of me, they widened, and her pale hands reached for my shoulders. We were the same height, and it took all my strength not to reach out for her shoulders, too, and collapse into her arms.

"My dear!" she addressed me, not with distrust or shock that I should be absent my prison and standing before her, but with genuine concern.

"I, I have to see Lorenzo," I stammered. "Something horrible has happened—"

"You must tell me," she said firmly.

I glanced over at her maid and at the two guards; Lucrezia marked the gesture. She waved a hand in dismissal: the maid disappeared, but the two guards remained, albeit at a distance that allowed our words to be private.

"Come," she said. She took my cold hand in her warm one and led me and the politely distant guards through a series of rooms, each one covered in paneled wood with outrageously ornate designs; each one, oddly, with a bed, and crammed with paintings and vases and statuary of gold and bronze and marble atop semiprecious pedestals, Persian and Chinese carpets, and curios from the East and jewels—a display of more wealth than befitted a king, more than I ever could have imagined existed.

I stumbled alongside her across a private loggia, then inside again and up a narrow staircase. She led me through another series of rooms, each slightly less cluttered with art and jewels than the last, until we arrived at the farthest chamber. The guards hung back at the doorway, reluctant to enter a lady's bedroom. Lucrezia's was paneled in a darker wood, with a few paintings and sculptures, religious rather than pagan in theme. A small bed curtained in heavy gold brocade was pushed off into one corner, as was a single wardrobe; the rest of the room was filled with padded chairs and low tables to facilitate the serving of refreshments: apparently, Lucrezia did far more entertaining than sleeping here. A chambermaid stood filling the bedside ewer, and a kitchen maid had just arrived with a flagon of what smelled to be hot mulled wine.

Donna Lucrezia gestured for the women to leave and close the door behind them and on the reluctant guards. When we were alone, she turned and put the softest palm I'd ever felt to my cheek.

"My dear, what has happened to you?"

I'd never known the touch of a maternal hand, and it took all my resolve not to cry.

"Abramo," I began, then stopped, unable to go on.

Lucrezia took both my hands and lowered me into a chair as she took the one across from mine. "I know," she said gently. "They had discovered his identity, Giuliana." She uttered my real name as if she'd always known it, as if the fact that I was female had come as no revelation, but was the most natural thing in the world. "His previous assistant had betrayed him. It was only a matter of time."

I knew that *they* were the Romans.

"Niccolo did it," I said, with much less conviction than I'd previously felt after seeing Niccolo magically appear in place of Stout.

Lucrezia sighed and let go of my hands. Her tone was soft and firm at the same time. "Niccolo did his part for us, my dear, no matter what you saw. He is now at great risk. But something more has happened, or you would not be sitting here." She paused, and the softness left her. In its place was an exquisitely sharp intelligence, and steely determination. "Why did your . . . protectors let you go?"

"I need to speak to Lorenzo," I said. I couldn't imagine relaying the horrid details of Albrecht's and the Nubian's murders to this gentle woman, nor could I imagine that anyone outside of Lorenzo would have any knowledge of the cipher wheel or the encoded talismans.

"As you wish," she said, not altogether pleased. She got up and called for a servant and whispered something to the chambermaid, who disappeared.

Donna Lucrezia sat back down, pulling her chair a bit closer to mine, and took my chin gently in her fingers, a caress. "I have been worried about you," she said, her kindliness returned. "It was not my choice to put you in such a situation."

I took her to mean that she regretted my imprisonment. I was wrong.

"You know too much," she said, in a way that did not threaten. "Which puts you in grave danger. We have to protect you. It is our obligation, as you are one of us."

"Us?" I shook my head, which forced her to withdraw her hand. "I'm not one of you."

She lowered her gaze to the fine carpet beneath us, her large dark eyes suddenly sorrowful, liquid, glinting in the hearthlight. She seemed to be struggling to make a decision, to find her voice.

When she looked up at me, her face composed, she reached for me again and clasped my hands—once more touching me, as if she'd found something so dear she dared not let it go.

"Magic is real, my dear," she whispered conspiratorially. "I'm sure you know this, having worked with Abramo. When I saw you, and your eyes . . ." She drew a quick breath, as if in pain, but caught hold of herself again. "And I heard your name, it was as though heaven had returned my Giuliano to me again. Even death cannot keep us from our loved ones."

I blinked at her as though I'd come abruptly on a lunatic, but the last of her words echoed Ser Abramo in a way that made my hair stand on end.

She must have read the confusion in my eyes, for she gently set my hands down upon my lap and withdrew her own, and sat back, smiling calmly, sanely, as if she had not just made an astounding confession. And then she rose, and rang for a servant, and ordered her to bring us bread and cheese.

"You must be terribly hungry, my dear Giuliana," she said. "Your hands are trembling badly."

She poured me a cup of mulled wine, as if she'd been the servant and I the mistress, and watered it down at my request before handing it to me with a calm smile.

Lorenzo finally came in and drew back, stunned at the sight of me. His eyes, like his mother's, were deeply shadowed, and his face seemed more gaunt than when I'd last seen it. It was the face of a man struggling beneath the weight of an entire city, beneath the specter of his own imminent death.

I had always disliked Lorenzo and his brother because they were wealthy, spoiled, and worshiped, to my mind, by an ignorant population who thought gold a sign of God's favor and occasional spectacle a sufficient distraction from daily misery. But I had never considered that their privilege had also brought them peril and was now forcing Lorenzo to confront one of his most dangerous enemies.

Lorenzo stood protectively beside his mother, as if I'd been a

threat. Lucrezia caught his sleeve. He started to pull away in irritation, but her grip was adamant, and he let himself be coaxed
into the seat beside her. Although he leaned forward so far, he
was scarcely sitting at all.

"What in God's name are you doing here?" he demanded, his
voice so loud that Lucrezia shushed him to get him to lower it. In
a calmer tone, he continued, "Where are my men?"

I directed a sidewise look at Donna Lucrezia, uncertain as
to whether she should—or wanted to be—included in the conversation.

"My mother knows more than I do at this point," Lorenzo
said. "How in God's name did you come to be here? Where are
my men?"

"Dead." Even I could hear the anguish in my voice.

Even Lucrezia leaned forward in alarm.

"Stout killed them," I said.

"Who?" Lorenzo was puzzled, if no less intense.

Stout had been my private nickname for the murderer. I cast
about and finally said, "The man who . . . questioned me that day,
trying to prove my loyalty, in the warehouse. Where you and
your mother saw me for the first time."

"Girolamo," Donna Lucrezia murmured to her son. "The stablehand."

Lorenzo directed a thunderous scowl at me. "Outrageous," he
said. "Girolamo has worked for our family for years."

"He killed Albrecht," I said, my voice catching. "He killed the
Nubian and . . . others. I think he's dead. At any rate, he's trapped
down in Ser Abramo's cellar. He has the written notes concern-
ing your plans—"

"What else, what else?" Lorenzo half rose from his seat. Even
Lucrezia's insistent tug couldn't make him sit back down.

Silently, I stood and tugged on the cipher wheel until it finally came free of my cloak pocket. I handed it to Lorenzo, who looked at it in honest confusion.

"The talismans are safe, already in your people's possession," I began.

"I have them," Lucrezia said. "All but one." She took the wheel from her son's grasp and said, "An invention of Abramo's and mine. It generates the code that goes on the amulets. If our enemies stole this, it would destroy our entire system of secret communication."

"So you are loyal," Lorenzo stated matter-of-factly, as if I hadn't proved myself a thousand times over. "Good. But now we must discover who else in our household has betrayed us, if anyone. And you . . ." He eyed me intently. "You must not leave our protection. The Romans are likely aware of you now, as they were of Abramo."

He stood up and pulled the long velvet sash that rang the bell for a servant. As he waited, pacing near the door, I begged: "Please, my friends . . . Where did you take them? Can I see them?"

The ever-present crease between his mahogany-dark brows deepened as he struggled to remember. "Ah yes. Your friends," he said. "The young woman and the baby and the little boy. They're where they've always been and well-fed and warm, but they don't know who their benefactor is."

I rose, aghast. "Then they're not protected?"

"Our people have checked on them from time to time. But I thought it best not to draw attention to them. I doubt anyone knows of their connection to you."

I sank back onto my chair, shaken and gripped by worry. A chambermaid arrived with a tray of bread and cheese and was shortly followed by a manservant, whom Lorenzo took aside and loaded down with murmured instructions.

"You must eat," Donna Lucrezia prompted, "and then you must sleep."

But I could hardly do either, thinking of Tommaso and Cecilia.

Somehow, I managed to do both, and I was curled asleep on Donna Lucrezia's bed when she shook me awake by the shoulder. Lorenzo stood over me, his dark shoulder-length hair hung forward framing his cheeks, making him look even more gaunt than before.

"Girolamo is gone," he said, and at my sleepy confusion, added, "Stout. There was no body in the cellar. The rendezvous locations are in the hands of the Romans, apparently."

Donna Lucrezia walked up beside him, the hem of her long overdress whispering against the carpet. The animated charm had fled her heavy-lidded eyes with the result that she looked worn and tired and older than her years.

I pressed my palms against the mattress and pushed myself up to sitting as she said: "The cipher wheel. Did he see it, Giuliana? Did he try to take it?"

"He tried, but I got it. He passed it over at first—I don't think he knew what it was, but then he went back and picked it up as an afterthought. He had to have been badly injured. I can't imagine he got very far."

Lucrezia and Lorenzo ignored my last two sentences and shared pointed glances.

"We're moving to another property," Lorenzo said; his tone invited no opposition. "Someone may have seen you come here. All the tools that you need to continue your work will be taken there."

"How long will I be there?" I asked.

"Indefinitely. Most likely until I can bring this war to an end."

"My friends," I pressed. "They have to come with us."

He was already turning away, intent on the matter at hand, and muttered over his shoulder, "They'll be fine where they are. We don't have time to waste."

It takes time for the Medici to gather up necessary things; time for servants to prepare for a journey, however short. I convinced Donna Lucrezia that I was desperate for sleep and so would, in one of the quiet guest rooms while she directed the ladies who crowded her bedchamber.

I did not sleep, of course. I had kept my cloak nearby and laid it beside me as I settled into another feather-soft bed as Donna Lucrezia watched. I'm quite good at feigning snoring, a necessary talent when it came to convincing an anxious little Tommaso to sleep or at least to be quiet. So I gave a fine performance for Donna Lucrezia, letting my jaw sag and my lips part, and snoring just loud enough, but not too, until she closed the door on me and went to take care of other things.

I waited for the sound of her tread to disappear and at once jumped up and folded my cloak over my arm. I cracked my door, peered both ways to make sure neither Lucrezia nor Lorenzo was anywhere in sight, and stepped out into the bustling hall.

The household staff, many of them dressed in the Medici livery, swarmed the rooms in a swirl of red and white. None of them had time for a well-dressed lad apparently sent on an errand. The palazzo was vast and I got lost a time or two in yet another curio-laden room with busy golden wood panels, but somehow I managed to hold my breath most of the way out and released it with a gust when I finally stepped outside the door I'd entered.

The bodyguard who'd stopped me the first time was lingering there. I forced a half smile and a nod as if to say *my work is done here, thank you.* It wasn't so easy to gain access into the Medici estate, but it was certainly a cinch to get out.

The all-too-brief nap I'd taken on Donna Lucrezia's bed hadn't lifted my fatigue one jot, but the bread and cheese and watered wine provided me just enough strength to cross the city once more, albeit it at a pace far too slow for a pickpocket's liking.

Cecilia screamed with joy at the sight of me, a sound so shrill it made my head hurt (although at that point, most sounds made my head hurt), and when Tommaso hurled himself at me, my legs gave way and I fell hard onto my backside, right there in the open doorway.

Giggling with glee, Tommaso fell on top of me and stayed there, wrapping his skinny arms around my ribs and trying to burrow his face into my bound breasts.

Cecilia's golden hair was down, unplaited and uncoiled; it spilled down her back as she threw her head back and laughed. She and Tommaso pulled me up so I could rise but her laughter stopped when she saw my face. I was too tired, too overcome with worry and grief and shock and desperation to even smile. I pushed myself up to a sitting position with effort. Cecilia saw, took my arms, and pulled me to my feet. It gave me time to see that Tommaso's front tooth had come in halfway now, brilliant white against pristine pink gums, time to drown in bittersweet relief at the sight.

"Giuli!" Cecilia crowed, and Tommaso chimed in—at which point Cecilia caught herself and shushed Tommaso as Ginevra, swaddled on the bed behind them, let go a plaintive sleepy mewl.

"Shhh," she told me in a whisper. "The baby's napping." In low voices, she and Tommaso babbled of worry and gratitude for the money, food, and fine bedding, and then Cecilia stopped herself abruptly. She put her hand to my cheek, just as Donna Lucrezia had done, and I had to squeeze my eyes tightly shut at the welling of tears, at the sudden painful tug in my throat.

"Giuli, my darling," she said softly, ignoring Tommaso's excited, slightly-too-loud chatter as he pulled at my clothes trying to get my blurry attention. "Tell me what has happened to you. Tell me what is wrong."

"Will you leave me again?" Tommaso asked, so pitifully, so near tears himself, that I sat down on the narrow bed and pulled him to me, winding my arms around him so tightly that he was crushed and near breathless, but he didn't try to squirm away.

"I'll never leave you again, ever," I gasped. "But we're leaving this place for a much, much nicer one." I looked over the top of his little straw-colored head at Cecilia, whose sweet face had grown abruptly grim.

"For two days, I thought you had died," she said somberly, "until the money started appearing. Packages. My landlord didn't know what was in them. I kept wondering if Tommaso and I should go to another city, like you told us, but I kept hoping you'd come back. And now you have." She paused. "You don't look well, Giuli."

I closed my eyes and managed to say calmly, "The men who killed my master are after me and—"

"*The men who killed your master*," she interrupted, her look stern and maternal. "Criminals?"

I shook my head. "Worse."

She frowned, confused.

"I'm in danger," I said. "Which means you might be in danger, too. But everything is going to be all right. We're leaving—I don't know if we're leaving Florence, but we're going someplace safe. Others will be protecting us."

Her dazzlingly blue eyes narrowed. "What others? Giuli, I'm

not getting involved with criminals or worse. I'll not let Tommaso get involved with them either."

I drew a deep breath. If I hadn't been so jagged, so near insanity, I might have answered differently. When I let go the rush of air, unexpected words rode on it.

"The Medici. It's about the war, Celia. It's about Rome."

It was her turn to let go a gust. Her pretty rosebud lips pursed into an open circle that grew until it was the size of her widened eyes.

"You're a spy," she whispered.

"Among other things," I admitted, then almost slapped my own face as I realized that Tommaso—chatty brat Tommaso, that little blond parrot—should never have heard such a thing. And by telling Cecilia, I had just endangered her, too.

"We need to get back to their palazzo *now*," I said. "They'll take very good care of us all. We have to go. I . . . I'm keeping too many secrets. And the Romans know it. They're after me, Celia."

Cecilia was still gaping as if she hadn't heard. Her gaze left mine and traveled to a spot beyond my right shoulder, where the door was still open. I turned my head away from her, from Tommaso, still in my grasp, and looked over my shoulder at the cowled man standing on the threshold. His face bore cherry bruises, and his black cloak, slashed and hanging down at one side, bore fat handprints where he had tried and failed to brush off all of the white powder.

"Funny as you should be blabbin' about that," Stout said. "You'll be comin' with me now, I thinks."

Sixteen

He wasn't alone. The lanky, silent man I'd nicknamed Lean was lingering behind him in the doorway, his mantle pushed back at the hip to reveal the steel hilt protruding from his baldric, his gaze intently focused on me.

Cecilia raised herself to her full height. She was far from dangerous, but she'd dealt with many a rowdy male customer, and the sudden frightening blaze in her eyes intimidated *me*.

"Get out," she ordered, her voice low and thick with loathing. "Get out now, or I'll call for the landlord."

Stout gave her a smarmy grin and raised his hands, palms out, to show he meant no harm. "I work for the Medici, dearie. I'm just here for her. You and the kiddies can stay here if you want. We just want to take her someplace safe."

Cecilia wavered and glanced back at me.

I locked gazes with Stout and gently pushed Tommaso away from me.

"I'll go with them, Cecilia," I said slowly. "You and Tommaso stay here. I'll come back for you later."

I'm a fairly good liar, but I've never been able to fool Cecilia for an instant.

"They're *not* with the Medici," she said, her voice quavering not with fear, but indignance. She turned on the two men. "Get out!" she shouted.

Stout actually took a step backward, and she tried to close the door on his boot, but he kept it on the threshold and used a powerful shoulder to push the door back open.

Cecilia screamed bloody murder, a sound louder than I thought her capable of making. "*Help!*" she shrieked. "*Police! He's killing me! Help!*"

Ginevra started wailing almost as loudly, while her mother picked up a bowl from the table and began, ridiculously, to beat Stout with it. He seized her arm with such crushing force that she yelped and dropped the bowl to the floor, where it split in two. He pushed her further back into the room so that he and Lean could step inside and close the door. Enraged, Tommaso let go a high-pitched roar as he lunged at Stout and started pummeling his thighs. I forced myself into the melee, trying to push the boy away, trying to pull Cecilia's arm free.

Lean stepped forward and drew his short sword.

"Tommaso!" I shouted. "Stop it!" To Lean, I yelled, "Don't you dare hurt either of them or I won't go!!"

"Shut up, all of you!" Stout bellowed, and shook Cecilia by the arm as he directed his next words to her. "Or I'll shut you and your kiddies up for good!"

He pushed Cecilia away and kicked at Tommaso. I guided both of them away before they got themselves hurt.

Cecilia was angrier than I'd ever seen her. "Don't you dare go with him, Giuli!"

"You have to stay with Tommaso and Ginevra," I said quietly, reasonably, turning to her and exposing my back to Stout. "Please . . ."

"You can't!" She sounded as petulant as Tommaso, who echoed her in a high-pitched whine.

"Celia," I hissed through gritted teeth. "He's killed. He's killed . . ."

Before I could finish, Stout threw a massive arm around my

chest and pressed my back hard against his upper torso so that I was thrown off balance, forced to lean against him—my head resting on his heart, pinned in the crook of his elbow. If I moved, I would be strangled. At the same time, he unsheathed his sword, one edge of it faintly crusted with a dark brown-red substance. Albrecht's blood. And now he had me in the same position as poor Albrecht when his throat had been slit.

I had no weapon, no more trick, no helpful visions of Niccolo. *So*, I thought sourly, *this is how it ends. This close to happiness.*

"Yes, I've killed," Stout told a horrified Cecilia, "and I'll run her and you and the kiddies through unless you back up and shut up."

"No matter what he does," I gasped at her, at Tommaso, "don't do anything. Just hold still, and let him go." Because I knew he was going to kill me, and I didn't want him to do it in front of them. Especially not Tommaso.

Wide-eyed, her hair tousled, Cecilia ran to the bed and protectively picked up her shrieking child, who pushed her mother's face away with chubby fingers.

"Don't you dare," Cecilia said, her voice quaking with outrage. I couldn't tell if she was speaking to Stout or to me. "Don't you dare . . ."

Tommaso surged forward again, screaming, "Let her go!" in a voice so loud and so shrill I was surprised the entire city didn't come bounding up the stairs to investigate. He pushed away Stout's tattered cloak to reveal one of his thick thighs, and then Tommaso bared his little teeth and sank them into Stout's flesh.

Stout yelped and tried to kick the boy away, but his grip on me never wavered.

"Stop it!" I roared and kicked at Tommaso myself. I finally managed to connect and sent him falling onto his backside.

"I'll kill you," Tommaso wailed. Tears streamed from the corners of his irresistibly blue eyes. He scrambled to his feet.

"Not before I kill *her*," Stout retorted, pressing his blade even closer against my neck. "And you, you stupid little bastard!"

Lean, heretofore a spectator, sidled past Stout and grabbed Tommaso's arms. The boy struggled in vain as Lean held him fast.

"No!" I gasped; the razor-fine edge of Stout's blade scraped off the tender flesh at my neck. "Let him go. I'll do anything you say."

Stout withdrew his sword a bit. "Oho," he said. "You're a tough one. I remember how you was so willing to die for Florence. But maybe there's something as you love more that'll loosen your tongue." He jerked his chin at Lean. "Bring 'im with us."

"No," Cecilia moaned. Ginevra echoed her wordlessly.

"No," I moaned, too. "I swear on God's throne, if you leave him, if you don't hurt him, I'll talk. Just please, please leave him alone."

"Well," Stout remarked cheerfully, slowly uncoiling his arm from around my neck. I stood up and rubbed the offended flesh there. "That cinches it, then." He winked at Lean. "C'mon, let's go."

Lean looked uncertainly at Ginevra, then back at Stout.

"She'll keep her yap shut," Stout said deliberately as he eyed her. "At least until we're back in the street, if she wants her baby to live."

Clutching the sobbing Ginevra to her, Cecilia stared at me, her gaze stunned, frightened, imploring forgiveness.

"It's okay, Cecilia," I said softly. "You're doing the right thing by Ginevra." And I truly didn't blame her, not at all, because I knew that if it came down to a choice for me between protecting Lorenzo de' Medici or Tommaso, Tommaso would win.

With Stout clutching my arm and Lean clutching Tommaso's, we marched through the outer rooms and down the stairs into the landlord's shop. The landlord was in the back firing new wares, but his wife and a pair of customers noted Stout's brandished sword and my and Tommaso's incapacitation, and gasped.

"Police," Stout growled.

"He's lying!" Tommaso piped, before Lean cuffed his ear.

There was a moment of silence as the others digested this. *Please,* I thought, looking as desperate and frightened as I dared, *please believe Tommaso and help us!*

"So that's what all that commotion was about," the landlady said huffily. "And me trying to do business! I *told* Cecilia that the lad would come to no good. Good riddance!"

Outside in the street, Stout's flatbed wagon awaited. A third man sat in the open bed. I marked his long, exposed baldric and the hilt of the weapon inside it, and crawled peaceably up to sit beside him. Lean lifted Tommaso up. The boy kicked a bit and seemed ready to fight the third man, who reached out and enfolded him tightly in his arms.

I looked pointedly at the man's baldric and, sotto voce, told Tommaso, "There's a sword in there with your name on it if you give him any trouble."

Tommaso scowled and thrust out his lower lip. He pulled away from his captor—not to escape, but only so that he could be next to me. The man—goateed, middle-aged, and weary-looking—kept hold of Tommaso's one arm but let the boy squirm in between us. His warm little body pressed against mine and I resolved at that instant that wherever we were ultimately headed, Tommaso would not arrive with us.

The wagon rolled toward the east, away from the richer part of town, and south down the vast and crowded Via de' Calza-iuoli. I drowsed. I tried hard not to fall asleep so that I could keep an eye on Tommaso, but the steady rumble of the wheels and the rocking of the cart overcame me. I dreamed of Niccolo, showing

me again and again how to thrust and how to fall. I dreamed of
Ser Abramo down in the cellar with the silver talisman I'd had
since childhood, studying it, realizing that it marked the position
of the constellations and planets on the day I was born, remembering the moment he had hung it around my tiny neck. I dreamed
of the moment I had first taken hold of Tommaso's hand when he
was sitting all alone at the fountain outside the orphanage, and
our first night together, when he had sobbed in my arms as he told
me the story about stumbling over his dead mother in the dark.

An agonized human shriek, an oddly sickening *thump thump*
of wheels and an ass's bray hurled me hard into waking, onto my
belly on the flatbed of the cart. Tommaso was no longer sobbing
in my arms but down beside me, the two of us clutching the
wagon bed's rear edge to keeping from falling down into the
street and gaping down over the crushed body of an urchin lying
on the cobblestones, close enough for me to reach down and
touch. It all happened in the space of a breath, less than a breath,
but in that instant I had never been so fully awake, so aware that
my captor had lost his grip on me, on Tommaso, and so clear on
exactly what I needed to do.

I rolled onto my side and with all my strength pushed Tommaso off the wagon so that he fell facedown into the street. I
would have scrambled after him, but the goateed man seized
my legs and held fast. I pushed my palms against the bed, lifting
my head and upper torso up so that I could scream: "Run, Tommaso, run!"

Stupid of me to make noise, since Tommaso already knew
what to do—I'd trained him well in the art of running away from
the law—but especially since it alerted Lean, who jumped off the
driver's seat and followed at top speed.

Lean was fast, but there was no one faster than Tommaso, not
even me. The sunlight caught his hair and turned it incandescent

white gold. I watched that shining little head bob through the crowd and, in seconds, disappear before Lean had even gotten a good start.

For the first time in days, I felt myself grinning. Ear to ear, with teeth brazenly bared, because that was a singularly happy moment, perhaps the happiest of my life. Tommaso was free; he would go to Cecilia, who would deliver him to the Medici and Donna Lucrezia's tender care. He would grow up an educated man, and the hard life of the streets—and I—would soon fade from his memory.

I didn't relish the notion of being tortured, or of dying, but at the moment, I was too joyful to worry about hell. Who knew, my saving Tommaso's life might even have qualified me for purgatory.

After the accident, my fellow traveler dragged me back by my legs into the cart—my sleeves picking up several splinters along the way—and pulled me to sit with him just behind the driver's seat, our backs pressed against Stout's as he drove. The goateed man pinned both my arms behind my back until I yelped in pain. He nodded, satisfied, as if to say, *You won't be doing* that *again, miladdo.*

Our pace quickened, despite the crowds. Stout, like many a heartless driver on an errand, would not be distracted from his mission by the possibility that the child he'd just run over might be in need of assistance or already dead.

We rumbled on past the massive orange tile dome of the great Duomo, southward past the distant Palazzo della Signoria in the west, the House of Lords, a grim fortress of rough gray stone. If the bulwark was a massive fist, then the slim toothy tower, visible from almost anywhere in the city, was a slim forefinger pointing accusatorily up at the sky.

I relaxed as best I could in my captor's grip. No point in trying to escape; if I did, they'd go looking for me, and in the process might come across Tommaso. Lorenzo de' Medici had no idea how lucky he was that the boy had escaped—because if he hadn't, I would have told the Romans everything, anything they wanted to know if it would have spared Tommaso an instant of pain. But now . . .

Now I wouldn't talk. I only had to bear the next few hours, or God forbid, days, but I could bear them now that Tommaso was safe.

The cart lurched and slowed again as we made our way onto the rougher surface of the Old Bridge, where the way grew narrower because of the scores of shops lining either side of the bridge, and the scores of pedestrians patronizing each one. The Arno River reeked of fish and garbage wherever you were, but the smell wasn't so bad at the north end because the merchants were mostly artisans, with a few goldsmiths and jewelers. But at midpoint came the fishmongers and dye-makers, and the vile piss-and-dung scented tanneries, which always turned my stomach.

The cart rolled right up next to a tannery and stopped. My captor dragged me from the cart and I sighed, thinking that the tanner whose marriage proposal I'd rejected so long ago was finally having his revenge. All my enemies had to do was threaten to lower me into one of those foul-smelling vats . . .

I sent up a formal prayer. *Dear God, anything but that.*

As if in reply, my captors' steps veered away from the tannery toward the butcher shop next door.

In front of the building, a lad was doing brisk business. His stand, being carefully inspected by half a dozen kitchenmaids and poorer housewives, was overflowing. Here, a basket heaped with the corpses of unplucked birds—chicken and gamecocks and pigeons with wrung necks, their stiff skinny legs sticking straight from their bodies. There, on the makeshift table, artfully arranged, a display of the furry heads of sheep and boar and cows with dark clouded eyes, all seeming to stare back at those inspecting them. Lumps of yellowed ivory lard sat nearby, hard as rocks in the winter and, above them, loosely looped around a trellis like a vine, hung lengths of gossamer white intestines, cleaned and ready for use as sausage casings. Next to them sat pails, some overflowing with lungs, some with hearts or livers or brains.

The lad, busy with a sale to a particularly suspicious maid, didn't even glance at us as Stout led the way past the stands and into the building. The goateed man didn't try to hide the fact that he was dragging me against my will by my arm. Perhaps everyone thought I was an apprehended thief brought back for the administration of justice. They would have been half right.

The shops on the Old Bridge weren't large, but crowded side by side, which necessitated a good deal of cramming of both people and wares into too-small spaces. The butcher shop was no different. The air inside was thick from the smell of human sweat and animal blood, piss, and the particularly pungent feces born of fear. It was also hazy with smoke from the apparently never-cleaned hearth. Even so, the fire was poorly stoked, so that the shop was cool enough for the meat.

Three different men, dressed in once-white aprons now stained yellow and dark brown and bright red, wielded ferocious looking knives and saws and cleavers as they sliced and sawed and chopped away at remnants of their recent victims. One of them glanced up, his plump round face red and sweating, and winked a deep-set eye at Stout; the two bore an uncanny resemblance. The other two men continued laughing and chatting with each other, eyes on their work and their fingers, as if we'd been invisible.

On either side of the workbench, thick wooden planks had

been nailed to the wall; attached to those planks were hooks with tips as sharp as wolves' teeth, from which hung slabs of trimmed bright red meat.

Behind the men, a dozen or so chains dangled from the ceiling, and from each chain, the half or whole carcasses of skinned and trimmed sheep and pigs and cows hung upside down from their ankles. A lad of perhaps ten years moved from the back of the room toward the front carrying a pail of fresh lungs, sidling through the narrow passageway between the carcasses—some of them twice his size—and setting them into gentle motion.

As we passed by the workbench, I saw the pails tucked beneath, heaped with yellow fat to be rendered into tallow for cooking, soap, and candles. Stout led the way fearlessly through the forest of hanging dead, his broad shoulders striking a pink-and-white corpse on either side, setting them swinging like pendulums that struck me and the goateed man as we followed him into the back of the shop.

We passed out the back door into a poor man's loggia, a small, walled-in patio sheltered by the building's rear eaves. The loggia looked down onto the Arno below. The only protection from inadvertently falling into the river was a brick wall the height of my hip—which made this the perfect spot for dumping feces and offal and unwanted urchins into the drink.

Against the wall opposite the river stood a workbench, and in front of the bench a cheerful older man, uncloaked with his sleeves rolled up and his balding head exposed to the weather, as he had apparently worked up a good sweat. On the bench lay the tools of his trade—knives, saws, pincers, and cleavers in all sizes, including some so large I could never have hoisted them. My fingers involuntarily retracted into fists at the sight of the great cleaver in his hand.

Next to the bench, a tall ladder had been propped in the corner. A great ewe had been lashed to it by her rear hooves with her belly exposed. Or rather, her backbone, as her organs had been removed, and she was splayed open like a book, her glistening spine exposed, her ribs spread like bony wings. She'd been relieved of most of her innards, which, still faintly steaming in the cold, overflowed from a bucket on the floor beside her. Only her dark little kidneys remained, nestled against a thick slab of fat covering her pelvis. Her face was hidden, but I could still see the last bit of her blood dripping from her nostrils onto the bricks beneath her.

In her, I saw my fate.

The butcher was whistling as he swiped his cleaver against a whetstone, and when Stout moved up and tapped him on the shoulder, he turned and smiled at us, as if it had been perfectly natural to find Stout accompanied by a man frog-marching a reluctant lad. The butcher set down the knife, quickly wiped his sleeve across his blood-spattered face, and his hand on his blood-and-fat smeared apron before thumping Stout's shoulder. This man, too, bore a resemblance to Stout—no surprise to me that it was a family business.

The butcher shot a quick glance at me, then back at Stout's bruised face and powdery tattered cloak. "He's a small one, but he looks like he gave you a bit of a go, Girolamo." Despite the sullen lack of reply, he continued, "I sent for 'em, of course. Uppity bastards sent back a message to call for 'em once you got here with your prize."

Stout grunted in annoyance.

"And who's your friend here?" the butcher asked pleasantly, as if we'd all come for a chat.

Stout shot the goateed man a narrowed, sidewise glance and opened his mouth to speak, but my reticent captor answered first.

"Giovanni," he said stonily, in a way that discouraged further conversation.

Stout snickered. Even I, in my drunken sleepless state that alternated between resigned euphoria and base terror, caught the sarcasm in the reply. Half of the men in Florence were named Giovanni because San Giovanni, John the Baptist, was the city's patron saint. Stout lifted his brows approvingly and nodded as if to say, *Giovanni it is, then.*

But the butcher remained oblivious and cheery. "Well met, Giovanni, well met." The butcher turned to me and his grin grew smug. "Have a seat, laddie," he said, gesturing graciously at the uneven brick floor, where a small puddle of blood lay congealing.

Relieved, Giovanni flung me down onto the slimy bricks. I sat down beside the crucified ewe and closed my eyes as the butcher took up a large cleaver and began hacking at her forelegs. A wave of nausea hit me, in part because of the poor ewe and the stink of blood and bowels, but also because of the acrid aged piss smell coming from the tanner next door. I put my freezing ungloved hand to my brow, took off my cap, and leaned my bare head against the cold stone wall.

I suppose I dozed. I was too tired to know if I was sleeping or waking, but regardless, the realization came to me that magic might be of use. Abramo had said that magic had brought me back to him. Perhaps now it could perform another miracle. At the very least, it might distract me from the nausea.

And so I cast a circle in my imagination. I wasn't physically facing east, but in my mind's eye I corrected my orientation and saw myself standing at the low wall overlooking the Arno, spreading my arms as if to fly or to embrace the waters. I chanted the Hebrew words of power silently, imagining that my voice was low and powerful as Abramo's had been, that the vibration of it went out into the air and surrounded me, filled every corner, expanding until it filled the entire sky.

My enemies had the daggers, not I, but Ser Abramo had shown me that I needed no weapons, no tools, no altar to save my own soul. I traced the circle and the stars carefully with my finger. Perhaps it was my teetering on the brink between sleep and waking that made the magic feel so powerful, more powerful than it ever had been before: strong enough to change the world and everyone in it, including me.

Your heart's in a furnace, Giuliano . . .

In the east, I summoned the Archangel Raphael, who appeared shimmering, yellow-flecked with tiny bursts of purple light. In the south, I called out to Michael, composed of red flames faintly tinged with green; to the west, watery Gabriel, in deep undulating blue glinting with orange from the setting sun. Uriel stood in the north, solid and earthen, her hair jet against terra-cotta skin, her pregnant body clothed in shades of forest and grain.

Silently, I spoke to them all. *Help me. Help me, and keep Tommaso safe. Keep Florence safe, and help Lorenzo.*

I felt as though I had imbibed a large dose of the poppy. The dreaming world intruded upon the waking, leaving me uncertain as to which was which. I called out to the one whose face I most yearned to see, the one to whom I most desired to speak, the only departed saint on whom I could rely.

Ser Abramo, I prayed. *Dear Abramo, come to me. Help me now.*

He appeared before me in the air above the glimmering river, like Christ interrupted in mid-ascension, his hands spread slightly, beneficently to either side as if to bestow a blessing. He was dressed as I'd last seen him: in the brown robes of a Franciscan friar. Shadows accentuated the severity of his strong hawkish nose, his coal brows, the lines around his lips. That face had frightened me once, but now I saw the kindness in his expression, the softness in his uncovered eyes.

His lips never moved, but I distinctly heard him say, *I never left you.* As I watched, his angelic apparition grew closer to me with each second until we touched, until he, shimmering like an archangel, sat down upon the bloody bricks beside me.

I don't want to die, I told him.

He answered: *It's not the worst thing that can happen, you know. But we won't let it come to that.*

I meant to ask him who "we" meant, but I was jostled awake, this time by a kick to my shoulder. The butcher had disappeared, but Stout was smirking down at me, smug in anticipation of my suffering and demise. Beside him stood three men, none of whom had made the slightest effort to fit in with their surroundings. One wore a mantle of the finest wool, trimmed lavishly with costly brown marten fur; his indigo velvet cap was edged with the same, as were the gloves on his hands, which pressed a perfumed lawn kerchief to his nose in an effort to lessen the stench. The first of his companions had neither a cap nor a strand of hair upon his head, nor eyebrows, nor even eyelashes, nor the faintest trace of a beard, which made his face seem naked, almost infantile, compared to his tall, overly muscular body. He wore a plain, black-wool mantle and gloves, and his posture toward the wealthier man was that of a respectful guardian. The second companion had the same mien and clothing, but was even taller, even more muscular, and definitely hairier, with an unstylishly long beard, brown with shocks of brassy gold. They had no kerchiefs and the stony, humorless expressions expected of professional bodyguards.

Giovanni was nowhere to be seen. I assumed he had been dismissed.

The rich man's black hair and eyes gave me pause. He seemed faintly familiar, and I struggled to place him.

I finally did: He had fled alongside Niccolo immediately after Ser Abramo had been murdered.

A Roman, Ser Abramo said helpfully.

"I know," I said aloud, which made Stout and his Romans lift their brows.

"She's mad," Stout explained to his visitors, who accepted this news without comment or surprise.

With a flourish, he produced a thin sheaf of partially tattered papers—the ones that he'd stolen from the cellar, the ones that contained the possible rendezvous sites where Lorenzo would meet *La Perla*, the king of Naples' ship. Stout fanned them out on the butcher's viscera-covered workbench, ignoring the fact that the edges of the paper had already started absorbing blood.

"For you, Ser Andrea," Stout said proudly.

The rich man, his expression one of distaste, leaned over the papers without touching them, the perfumed kerchief pressed fast to his nose. "And you found these . . . ?" His voice was muffled, but his faint accent identified him as having been born in the Romagna, the countryside just north of Rome. It wasn't thick enough to decisively incriminate him as being from the Holy City, but it was thick enough for my keen ears.

"In a secret workshop," Stout said proudly. "It was locked up tight—none of yous could have got in. But see, the guards, they knew me. I even drove some of 'em there from the Medici palace. That's how I got in and killed 'em, see. They wasn't expectin' it, but they wasn't afraid of me. They thought maybe I had a message fer 'em. I got the keys off the first dead man and let myself in."

The dark-haired Roman waved an impatient hand for silence. "I don't need details of your heroic exploits. Just tell me where this damned workshop was."

"In the Oltrarno, back in the countryside. Not an easy place to get to, but I can take you there if you want."

"Where *is* it?" the Roman snapped.

Stout's red face grew even redder. "You goes to Santo Spirito in the Oltrarno. And head due south as the crow flies, through some fields and a dead orchard, about four miles beyond where the road stops. There's a wall with tangled vines onnit, and normally you needs the keys"—he pulled at his neck and they jangled, muffled, beneath his mantello—"to gets in, but I din' bother to lock it back up. In a bit of a hurry and preoccupied with this one here, y'know." He jerked his chin in my direction. "As I says, I can take you—"

Ser Andrea waved his hand imperiously again, cutting off Stout, who twisted his lip, pouting at the snub. "Niccolo's coming. He has been there before, yes?"

"Yes," Stout answered reluctantly.

"Then we have no immediate need of your services in that regard. This is all there was?" the Roman demanded. "Nothing else?"

Stout's tone was deflated, faintly petulant. "There was a funny-lookin' block of wood, with magical writin' on it. I told you, they did magic in there. Devilish stuff."

My heart felt as though it had tried to flip itself over in my chest. With the sensation came a wave of fresh nausea. Now the questions would begin, and my refusal to speak about the funny-looking block of wood, and the torture . . .

But the Roman merely smiled beneath his kerchief. I supposed he thought the cipher wheel to be some sort of magical implement. "I'm not surprised to hear of it here in this godless city," he said. "Magic and men carrying on with boys the way you do. In Rome, the lad would be burned in the public square."

"I'll put a curse on you," I hissed drunkenly at Stout.

Stout crossed himself—a performance, perhaps, for his visitors. "I dunno why you set such store on Niccolo, Ser Andrea," he said grudgingly. "*I'm* the one you should've trusted with the murder. I'd a seen to it that both the crypto—crypto-man or whatever he's called—and 'is little sidekick 'ere would both be dead and buried, no question."

"Niccolo is of especial use to us," Ser Andrea said. "He knows the Medici compound intimately. He knows Lorenzo's habits."

"Then why isn't Lorenzo dead yet?"

Stout's question evoked an uncomfortable pause.

Ser Andrea finally answered, "I haven't time to discuss this. Lorenzo is never unattended by bodyguards, and there was a great falling-out between Niccolo and certain . . . members of the household, which led to his coming to us." Ser Andrea cleared his throat and shot a fleeting glance at the wiry-bearded bodyguard, then back at Stout. "Your services are appreciated, but they are no longer needed, Girolamo. That will be all."

Stout looked rather deflated by the dismissal, but a thought made him suddenly cheerful again. "There's one thing you *will* be wantin' to know—about Lorenzo, that nobody but me and those in the Medici palace know. *If* you want to speed things up and catch the bastard yourselves instead of worryin' over all this silly spying. Because *I* know where he's gonna be, and *I* know when he's gonna be there. But first I want money. Five florins, no less."

In other words, a small fortune, an amount of money no one would be walking around with.

The inner edges of Ser Andrea's eyebrows rose in skepticism. "Please. We both know he'll be heavily guarded. He never goes anywhere without guards."

"You has archers, don't you? There's a way for 'em to get a clean shot when he leaves the house, but there's a secret only I knows." Stout's devious enthusiasm convinced even me to believe him.

"All right then. Five florins. But if your information is useless, we'll take it back, along with your life. So what is this information?"

Stout's tiny eyes narrowed even further; one side of his lip curled up in a smirk. "I ain't as stupid as this one here," he said, nodding at me. "Money first."

He crossed his arms—clearly expecting to have to wait for a while as one of Ser Andrea's men headed for the bank. Instead, Ser Andrea stuffed his kerchief into the top of his leggings, reached under his mantello, pulled out a purple velvet purse, and set five gold florins, one by one, in Stout's waiting hand while I gaped.

Dazzled, Stout smiled down at the gold.

"Details, please," the Roman said, as he put his purse away and retrieved his kerchief.

"Talked to a stablehand myself as I was followin' this one today," Stout replied, with a tilt of his head to indicate me. "A small group leavin' today, in two hours or so, though I don't know where. Lorenzo and his mother. He tries to throw folks off by riding alongside the carriage, on a horse, like he's one of the guards. You put an archer on a nearby roof—the Church of San Lorenzo, across the way, maybe—and he can pick 'im off just like that." Stout snapped his fingers.

"Two hours or so," the Roman murmured, apparently so distracted that he lowered his kerchief to reveal a handsomely formed nose and chin. "Not much time to alert archers and get them into place."

"My wagon's out front," Stout said. "I can get 'em there. Just tell me where to go." He turned, ready to leave, but said rather snidely over his shoulder, with a nod at me, "Good luck gettin' that one to talk. He had a blade right to his throat, and all he'd sing was *palle, palle.* Crazy loyal to the Medici, for God knows what reason."

"Then pray tell, dear Girolamo," the wealthy Roman countered, "what we must do to make him speak."

Stout shrugged. "He 'ad a little boy with 'im. Don't know as they're brothers or what, but he begged us not to bring 'im with us. Ready to die for the little one, 'e is, but doesn't give a worry 'bout his own life."

Ser Andrea drew back, aghast. "Then *where* is he, you imbecile? Why didn't you bring him?"

Stout bristled. "I ain't stupid! I brought 'im. The little bastard escaped. But not to worry, Renato went after 'im. They'll be here soon enough."

"I see," the Roman said, somewhat mollified. "Is there anything else you have to tell us?"

"That would be it," Stout admitted.

"Well, then," Ser Andrea said briskly, "As I said, that will be all. We have no need of your wagon. Claudio's horse will be far faster." He gestured with his handkerchief at the hairy bodyguard. "Claudio, would you please?"

Stout turned expectantly toward the bodyguard.

In a display of fine swordsmanship, Claudio lunged forward on his right leg, his left flexed and ready to power a spring, his left arm out to perfectly counterbalance his forward movement. A long stiletto—of the sort Ser Abramo had once wielded against me—had magically appeared in his hand, and he delivered it emphatically into the center of Stout's formidable gut. Stout's little eyes bloomed into great circles, as did his pink lips. His shoulders hunched forward and he gripped the top of the long blade as if to stop it, as if it hadn't already been piercing his innards. Claudio pulled out his weapon with the same swiftness, with a sucking sound.

Still looking startled, Stout dropped to his knees and stared down in alarm at the blood darkening his tattered mantello and dripping from his half-severed fingers. He keeled forward like a felled calf.

I closed my eyes and didn't open them again until I heard a splash and saw the two bodyguards returning from the low wall meant to protect people from falling into the river. Stout was, of course, nowhere to be seen.

The rich Roman was just closing his purse, presumably after replacing his five gold florins. Without looking up, he said, "So, Claudio, top speed. Advise Lauro and Luca to be armed and on the roof of the Church of San Lorenzo within an hour."

The wild-bearded man nodded and disappeared without a word.

In the interim, Ser Andrea retrieved a pair of spectacles from beneath his mantle and put them on. With extreme distaste, he leaned over the workbench and lifted up one of the pieces of paper by the corner, using only the tips of his gloved forefinger and thumb. He kept his kerchief pressed to his nose as he read silently.

He finally looked up and noted my amazed expression. "Never trust those easily turned by money," he said, bemused, the very edges of a smile visible on either side of his kerchief. "I questioned Girolamo's devotion to His Holiness. At any rate, let him be a cautionary tale for those who speak too freely." His grin broadened briefly at the irony before he turned back to the paper in his reluctant grasp.

"We have times and dates here, but no final destinations. And we have a number of magical symbols jotted down on the paper, which appear to be notes."

I stared at him and said nothing.

He spoke as if he were lecturing the guard or a class of assembled students. "These symbols aren't necessarily devilish. The Hebrews have their own form of sacred magic, which invokes

angelic forces rather than demonic. This is the writing of someone very learned, not of a superstitious charlatan. However, as
much as the Florentines like to look the other way on these things,
in Rome this is heresy, punishable by death."

He smiled at me as he set the paper back down on the bloodied workbench. "I suppose you think yourself on the side of the
angels?"

I nodded wearily.

He snorted softly. "Nothing could be further from the truth.
No angel, light or dark, can help you now."

He's wrong, Ser Abramo said. I started. I had forgotten his
ghost was still sitting beside me.

"These dates and times," Andrea went on, "are written in a
different hand. Which did you write: the message, or the magical symbols noted beside them?"

"The symbols," I answered dully, and then cursed myself for
answering at all. I had intended to remain silent so that my torture
and death would proceed swiftly and be done with.

The Roman raised his eyebrows, faintly impressed, and lowered his kerchief in order to be better understood. "You are perhaps not so foolish as you look. I have no desire to make this
unpleasant for you. I see that you were instructed to create four
different messages, the first of which was to contain a key. I daresay your departed master was rumored to possess an exceptional
intelligence. It's possible that you know nothing more than pre-
cisely what you were instructed to do, but then, you were working in the cellar after his death. From the looks of you, you were
working very hard and for a long time without sleep.

"The instructions here say that you are to create a new key.
The key to deciphering a system of code.

"Clearly, even if one is a magician and the creator of talismans
for the elite public—and by coincidence also a cryptographer—one

does not use such a dangerous and critical piece of paper for jotting down random notes when creating, say, a love charm for a young lady. Certainly not *unrelated random* notes. Which means that the numbers you have written here—and the symbols for Venus and Saturn and various Hebrew letters—have nothing to do with the production of a charm, but rather with the requests made in this letter. Some of them, no doubt, used in the creation of the aforementioned key."

He paused. "I believe that I have an admirable talent for being able to look into a man's eyes and see what lies beyond the outer appearance. You, I perceive, have an intelligence equal to that of your master.

"Girolamo is hardly a convincing proselytizer; hardly the sort of person one would want to confide in. I wonder . . . With your fine brain, you could be of enormous use to us—not to mention the fact that by working with us, your excommunication would be rescinded and His Holiness Pope Sixtus would grant you a pardon for all of your sins." He waited a moment for his words to register in my disoriented brain, then delivered what he clearly felt to be the most attractive part of his argument: "We would make you rich. It's possible you might even be made a cardinal, which would guarantee a life of luxury for you and your friends."

I yawned. Poor timing. His chin jerked up and his eyes flashed at me, but they didn't stay focused on me for long. He turned toward the figure coming out the rear door, who was already being sized up by the hairless man guarding it.

"Niccolo," he said, his tone at once welcoming, sly and vaguely threatening. "It's good that you are here."

Seventeen

There stood Niccolo, dressed in a pleated dark green tunic that hung halfway down his thighs, black leggings, and a scabbard clearly visible beneath his short burgundy mantle. The goatee that had once been a shadow had filled in nicely, complimenting his short black curls. His eyes—those pale celery eyes, ringed with forest green and thick black lashes, the envy and desire of women—his eyes betrayed a flicker of recognition at the sight of me.

Yes, I was drunk with sleeplessness. Yes, he was beautiful; yes, I wanted him—or would have wanted him, if I hadn't been in a wildly fluctuating state of fear.

There was another emotion in Niccolo's eyes, too, one deep and dark but quickly dismissed in favor of polite attention to Ser Andrea.

"So I am," Niccolo said, with a slight bow from the shoulders. "Is this"—he lifted his brows and directed a pointed glance at me, sitting on the cold bricks there beside the poor crucified ewe—"the reason you sent for me?"

"It is," the Roman replied, smiling smugly. "I hear that you two know each other. From that fleeting look of interest on your face, I'd guess you know each other *quite* well. I also thought you were one for the ladies, but this is Florence."

Niccolo shrugged, indifferent. "I've seen him before," he admitted, without looking at me. "He worked for Abramo."

"Does he have a name?" Ser Andrea pressed.

"Giuliano," Niccolo said simply.

"Giuliano," Ser Andrea repeated, and showed a row of yellowed tiny teeth at the mention of Lorenzo's dead brother's name, as if the assassination had been vaguely amusing and not the tragic spilling of an innocent's blood in the most sacred of spaces. He looked down at me. "What an unfortunate choice of name for you, but how very indicative of your fate."

"What do you mean to do with him?" Niccolo asked, again casually.

"There are questions to be asked," Andrea said. "And not just of him. I've always wondered what happened to Giuseppe, after he went chasing after the lad when you killed Abramo. Or at least, seemed to kill Abramo; only Giuseppe and this one"—he nodded again at me—"really know exactly how . . . effective you were. It just seemed to me convenient that Giuseppe disappeared after that, never to be seen again."

My mind was so fuzzy I had to work hard to understand every word, but I was able to understand who he was talking about: Red Beard, the man who had run after me. Red Beard, the man that Leo had killed while protecting me.

I squinted my eyes half shut and remembered Ser Lorenzo next to me in the carriage, saying, *You killed one of my men . . .*

Spies and counterspies. Too bad that Leo hadn't realized that Red Beard had been on our side.

Niccolo let go a sound that lay somewhere between a dismissive laugh and an outraged gasp, but he was still smiling. "Ask *him!*" He pointed at me. "*I* risk my neck for you by killing Abramo, and all you can do is ask me whether I'm loyal?"

Ser Andrea wore a taut little grin. "Girolamo said you couldn't be trusted."

Niccolo swung from side to side, searching his surroundings, his tone flatly angry. "Where is he? I'll have a word!"

"Indisposed," the Roman said.

The hairless bodyguard snickered.

Ser Andrea grinned at him, enjoying a private joke. "Or should we say disposed, eh, Donato?"

Niccolo wasn't laughing. "It's not funny," he said. "I killed a man—a man I knew well, who'd never done me harm. The Medici are looking for me. They'll have my head on a pike the minute they find me. And *you* doubt my loyalty?"

"Well, I never thought much of Girolamo's character," Ser Andrea allowed. "But it's clear that you know this one"—again, referring to me—"so I'll let you do the honors instead of Donato. Here." He gestured Niccolo toward him and showed him the papers. Niccolo read them, his expression a blank.

"Rendezvous points," he said finally. "For couriers, perhaps. These are instructions for a cryptographer."

"I think it refers to Lorenzo himself," Ser Andrea said. "I think he either intends to go begging for help again or to escape like the coward he is. He knows he could end this war at any time by surrendering himself."

Niccolo looked wryly at him. "To publicly be drawn and quartered, of course."

"Which he deserves, after what he did to His Holiness's friends," Ser Andrea countered. "Regardless, Florence is almost in our hands. She has no strong allies, and certainly no time to use traditional diplomacy to make them. But it's impossible for Lorenzo to head off in all directions. I want to know: Which of these rendezvous points is the right one? What is the ultimate destination? Who is meeting with him, if anyone?

"I believe young Giuliano here knows the answer to these

things, or at least some of them. He has created a new code key so Lorenzo can communicate safely with another party. The question is, have the key and the messages already been sent to the other party?"

"Yes," I said abruptly, as Ser Abramo's ghost, Niccolo, and Ser Andrea turned their heads sharply toward me at my answer. I may have been hallucinating and half mad, but I knew the answer didn't really matter. Either way, the Romans could figure out how to get what they wanted. At least, by pretending to cooperate, I could play for time, as any good thief and liar would.

Niccolo's handsome face revealed no emotion other than vague interest. Ser Andrea looked pleased.

"Girolamo said you would be difficult to work with, but then, he was deeply stupid and mistaken about a good many things," he said. "So then you can understand, dear Giuliano, why we need to know both the code and its key, as well as the method of transmission. In other words, what sort of couriers deliver the messages, and whether the messages are hidden on the couriers' person or incorporated into apparently innocent documents or letters—"

"I know what *transmission* means," I said drowsily. Ser Abramo, sitting beside me in a shimmering aura, his elbows propped upon his knees, as mine were now, whispered, *You needn't be flippant. He could easily decide to kill you.*

"I know," I said to him, but the others clearly took me to be repeating myself.

"So then," the Roman said, turning to face me and smiling down at me with mock benevolence. "Let's start with the basics: The dates written there." He nodded at the workbench to his left. "Kindly tell me what the dates and places indicate. Rendezvous points for Lorenzo? An army? A diplomat?"

A thrill of fear pushed me further toward wakefulness. "I don't know," I said, hearing the panicked catch in my own voice.

"I'm only a cryptographer. No one tells me anything about Lorenzo's plans."

Ser Andrea nodded at the impressively tall and muscular Donato, who apparently needed no words to understand what his master meant; his eyes, dark gray agates against his lashless lids, sparked with unhealthy anticipation. Donato moved in front of the butcher's bench and, after a moment of contemplation, picked up one of the larger cleavers.

"I'll let you do the honors," Andrea told Niccolo, "since you're so very talented at cutting up those you know."

Clearly disappointed, Donato handed the cleaver to Niccolo, who moved up to the bench, his expression relaxed but otherwise unreadable.

"Get up," Ser Andrea said to me.

I straightened my bent legs, but after a glance at the freshly sharpened cleaver, didn't move.

Another nod from Ser Andrea, and Donato lumbered over to me and yanked me to my feet so hard I stumbled forward and collided with him. It was like striking a stone wall. He led me by my wrist over to the workbench so that I stood beside Niccolo and pressed my right hand down against the wood, flattening it with the heel of his and fanning my fingers out like a starfish.

Even the crushing pressure he applied couldn't keep my fingers from trembling while Niccolo eyed them, cleaver in hand.

"Just one," Ser Andrea said graciously.

Niccolo's gaze flickered at me. We were standing side by side, my right shoulder pressed against his left, both of us facing the workbench. He brushed against me as he turned his upper torso sideways, toward me, so that his right arm could wield the cleaver over my outstretched hand.

He shifted slightly so that his left thigh pressed against my right; his muscles loosened as his knee bent ever so slightly.

I understood that sort of touch. It was a wordless communication between cohorts in crime—just like me wiping my nose to signal to Tommaso that the Game should commence.

Bend your knees, bend your knees, I heard him say. *So your left foot is forward, but now shift the bulk of your weight onto the back foot, your right foot. You see? You have more speed, more power moving forward.*

He raised the cleaver while the Roman watched critically.

I was confused. Whatever Niccolo was planning to do to the monstrous Donato, I was in the way, and Ser Andrea was standing on Niccolo's other side. I was weaponless and too clumsy to protect him from either man, which wasn't good.

Still, I appreciated the gesture.

"Wait," I said to Ser Andrea, before Niccolo could spring. "You want the cipher key—it's a long document—too long for me to tell you. I have to write it down. I won't remember it all any other way."

Andrea raised his eyebrows in bemusement. "You make a good point. Donato, the left hand, please."

This was not the response I'd hoped for. Donato released my right hand, which I curled into a fist and shoved protectively beneath my mantle, against my sickened heart. I strained against Donato's grip on my lower left arm, but it was useless, like resisting a charging bull. He slammed the inside of my wrist down against the wood. I curled my fingers tightly, forcing him to pry them apart, one by one. He put the heel of his massive paw against my pathetic little hand so that I couldn't move it, couldn't even wiggle the tip of my pinky.

The shift required Niccolo to lean further forward, putting us in an even more awkward position than before. I looked up into his eyes, found that little golden fleck floating in that beautiful celery sea, and tried, without giving anything away to either

Roman, to summon an expression that would let him know that it was okay, that I knew he had no other choice, that it wasn't his fault.

I felt Ser Abramo standing behind me. *Trust him.*

But it was a cleaver. And it was my finger.

"I'll talk," I said swiftly. I wouldn't of course, but I wanted to end the moment of awful anticipation for me, for Niccolo. Perhaps if I distracted them enough with talking, there'd come a better moment for me to get out of the way, for Niccolo to spring.

Yet at the very instant I said I'd talk, the back door to the butcher shop opened, and Lean stepped in, dragging Tommaso with him. Lean looked exhausted; Tommaso, defiant. He saw Niccolo still holding the huge cleaver over my fingers, saw Donato holding my hand steady, and he let go a piping shout loud enough to raise all the dead sleeping in the Arno, Stout included. He pulled away from his captor and ran toward us.

"Where's Girolamo?" Lean asked, clearly glad to be rid of his burden.

"Headed home. We had no further need of him. Or you, for that matter," Ser Andrea said pointedly. Lean nodded gratefully and disappeared.

In the meantime, Tommaso was beside himself. "Leave her alone!" he yelled. He ran to Niccolo and started beating on his legs and hips. "Put that down! I thought you were nice!"

Niccolo set down the cleaver in order to seize Tommaso by the arms. Ser Andrea did a doubletake. Donato held on to me fiercely.

"*Her?*" Ser Andrea marveled. "*Her?*" He looked over at me and grinned, shaking his head with amazement. "Isn't this just like sinful Florence? Men in love with men, and young ladies with unnatural intelligence dressing as men, the whole of it forbidden by Scripture. I daresay the Holy Father's excommunication of you all was redundant." He paused. "But maybe fat old Girolamo was right about one thing: the boy being your weak spot. Was he speaking of a mother's love for her child?"

Through it all, Tommaso was still squalling at Niccolo. "How can you be so mean? I thought you were nice, bringing us all those gifts from Giuli—and now you're hurting her!"

Ser Andrea recoiled in surprise again, his chin half disappearing into his luxurious fur collar. This time his expression held no amusement at the revelation. He bent down with the agility of a trained swordsman, not a pampered rich man, and pulled a dagger from his handsome gleaming boot. He would have stabbed Niccolo with it had Niccolo not caught hold of Tommaso and pulled him away toward the river wall.

Niccolo drew his own dagger—training it not on Ser Andrea, nor on Donato, but on Tommaso's tender little neck. "I had to befriend the boy to get to her! Go ahead, kill me, and chop off her fingers while you're at it—you won't make her talk. Threaten her, and she'll die before she betrays Florence. But she loves the boy! *This*"—he waved the dagger in front of Tommaso's throat— "*this* is the only way you'll get her to talk!"

For more than two years, I had spoken only in my low boy's voice until it had become habit, but at that moment I shrieked in a breaking little girl's voice. "I don't love him! I don't! I don't love anyone at all!"

"But Giuliano," Tommaso wailed, his little mouth a rictus, "*I* love *you!*"

I broke. The sleeplessness, the physical exertion, the shock and the grief finally had their way. Reality fled, leaving in its place Ser Abramo's shadowy cellar, and the flickering light that illumined the page in my trembling hand.

You are my daughter; it was indeed my hand that cast the silver talisman for you.

I am indeed the Magician, and death cannot separate us.

My knees against the cobblestone, Abramo's face horribly slack, his eyes staring sightless at the Florentine sky.

Tommaso in the darkness, sobbing in my arms.

Oh, I'd been such a liar for so, so long, and I my worst victim.

Niccolo had visited them, taken care of them when I could not. His blade was at Tommaso's throat now, but all I could hear was the Magician whispering into my ear.

Trust him. Love him.

I can't, I answered Abramo silently, my imaginary voice coming out as gasps, a little girl on the verge of crying. *I'll get hurt again.*

But I couldn't help it: I trusted him despite myself.

It all happened with impossible, magical speed—Niccolo's grabbing Tommaso, Andrea's reaction, Niccolo's shouts and mine, and the visitation of the moments that had broken my weary heart.

And that instant, that ever-so-fleeting instant when Donato twisted his upper torso in surprise to gaze at Tommaso and Niccolo behind him, that instant when the Magician whispered, *Now.*

Donato lunged at Niccolo with the cleaver meant for my trembling fingers, trying at the same time to keep one hand on me, but his grip loosened just enough for me to pull away. To take up the nearest butcher's knife in reach—the long knife that the butcher had been sharpening against the whetstone, the great long knife used to split open the poor ewe—and, whirling, to direct myself at Ser Andrea's exposed back and swing the great knife's blade at the backs of his knees. Tendons snapped. Ser Andrea went down screaming.

His fall gave me clear view of what was happening in front of me: Niccolo, flinging Tommaso past the hairless monster Donato, toward me; Donato swiping at Niccolo with the huge cleaver.

Niccolo was dancing like I've never seen, weaving toward and away from the cleaver's bite. He made a lunge at Donato with the dagger, but the giant, though heavier on his feet, was also well-trained and caught the dagger's tip with the flat of the cleaver with a crashing clang. Niccolo and I both watched as half his blade flew away.

The distraction was enough for Donato to lunge at Niccolo, force him down on his back, and straddle him. I pushed Tommaso out of the way and ran up to see Donato bearing down on Niccolo with the great cleaver, while Niccolo reached up and—overhand, with his left hand, as we'd done so many times in practice—clutched the inside of Donato's forearm. I'd never been able to push past that hold with Niccolo and stab him with my wooden dagger in practice, but if anyone could break a grip, it was the mighty Donato.

Niccolo's teeth were bared; his arm was shaking violently. Sensing victory, Donato bared his own teeth in a smile.

I saw the massive cleaver hovering over Niccolo's head and everything that had been so murky before now seemed so clear: There were people worth living and dying for.

And people worth killing for. I was already going to hell, after all.

I stood over Donato's broad back, which strained beneath his black mantello as he pinned Niccolo down, as the cleaver gradually closed in on Niccolo's beautiful face.

It was easy, really, now that I was clear about everything.

I poised the tip of the long knife at the level of Donato's kidney, and I pushed down hard with both hands, rising on tiptoe so that I could bring the full weight of my body down on the weapon. Even then, the blade didn't sink easily, but required my extended effort.

Niccolo squeezed his eyes shut and turned his face away as

Donato dropped the cleaver, which struck Niccolo—whether with the flat or the blade, I couldn't see because Donato pushed himself up on his arms.

Niccolo wriggled away on the ground until his head touched the river wall, his face bright red but thankfully unbloodied.

"Mother of God!" Niccolo yelped indignantly. "Be *careful* with that!"

He was yelling at me, and that's when I saw, as Donato stood swaying, that the long blade had sunk deep. His mantle was twisted, revealing his tunic and his scabbard and baldric—beneath which the front half of the blade protruded a hand's length.

Niccolo had pushed himself up to sitting, revealing a slowly growing red spot on the hip of his green tunic. The butcher's blade had actually pierced him, but his clear lack of concern about it boded well for him. He scrabbled after the cleaver lying on the bricks where his head had so recently been.

Donato dropped like a stone to his knees and then forward onto his elbows. The tip of the blade scraped the bricks as he started crawling in confusion toward the butcher's bench and his keening employer. I pushed him down with my foot and pulled out the blade. It was work, but it finally came out with a mighty sucking sound. I fell backward as it came out, but I pushed myself up in time to see Niccolo use the side of his boot to push Donato onto his back, to see if he was still alive.

I doubted he was. His eyes were open, but they didn't seem to see any of us. His mouth was open, too, but he made no sound. Peeking out from the slit in his gut was what looked to be a loop of bloodied red sausage.

Oddly, the sight was accompanied by something slammed against my skull, causing my teeth to strike each other so hard I feared them shattering, my ears to throb so loudly I feared their bursting.

It was the stone ground. I must have fainted from the shock and exhaustion, because at some point I found myself watching a very animated discussion between Ser Abramo—who appeared quite human, not ghostly—and Niccolo and Cecilia and Tommaso.

"I've seen this before," Abramo said sadly.

Cecilia nodded knowingly. "It comes from the streets. Bad things happened to her, I think. She won't talk about it, but there was one night when she came home and she was hurt. Badly."

Niccolo spoke softly, almost a whisper. "She doesn't even know she cares."

Tommaso looked down at me wistfully. "She loves me. I know she does."

Someone else knelt beside me and let me settle against them for support. I opened my eyes.

"I'm right here," Abramo said. He looked deeply relieved. "I'm right here."

He kept saying it until his face metamorphosed into Niccolo's. I was resting in his lap. His cool ungloved hand was upon my forehead. Beyond him was sunlit sky, fading to afternoon, and Tommaso's sweet, frightened face. There were two little tears trickling down Tommaso's cheeks, one on each side, and they weren't the bratty, manipulative ones that he could spew at will, but the little ones that slid down when he was truly frightened.

"Are you okay, Giuliano?" He tried to stifle a sob and failed. "Are you okay?"

"I'm okay," I said softly. "Don't cry, Tommaso. Please don't cry."

Niccolo's arms were around my shoulders, my head cradled against him, a pietà with me as Christ and him as the Virgin.

I blinked up at him and said with sudden urgency, "*Lorenzo.*"

Eighteen

The Via de' Gori runs east to west. One flank of the Medici Palazzo sits on its northern side; the Church of San Lorenzo sits on its south on a diagonal to the estate, lying slightly east of the palazzo. Like the great Duomo, the basilica bears the shape of a Roman cross, or *tau*, with the altar positioned at the crux of the *T*. The long leg of the *T* runs lengthwise to the street, ending in the public entrance and the plaza in front of the church, the end closest to the Medici home. Like most buildings in Florence, San Lorenzo has a roof that is almost flat, with only a slight crest in the center—flat enough to allow men to sit or stand atop it with little fear of accidentally rolling off.

The two buildings—the family palace and the church where Lorenzo's brother, father, and grandfather are entombed—sit only a short walking distance apart. On a quiet night, a man shouting on one roof could be heard on the other.

The streets were emptying quickly in the wake of sunset. As Niccolo steered Stout's careening wagon off the Via Larga, which the palazzo faced, onto the narrower de' Gori, I clutched Tommaso with one hand and, with the other, shaded my eyes against the blood orange disc in the sky, against the rays that streamed unobstructed down the length of the street. Niccolo tugged on the reins, bringing the wagon to a rocking halt alongside the great stone bulk of the Medici compound. Beyond us, at the end of the block, lay the back corner of the compound, and just beyond it, San Lorenzo's basilica.

I squinted into the light. Backlit everything looked black against an incandescent backdrop. A pair of monks hurried from the street into the church's plaza so as not to be late for vespers, but otherwise, the area was quiet and blessedly absent any sign of a Medici caravan—and, more blessedly still, any archers on San Lorenzo's distant roof.

"Take Tommaso and go to the front Via Larga entrance," Niccolo said quietly, as if he'd been in charge. His grim gaze was focused further down the street as he hopped off the donkey and Tommaso steadied me as I clumsily half jumped, half climbed down from the wagon. "Make them tell the archers stationed on their roof to look for those on San Lorenzo's. I'll stop them from leaving on this side."

Without waiting for my response, he began strolling down the street with a remarkably casual air. I was relieved to learn that Lorenzo and his own were capably defended, but not at all happy with Niccolo's plan.

"You'll get yourself shot," I hissed, but he was already out of earshot. I turned to Tommaso and said with all the firmness I could muster in my deranged state, "You heard him. Go to the front door. It's very important that you tell them *Giuliana*, not Giuliano, sent you. Got it? *Giuliana*. The girl's name. You tell them that Guiliana says there are archers on the church roof who are planning to kill Ser Lorenzo. Go."

I gave him a push. The momentum forced him to take a few staggering steps away from me, but then he balked and turned.

"Where are you going?" he demanded, glowering at me. I didn't say a word, since he already knew the answer. "You just said Niccolo was going to get shot!"

I growled in frustration. "Just do as I say!"

His lips twisted, trembling. "You're not my mother!" he said, not as much with anger as with regret. But he finally turned and ran off, crying, to the door, I think because he knew it was important.

I trotted after Niccolo—slowly, as if I'd had an afterthought and wanted to convey it to a departing friend. I tried to keep my face pointed straight ahead at Niccolo and not tilt my chin up or crane my neck to reveal that my gaze was actually locked on the roof of the sanctuary beyond him.

The sun left me half blinded and uncertain as to whether the swift and sudden motion of what looked like a black insect against orange tiles was actually an archer atop the church or a trick of the shifting light or my tired eyes.

Niccolo immediately started whistling a bawdy tavern song. I slowed my pace and hung back, uncertain.

As I did, the dark profile of a horse and rider emerged from behind the wall at the rear corner of the palazzo. Amazingly, Niccolo continued his pace and his whistling without a break in either, not even when a second horse and rider immediately followed. Both turned to their left, north, toward us, with their backs to the church.

I heard the creaking wheels before I saw the carriage emerge. Colors had already begun to fade to varying shades of gray, but the tarp covering the carriage was still red, the flap fastened shut to ensure the privacy of the riders, just as when I had ridden with Lorenzo.

Four more horsemen emerged in rapid succession and took their places, two on either side of the carriage.

Niccolo ran to the middle of the street and raised his hands for them to stop, prompting the first two horsemen to draw swords. I ran, too, but didn't stop alongside Niccolo. I loped past him, eluding the outer guards on their whinnying charges and

coming alongside the carriage. My gait was clumsy, almost staggering. I must have looked a drunk.

"Take cover!" I shouted. "Ser Lorenzo, take cover!" Like Niccolo, I raised my arms at the driver to stop, at a second emerging
wagon not to follow, waving them back, back. I ran directly up
to the outer pair of riders flanking the carriage. Unlike their forward counterparts, they drew no weapons; I looked up at one of
them and dreamed I saw the face of Ser Abramo half hidden by
his cowled mantello. I turned to the other, and saw Lorenzo,
scowling not in anger but concern.

"Shield yourselves!" Niccolo echoed in the near distance.
"Take cover!"

An arrow split the air between us, so close I felt its breeze
upon my face, its whistling song vibrate in my ear. Was it from
the enemy aiming at Lorenzo or Lorenzo's archers aiming at me?
It scarcely mattered. I threw myself upon the nervous stallion
and yanked Lorenzo's lower leg from the stirrup, downward and
hard, so that he fell sideways from his mount. He recovered
enough to keep his footing upon landing.

"Get down!" I shouted. "Get down!"

I caught him by the shoulders and tried to pull him to the
ground, but he was strong and shook me off with a single move.
I lost sight of him as the second arrow shrieked past and grazed
the horse's shoulder. More terrified than injured, the animal
cried out and reared. One of its hooves found the side of my head
and I fell hard against the cobblestones.

There I lay, unable to breathe, unable to move, able only to
watch the wild dance of shadows made of circling human,
equine, and wooden bodies, to listen to the chaotic song of men
and horses and a hundred loosed arrows all screaming, of wood
and hooves and boot heels crashing against stone, the whole in-
fused with light born of an incandescent bouquet of marigold,

rose, and lilac. It was the worst of dreams, in which powerlessness always prevails.

I could not gauge time. I could not understand all the shouting voices, although I recognized Lorenzo's, Niccolo's, the disobedient Tommaso's, and, in my stupor, Ser Abramo's. I may have fallen into a faint. My awareness faded along with the maelstrom, gradually, and returned abruptly when I realized the street was in near silence and the whirling motion around me had ceased. I opened my eyes to the fiery sun and was instantly blinded, but I could sense the bodies kneeling around me and could hear the voices clearly, gently calling my name.

Giuli.

Giuliano.

Giuliana . . .

The bright blot in the center of my sight went black; the blackness gradually faded to gray. Three faces loomed above me, blotting out the sun, their features softened by the dying light.

Giuli . . . Niccolo's cheeks were wet with tears—not fresh ones on my account, which I wouldn't have expected anyway, but drying ones. The sight of them brought a sudden sting of fear: Had Lorenzo been killed? Donna Lucrezia? Both? Had we failed them? But the concern on his handsome face was real enough.

Giuliano . . . Tommaso was all eyes and a tight, solemn little mouth, too scared even to cry.

Giuliana . . .

Giuliana, forgive me.

My third petitioner was penitent, his cowl thrown carelessly back despite the cold to reveal a shaven, noble skull; his worried brows knitted a thick black slash beneath a deep vertical furrow. His eyes, an indeterminate color in the failing light, were large and heavy-lidded and liquid with heartbreak.

"Forgive me, Giuliana."

Ser Abramo's ghost had never looked so alive, so solid, so human. I felt the press of his strong hand against my limp one. I supposed I was dying, then, or already dead, to find his touch so warm.

"Breathe, Giuliana," the Magician begged. "Please breathe."

Nineteen

I breathed.

Is she all right? a male voice asked.

She's sleeping, another replied.

When she wakes, she's going to hate you, the first said, *just like I did. It's a cruel thing you did to both of us, you know.*

Do you hate me still, Niccolo? asked the second wistfully, and the former choked before answering,

You know I love you, old man.

And I woke up in a fine cozy bed, my gaze by chance focused on the half raised wooden shutter covering the window and the bright afternoon light shining through beneath. It hurt my eyes a bit and made me realize I had a headache. It also confused me, because I'd thought the sun had already set. The room was unfamiliar, airier than those in the Medici Palazzo because the walls were plain whitewashed stucco, without the busy wooden panels, and less cluttered, with only a few oil paintings on the walls and not a single priceless curio.

I wasn't dead—the headache was proof enough of that—but I was someplace I'd never been before. Not in Florence, nor any other city because it was so profoundly *quiet.* I was so used to the clanging of church bells and nonstop clatter of wheels and hooves, the chatter of pedestrians and songs of merchants that the absence of them all was remarkable.

The light streaming through the window made me direct my

gaze downward, where a large gray dog with a coat like close-cropped velvet was dozing, his great square muzzle resting on his forepaws, his pendulous jowls fanning out onto the tile floor.

"*Leo,*" I croaked with joy.

Leo drew his head up with a start, his pale eyes ferally alert. At the sight of my face, his stub of a tail began to thump wildly, and he grinned so fetchingly I gave a soft laugh, even though the effort made the throbbing in my temple worse. He pushed himself to his feet, his nails clicking against rustic tile, and began dancing in place, looking over his shoulder at the man sitting on the daybed pushed against the wall beneath the window. Leo clearly wanted to jump up on the bed with me, but either needed permission or feared rebuke.

Like the dog, the man on the daybed woke with a start, and closed his half agape mouth. His bare head and cheeks caught the daylight, revealing the very beginnings of silvery stubble.

"Giuliana," Abramo said. The sound held concern and hope edged with shame. He seemed not to see the mastiff vying frantically for his attention.

"You're real," I rasped. Just like laughing, talking hurt. For some reason, my throat was terribly sore.

"I'm sorry that we had to fool you," he said, and whatever he said next, I didn't hear, because I started to cry. Not so much out of relief, although there was definitely some of that, but out of rage and grief over my needless suffering.

"I thought you trusted me," I wept. "Why didn't you just take me with you? Why did you have to be so cruel?"

He leaned forward, elbows on his knees, his expression stricken, puzzled. "I didn't think . . . I didn't know . . . that you would care that much." He cleared his throat. "But when you knelt over me when you thought I was dying, when you whispered to me, I wanted so badly to tell you then. But of course, they would have killed us both." He drew in a breath. "I thought—I thought that you were playing along with me. For the money."

True, of course, not that I was going to admit to it.

"Is it even true?" I asked, sniffling, wiping my tears on the edge of a woolen sleeve of a lady's fine nightgown that I'd never seen before. "That you're my father? Or was that a trick, too?"

He stood up, walked to the edge of the bed, and sat down beside me. Leo followed, pressing against his thighs.

"I'm your father, Giuliana," he said gently, and took up my hand between his. "What I told you was the truth."

"Why'd you even tell me, then, if you knew you were going to be dead?"

He lowered his gaze, sorrowful in the face of my pain. "I was hoping it would *make* you care. I was hoping it would make you seek out the Medici for answers, so they could take care of you."

I hiccupped, the way Tommaso sometimes does after a long cry. "You really are my father?" My voice sounded so small and wistful, just like Tommaso's, and it wasn't even an act.

"I really am," he said, in his deep beautiful voice, and he brought my hand, clasped between his own, to his lips and kissed it.

I cried. I cried the way Tommaso used to, mouth open and contorted, eyes and nose streaming as I let go ugly hitching sounds. I pressed my sore, aching cheek against Ser Abramo's shoulder and let him hold me, let him pat my back and murmur to me until I couldn't cry anymore. Leo panted happily beside us, pawing at me from time to time.

"It's magic," Abramo said solemnly, holding me. "Magic that you are here. Magic that we are here together."

"The notes you left me," I said, my words partly muffled by his damp shoulder. "In the magical tent, on the altar. How did you do that? The tunnel beneath the carpet, right? It must lead up to the hidden chamber where I found the cipher wheel. You must have been at the house when I was working on the talismans. You must have . . . you must have heard me talking to you when I was in the tent somehow."

He shook his head. "That was real magic, Giuliana."

There was not the slightest shift in his posture, his tone. He seemed as utterly serious as when he'd confirmed he was my father. Even so, I let go a feeble snicker, to which he failed to react, and pulled gently out of the embrace, leaving us to study each other at close range.

"My mother," I ventured. "Is she dead?"

He held very still, and paused for so long that I needed no further answer.

"She's *alive,*" I said, marveling, indignant. "Who is she? Where is she? Is she—"

He cut me off. "It's not my choice to tell you. It's hers. The note explained that it's not my place to speak of it. She is a woman of uncommon reputation and importance and I will never do anything to see her or her loved ones hurt."

I pressed a hand to my aching head and began to cry again, out of frustration but oddly, not a desire to influence.

Abramo's expression was one of helplessness. "It's out of my hands. Just know that you are loved, by both of us." He wrapped his arms around me and held me to him briefly, then rose and paused at the door.

"I'll send someone with food. In the meantime, you need to rest. You've gone through more than any young woman should ever have to."

He took a final glance at me and left, Leo ever by his side, while I was still crying bitterly.

·   ·   ·

Eventually I cried myself back to sleep until the sound of a door opening woke me. The sun had set again, and the candle lamp on the table beside my bed had been lit without my knowing it. The half open shutter revealed a full moon, which cast a silvery pane of light across the floor and the center of my bed.

I didn't pay much mind to the woman who carried the tray of food in and set it carefully down on the bedside table—not until she bent down and her face entered the pane of bluish incandescence, making her weathered face look magical. The veil over her gray hair was pure colorless gossamer that caught the moonlight like a halo. At that moment, she looked more ghostly than any apparition I'd seen of Ser Abramo in my delirium.

Donna Lucrezia's face passed from the silvered light into warm candleglow, and became warm, human, wistfully aged. There were pockets of slack flesh beneath her dark, impossibly intelligent eyes, and purplish shadows, and lines bracing her mouth, its edges curved ever so slightly upward and trembling.

She sat down on the daybed where Abramo had so recently been and folded her hands in her lap. She wore a housewife's simple apron and a dress as simple as any servant's. She did not look like the matriarch of the powerful Medici family or the brilliant architect behind the cipher wheel. She looked timid and small.

Yet there was no denying the infinite love in her eyes as she stretched her hand out to my cheek and said, her voice unsteady with maternal emotion: "My Giuliana. Oh, my Giuliana . . ."

I asked her no questions, demanded no confessions. Whatever shame and grief she had felt over the past two decades had certainly been enough. I simply pushed myself up to sitting and swung my legs over the bed and reached for her, reached across all those years of pain and misunderstanding.

Before we embraced she paused to draw something gleaming

from her apron pocket: a talisman, a silver one, just like the one from my childhood. For the second time in my life, she lifted it over my head and settled the charm gently so that it came to rest over my heart.

Despite the emotional encounter, when my mother left the room, I discovered that I was ravenous, and I made short shrift of the supper of bread, cheese, and soup. I left not a crumb of bread or cheese, licked the bowl clean, and drank sufficient wine to become a bit tipsy. As I'd had more than enough sleep, I decided to explore my surroundings. I slipped out from beneath the covers and discovered a shawl thoughtfully placed on the nightstand so that I could maintain decency.

I made my way through a series of rooms—a library, an office, a guestchamber—all of them containing at least one bed, just like the Medici Palazzo in town. The shutters were closed, but the light outlined their edges brightly enough that I could make my way surely. I eventually came to a large sitting area for entertaining crowds. Despite the cold, someone had raised a shutter to reveal the dazzling moon, partially blocked by the dark silhouette of a man. He stood with his back to me, staring up at the dazzling moon.

"Niccolo," I said, my tone hushed.

Startled, he drew in a breath and turned, his wide green eyes rendered pale gray in the light.

"You're up," he responded quietly. "How do you feel?" His expression was more vulnerable, gentler, than I'd ever seen it. He stepped from the window toward me, his movements stiff after the previous day's battles. The outline of a bandage over his abdomen was clearly visible beneath his silk tunic.

I moved to stand beside him, ignoring the throbbing in my head and the ache that consumed my entire body.

"I'm fine," I murmured dismissively and paused. "Thank you for saving my life. I take it Ser Lorenzo is well?"

He nodded. "On his way to his destination." He paused. "No need to thank me. I would have had to fight those men sooner or later. I may have saved your fingers, but it was you who saved *my* life, if you recall."

I gestured with my chin at his half hidden bandage. "And left you with a memento. Actually, I wasn't thanking you for that—I was thanking you for teaching me the leg trick. It saved my neck."

He frowned, puzzled. "Leg trick?"

I moved in even closer, and twined a leg around his to remind him of the maneuver.

"Oh. Yes," he said, staring directly into my eyes in a fashion I might have found unsettling had I not been doing the same to him. His breathing and mine had grown more rapid. Instead of stepping back, I kept my leg pressed against his and put my arms around his thick chest at the same instant that he wound his arms around my shoulders. I gave a small, sharp gasp as his hands found the burn left by Stout's pincers, but he took it for passion and pressed his lips to mine. His were incredibly soft and smelled of good wine.

My head throbbed, and the kiss reminded me of how bruised and sore my lips were. Yet I cared not one whit. A blaze was kindled in my core and radiated outward until it contained me, until it contained both of us. We stayed enmeshed for a timeless moment, until I felt the kindling of an internal blaze and myself melting, until my body was possessed of an entirely different sort of ache.

I pulled gently away from him. "Not here," I said.

"It's all right," he whispered. "Everyone is asleep." He gestured at the wing opposite the one I'd come from.

I stared in disbelief for a moment. It was uncommon for a

young unmarried woman like myself to be sleeping alone, without a servant or chaperone within hearing. It was almost as if Donna Lucrezia and Ser Abramo had known that this moment would come and were giving tacit approval.

I offered him my hand, and he took it, and let me lead him back to my bedchamber with its whitewashed walls. As I closed the door behind us, he hesitated.

"Are you sure?" he asked.

"You wouldn't be here if I weren't."

"But we haven't even . . ." He hesitated, suddenly endearingly shy. "I've only kissed you the once now, not even properly. And I haven't even asked for your hand."

I laughed with something suspiciously akin to joy. "I know just the man you should speak to about that," I said, and he grinned and reached for me.

But another thought stopped him. "I'm not at my best," he said wryly, and lifted up his tunic to show the bandage on his abdomen.

"You mean you can't—"

"I didn't say *that*," he countered. "It's just that . . . I want you to know that . . ."

"That you'll do better next time?" I grinned.

He grinned back and said teasingly, "And you and your head. Your poor face is quite bruised, you know."

"I'll look better next time," I quipped. "In the meantime, you'd better kiss it. A proper kiss, now."

He leaned down and obeyed, taking me into his arms, wincing only a little when I pressed myself against him—my waist straining against his wound, my breasts against his hard ribs, my face upturned, a flower seeking the sun. He put his lips tenderly to mine. His clothes smelled of horses, his face and neck of rosemary and soap. He hadn't shaved, and the stubble on his cheeks pricked my skin, but even that discomfort was a delight. His wiry goatee brushed my chin and, despite myself, I giggled, my lips still against his, and felt my own warm breath on my cheeks. He playfully caught hold of my lower lip ever so softly with his teeth before letting go.

"It tickles," I mumbled. I could feel the bright flush on my face, my body, could hear my own quickened breathing. Stranger still was the sensation of pure happiness.

"Would you mind very much," he began, and stopped.

I drew back, our noses less than a hand's breadth apart. "Yes," I said.

He laughed quietly. "I haven't even told you what I wanted."

"It doesn't matter," I said. "The answer is still the same."

I felt a thrill at my own bold words, one of yearning mixed with a distinct undercurrent of fear. I looked at his eyes, pale gray ringed with charcoal in the silvered light, and realized: He was all too mortal, in a dangerous profession, and if I allowed that I loved him, would God then conspire to take him from me?

Perhaps. But perhaps not. He had restored my mother and father and spared Tomasso, Celia, Niccolo, and me from the direst situation. Perhaps even Lorenzo and Florence would survive.

I glanced sidewise at the moon, half hidden by the shutters, and felt a pang of sorrow for Paolo and Old Sot before turning back to Niccolo.

He was smiling. "Then would you mind terribly if I removed your nightgown?"

It was unsettling to want someone so badly, but I drew in a breath and braved it. Niccolo was here, now, and so was I, and I was determined to experience the bliss of this moment, no matter what came next.

"Please," I said. I let the shawl slip from my shoulders onto the floor.

His fingers were unsteady as he gently gathered the woolen fabric into his hands and awkwardly lifted it up over my head. It took a bit of struggling on both our parts to free me of the long sleeves.

The nightgown dropped silently into a small heap. I wore nothing beneath. I stepped out of the pool of fabric and kicked it away with decided irreverence.

By then, he had removed his tunic and the plain *camicia* beneath. His shoulders were broad and beautifully sculpted, tapering down to a deliciously small waist. A thicket of dark hair covered his chest from his nipples and thinned to a vee above his navel. The moon painted his skin bluish white.

I reached for him at the same time he reached for my breast. We both froze in unison, our hands wavering in midair.

"May I?" he asked again.

"If I asked the same of you, what would you say?" I countered, impatient.

He chuckled. "I'd tell you to stop asking silly questions."

I raised my eyebrows to say, *Well, then . . .*

Sheepish, he half smiled. "It's just that . . ." I couldn't see him blush in the light, but I could hear it in his tone. "When I first met you, I thought you were a boy. And I'd never been attracted to a boy that way before. I began to wonder what was happening to me. And then when I touched—that is, when I realized you were a young woman . . ."

I stared up at his beautiful face, utterly charmed by his words, not quite able to believe that someone I'd loved from afar—so far, in fact, that I hadn't fully admitted to myself until that instant—actually returned my feelings.

"Will you lie down?" he asked.

I would. And when I settled my naked body down into the

pane of blue light that fell across the bed, he removed his leggings and lay down beside me. Propped on one elbow, he ran his hand over my flesh, over my breasts, down to the mound between my legs. I sighed and pulled him down on top of me.

"Is this . . . ?" Niccolo began; once again I didn't let him finish. I nodded. "My first time."

I reached between us and found that part of him that was impossibly firm yet velvet to the touch and guided him.

When he entered me, I gasped—not with pain or discomfort, but pure amazement that I had lived long enough to feel such pleasure, such happiness.

As he moved inside me, and our bodies began to rock together in that most primal of rhythms, I stared past him at the glorious moon.

Even now, when the moon shines I remember poor Paolo and Old Sot and embrace the sorrow I dared not feel before. But I no longer see only their suffering. I see Niccolo's face, contorted by passion. I see beauty, too, and love, and magic.

They make me dress like a woman now. I hate it. I'm used to wearing the *camicia*, the long undershirt, because everybody does, but the women's are longer, and they wear an underskirt, too, and over that is the *gamurra*, the gown proper, but that doesn't include the overgown or the sleeves, or any one of the hundred possible additions to the layers and layers, which all end in the ubiquitous mantello, draped in a hundred possible ever-so-stylish ways. Don't even get me started on the headpieces. If I go out at all, even if it's just to the chapel, Donna Lucrezia insists I wear a wig. It's a fine one, done up in coils and braids, which are the fashion now, but I call it the rat, in part because it makes

Celia laugh when I do. I wear a veil over it, of course, and look so terribly convincingly female that when I first appeared in it, Tommaso didn't recognize me for a full minute.

Any Roman spy who might recognize me or Ser Abramo is supposedly dead now, except for the wicked Ser Andrea, who resides in the bowels of the Bargello these days and has proven very helpful in helping us to crack Rome's most recent code. For that reason, we all dared to go back to the city once—just once, with me in my cunning new disguise—because there were things Ser Abramo needed from his estate that he apparently trusted only himself to get. I never understood what it was. But Celia was eager to go to the Duomo for Mass to thank God for everything— our new wealth, our kind benefactors, and the fact that none of us wound up good and really dead—and so she, Niccolo, Tommaso, Ser Abramo, two bodyguards, and I all rode into Florence one mild winter's day and we dropped Celia, Niccolo, and Tommaso off with one of the bodyguards at the great cathedral before continuing on to the estate. Tommaso clutched Niccolo's hand as if they'd been father and son, which clearly pleased Niccolo, judging from his abrupt affectionate grin. The two had taken to each other so quickly, I was worried Tomasso would get too attached and get hurt.

But then, I was already too attached to Niccolo myself. He and I shared warm, furtive glances when he turned his head to look back at me.

When we returned to pick them up later, they weren't where they were supposed to be, so I climbed out of the wagon to hunt them down. It took me less than a second to figure it out: they were at the Baptistery, of course, looking at the bronze doors—at Tommaso's favorite panel, *The Sacrifice of Isaac.* Niccolo and Celia turned to smile at me as I approached, but I held my finger to my lips and snuck up behind Tommaso before squatting down to coil an arm around his shoulder. He gave a startled little laugh and pointed up at the metal bas-relief as if it'd been the first time either of us had laid eyes on it.

"It all turned out okay," he announced emphatically. "Isaac didn't die. And Abraham took him home."

I nodded, thoughtful. "You know what I think? I think Abraham knew all the time that God wouldn't make him kill his own son. He knew God wouldn't be that mean."

Celia shot me a startled sidewise look, which I scrupulously ignored.

"I'm glad you're alive, Giuli," Tommaso blurted, and grabbed me with unashamed ebullient affection.

I hugged him back. "I love you, Tommaso." The words slipped out so easily and fast, even I was shocked. I was shocked even more when my gaze caught Niccolo's and I did not look away but smiled invitingly, silently repeating *I love you*.

Not noticing the electric glance between Niccolo and me, Tommaso drew back and crowed, "I knew it! I always knew it!"

He's a smart boy, our Tommaso. He'll go far in this world.

It was funny, finding Tommaso standing in front of the Abraham and Isaac panel, because I'd been thinking about the biblical story earlier, when Abramo and I were riding in silence to the estate. Lorenzo had left for Naples the day before, and I kept seeing that damned panel over and over in my imagination, but instead of young Isaac stretched out on that stone altar, I saw Lorenzo. Only Isaac had a much, much better chance of surviving at his father's hands than Ser Lorenzo had at that madman Ferrante's. It had seemed incredibly brave and daring to me at first, his going there unarmed, relying on nothing but his charmed tongue, and daring, and vaguely romantic. But once he'd gone,

I was—like Donna Lucrezia, although she won't say it—sick with fear. It no longer seemed brave, but idiotic. Insane.

The closer we grew to the estate, the darker my mood grew. The glorious new existence that had befallen me, and Celia, and Tommaso, and the city we so loved had never been in greater danger and, at any minute, a courier might come riding with word that both were lost.

Ser Abramo must have felt some misgivings as well, because not a word passed between us as we followed the guards onto the old estate. Each room we passed through brought a fresh reminder of bloodshed: of the deaths of Lorenzo's red-bearded spy, of the Nubian and the kitchen maid, and—when my master and I climbed down into the cellar unaccompanied—of poor Albrecht. I was grateful that our visit had been preceded by others' who had erased the worst of the evidence, the blood and corpses. Even the obscene mess created by Stout's toppling of the supply shelf had been carefully cleaned up, the broken shelf pushed off to one side and the supplies themselves organized in piles upon the floor behind the bowed worktable. The only sign was a faint scattering of white dust on the floor, the last remnants of plaster powder that stubbornly resisted the broom.

Abramo had brought with him a basket and a lamp. I lit a second lamp, on the ground near the chair where Albrecht had not so long ago sat. There were supplies that we needed—scrolls and books and herbs from the apothecary, the last of which Abramo set himself to gathering. I quickly found the desired books and scrolls and began to pace restlessly, unnerved by the memories contained in the gloom. At last, I went to stand behind Abramo.

"You were dead, you know," I blurted. "Really dead. I reached underneath the pig's bladder, and you were bleeding under there."

"A shallow wound, self-administered," he said with his back to me, still focused on his task. "I thought it best, as Niccolo said the Romans were a suspicious lot and likely to make sure I was dead." He paused and glanced over his shoulder at me. "Just as you did."

"But the man with the red beard . . . he stabbed you so many times—"

"With a retractable blade," he murmured, kneeling down to open a drawer near the floor. "Thank God it worked as well as it did." He took what he needed from the drawer, rose, and turned to face me, his expression clouded. "If only I'd introduced him to Leo, he might still be alive. He was going to retrieve you after our little play and take you to Donna Lucrezia and safety. You would have learned the facts about my death that afternoon, but you ran away. Because of that, Lorenzo had to be persuaded to trust you."

"What was the point of keeping me here like a prisoner?" I pressed. "Yes, I know, you were protecting me. But why have me make all those talismans and create a new cipher key? Did you not trust me by then?"

Abramo was peering into one of the little labeled drawers. He answered without looking up. "It wasn't a question of trust. We needed those things."

I snorted. "You were perfectly capable. Why didn't you make them? You had more experience. The process would have gone faster."

He sighed and looked over at me, his fingers still digging in the drawer. "I was creating other things. Things Lorenzo needed far more than those you created."

I felt stung. "How could anything possibly have been more important than those four talismans?"

He withdrew his fingers and turned his body toward me. "Here," he said. He set down the basket and walked over to the worktable, looking first at the jumble of supplies before deciding against trying to find quill or pen or paper. He squatted down and with his finger wrote a symbol in the pale dust.

"Mercury," I read aloud, and like a good student said, "For eloquence."

"A most powerful eloquence," he said, drawing a numerical square and more symbols, "to bring about a lasting peace." He looked up at me. "The timing had to be exquisitely precise, when Mercury was at his greatest possible exaltation. There had to be a second talisman for protection, too, one compatible with the first." He paused. "And there were a number of rituals beyond the charging of the talisman."

Something broke in me then. "You're letting our fates, the fate of an entire city, ride on this? On charms and ceremonies?" I shook my head, feeling the old anger swallow me. "It's a sham, all of it. You weren't really dead—it was just playacting with Niccolo. All of this is just playacting, but now everything is at stake."

Clutching my lamp, I pivoted on my heel and stomped off to the magical tent. With an utter lack of reverence, I threw the flap aside and stalked in. Abramo followed, chiding me.

"Your shoes," he said. "At least take off your shoes."

But I was too angry. I set the lamp off to one side on the floor and pushed back the black altar, rolled back the carpet, and gestured angrily at the revealed wooden hatch.

"There!" I snapped. "All those notes that magically appeared on the altar—those notes that you wrote me after I spoke to you, thinking you were dead—they were just a cheap trick! I have no doubt this leads up to the chamber where I found the cipher wheel. I know it. You must have been hiding up there, somehow listening to me! Playing me for a fool!"

I yanked on the leather handle and flung the hatch open with more force than was needed. It struck the furled carpet with a muted thud. I knew the depth of the pit this time, and jumped in unafraid. Fearless of spiders or vermin, I got onto all fours and moved at top speed into the utterly dark crawlspace.

And almost immediately hit my still-tender head against hard earth. The tunnel ended as quickly as it had begun. Confused, I crawled backward and turned around, thinking I must have made an error and the tunnel must have led in the opposite direction. But on either side lay nothing but implacable, long-undisturbed earth.

I looked up at Abramo, who stood expressionless, absent the bemusement I expected.

"It doesn't go anywhere," I said, at an utter loss.

"It never did," he said. "The previous owner never completed it. Nor did I."

"But the notes"—I broke off. He gazed at me evenly, steadily. He knew what I was speaking about, of that I was sure, but he wasn't going to say a word about it. He was going to force me to say what I was thinking.

"You left written messages for me. You know you did. I figured this tunnel was connected up to the room where I found the cipher wheel. I . . . prayed to you for help. And you answered me." I patted the surface of the altar. "I came in here to charge the talismans, and the notes were *not* there at first. Then I'd talk to you, and the notes appeared. Telling me to trust Niccolo. To trust Lorenzo."

"And you did," he said approvingly.

"They didn't appear out of nowhere," I said, my tone scathing, bitter. I stared up at the ceiling, looking for a way they could have dropped down from above, and saw nothing but black velvet sky.

"Go ahead," he urged softly. "Look. Shall I lift you on my shoulder?" It was a sincere question, without a trace of sarcasm.

Instead of replying, I retrieved my lantern and held it aloft as

I studied the velvet ceiling of the tent. The fabric was of a piece; there were no slits, no tears.

When I finally looked back at Abramo, he wore a faint smile. Even so, his tone was serious.

"My death could not separate us," he said. "Nor could yours." He walked over to the tunnel and closed the hatch. I helpfully rolled the carpet back into place with one hand.

He held the tent flap open for me so that I could exit ahead of him, but as I ducked my head to pass through, he spoke again. The lamp in my hand lit his face from below, making him look faintly menacing, ghostly.

"What if I told you that we had both been dead?" he asked. "What if I told you that magic had brought us both back to life, dear Giuliana?"

A shudder passed through me like the hair-raising thrill of a nearby lightning strike, leaving me speechless.

The Magician of Florence studied me with his ageless gaze.

"Lorenzo will return victorious from Naples against impossible odds," he said. "Just as a dead child was returned to its mother and father. Just as messages appeared out of thin air, written by a dead hand. Just as a wounded heart was made whole." He paused. "And how was this accomplished, my brave apprentice?"

"Magic," I said, and believed.